A NOV

THE SUGAR HOUSE

Jean Scheffler

Printed in the United States of America

Published by: Jean Scheffler
www.jeanscheffler.com

First Printing, 2013

ISBN: 978-0-9911925-0-2

Book Design by KarrieRoss.com

For Joe Sczytko, who inspired this tale and taught me that anything is possible with a little hard work and a sense of humor.

PROLOGUE

Detroit. To many modern persons the name implies poverty, decay, corruption and violence. To lovers of the city's rich history the name means much more. I grew up in the suburbs of this unique city, listening to the stories of the exciting place it had been before my birth. Many of the tellers had lived there during the time when it was a bustling, exhilarating place... "The New York of the Midwest" it had been called. From the back seat of my parent's brown Pontiac Phoenix, this little blonde haired girl would look up at the enormous skyscrapers and even then, I could see the beauty of the architecture and thoughtful care that had gone into the storefronts, parks and homes. Much has been written about why Detroit crumbled and how to rejuvenate the once great town. Both are difficult topics with no simple answers that I or most are able to answer.

To be truthful, my interest in the city's history began with a love for the romantic feel of the 1920's; a party atmosphere where men were gentlemen and women were ladies and dressed the part. The beautiful cars, glittering movie palaces, the doormen and valets. Even the double-dealing gangster dashing down the brick paved streets had a glamorous feel. But as I watched old movies, read as much as I could find on the topic and begged anyone over the age of eighty to share their stories, I learned much more.

And I remembered back to a time when I would wake early in my Grandfather's cottage on a little lake in Northern Michigan and crawl onto his lap where he was rocking by the stone fireplace. There in the quiet of the morning before my sister or my seven girl cousins would awake he would share with me his stories of growing up in Detroit. These were not the romantic stories of the black and white movies that I loved to watch. His story was one of poverty (although he didn't tell it that way), and street smarts, and neighborhood unity, and hard work with some occasional mischievous fun thrown in. A world where a third grade education didn't define a man's worth and bending the law to try to survive was not looked down upon.

When I became a gerontology nurse at the young age of twenty-one I was lucky enough to again learn from this country's greatest generation. Any down time I had during a shift I would search out a patient who wanted to talk for a little while. On those late evenings after the last medications were passed, as I'd sit at the bedside of a World War Vet or hold the hand of a ninety year old housewife I'd feel a warmth in the dark ward as they quietly shared the story of their lives. I learned not only historical facts but the true feelings, emotions and struggles their lives had held.

As I entered my thirties and the decline of Detroit became the main focus of the evening news, my mind wandered over all the accumulated history I had had the privilege to learn. True, I had never lived during the time when Detroit was the jewel of the Midwest but I could definitely imagine it as it had been. And when I found during conversations with coworkers, friends and strangers of my generation that most were unfamiliar with the history of our great city I was saddened. I wanted to record it as I saw it for the grandchildren of the citizens who created it and for the great grandchildren who will hopefully see it rise again.

Confucius says, "Study the past if you would define the future." I honestly believe this to be true. I hope by my telling this small story based loosely on a few facts from my grandfather's life I can contribute to the next generation's is commitment to keep Detroit and its history alive. For it is their ancestors who built, worked, played, slept, cried, laughed and loved there also.

THE
SUGAR
HOUSE

CHAPTER ONE

1915

P*ospiesz sie , pospiesz sie!* (Hurry, Hurry!) thought Joe as he rushed down the tree-lined street. His father was expecting him to bring his dinner, and if he did not hurry Ojciec (Father) would not have time to eat the kielbasa sandwich Matka (Mother) had prepared. He'd been watching his two-year-old brother, Frank, while Matka gossiped at the market. Now he needed to run to avoid a reprimand from Ojciec. His small frame weaved quickly down the wooden sidewalk between neighbors, strangers and children. Watching for cars and horses, he crossed the street and headed north. He could see the steeple of St. Josaphat's looming two hundred feet above the houses, and he was anxious to arrive at the construction site.

Strangers he passed on the busy street would not have noticed the small boy. He looked like all the Polish boys in the neighborhood. His clothes were fairly clean—short brown pants with stockings, a small brown overcoat and a flat hat pulled over his shaggy blond hair. But anyone who stopped him to ask for directions or to say dzie dobry (Good Morning) would probably have blinked a few times and stared. Under his cap were eyes the bright azure of the sky on the Fourth of July, the sparkling sapphire of the water surrounding Belle Isle Park, the aqua of a little girl's traditional costume on a saint's day and the powder blue of a morning sunrise when the day holds all possibilities.

Small shoulders squared, chest out, he walked confidently with his chin held high. His stature was average for an eight-year-old, and he didn't stand out at school when it came to marks. But he was strangely self-assured. His aunt whispered that he was a stary dusza–an old soul. However, steadfastness and the will to fight ran thick through his blood. A century of poverty and oppression in the old country had fused a thick rope of determination into his genetic code. When he was a small child sitting on his mother's lap, she'd told him she believed he had a special fate and was destined for great things in this new country. Joe was special.

When he greeted an adult at the five-and-dime or at the market he looked the person straight in the eye, reached out his hand, smiled and addressed the person as an equal. For a child so small to behave this way could have been off-putting, but Joe seemed to put people at ease with this tactic. Men would smile and shake his hand; women would lean down to further inspect his beautiful eyes and compliment his manners. Even older children would listen to his stories and let him lead their games.

As he neared the construction site, the noise of the city grew much larger. St. Josaphat's was the newest Polish church the archdiocese had commissioned to be built. There were two other large Polish churches within two miles, yet the population of Polish Catholics had become so large in Detroit that the Church was continually erecting more houses of worship. The original wooden chapel had been rebuilt into a massive cathedral only fifteen years prior, but the school was updated only this year. The school was almost complete, and Joe and his classmates would soon move from the old school.

Crossing the red brick street, Joe stepped onto the site and searched for his father. He was careful, as he knew that bricks falling from above were a common occurrence. The men joked that a brick that landed on a Polish man's head would bounce off. But Joe knew this was only a barb that helped alleviate their fear of injury. He'd recently heard of a neighbor who was killed when a bucket of mortar fell from a second story. His widow and five children now depended on the church's and the neighborhood's charity to survive.

Jumping over a mud puddle, he made his way closer to the new school. His father volunteered his labor at the site on Saturdays. The Jopolowski family was proud to belong to St. Josaphat's, as it was one of the larger churches in the area. The Felician sisters who taught in the school were highly educated. Joe's parents revered the teaching nuns; Joe, however, did not feel the same adoration. The sisters insisted on calling him Joseph despite the fact that his birth certificate clearly stated his name was Joe Jopolowski. He'd even brought it to school and shown it to Sister Mary Monica to no avail. She had responded curtly, "Joe is not a given name," and there was no further discussion.

Joe slowed down to say hello to Mrs. Stanislewski, who was carrying her husband's dinner in a small woven basket in the crook of her arm. The hem of her long, dark dress brushed the dirty sidewalk as she leaned down to kiss his flushed cheek. She stood up and grabbed the edge of her embroidered apron and patted her face. Joe complimented the bright red babushka that donned her head.

"Oh this?" she said in Polish, patting the pretty cloth. "It was a gift from my grandmother. She gave it to me the day I left for America. She passed last year. I was thinking of her this morning as I got dressed, so I pulled it out of my drawer. Of course, I hadn't seen her in ten years; but I can still see her standing at her cottage door waving goodbye like it was yesterday." Joe nodded and politely said goodbye as he moved on. He heard stories like Mrs. Stanislewski's every day. Many of the parishioners hailed from the same area of Poland as Joe's family. It seemed that every adult he knew had left someone behind in the old country.

The noise and commotion of the construction site had a celebratory feeling. Men shouted out in Polish and laughed and joked with their friends. Some whistled folk songs while they worked. Some waved to Joe and called out greetings. "Dzie dobry maly czlowiek! (Good Morning, little man" Older men teased. "Pozno? Ha! To s na to! (Late? Ha! You are in for it!) Scurrying over the piles of bricks and wood, Joe quickly found his father.

At five foot eight, Mikołaj Jopolowski was not a large man, nor was he demonstrative with his affections. He loved his young son, but he had left the raising of him mostly to his wife, Blanca, until recently. Growing up in a poor village, Mikołaj had scrimped to save enough money to make the passage to America. He'd arrived in New York ten years ago and had made his way to Calumet, in the Upper Peninsula of Michigan, to work in the copper mines. Nine months ago, Mikołaj and his two brothers had heard of Henry Ford's five-dollar-a-day jobs and had brought their families to

Detroit to work in the automobile plants. As an unskilled workman, Mikołaj was making almost twice what he'd been paid to labor in the cold, dark mines.

There was a price to pay for such a high wage, however. Joe's father had many scars from droplets of molten iron searing his skin as he poured the red-hot metal into molds for engine blocks. Blanca told Joe that before coming home at night from work, Ojciec would pull the balls of iron out of his skin. Mikołaj was lucky in one small respect: he worked with his two brothers, Alexy and Feliks. Working together gave the men confidence that they could avoid the kinds of fatal accidents that occurred in the factory.

Nearing the front steps of the new school, Joe saw his father laying bricks for the entryway.

Joe shouted hello to his father above the noise of the hammering and sawing. "Cze , Ojciec! (Hi, Father)"

Ojciec turned to him and smiled. "A little late, Joe, are we?"

"Yes sir. Matka took longer shopping than expected."

Ojciec laughed under his dark handlebar mustache. "Gossiping again at the market, I am sure. Well, what can I expect for supper when I get home this evening, for all the time spent in getting it? Maybe golabki (stuffed cabbage) with rice and mushrooms, or perhaps ox tongue in gray sauce?"

"No, Ojciec. We're having cheese pierogi with fried onions and cucumber salad."

"Ahh . . . always a favorite dish of mine when your mother makes it."

Tossing a quarter into the air, he said "Find a milk truck and buy some fresh sour cream for the pierogi. Let's surprise

Matka and your little brother. Small extravagances make life worth living, right Joe?"

"Yes! Oh yes, Ojciec!" Joe said, smiling ear to ear. Walking away he wondered the reason for his father's good mood. During the week, he came home tired and worn out, staying awake only to eat supper and then retiring before Joe went to sleep. Ojciec was usually more relaxed on Saturdays, but to splurge on sour cream was extraordinary. Joe walked to the sidewalk and began to search for a milkman delivering his wares.

Avoiding two horse drawn carriages, a Model T and a Liberty-Brush runabout, he crossed the street. Heading south toward the busier part of the city, he allowed himself to sightsee a little and enjoy the revelry of a sunny Saturday. The windows and doors of the houses lining the street were propped open on this mid-September day. Cabbage, sauerkraut and onion aromas drifted onto the sidewalk as the women in the neighborhood prepared supper for their families. Searching but finding no sign of a milkman, Joe continued toward the Irish district, a few blocks south.

Rounding the corner, he saw two red-haired boys playing with a Ouija board on the front porch of their home. He crossed to the other side of the brick street, not paying attention to the road; he almost stepped in horse dung. His priest, Father Gatowski, had just preached about the evils of the Ouija board last week at Mass.

"Ouija boards are the Devil's toy! God has spelled it out for us in the Holy Book." Father Gatowski had shouted from his pulpit. "'There shall not be found among you any one that maketh his son or his daughter to pass through fire, or that useth divination, or an observer of times, an enchanter, or a witch, or a charmer, or a consulter with familiar spirits, or a wizard, or a necromancer. For all that do these things are an abomination unto the LORD: and because these abominations the LORD thy God doth drive them out from before thee. Thou shalt be perfect with the LORD thy God.' Deuteronomy 18:10–13."

The priest had slammed the bible shut on the pulpit waving and pointing his finger at the congregation as he continued. "God has forewarned you in his most righteous way of knowing what is to come. Listen to his teachings! These modern toys being sold to our young souls in the false title of entertainment are a straight path to Hell! Do not allow your young children to surround themselves with the evil spirits of this world."

Of course, Joe being a young boy, he had not paid attention to the sermon until the priest yelled "Hell!"; and even then he hadn't understood what the priest was speaking about until his mother sat him down in the kitchen after Mass. She told him that if he ever played with a Ouija board that his soul would burn in Hell for eternity.

Joe hastened away from the sinful game and stepped onto the opposite sidewalk, colliding into a young woman with a parasol. She started to fall forward, unable to keep her balance thanks to her hobble skirt. Joe snapped out his hand at the last moment and grabbed her by the elbow to help right her.

"Are ye not an imp and angel in one crib?'" said the pretty lady in a lilting Irish accent, once she regained her balance.

Puzzled by this response, Joe stared into her eyes and quietly said in his best English, "I'm sorry, ma'am.

I should've been paying attention to what was ahead of me and not behind."

Laughing, the young woman responded by straightening Joe's cap and said, "Now if that were the advice we all followed through life, I know, by God, all us folks down here on Earth would have an easier time of it, to be sure." Fixing her large light pink hat upon her head, confident that her wardrobe was returned to order, she turned her attention fully to Joe. "My! What an amazing color your eyes are. They remind me of the sea by my village in Ireland, they do."

"Thank you, ma'am. And again I am sorry to have bumped into you." Joe turned to go.

"No use worrying yourself, young lad. Tis only a stepmother would blame you. Now before you rush off again and injure some other innocent lady, perhaps you should tell me where ya' were headed in such a hurry."

"Well. . . . I was . . ." Joe started.

"Out with it, wee one. I am just trying to head ya' in the right direction, I am. Obviously you are not in your own neighborhood." She smiled kindly down at Joe as she twirled her parasol behind her shoulder.

His eyes dimmed slightly at her comment, as he had been feeling confident that he'd perfected his American accent during the last school year. "Well, I *was* looking for the milkman, but I had to run from the other side of the street to get away from a board game."

The pretty lady started to laugh again but stopped when she saw how seriously Joe was staring at her. "Why on God's green earth would a fine, smart young chap be afraid of a child's toy?"

"Because the Devil lives in it!" Joe responded assuredly. He pointed across the street to where the two boys were still playing the game.

She pulled the light pink rim of her hat up and peered across the sunny street and saw what Joe was referring to. "Those two monkeys are my little brothers, full of mischief and snake tails as they are. They're trouble to be sure, but no more possessed of the Devil than any other ten-year-old boys. 'Tis just a game, it is. No more worrying for ya'. Now, I saw the milkman headed left on the next street just before ya' jostled me, my lad. Scurry along and you might catch him yet."

"Thanks, ma'am!" Turning to run toward where the milkman had headed, he heard the woman call, "And watch out for evil toys and lasses out for a stroll!"

Joe found the delivery truck on the next block and bought the sour cream. Carrying the glass bottle carefully, he headed directly home to avoid any further difficulties.

CHAPTER TWO

Joe bounced up the steps of the two-family house his family shared with his uncle and aunt, Wujek Alexy and Ciotka Hedwig (Uncle Alex and Aunt Hattie). Joe could smell onions simmering in the kitchen, and he heard his three female cousins playing next door. He opened his own front door and hung his hat in the hallway.

The house was typical for this area of Polonia, as his neighborhood was called in Detroit. Each home had a separate entrance, its own kitchen and living area downstairs and bedrooms upstairs. Matka and Aunt Hattie were good friends, and both enjoyed gardening in the backyard and gossiping in their wooden chairs on the porch in the evenings.

What Joe did not enjoy however, was sharing *anything* with his cousins, Marya, Pauline and Emilia. Marya was ten years old, extremely bossy and always telling Joe what to do and how he should do it. His mother had instructed Joe to pretend to go along with the older girl for the peace of the family. He *was* two years younger after all. Occasionally when Marya had to watch Emilia for his aunt, he and Pauline would play stickball in the backyard or on the street with the other children from the neighborhood. But ordinarily, Marya would yell out the window for Pauline to come back inside to help with some kind of cleaning or cooking. Emilia was two years old, like Joe's brother Frank, and therefore was inconsequential to the mind of a busy eight-year-old boy.

Joe walked into the kitchen with the sour cream behind his back. Luckily for him, Matka was giving Frank a piece of a sugar cookie, and her back was turned toward the door. Joe slipped the sour cream into the icebox, on the top shelf, behind the milk bottles. He wanted to let his father have the gratification of presenting it at supper. It was all Joe could do not to tell his mother. Relieved of his surprise, Joe turned his attention to the goings-on in the kitchen.

Aunt Hattie was rolling dough for the pierogi. She was a short woman with a wide girth. Her sleeves were rolled up to her elbows, and her traditional black dress swayed at her ankles as she pushed the dough on the wooden kitchen table with a rolling pin. Perspiration had formed on her brow and she wiped it off with the hem of her apron while humming *Czerwone Jabłuszko*, a cheerful folk song. Hattie had married Joe's uncle in Poland and had stayed behind with his cousin Marya until Uncle Alexy had saved enough money for their passage. Two years in a turbulent country without her husband had given Hattie a strong independent streak that Uncle Alexy found challenging, to say the least. Although not yet a citizen, Aunt Hattie spent any spare time she had campaigning for women's suffrage. She witnessed the atrocities committed by the Prussian army, and as a result she believed that all citizens should have a say in their government's activities.

The large, shiny black stove on the back wall had been left by the previous tenants and was fairly modern. The oven door had Detroit Stove Works in ornate raised lettering on the front. The stove was burning coal and generating more heat on the already warm late summer day.

Matka dipped a cloth into the hot water reservoir next to the stove's firebox and wiped down the sink.

The kitchen was narrow and dark with only one window, above the sink, that provided little light. Matka washed the small window every week when the smoke from the stove and kerosene lamps began to darken the panes. Joe's mother had selected a dark wallpaper for the kitchen in an attempt to camouflage the smoke stains. A large wooden tub, used both for the family's weekly baths on Saturday night and for washing the family's laundry sat in the corner with the washboard. (It was Joe's job to draw the water from a pump in the backyard for cooking and cleaning.) One lone picture, of Our Lady of Cz stochowa, hung on the wall near the table. Matka had hung a pretty flowered cloth in front of the sink to hide shelves underneath which held her pots and pans. She'd sewn a matching tablecloth that was used for suppers in the small kitchen.

Matka opened doors of the hutch which held the family's few dishes, pulled out a glass tumbler and crossed the worn wooden floor to the kitchen table. Ciotka Hedwig and Matka were preparing supper in Blanca's kitchen because Aunt Hattie's stove was small and difficult to cook on.

Frank was satisfied to chew on his cookie, and Matka sat at the table. She turned the tumbler upside down and used it to cut out circles for the pierogi.

Joe greeted his mother. "Cze   Matka."

"Joe. You're back. How was Father?" she asked in Polish. Matka knew almost no English and Ojciec spoke only a little.

"Ojciec's in a good mood. He didn't care that I was a few minutes late," replied Joe.

Blanca turned to Hedwig and said, "Well, what could be causing this cheery mood, I wonder?"

"Who cares?" said Aunt Hattie. "Just be glad for it. Perhaps it will help with the news about . . . well, you know."

"Yes, let us just thank the Lord for it. Perhaps God did hear me praying last night," replied Matka.

Joe held his tongue and didn't ask his mother what the news was. Children could not interrupt adult conversation, and the women were obviously trying to keep something from him. Of course, being a young boy and being Joe he was all the more curious and determined to figure out what was going on.

"Matka?"

"Yes?"

"Can I help put the filling in the pierogi?" Joe said, looking up sweetly at his mother.

"Why, yes. Thank you, my son. I can't remember the last time you helped me cook in the kitchen, especially on such a lovely day, and a Saturday at that!" Joe thought he saw her turn to his aunt and wink.

Joe began scooping small amounts of a cottage cheese and egg mixture onto the small dough circles. As he did this he peered at Matka from the corner of his eyes. After a couple of minutes, the two women appeared to have forgotten he was there and began discussing a neighbor who lived four doors down the street.

"I saw five men come out of Mrs. Ludwicka's house at six yesterday morning," his mother said to Aunt Hattie. "Then, not forty-five minutes, later I saw two men going in. Ten minutes later, three more went in the front door, and when I left for the market a half-hour later, another man, very large this time, walked up the stairs and went in. All were dirty and tired, looking like they had just got off work at the automobile plant." Matka continued pushing the round drinking glass into the rolled out dough and pressing out small circles which she handed to Joe.

"Oh, my" replied Hattie. "I was meaning to tell you, Blanca, I saw three men leaving around two o'clock yesterday. They were carrying dinner pails and looked like they were on their way to work."

"Her house is the same size as ours," Blanca said. "We fit quite nicely here, but I can't imagine all those grown men in a house this size. What on earth do you think is going on over there? She couldn't possibly be boarding all those men, could she? I know she lost her husband last year; poor man, falling off that steel beam building the Statler Hotel. Dear Lord—falling fourteen stories down," she said, making the sign of the cross over herself. "But there has to be another way to earn money than taking in all those men."

"Fourteen men in one house! Disgraceful! Where can they all sleep? Surely there are not fifteen beds in that house? And what about her little boy? Isn't he around Joe's age? Even if her boy slept with her, she'd need her own room. Isn't the St. Josaphat civic committee always bringing her a food basket or two during the week? I donated a bag of potatoes and a pound of oatmeal to the church last Monday myself."

"Matka?" said Joe. Matka looked at Joe and he continued. "I was playing baseball with Sam and the other boys yesterday after school in the street, and he told me that all those men living there share beds."

"Whatever can you mean, Joe? Share a bed?" Matka looked sharply at her son. "Did you ask him about the men going in his house?" Neighbors that meddled in others' business were looked down upon.

Joe's other uncle, Wujek Feliks, lived in a boarding house a few blocks from the Jopolowski clan. Ojciec and Uncle Alexy felt Feliks should live with the family, but Feliks said he didn't want to burden his brothers. To Joe's thinking however, his uncle liked to live without the interference of his sisters-in-law. He'd overheard the women tsk-tsk in hushed voices, as they prepared food in the kitchen, about taverns, gambling and burlesque shows.

"No, Matka, Sam was telling me that he was going to Belle Isle Park today, and I asked him what he was going to do there. He told me his mother and he are taking a ferry to the island and renting a canoe to paddle through the canals. There's a zoo too, Matka, did you know that? Sam and his mother are going to go to the zoo and an aquarium. Then they are going to eat a picnic lunch and watch the big steam ships go by."

"That's nice" Blanca interrupted, "but what does that have to do with the men living in their house?"

"I'm getting to that, Matka" Joe replied. "Well, it sounded like a terrific time to me, so I said, 'Sam, how much does it cost to go to this park?' and Sam said it costs ten cents for the ferry, and the zoo and the aquarium are five cents apiece. His mother packed sandwiches for lunch, and after they take the ferry back to the city, Sam said they are going to the Sanders Palace of Sweets for an ice cream soda!"

"My goodness, sounds like a lot of money to spend. What a waste when Mrs. Ludwicka must provide for her and Sam."

"That's the thing Matka; Mrs. Ludwicka has lots of money now. Sam told me she has seven beds set up in the living room of his house. The day shift men share a bed with the night shift men. That way Mrs. Ludwicka gets two times the boarding money. The men don't care 'cause they only sleep there and get one meal a day. They have no families 'cause they just got here from Poland and they left them behind."

"It's hard for men to leave their families and come to a new country alone; hard for the families left behind too," Hattie interjected.

"So I asked Sam if I could look in his house and see all the beds and he took me over there," Joe continued. "What a sight. All the windows are covered so the night shift men can sleep during the day. Each man has a hook over the bed he shares to put his clothes on, and they keep the rest of their stuff under the beds. There were five men sleeping when Sam and I snuck in, so we had to be very quiet. Mrs. Ludwicka was in the backyard hanging laundry, because she cleans their clothes as part of their room and board. So she didn't see us."

"Can you believe this Hattie? What a shame. All those men living in her house . . . I don't care if I was left with both those boys by myself, I would never . . ." Blanca was becoming upset, and Joe felt like he had ruined what had been a pleasurable day.

"Don't worry, Matka. Sam says it's just for a little while. His mother is saving most of the money and is learning English so she can get a job downtown. Sam said his mother doesn't like all those men living there, but she has no other choice until she can learn English," Joe explained, anxious to change the mood back to a lighthearted one.

"Well, I surely hope so. Imagine!"

Hattie laughed. "*One* man in my house is one too many sometimes."

"Oh, Hattie, stop now." Blanca giggled.

Joe folded the filled circles of dough in half and pinched the edges together to finish making the pierogi, and the conversation changed to talk of some cloth Aunt Hattie wanted to buy to make Marya a new dress for Christmas. Joe was uninterested, and his mind began to wander back to the Irish boys playing with the board game on the porch. He wondered if they would go to Hell or if an evil spirit would come to them at night and possess them. Maybe nothing would happen and it was just a board game after all. *Well,* Joe thought, *it sure wasn't worth the risk for a silly game.*

Hattie grabbed a large spoon and dropped the stuffed dough into a pot of boiling water. After a few minutes she pulled them out and gave them to Blanca to brown them in the cast iron skillet that Matka had retrieved from a shelf under the sink. She placed the skillet on the right front corner of the range, just the right spot to get it to a medium heat while she chopped onions on her wooden cutting board. When she finished chopping, she took a few tablespoons of butter from the icebox and put it in the skillet with the onions. A delightful sizzling accompanied the delicious aroma of onion. . As she was browning the pierogi in the same pan, Mikołaj came into the kitchen.

"What delicious smells greet me after a day of hard work! And two such lovely peasant girls to look upon! A man could not ask for more," he said. Joe poured his father a beer from the small keg next to the icebox and handed it to him. "*And* a good son to bring me a drink, God must be smiling down on me."

Hattie laughed as she gathered her portion of the meal to take next door. "I am glad to see someone appreciates my healthy figure," she said, as she balanced the bowl of pierogi on one of her ample hips and swished her skirt in a flirty fashion as she went out the door.

Joe sat next to Frank's highchair at the kitchen table. Ojciec sat down next to Joe. Matka placed the fragrant pierogi on the table and brought out a cucumber salad she had made that morning from the bottom shelf of the icebox.

"I'll get the milk," Joe volunteered so Matka wouldn't discover the surprise hidden on the top shelf. Joe looked at Ojciec and Ojciec winked playfully at him. After pouring a glass for Matka, Frank and himself, Joe sat back down. Ojciec began the prayer over the meal, "Thank you Lord, for these gifts: for the health of this family, for steady work, a solid home and nourishing food. Amen."

Matka dished out the pierogi onto each plate. Ojciec took a bite and said "Blanca, something is missing. . . ."

"Oh no, did I forget to put in the egg?" she asked cutting a pierogi apart and looking at the filling.

"No, no . . . hmmm . . . I think it needs a little . . . whatta you think, Joe?"

Joe jumped up, ran to the icebox, pulled out the sour cream, and put it on the table.

"Oh, Mikołaj! How exciting! Joe, you did not even give me a hint!"

Pouring a spoonful of the heavy cream on his pierogi, Joe began to eat. The warm cheese and dough tasted like heaven, and he ate them quickly. After only three or four he began to feel full. Slowing down now, he took a bite of the cold cucumber salad. It had a refreshing feel after the warm pierogi.

"Blanca, you do make the best pierogi in Polonia," said Mikołaj, taking a bite of his seventh dumpling.

"Mikołaj, you are just full of compliments and surprises today. What is going on in that head of yours? Are you just happy tomorrow is your day off, or have you been elected to be the next president of America?"

"Well, if you must know, the supervisor of the school building project let us know this morning that the school should be completed by November. Just in time too, as I see it. That old school is not well heated and our Joe needs to be warm so he can concentrate on his studies and become a great man someday. Right, Joe?"

"That *is* good news," said Blanca. "A couple of months ahead of schedule isn't it?"

"Yes, but the best news is that the school will be dedicated by the bishop on November 14, which is St. Josaphat's feast day. What a celebration we will have!"

"How wonderful—the Bishop!"

"Oh, and I have one other small thing to share with my fine family . . ."

"What, Mikołaj?"

"What is it, Ojciec?"

"Father Gatowski gave me five dollars in thanks for volunteering every Saturday. So I decided to take our family to Bois Blanc Island next Saturday!"

Joe could hardly believe it. He had heard about Bois Blanc from an older boy at school named Franz, the only child of a butcher. Franz had experienced more of the city's entertainments than any other kid at school. Franz and his parents had picnicked at Bois Blanc that summer, and he'd told Joe all about the steamship that took them there and the fun things they had done during the day. It sounded like paradise to Joe, and he couldn't wait to see it for himself. Waiting seven days would seem like eternity.

CHAPTER THREE

Sunday morning, refreshed from their weekly bath the night before, Joe and his family left for church. Wearing freshly laundered short pants, stockings, shirt and jacket, he was on top of the world. His shoes were too small, but he dared not complain lest his mother think new shoes more important than a trip to Bois Blanc. In the morning sun, they walked tall and proud in their Sunday best. Mikołaj smiled as he carried Frank in the crook of his arm and held his pretty wife's elbow. Life had become a little easier since moving to Detroit, and they felt like they belonged. Blanca and Mikołaj greeted other families as they, too, left their homes and started toward the great steepled cathedral. They passed several Polish Catholic families who were headed in the opposite direction towards the Sweetest Heart of Mary or St. Albertus, both located two blocks down from St. Josaphat.

St. Albertus was the first Polish church built in Detroit. It had served the community for several years when the handsome, young priest, Father Kolasinski, was assigned as the head priest in 1882. After only a few years, reports began to circulate that his live-in housekeeper was not his sister, as he had declared, but his lover. The radical priest was thrown out of the Catholic archdiocese; however thousands of parishioners remained loyal to Father Kolasinski and banded together to build a second Polish Catholic church only a block from St. Albertus. With their own hard-earned money they built the largest cathedral in Michigan, Sacred Heart of Mary, without the help or blessing of Rome. All who followed Father Kolasinksi were excommunicated. In reprisal, the Detroit archdiocese began to build St. Josaphat, just one block south of the rogue church, for the burgeoning Polish population. After a few years and much protest and discussion, the Vatican recanted the excommunications and allowed the priest and his followers back into the Catholic faith. The exquisite church was renamed the Sweetest Heart of Mary, and in the end three mammoth churches lay within four blocks of each other on the same street.

Joe looked up at the three steeples of St. Josaphat as he heard the three mighty bells begin to ring, calling the devoted to worship. Two young women in slim-fitting dresses and babushkas chatted and laughed as they walked on the sidewalk in front of him. One was telling the other how a would-be suitor's overzealous attempt to impress had resulted in his landing on his rear in a pile of horse manure. Joe chuckled to himself and turned his attention to a conversation several men were having with his father, behind him.

"Falling down drunk," a small man was saying to Mikołaj.

"The foreman threw him right out into the street in front of the Piquette plant," another added. Joe's ears strained to hear over the sound of the giggling women in front of him.

"Everyone knows Jacob drinks at lunch," Mikołaj replied. "But how was he drinking in the plant without being noticed?"

A gruff voice answered, "Apparently he'd somehow fastened a flask to his back, attached a long tube and pulled it over his shoulder down his sleeve to his cuff. He'd just put his wrist to his mouth and suck on the tube and take a drink and no one was the wiser. Till he over-served himself, that is!" The gravelly voice guffawed. Joe slowed his pace so he wouldn't miss anything.

"Too many men hooked on booze lately. Seems everywhere I look there's some drunk in the gutter or harassing a lady as she tries to go about her errands," Mikołaj said. "They don't know the difference between having a nice glass of beer and drinking a bottle of whiskey. From what I read in the paper, the whole country is drowning themselves in it. Just adds fuel to the fire for those Temperance ladies. Watch my words boys—this keeps on the government *will* decide to outlaw booze."

"No way, Mikołaj" the small man replied. "Never will happen. Those women have been trying to ban liquor for twenty years. It's no business of the government's if a man has a drink or two. A man has to set his own moral compass." Several other men joined in to voice their own opinions, but they were now nearing the cathedral and the conversation dimmed into a respectful murmur and then to silence as the parishioners ascended the stairs into church.

The smell of incense drifted into their nostrils as the large wooden doors opened and they entered the sanctuary. Pulling off his cap, Mikołaj nodded a greeting to the ushers in the vestibule, and the family entered the nave, bathed in a soft light from the stained glass windows lining both sides. They headed to a pew, on the left, near the back, with the number 143 intricately carved in its side of white oak.

Joe's father paid a monthly pew rental to occupy a designated seat, as did all parishioners. New members to the parish were typically assigned seating in the rear of the cathedral. However, people whose weekly tithing was deemed generous or were important members of the community would quickly find themselves near the front. Visitors to the parish could occupy seats in the back of the church if they were available.

Bright golden angels gazed down at Joe from every nook and arch of the nave ceiling. Murals of saints, Christ and his apostles decorated the vaults above his seat. Myriad electric bulbs twinkled on a great chandelier suspended in the middle of the church. Candles glowing in red and blue glass flickered on the five altars. A cloud moved in the sky outside, and a beam of sunshine shone through the stained glass windows.

The warm weather combined with the body heat of nearly twelve hundred attendees had women fanning themselves with their prayer books throughout the hundreds of pews. Joe pulled his handkerchief from his pants pocket and wiped the perspiration from under his collar. His gaze drifted from the oval rose window, with its rose, violet, and blue petals stretching out from the central picture of Jesus, to the ostrich feathers trimming the ladies' hats in the pews before him. Looking around the crowd he spotted Sam and his mother kneeling in prayer a few rows behind his family. Joe coughed quietly to try to grab Sam's attention, but the boy and his mother were deep in prayer. Matka looked down sharply at Joe, and he looked to the front of the church.

Scarlet carpeting down the main aisle ended at the alabaster altar. This too was illuminated with electric lights going up the sides and culminating in a vibrantly lit cross thirty feet above. Two angels blowing trumpets flanked the outer corners. Images of Our Lady of Cz stochowa, Saint Stanislaus and Saint Aloysius adjoined a painting of the church's patron, Saint Josaphat.

Above the high altar a mural of the Trinity was depicted on the domed ceiling, bordered by images of the Nativity and the Last Supper. Detailed paintings of significant biblical scenes adorned the ceiling above the four confessionals in the transept. The décor, murals, lights and vastness of the sanctuary could easily sway a man back into the arms of God. The building was intended to elicit humility and worship. To a small boy, St. Josaphat's cathedral was truly God's house.

Joe stood, as loud chords began to reverberate throughout the church from the massive organ. Two lines of nuns in long, black habits started the procession down the aisle, followed by six altar boys wearing white surplices over black cassocks and carrying flickering ivory candles. Four priests conveying tall golden crosses preceded the head priest, Father Gatowski.

Joe followed along in his missal, singing the sacred songs with reverence and joy. Though he couldn't understand the language, he was familiar with the rites and traditions. Not many in the church could comprehend the old language. Most of the older parishioners couldn't understand English much less Latin, but Mass had been conducted in Latin in the old country, so all were familiar with the liturgy.

Joe had much to be thankful for this week. He thanked God during the time of prayer for his kind, hardworking parents, for Frank not bugging him too much last week and especially for the adventure that awaited him. He finished his prayer with a request. “Dear God, please help the nuns be nicer this week, so I don’t get a note home that’ll mess the plans for Saturday.”

Following the readings, Father Gatowski climbed the curved steps of the pulpit at the center of the front pews. He stood fifteen feet above the congregation, his ivory robes billowing about him. The people near the bottom of the pulpit craned their necks to see the monsignor.

Father Gatowski was a kind man, and the children of St. Josaphat’s often brought him treats from home, which only helped to enhance his round girth. Frequently, he could be seen behind the school throwing a football with the boys or pushing a couple girls on the swings. He was average in stature though a little generous in the belly and had a shock of thick white hair that stood straight up when he was running on the small playground.

Switching from Latin to Polish, Father Gatowski began, “Dzie dobry, St. Josaphat’s! Today I have great news to share with you. Just as Jesus walked through Jerusalem pronouncing the good news of his Father’s love, I want to follow in his footsteps and walk through our streets shouting our good news. All thanks to the donations of money and time from you, our friends and neighbors, St. Josaphat’s new school will be finished in less than a month’s time. All the sacrifices given by you to build a place where our young can learn and be educated in the ways of the Catholic Church are coming to fruition. The school building will be officially dedicated on Friday, November 12, the feast day of our patron saint. There will be no school for the children that day. The sisters and the children will march in procession from the corner of Beaubien and St. Antoine Streets, turning onto Canfield and ending here at the church. They will begin the procession at nine o'clock in the morning. For those that can attend; there will be a ceremony and benediction given by Bishop Foley. Following Mass there will be a dinner held at Polonia Hall. Ladies, please plan to donate a dish to pass, and at that I only request one thing . . . that no meat will be served or eaten on this day in honor of St. Josaphat, who abstained from meat throughout his life out of devotion to our Lord. The weekend will include many celebratory events that the parish social committees are planning. Please stop in the vestibule after Mass to look over the scheduled events and sign up to work at one or two functions. With God's blessing it will be a wonderful occasion. So, as I again thank all of you, let us ask the blessing of St. Josaphat and our Lord Jesus Christ and we pray. . . ."

After the blessing of the gifts, Joe followed his parents out of the pew for Communion. He crossed his arms over his chest as he knelt next to Matka at the altar. This signified to the priest that he had not received the First Holy Communion sacrament, so Father Gatowski instead, lay his hand on Joe's head, giving him a small blessing for the week, and moved down to distribute a holy wafer on the tongue of Ojciec and the others kneeling at the altar.

After Mass, Joe walked as quickly as he could to the back of the church but not so fast he'd be noticed by one of the nuns who were always watching. Reaching the vestibule, he saw the plans for the big festival posted on a large easel. A polka band would play for a dance on that Friday evening.

Joe had never been to a dance before, and he wondered if he'd be allowed to attend. On Saturday morning a baseball game for the boys from the school would be held at a small park near the church. After a picnic lunch, the men of the parish could join a team that would play in the afternoon. Later, the parishioners would reconvene at the church for an evening of song. Tunes from the old county were to be sung followed by dessert and coffee in the basement. The festivities would end with a special Mass on Sunday. Proceeds from a weekend long bake sale would go to buy supplies for the new school.

Joe swiftly wrote his name on the signup sheet for the boys' baseball game. He wanted to make sure he secured a spot on one of the teams. As he turned to walk away, he was surprised to see his father signing up for the baseball game on Saturday afternoon. "Ojciec, have you played baseball before?" asked Joe.

"No, Joe but I've wanted to since I first heard about it when I came to this country. I see you and the neighborhood boys playing in the street, and I think I could learn to play. I am not too old, you know. Twenty-eight is not too old of a man yet, my son. Perhaps you can teach me a couple of the rules in the backyard this afternoon?"

"Yes, Ojciec. Sure! That will be fun!" Joe could hardly believe it. Ojciec had never played a game with him before. When they'd lived in the Upper Peninsula his father had always been too tired from working in the mine, and seven months of snow prohibited much outdoor playing time. Walking home from church, Joe felt that his family was truly on their way to living the American dream.

CHAPTER FOUR

Joe's parents stopped to talk to their friends Mr. and Mrs. Stanislewski, who were sitting on their front porch. The Stanislewski's had lived in a village near where Mikołaj and Blanca had come from in Poland. The couples liked to compare stories and war reports they heard throughout the week from newspapers and from new immigrants arriving in Detroit. The Prussian army was heavily entrenched in the region where they'd lived, and accurate reporting on the state of their villages was difficult to ascertain. Joe sat on the porch step for a few minutes until there was a small break in the conversation.

"Would you like a sugar cookie, Mrs. Stanislewski?" Blanca ventured, pulling the sweet smelling treat from the basket she had taken to church.

"I'd love one, Mrs. Jopolowski! You do make the finest sweets on this side of Detroit, Blanca."

"Oh, I don't know about that . . ."

"Blanca, please don't be so humble! Mikołaj! Aren't Blanca's pastries the best in the city?" Mrs. Stanislewski asked.

"Absolutely! And they should be, for as much sugar she goes through in a week." He smiled. "Pretty soon I'll have to buy a car so I can carry it back from the market."

"If she sold them you probably could buy a car, Mikołaj," Mr. Stanislewski interjected.

"Now stop, all of you," Blanca said. "I could never charge for my baking. I just enjoy it, and I enjoy sharing it with others. Here, Joe, why don't you take two cookies and give one to Walt," she said.

"Is Walt home?" he asked Mrs. Stanislewski hopefully, as she fanned herself on a chair in the shade.

"Go on upstairs," Mrs. Stanislewski replied, smiling. "He's in his room." Joe ran up the narrow staircase to Walt's room. Walt was three years older than Joe and a friendly kid who didn't mind hanging out with Joe while their parents visited. Joe found Walt sitting on his bed, glasses lying crooked on his nose, looking at postcards of the Gold Cup boat races in Manhasset Bay, New York.

"Hiya Joe! Hey, look at this. These are from August fourteenth of this year." Walt pointed at a black and white picture of a hydroplane boat named the Miss Detroit. "This girl has a two hundred fifty horsepower Sterling engine!"

"Wow! Two hundred fifty horses! How fast can she go?" asked Joe.

"Almost fifty miles per hour, but she averages around forty-two in a circular course. The Miss Detroit won the Gold Cup this year. First time a boat from Detroit has won since they started racing eleven years ago. Look, see this other postcard? That's a picture of Jack Beebe standing on her bow. Last year he was the riding mechanic on the Baby Speed Demon II, but that boat wasn't from Michigan.

He's a master mechanic. He rebuilds all his engines to make them faster and lighter for racing."

Walt walked over to a small desk and picked up several books that were piled high on the corner. Papers fell to the ground, and Joe saw several drawings of engines and boats as he lent a hand picking up the sheets. Joe knew better than to ask his friend if he was going to play in the St. Josaphat baseball game. Walt always refused to play games or baseball with the other boys. He spent half his time tinkering with small machines and kitchen tools and the other half down at the river watching boats and ships.

"What's a riding mechanic?" Joe asked.

"That's the guy that sits in the boat with the driver. He operates the engine and fixes what breaks while they're racing. Last year Jack Beebe whittled a washer for the air pump of the Speed Demon while they were racing!"

"Boy, how long is a race?"

"Depends on the race," Walt said. "This year the Gold Cup was five miles."

"Does Jack Beebe ever drive the boat or does he always just work on the engine?" Joe was very interested; he hadn't known a boat could go so fast.

"Well, actually this year, when he won again, he was driving. See, Miss Detroit's driver didn't show up for the race and five minutes before the starting gun they still had no one to drive. So the owners of the boat say 'Hey! Can anybody here drive a boat?' and this guy Johnny Milot says he can. Johnny'd come to the race to be a mechanic's assistant and had driven the boat a couple times to test it out but he'd never driven in a race and didn't know the course."

Joe stared hard at the facial features of the mechanic on the postcard as Walt continued. The man's face was wrinkled, and his cap was tilted up above his forehead.

"So the race starts, see? And Johnny decides to follow the other boats so he can figure out the course. After a few times around, he tells Jack to let it out. Jack pulls out the throttle and they start gaining. Then the water starts getting really rough and young Johnny starts getting banged up and he's getting sick from the smell of the exhaust from the other boats. So old Jack takes over driving while still operating the engine. On top of that, he's holding Johnny in the boat so he won't fall out! But old Jack just keeps the throttle open and gets in the lead. Finally, he's gotta pull into the pit for some gas and someone yells 'Why didn't you stop? You won the race long ago.' And Jack says 'We forgot to count the laps.' Can you believe that? Yes sir, as soon as I'm older I'm going to drive a boat like that!"

"Do you really think you will?" Joe asked. He handed the postcard back to Walt, who put it on the crowded desk.

"Sure. Next year I'll be eleven, old enough to help with doing something around those fast machines—*anything*. Even if it's just washing 'em up. Next summer they're having the Gold Cup right here on the Detroit River on account of the Miss Detroit winning last year. I'm sure I'll be able to work my way in somewhere."

Joe left the Stanislewski's a little while later, thinking about speed boats and races the entire way home.

Exciting things were happening in Joe's city. Detroit was growing; new high-rise buildings, stores, theaters and auto plants were going up everywhere, along with new homes to house all the people that were arriving daily at the train station. Every week there were new faces at church and almost as often a new kid at school. Good thing the new school was almost finished. Joe's classroom was getting pretty full. Lately, he had gotten into the habit of getting to school early so he'd be one of the first in line when the bell rang to make sure he'd get a desk for the day.

After a dinner of ham, green beans, bread and some poppy seed cake, Joe and Ojciec went in the backyard to throw a ball around. The yard was small and they didn't have a mitt, but it didn't matter. Ojciec lobbed the ball at Joe. With concerted effort, Joe jumped a couple feet to make the catch. As they played catch, Joe tried to explain the rules of the game to his father.

"A pitcher can spit on a ball and throw it at the batter?" asked Ojciec.

"Sure, it's called a spitball," Joe explained. "The pitcher can spit or rub some Vaseline from inside his baseball cap on the ball. When he throws the ball the batter can't be sure where or how it's going to come into the plate. Sometimes the pitcher smears the ball with tobacco spit and dirt so the ball is the same color of the infield and it's hard to see."

"I think I'm following you on the basic rules. Three outs, three strikes, four balls, nine innings, both teams go up each inning. Guess it'd be easier to understand if I could see a game before I go out there and make a fool of myself, huh, Joe?"

"Well, I heard they have baseball diamonds on Bois Blanc. Maybe we can catch a game there on Saturday, huh

Ojciec?" Joe thought this was a good way to solidify the family's upcoming trip.

"Really? Yeah, I think I heard a guy down at the plant saying he played there this summer. Well, I guess our little boat trip comes at a good time, right Joe?" Ojciec said as he winked at his son.

"Yes sir!" Joe replied.

CHAPTER FIVE

The school week passed slowly. A cold drizzle fell over the city the first three days and turned into a steady downpour on Thursday. The streets were a muddy mess. Walking home from school on Thursday, Joe stopped to watch two men attempting to free a carriage that had gotten stuck in the mud. Rain poured off their hats and down the backs of their long overcoats as they swore and cussed at the unmoving wheels. The carriage horse stood to the side observing their labor, shaking off the water from his mane and stomping his hooves to release the mud caked on his legs.

The brick streets were not much better than the unpaved ones, as the sewer system could not seem to keep up with the deluge. Cars and streetcars plunged through great streams of rain, splashing any poor pedestrian with a wall of water.

Joe's Sunday prayers went unheard. The nuns' demeanor was soured by the weather as well. Several boys in the class had their fingers rapped with rulers for small indiscretions like swinging their feet at their desks or not finishing all their milk at dinner. Joe's neighbor Sam was made to stand at the front of the class and hold his arms straight out to the side for half an hour. At first, Sam thought this to be an easy punishment for pulling the pigtails of the girl who sat in front of him. But after half an hour, pain began to show on Sam's face. At the end of the hour, his small arms were trembling uncontrollably with muscle spasms. Joe felt bad for his friend but said nothing. He sat quietly working on his arithmetic and American history assignments. Too great a gift awaited him on Saturday to jeopardize his standing with Sister Mary Monica.

The clouds finally parted on Friday afternoon, and the class went out to recess after eating dinner. Franz, one of the older boys, found a stick and drew four large circles in the wet dirt beside the school. Another pulled a small, closed sack filled with barley from his pants pocket.

"Zo ka!" Joe said when he recognized the game. "Can I play?"

"Sure" replied Tall Paul, the boy holding the zo ka sack. Joe stood in the middle of one of the dirt circles, and Sam raced over to the remaining one. Paul dropped the zo ka on his foot and tossed it to Joe, who caught it in the air with his left foot and tossed it to Sam, who immediately dropped it.

Franz, the boy who had drawn the circles stated, "That's a fault, Sam. You're out!" Franz said. He took the sack and passed it to Tall Paul, who deftly caught it between his knees.

"Good one, Paul!" Franz said. Tall Paul tossed it to Joe, who again caught it on his foot. But when Joe attempted to pass it to Franz, he crossed his dirt circle, and the other boys called a fault, so he had to leave the game. The older boys passed the zo ka back and forth several times until Franz was also out and Tall Paul declared the winner. They played for the entire recess, and Joe smiled to himself, feeling the warm sun on the back of his jacket. The sun was shining, he'd managed to stay out of Sister Mary Monica's line of sight that week and tomorrow was the big day.

Eating a supper of kielbasa and sauerkraut that evening with his family, Joe noticed his matka and ojciec secretly smiling at each other when they thought he wasn't looking. "Now what could be going on?" he wondered. He was about to ask, when his mother mentioned the picnic lunch she was going to pack for the next day.

"What time does the *Columbia* leave for Bois Blanc, Ojciec?" Joe asked. He could already picture the big boat chugging down the river with him on it.

"Eight-thirty a.m., Joe. We'll have breakfast and head for the streetcar at seven-thirty. That will give us plenty of time to get to the dock and buy our tickets. Matka made our picnic lunch and it's in the icebox ready to pack for the morning. Now," he said when they had finished the meal, "empty the water from the icebox and get ready for bed. Matka will bring Frank up in a minute."

Joe retrieved the metal pan containing the melted ice from the bottom of the icebox and carefully carried it to the backyard. He threw the water on what remained of their summer garden. As he carried it back down the hall to the kitchen he overheard his father say to his mother, "I know, I know . . . it can wait till tomorrow. Let's do as we planned, Blanca. One more day is nothing in a lifetime."

Joe returned the pan to the icebox and climbed the stairs to the room he shared with Frank. He undressed and, with a running start, leapt into the small, metal framed bed he shared with Frank. Now that his brother was almost three, his parents felt it was time for Frank to be out of his crib. The last two months had not provided Joe with much sleep. The weather had been warm and Frank had a tendency to push his hot little body against Joe all night. No matter how many times Joe would push his brother away or even arrange him down at the foot of the bed, Frank squirmed his way up next to Joe. Exasperated, Joe would occasionally grab a blanket and sleep on the floor next to what had been, up until July, his own bed.

When Matka brought Frank up to bed, Joe moved next to the wall to make room for his little brother. He thought that for once it wouldn't matter how much Frank kicked and squirmed. He was too excited to be able to sleep anyway. However, when Frank fell asleep a little while later, Joe found his eyes closing too. It had been a long week, and even the great event could not compete with a little boy's need for rest.

The following morning, Joe was up, dressed, washed and downstairs by six-fifteen. "Can I wake up Frank, Matka?" he asked.

"It's too early, Joe. Ojciec is still asleep. Why don't you go to the garden and see what is left to harvest. If you stay in here, I can see you will pester me to death."

Joe surveyed the remains of the small backyard garden they shared with his aunt's family. Joe walked past the string beans. He didn't like picking them because they made his palms itch. The early cabbages had all been picked and the big, late cabbages for sauerkraut wouldn't be ready for another month. But he found two cucumbers, several yellow hot peppers and two green sweet peppers. Piling them on the ground, he looked at the twenty tomato plants near the fence. There were still dozens of ripening tomatoes on the vines. He picked four large red tomatoes and thirty small cherries and brushed the dirt from the bounty. Untucking his shirt, he put all the vegetables in it, using it as a basket. In the kitchen he rinsed the harvest with water and placed it in the sink.

Matka turned from frying eggs on the stove to ask, "Was there no squash, Joe?"

"No, Matka. Not that I could see."

"Maybe Hattie grabbed them yesterday. I'd have you go next door and ask, but it's early yet. Also, I think Hattie is a little jealous of our trip today. We asked them to go, of course, but the girls need new shoes and dresses for the winter and Uncle Alexy felt they couldn't spend the money right now."

Thank Jesus, Mary and Joseph, thought Joe. If anything could ruin his trip it would have been his vexing cousins. A small stab of guilt about his small shoes crossed his mind, and he thought about telling his mother he needed new shoes also. But he couldn't fight the excited voice in his head telling him to keep quiet.

Matka was percolating the coffee when Ojciec walked down the stairs. He was washed, shaved and dressed to go out on the town.

"Now can I get Frank, please?" Joe pleaded.

"All right, Joe, go ahead and get your brother ready."

Joe ran up the stairs two at a time and down the hall to their room.

"Come on, Frank, wake up. Ya wanna go on a boat today?" he said, trying to raise his little brother from a deep sleep. Frank's hair was standing up all over his head, and one of his cheeks was bright red.

"Boat?" he said sleepily.

"Yes, a great big boat! Come on and get washed up. We're going after breakfast. Hurry now; let me help you get your clothes on." Joe quickly got his brother ready to go and tied his small brown leather shoes. Holding hands, they walked down to the kitchen.

Matka had the packed picnic basket on the counter. She was wearing a bright lilac dress that came to her ankles, and her blonde hair was up in a pretty bun. Most days she wore a babushka, but today her hair was prettily coiffed. It shone like a jar of honey in the sun. A quick prayer over the meal, three bites of toast with jam and a scrambled egg, and Joe was ready for the door.

"Joe, slow down, get a bucket of water from the pump so I can wash these few dishes before we leave." Matka said.

Can't she wash them when we get back? he thought. Obeying his mother, he grabbed the bucket from under the sink and went to retrieve the water.

Many houses had running water but the Jopolowskis' home had been built without plumbing. An outhouse directly behind the home was their toilet. The family had never had indoor plumbing. Joe sometimes wished they lived in a more modern home, but knew better than to complain.

Quickly pushing up and down on the pump handle, Joe soon filled the bucket.

"Thought you'd be gone by now," came a snotty voice from the back of the house. Joe looked up and saw his older cousin coming down the steps carrying her own bucket.

"We're leaving in a minute, Marya" Joe replied.

"Better hurry or you'll miss the boat," she taunted.

"Don't worry, Marya, we'll make it. Have fun hanging around here all day. Looks like it's going to be a hot one." Joe enjoyed the fact that he was going to escape the heat for once. "If the iceman comes by, could you get a block for our icebox? I'm sure it will melt by the time we come back from the island. Thanks, Marya." Joe walked up the stairs and let the door shut in his fuming cousin's face.

Joe raced inside, sloshing some water in the hall. Joe emptied the pail into the sink, grabbed a rag to clean up the water on the wood floor and returned the rag to its rightful spot before Matka noticed.

Ten minutes later, dishes clean, kitchen in order, they were on their way. Walking south toward Gratiot Street, dressed in their best clothing, they were the perfect portrait of a good, hardworking immigrant family. Ojciec carried Frank on his shoulders, smiling under his mustache. Matka carried the basket with tasty treats for their outing. And Joe ran ahead and then back. They turned on Gratiot.

"What is that construction noise I hear, Matka asked Ojciec. The noise came from a few blocks away.

"Crowley's department store is expanding. They're taking over the whole block." Crowley's was a nine story building taking up half a block from Gratiot to Monroe Street. Ojciec had not been there but had heard the men at work talking about what a large store it was.

Matka said, “A couple of the ladies in the neighborhood shopped there and had afternoon tea in the mezzanine dining room. There are ladies’ lounges on several floors and even a sick room staffed with a full time nurse.” She laughed. “Can you imagine getting ill in a store and not going home to care of yourself?”

A few blocks later the family arrived at Woodward Avenue. This main artery through the city was three times as wide as a regular street. They waited at the corner for the electric streetcar that would carry them to the Bois Blanc dock. The street was bustling with horse-drawn carriages, Model T’s and bicyclists, and there were people everywhere.

Matka grabbed Joe’s hand as they climbed into the next streetcar. She sat down with Frank on a polished cane seat. Joe and his father stood nearby and grabbed onto a brass pole. The streetcar driver swung a knob that closed the folding doors. Joe had never seen an automatic door before and stared at the knob mechanism in amazement. *Clang! Clang! Clang!* the bell rang out as the driver stamped his foot on a button in the floor. He pulled a big lever with a wooden knob, and the car started down the tracks. The motorman pulled the lever again, and the car started speeding up. Joe started swinging side to side with the car’s motion. The motorman turned and smiled at Joe. “Hello, good morning to you. Welcome aboard,” he called in a friendly voice that had an unmistakable English accent.

“Good morning, sir” Joe replied.

“Looks like you are on your way to an adventure today . . . the Palace of Sweets or maybe Electric Park?”

“No, sir,” replied Joe looking the driver in the eye. “We’re going to Bois Blanc.” He pronounced it like the French name it was, *bwah blanh*.

"Oh, you mean Boblo Island No one says Bois Blanc anymore. No one round here can seem to pronounce it right, so folks have been calling it Boblo. All these different languages pouring into this fine city, and yet no one seems to speak French." He laughed. "Don't know why, but it seems to fit, and everyone can say it." The motorman was tall and slim, with auburn hair and light brown eyes. He was Mikołaj's age or perhaps a few years younger. Joe admired the motorman's ability to balance on one foot and clang the bell with the other as he drove down the street.

"How long have you worked on the streetcar?" Joe asked.

"Oh, about three years now, I'm guessing. It's a nice job when the weather's good. Bit dirty and cold in the winter, but I meet lots of nice folks like yourself. Name is William Gribble."

"Joe Jopolowski." Joe extended his hand.

"That's a mouthful to be sure, Joe." William laughed.

The trolley's pantograph sparked and crackled as it met the copper catenary lines strung down the middle of the avenue. An oncoming streetcar passed them on the other track, pulling both cars slightly toward each other. What a rush! Joe turned and waved at the passengers riding the opposing trolley.

The noise on the street turned to a din as they traveled farther down Woodward Avenue. The ringing of the bell on the streetcar, the horns of the cars, the people and horses, musicians playing in front of a store to attract customers—it all fascinated Joe.

Joe translated what the conductor said about the island's name to his parents. He didn't want them to feel ignorant when they bought the tickets.

"How long has your family been in Detroit?" William said.

"About eight months—my father is working for Mr. Ford," Joe replied.

"Mr. Ford hires a lot of Poles, and the Dodge brothers are building an enormous plant in Hamtramck, and that whole city is mostly made up of Poles. They're even taking over the taverns the Germans always own. When I drive that route, I'm not sure if I'm in Poland or America."

"It's like that in my neighborhood too," said Joe.

The streetcar rails took them directly down the center of the avenue, with its multitude of businesses and stores. Tall wooden poles stood every twenty yards or so down the city sidewalks, shouldering a maze of electric wires. Huge signs stood on the rooftops of the large buildings advertising Light Vaudeville and Photo Plays for 10 cents. Delicious smells drifted out of the restaurants and bakeries into the streetcar.

Nickelodeons, barber shops, arcades, restaurants, (even a Chinese Restaurant!) crowded the city blocks. A sign for Heyn's Bazaar outlined with hundreds of electric bulbs competed with Weitz Clothing, Himel Hochs and B. Siegel's for customers' attention. Eureka Vacuum, Grinnel Brothers Music Store, Wright Kay Jewelers, Annis Furs and Fyfe's Shoes advertised their goods on giant signs hanging above their entrances. Taverns and saloons crouched between enormous emporiums on every block. Karsten's Cascade Room, Dolph's Saloon, Churchill's and the Hotel Delmar promoted locally made beers for a nickel in their windows. Detroit was known as the City of Saloons; it had over thirteen hundred taverns.

Joe read the marquees for the Wonderland, Temple, and Empress Theatres that offered vaudeville shows and short films inside. As the streetcar entered Campus Martius Park, Joe saw the Detroit Opera House perched on the corner.

The city's street plan had been redesigned by Augustus B. Woodward, a prominent judge, after a huge fire destroyed ninety-five percent of Detroit a century earlier, in 1805. Campus Martius was the hub of the city, with five major streets striking out from there like wagon wheel spokes. According to the motorman, Judge Woodward had simply taken the city map from Washington, D.C., and tried to emulate it.

"Look, Joe!" Matka pointed. "Why is there a giant chair in the middle of the park?" Joe turned his head and saw an enormous dark red chair that was nearly twenty feet high and eight feet wide.

"Why on earth would anyone build a chair that big?" Matka asked. Joe thought it also strange but in a good way. William said the monument was the Cadillac Chair of Justice and had been erected in honor of the city's two hundredth anniversary.

"More like the Cadillac Chair of Wasted of Tax Dollars," he said, laughing as they passed the huge sculpture.

Joe related what William had said, and his mother laughed. Passing the park, Joe saw a sign for J.L. Hudson Clothiers. The elaborate window displays of the enormous store enticed pedestrians to come inside and purchase a hat or fine china. A dark-skinned doorman wearing a sharp red uniform stood at the entrance welcoming customers. As the streetcar passed, he opened the set of large doors for a lady balancing several packages.

"See those big red and white awnings down there?" William asked Joe. "That's the famous Palace of Sweets, also known as Sanders Candy." This was the place that Sam and his mother had visited the week prior. Sam had told Joe of the beautiful marble counters with every conceivable kind of sweet displayed behind glass. Joe just knew he had to get there as soon as he had a chance. Men in straw hats and women in large feathered hats holding small children's hands were pouring in and out the front doors. How big could a candy store be to hold so many people? Joe had to find out. And soon.

Now he could see the river looming ahead. Large signs for Bois Blanc were mounted on the roofs and sides of buildings.

"This is your stop coming up, lad," William said. "Next time you need a ride, find car number 12. That's this one you're on. Take good care of you, I will. Hope you have a terrific time today."

Joe said goodbye. Ojciec instructed Joe to take Frank's hand, and they made their way to the back of the trolley. The conductor sat in a small cage collecting fares. Ojciec dropped four nickels in a glass box, and Joe watched as the coins bounced back and forth down the staggered chute. The conductor pushed another button on the floor to open the back door. The trolley stopped, and they stepped off. Ojciec assisted Matka so she would not trip on her long skirt.

CHAPTER SIX

It was a short two blocks north to the end of Bates Street to purchase the tickets for the boat. The sidewalk here was cement and easy to maneuver. They had to stay close to each other, as there were so many people walking alongside them. When they reached their destination, Matka, Joe and Frank walked to the railing by the river and looked down at the water. Matka picked up Frank and held him in her arms, as the railing provided little protection from falling over the side. The river was a swirl of blues and grays as it traveled southward toward Lake Erie in a great rush.

A young couple standing next to them pointed across the waterway toward the land on the other side, not a mile away. "I can't believe we can see Canada from right here!" they were saying. Joe looked, too, and marveled that another country was right before his eyes, within swimming distance. He felt he could easily swim across the river and walk right up the shores of the other country. His bravado was much stronger than his ability however. He had learned to swim fairly well in the Upper Peninsula, on a small lake near his family's rental cabin. But here the river was very swift, and many men had died trying to swim across.

The greatest feast for Joe's eyes was the large steel steamer, *Columbia.* She was three stories high and could carry 3,500 passengers. Joe looked at the three open-air decks teeming with people already aboard. The steamboat and her railings were painted the bright white of the wispy clouds passing above. Two ten-foot-long sunlit red flags waved cheerily in the breeze on the top deck. Her great smokestack was painted a matching red, and she shined and sparkled like freshly polished silver. Well-dressed passengers continued to cross over the small gangplank. The crowd was excited and jovial. The sun, which had risen two short hours before, reflected on the water, creating millions of tiny jumping points of light.

Ojciec joined them with the tickets—twenty-five cents apiece for Joe's and Frank's passage and thirty-five cents each for his and Matka's. The family walked toward the line of passengers crossing the gangplank, as music drifted onto the shore. Walking onto the boat, Joe saw a sixteen-piece orchestra playing a lively rendition of "Anchors Aweigh." The musicians—dressed alike in white seersucker suits, red bowties and white straw boaters with a red ribbon to match—swayed and tapped their feet, encouraging the boarding crowd to dance along to their song.

"Can we ride on the top deck, please?" said Joe. Ojciec nodded his approval, and Joe took off running toward the ladder in the middle of the boat. Not stopping to glance at the second deck, he arrived on the third deck, found a bench with a view of Canada and sat down. Matka found him sitting there, ferociously swinging his feet, as if the force of his small legs could encourage the captain to power up the engines for the trip down the river.

Ojciec stood in the center of the deck talking to two men in Polish. His father seemed to have a knack for finding his countrymen wherever he went. It was his way of feeling comfortable in a new country and learning of new employment possibilities. Not that Ojciec wanted to leave Ford Motor Company. He'd never earned a higher wage and was hoping to be promoted to a safer part of the line after his year anniversary. But foremen in the plant had much control, and any worker could lose his job with no notice. Ojciec had seen several men fired for such small indiscretions as missing one bolt on a wheel well or struggling to keep up as an engine moved down the line. The foreman, not always of the highest ethics, might have had an altercation outside of work with one or perhaps feel a line man was trying to take over his own position and would dismiss the employee for the smallest infraction. So Ojciec always kept his ear to the ground to stay abreast of the goings on within the labor community.

Joe's bench trembled beneath him, and he could hear the engines come to life as the boat began to get under way. Slowly at first, then faster, the *Columbia* began her journey to Boblo Island.

"May I go look on the other side of the boat, Matka?" asked Joe. He wiggled in his seat and craned his neck at the river.

"Be careful, and meet me at this bench when we near the island," she replied, smiling.

Weaving his way through the long skirts of the women on board, Joe made his way across the sixty-foot-wide wooden deck to the Detroit side of the boat. Nearing the front of the boat, he grabbed a vacant spot on the railing with his small hands and stepped up on the lowest bar to increase his field of vision.

He watched the activity on the riverbank. The sprawling Wayne Hotel grabbed his attention first. A large sign on the top floor touted that it was the newest mineral bathhouse in the city. Bright blue awnings hung above hundreds of windows, and a pavilion and large cafeteria were located directly in front of the hotel.

A smaller ferry was pulling away from its dock and heading north on the river. Joe waved at the riders as they passed by the *Columbia*, and they jovially waved back.

A man in his early twenties standing next to Joe leaned down and asked, "Ever ate at the Gardens, boy?" His thick Hungarian accent sounded similar to the Polish accents of Joe's neighborhood. Joe looked up and saw a pair of warm brown eyes looking at him. The man's light brown hair was a bit too long and hung in his eyes when he looked down at Joe, but his face was friendly.

"No, sir. Never ate at a restaurant before."

"No? Well, nothing so great about it, anyhow. Probably nowhere near as good as your mama's cooking. I myself haven't eaten there either. I heard it's a decent meal but a bit pricey for my taste. Friend of mine went to the bathhouse to try to cure his bad back. Aches him all the time. Well, Old Serge paid three dollars to stay there for a day and get treated with this Sulpha-Saline water that's supposed to come from a spring on the property. Said he felt better the next day but by the next week it was hurting him same as before. Maybe that's how they make their money. Keep ya coming back every week." He laughed at this and continued, "Course don't know anyone who could afford that!"

"My mother says the best thing for a sore back is to lie on the ground outside, and when you hear the call of the whip-poor-will roll over three times," Joe replied, trying to be helpful.

"That so?" replied the man. "I'll have to let Serge in on that one. Worth a try and a lot cheaper than the bathhouse, that's for sure. Say boy, what's your name?"

"Joe Jopolowski," he replied, extending his hand. The man grinned and took Joe's handshake, introducing himself as Vic Starboli.

"Ever been to Boblo, boy?"

"No, sir. Today's my first time. Heard about it from a friend of mine though."

"You sneak on the boat? You can let me in on it. I won't tell no one," Vic said.

"No, sir. My father bought my ticket. How can someone sneak on a boat? There are crewmen standing at the gang-plank," he answered.

"Well, a grown man would have a hard time of it, but a small boy could hide himself in between a couple of ladies' skirts and just walk right on without being noticed."

"But that would be stealing, Mr. Starboli!"

"Course it wouldn't . . . just taking a ride on a boat that's already going somewhere." Looking at his worried expression, Vic lightly jabbed Joe in the arm and said, "Now, you forget about what I said, and don't be worrying your folks about it. I was just teasing you. Let me show you a couple of sites along the way if ya want." Changing the subject, Vic pointed to a large building with fortresses on either side.

It was surrounded by several small buildings along the riverbank.

"Now that's Fort Wayne. It's not much of a defense against enemies, but soldiers still train there. It's over seventy-five years old and never had one shot fired in anger. They built it before we started getting along with those Canucks. Drank with a couple of enlisted men one time, and they said they like being stationed there because the work's easy and the city life is the greatest when they get furloughed." Joe hadn't known there was a fort with soldiers in Detroit.

Vic pointed at large factory after factory flanking the water front. Huge cranes and smokestacks rose above the buildings. One chimney reached up two hundred sixty feet into the sky, blocking out views beyond it. A sulfurous smell drifted into the open boat, and the ladies on board covered their noses with handkerchiefs. Two boys near Joe laughed and pointed at one another, blaming one another for the smell.

"Those factories are processing salt they pull up from under the ground. Detroit is sitting on a giant bed of salt, and it's just there for the taking. Ten thousand men work at that plant alone. But the salt mines reach outside Detroit." The boat had passed the outer limits of the city now. "That's River Rouge, and just ahead is the village of Ecorse." Joe watched the men working around the plant. Despite being Saturday, it seemed the plant was in full work mode.

Beyond the factories a small park appeared on the river's edge, and several grand houses with large yards dotted the shoreline. Many had docks with a small motorboat or rowboat tied to the side. The *Columbia* floated by a large shipyard. Men were hammering and sawing wood, constructing a large ship that was almost finished.

"Ford City," said Vic.

"I thought Henry Ford's city was Dearborn" said Joe, referring to the small city just west of Detroit that Henry Ford had founded. Mr. Ford had built a large mansion outside of the city because his wife didn't like the noise and pollution.

"Different Ford," replied Vic. "This one is John Ford. He manufactures glass in Pennsylvania, and he uses the salt mines here to make chemicals for the glass somehow. Well, his sons do anyway. He's dead now. I'll show you where they live; you can see their houses from the boat."

A little further down, after passing another large hotel, Vic pointed out two mansions. One sat directly on the water, and the other could be seen behind it, facing the avenue that ran along the river. "That's how the other half lives, my boy." The three-story homes had towers and ornate balconies, and turrets. Passing in front of the second mansion, Joe could see a streetcar lumbering along the middle of the avenue headed north.

"Does that streetcar go to Detroit from all the way down here?" he asked his companion.

"Sure does. Actually starts out farther south than here though."

"Where'd you learn all this?" Joe asked. The breeze from the water poured into the open side of the boat and Joe took off his cap to let the soft wind ruffle his blond hair.

"Well, don't have much of an education. Been working in factories or such since I was your age. My pa couldn't get much work when we got here. Back then, immigrants were the last to be hired, but children were a good commodity 'cause they don't cost as much to pay. I had little fingers for jobs that were in tight places, and I learned the language quick. Worked for the Detroit Stove Works starting at age seven, putting small pieces on the stoves. My ma took in laundry and seamstress work at home, but she died a few years ago. Pop finally got a steady job with the city in the Public Works Department. Ha! Ya know what he does all day? Walks the streets with a barrel wagon and a shovel, cleaning up after the horses. But he was happy to get it. Steady pay, and he likes being outside. Says working in a factory would kill him. Doesn't smell like a garden when he gets home, but he's happy as a rose, he says."

"I think I'd rather work outside than in a hot factory too," Joe said.

"Not sure how much longer he can go on with that work though. Lately there are more cars than horses on the streets. Well, by the time he got steady work it was too late for me to go back to school, so I've been working ever since. I started thinking I was going to be one ignorant son of a gun on account of not having any learning, so I set out to educate myself. Learning about my surroundings was one of the first things I did. Started riding the steam boats on my days off and listening to all the folks who knew what they was talking about while I rode up and down the river. Been down as far as Toledo, Ohio, and north to St. Clair Flats. Sometimes I take the interurban to Monroe—that's about forty miles south of Detroit—and see what I can in the country down there. Talk to the farmers and the fisherman; wander about and grab a ride home before it's even dark out. Don't cost much and I like to get out of the city sometimes. Don't get me wrong. I love Detroit and there's always something going on, but a fellow likes to breathe some fresh air sometimes, hear a little nature and have a little bit of quiet."

Joe agreed. He hadn't left the city since arriving almost a year ago and had almost forgotten about the quiet solitude that Mother Nature provided. With the *Columbia* leaving Detroit far behind her, Joe realized how accustomed he had become to the dirt and grime of the city. For all its glory, Detroit was a loud, steaming town with smells of burning rubber, ash, chemicals and smoke.

"You still work at the stove factory?" Joe asked.

"Nah, I work for Stroh's now; biggest brewery in Detroit. Pays more, and I get two free beers on my lunch breaks. I'm saving up to buy a farm outside the city. Maybe down this way."

Looking at the blue sky, trees, green grass and animals on the river banks, Joe took a few deep breaths and filled his lungs with the fresh county air. It was cool on this side of the boat, as the sun had not reached overhead. The orchestra downstairs continued to play, but even their songs had become gentler and slower as the *Columbia* moved closer to their destination. The passengers relaxed as the boat moved beyond the factories and boatyards and the land became greener and the trees denser on the riverbank and westward beyond it. When they passed a final small shipyard, Joe could see a three-story hotel a block from the river.

"That's the Grand Hotel of Trenton," Vic said, when he saw Joe eyeing the pretty structure. "Trains come up from Ohio and stop at a small depot in the city. The railroad brings hundreds to Detroit every day. Some passengers stop farther south in a town called Flat Rock, just a few miles from here. There's a unique place there called the Huron River Inn. It sits five feet from the railroad tracks. When a train roars by the barkeep rings a bell above the bar and a shot of whiskey only costs five cents. It's more tavern than inn, and I must confess I had one too many whiskey specials one night and had to rent a room for the night. Maybe that's the master plan for making a profit. The Grand Hotel however, is for a more respectable crowd from what I've heard. Not much more to see from here on out on this side, Joe. Let's walk to the other side of the boat."

Before turning to cross the deck, Joe noticed a large area of trees and grass with several elaborate bridges elegantly crossing over canals. "Hey Vic, what's that? A park?"

"Nope. It's owned by Elizabeth Slocum Nichols. She inherited it from her parents, and she owns the whole small island. Her father owned a couple of those shipyards we saw on the way down here. Now, come on. We are almost to Boblo and I want to show you one more thing." On the other side of the ship, Joe saw another island, but this one was a lot larger.

"That's Grosse Ile, or Big Island in French. You can take a train from there and cross over to Canada. They built a train track on the other side of the island and it crosses over part of the river. Then you take a ferry the rest of the way. Took it myself a year or so back. Stopped and wandered about the island a little. Not much to see; only has a horse stable, a small marina and one market on the whole island; but I caught a fifteen pound large-mouth bass right there off that little dock," Vic said, pointing to a small dock reaching out into the river. Behind the dock a large home with many windows and a wide covered porch overlooked the river.

"You know who owns that house?" asked Joe.

"No, don't think he was home. Lotta those guys only use those homes in the summer. They got big houses in Detroit too, but when it gets too hot in the city they come and stay on the island where it's cooler. They build a big old house to stay in for the summer. Man, the good life must be really good." Vic stared at the mansions sitting on the water and became quiet for the first time that morning.

The orchestra started playing "Let Me Call You Sweetheart," and the instruments became louder, signaling to the crowd that the ship was nearing its destination.

"Nice to have met you, Vic. Thanks for telling me all that stuff. You sure know a lot. I gotta go find my mother and brother now, OK?" Joe put his cap back on and turned to leave.

"Sure, kid. Have fun. I'll see you around sometime." Vic waved as Joe walked off to find Matka.

He found his family sitting on the bench where he had left them.

"Well, there you are Joe. Thought you went overboard," his father joked, patting him on the head. "Having fun? I think we're almost there."

"I hope so," Joe replied. "I can't wait to get there! Yes, I see it, Ojciec." Joe pointed at the island, which was peppered with small buildings. "We're here!"

CHAPTER SEVEN

As the great steamboat rounded the south end of Grosse Ile and headed into open water, the family descended the ladder to the bottom deck. When they reached the promenade deck, Joe saw many couples dancing on the large hardwood dance floor. Men and women floated over the floor, stepping in time to a waltz as the Zickels orchestra played. All aboard were in high spirits.

Joe observed one young couple dancing differently than the others on the floor. With their elbows bent at shoulder height, they circled each other and came together again, embracing with their arms held high. Joe pointed them out to his mother, saying the couple looked like a couple of dancing bears. A moment later, a uniformed employee approached the couple, saying they must stop the odd dance. The man who had been dancing became upset, and his voice grew louder, allowing Joe to overhear the conversation.

"We paid our money same as everyone else!"

"Company policy. No ragtime dancing on the boat or on the island," replied the ship's officer.

"It's just a dance. We're not hurting no one. We have the right to dance how we want!"

"Sir, stay calm. No one wants any trouble. Just dance a nice waltz with your pretty lady, and have a nice time."

His female companion grabbed the man's hand and pulled him to the back of the boat to try to calm him down and avoid further confrontation.

Matka observed the incident with a small smile. "Thank goodness the company has the good sense to control these young delinquents. One must watch these youngsters all the time these days."

An older Polish woman overheard Blanca's comment and joined in. "Dancing like animals! Why, they look like Negroes dancing on a plantation! Can you imagine? They probably snuck some liquor in a flask on board too. Thankfully the island does not allow alcohol on land or on its boats. Makes it free from rowdy and boisterous youths like those two. A place you can take your family and feel at peace."

The boat began to blow its steam whistle at it approached Boblo Island. Joe looked over the railing and watched as they closed in on their destination. Groves of green trees were interspersed between large buildings, and pretty paths circled the area. A large, white two-story building hovered over the water on stilts, and its many arched windows reflected the sparkling blue of the water. Grassy lawns created a rich carpet on the island's small embankment.

The boat docked, and the Jopolowskis listened to conversations of their fellow passengers as they waited in line to disembark. German, Italian, Russian, English, Yiddish and Polish conversations mingled. Ojciec laughed and shook his head. "Sounds like the Tower of Babel on this boat!"

The family stepped off the gangplank and walked down the long dock. A soft breeze blew over the island, and seagulls swooped down, diving into the water. The sky was dotted by only a few white puffy clouds; the weather appeared to be cooperating for the outing. The shore was planted with beds of roses, mums and marigolds. Delicious aromas wafted from the cafeteria. Throughout the park hundreds of rustic seats and hammocks were scattered to allow the patrons a place to sit and rest. Laughter, music and squeals of delight mingled with the sound of the river passing gently by.

A few hundred yards to the right lay a massive, three-story stone dance hall. Its four corners were anchored by square turrets with tall, arched windows. Covered balconies ran the length of the building on four sides.

"How about a polka, Blanca? We'll show these kids how to really dance," Ojciec said.

"Not now, Mikołaj. Let's explore a little."

Passing by the dance hall, they came to a smaller stone building that housed the carousel.

"Here's a dime, Joe. Take your brother and watch him close. Get in line over there." Ojciec pointed to a line of children waiting for their turn. The line moved quickly, and Joe lifted Frank over the lower edge of the carousel as they climbed aboard. Colorful chariots and carved horses stood amid the shiny gold poles on the deck. Forty-four white, brown and black horses, two goats and two white-tail deer stood proudly, reins beckoned the young children to grab and hold on for a thrilling ride. Sparkling mirrors positioned above the merry-go-round reflected the electric lights that flashed from the middle of the ride in a dazzling display of white light.

Frank chose one of the slender deer and Joe gave him a push up onto its back. Joe climbed onto an elegant white horse next to the white-tail and grabbed the reins. Cheerful music flowed out of the steam organ from the middle of the carousel. The ride began to move and the animals rose slowly up and down. Frank's face lit up with joy as his animal began rising toward the ceiling.

"Let's race!" Joe said to his brother.

"OK. Mine's faster!" Frank replied.

Circling around a second time, Joe saw his parents sitting on a wooden bench watching the boys. They were holding hands and smiling, enjoying their sons' good time. When the ride was over, Joe helped his little brother down and walked over to their parents.

"I won! I won!" called Frank. "My deer beat Joe's horse!"

"What a fine rider you are, son. Now let's see how you do on a live animal, shall we?" Ojciec replied. "Next stop . . .the pony rides!" Walking down the stone path they passed many families strolling about the grounds. Children ran through the fields playing made up games and throwing balls in games of catch. Nearing the small stable, Joe looked at a group of children hitting balls on the ground with wooden bats. "Look Ojciec!" he said pointing at the well-dressed group. "What are those children playing?"

"That's called croquet, Joe. You hit a ball through those wire hoops and the first person to reach the peg wins," he replied.

Matka sat on a bench under the shade of a large hickory tree while Ojciec took the boys into the stable. The stable hand found a small pony for Frank, but when Ojciec lifted him up to set him on the pony's back, Frank started to cry and said he did not want to ride the "real horse."

"Just one then," Ojciec told the stable man. Joe picked out a tall, handsome chestnut pony, and his father gave him a boost. The man led the pony around a small ring a couple of times while he explained to Joe how to hold the reins and how to steer the pony with his feet. Then he told Joe he could take the pony out for a trail ride for an hour if he promised to follow the rules.

"Stay clear of the bike track and the baseball diamonds, young man," the caretaker instructed.

"Yes sir, I will," Joe said.

Leaving Frank and his parents, Joe trotted off to explore the park. Joe headed south, the pony leading him along the shore of the river. He was on the Canadian side of the island and could look out over the water and see Amherstburg. It was much quieter here. Blue jays and cardinals sang in the trees as his pony clip-clopped along the sandy coast. As it was September, no swimmers had been brave enough to enter the water, and he had the beach to himself. Joe's small animal was gentle and obedient, and he had no trouble directing her toward the lighthouse that loomed ahead. The tower stood over forty feet in height and was flanked on one side by the light keeper's house. Joe steered the pony into a field of cornstalks and traveled down one of the rows to the bottom of the tower.

"Hey, you!" Joe heard a voice shouting at him. "Hey, you! You can't bring that animal over here!"

Joe turned toward the angry voice and saw a young boy marching toward him. Dismounting from the pony, Joe faced the hostile youth.

"Gee, kid. I'm sorry. Didn't mean anything by it. Didn't hurt anything either. I'll take off. Just wanted to take a look at the lighthouse is all,"

The boy neared. "That's our garden you just rode through, dummy. We don't need a bunch of pony dung fouling up our vegetables."

"OK, I said sorry. You don't have to have a fit. Here, I'll give you my best marble if you don't tell no one I was here," Joe said and reached into his right pants pocket for one of the glass marbles he always carried. Palming a green one, he reached out to hand it to the boy.

"Wow, that's a nice one. You sure?"

"Yeah, don't want any trouble, and didn't mean to cause any. Now take it and I'll leave," Joe replied.

"Gee, thanks. Sorry I yelled at you. I just get tired of people running around here like they own the place. I'm not supposed to say anything, but by the end of the summer it really wears on me. Name's Jimmy Hackett. My dad runs the lighthouse and me and my ma live here."

"I'm Joe. Do you live here all year long? Don't you get lonesome in the winter?"

"No, still gotta go to school. Take our boat over to Amherstburg in the mornings and back again after. When the river freezes I take our horse and sled over the ice. Only time I don't have to go is when it's storming bad or the ice is real thin."

"You drive a boat by yourself?" Joe asked.

"Sure. It's just a small thing. Not hard to steer."

"You ever help your Pa in the lighthouse?"

"Sure. All the time. He's a sailor too, so Ma and I got to tend the lights ourselves when he is gone. You want to go up and see?"

"You bet I do!" Joe said excitedly. They tied the pony to the outside of the garden gate and headed toward a wooden door at the bottom of the tower. Jimmy turned the handle and led them into the dark stairwell. As they climbed the stairs Jimmy explained to Joe that his family had been running the lighthouse for over seventy years.

"My great-grandfather was a ship's captain before he was appointed to operate the lighthouse. My great-grandmother got tired of him being gone all the time, and she wanted him to apply to run the light when it was being built. But he didn't think he would get picked so he didn't try for the job. Well, she got real irritated and was sitting on her front porch with her dog, just fuming about her lazy husband, when she saw the governor of Upper Canada drive by in his carriage. All of a sudden the carriage stopped and the governor got out and walked up to the porch. He said, 'That's a fine dog you have, madam. Is it for sale?' So my great-grandmother said, 'No, hadn't thought of selling him. But my husband is a lake sailor, and if you appoint him as keeper to the Bois Blanc lighthouse you can have the dog.' So the Governor agreed, and we've been here ever since."

"Talk about being in the right place at the right time! Too bad she had to give up the dog, though." replied Joe. Reaching the top stair, Joe stepped into the bright glass room and looked out over the water.

"I can see forever. Hey, I think I can see my house all the way in Detroit."

"Probably not quite that far, but on a clear day you can see almost seventeen miles," Jimmy replied. After he showed Joe how the light was lit and how it signaled ships in the river, they headed back down the stairs.

"Wanna go down to the beach?" asked Jimmy. "Sometimes I can find old Indian spearheads that wash up on the shore."

"Wish I could, but I'd better head back. My family's going to wonder what happened to me. Maybe I could meet you after we eat lunch."

"Yeah, sounds good. I'll meet you by the north baseball diamond around one o'clock. OK?"

"All right," Joe called, getting back on his pony and heading toward the stables. Joe found his family buying soft drinks at a small log cabin store that sold refreshments.

"Have a good time, Joe?" his mother inquired.

"Yes, ma'am. I met this boy who took me upstairs in the lighthouse, and I could see for miles! Thanks for letting me ride the pony, Matka."

The foursome headed toward a shady picnic spot near the baseball diamond. "Let's watch the game while we eat our lunch, shall we?" said Matka.

Ojciec took a blanket out of the basket and spread it on the grass under the trees. Matka handed everyone a ham and cheese sandwich on bread she had baked the day before. Joe took a sip of the lemonade his parents had bought for him and sat down on the blanket. The drink was cool and sweet and he had to sip slowly so he wouldn't drink it down in one gulp. Sitting on a small rise under the trees, they had a perfect view of the game that was already in progress.

Joe pointed out some of the finer points of the game to his father. "See, Ojciec, that guy on first base starts to lead off when the pitcher is about to throw to the batter. If he gets a real good lead he can steal second base. But he's gotta be real fast, cause the pitcher can throw it to first or second and get him out." Ojciec continued to ask questions as he observed the game and Joe answered with best of his limited knowledge, having learned mostly on the playground and on the street in front of their house.

The game became slightly heated when one of the players rounded third base and slid into home plate just as the catcher caught the ball coming from the infield. Shouting ensued and both teams stormed the plate and began to argue that the player was out or safe. After several tense moments, the player was deemed safe and the game continued. Joe explained that in professional leagues there were two umpires that determined the close calls.

When he finished his lunch, Joe asked his parents if he could meet Jimmy down by the baseball field. Agreeing, they told him to meet them at the cafeteria at five o'clock. Joe hadn't known they were going to eat at the restaurant, and he felt as though clouds were riding beneath his small shoes as he ran down the hill toward the game. He found Jimmy already waiting for him behind the bleachers by the first base line.

"Hi Jimmy. You want to watch the game?"

"Nah, these guys aren't very good. Let's go try to find some arrowheads on the beach." The boys headed through the trees to cut across the island. The stillness of the grove encouraged a quiet atmosphere, and the two boys walked in friendly silence. Suddenly, Jimmy put his hand up, signaling Joe to stop. With a finger at his lips to let Joe know to be quiet, he moved off the little path into the brush. A mosquito buzzed in Joe's ear as he followed him into the small woods. Then, he heard what Jimmy had heard; the sound of a woman's laugh and a man's mumbled voice coming from within the copse.

Jimmy led them closer, keeping out of sight of the voices. Hiding being a bush, Jimmy waved Joe over. Joe peered over the shrub and saw a young couple lying on a blanket between two trees. The young woman stood up and pulled on her long skirt over her petticoats; the man sat on the blanket buttoning his shirt. He leaned over and reached for the bottom of the lady's skirt and tried to pull it down in a teasing manner. "Stop Kurt! I have to get back before my mother notices I've been gone so long. Now help me button the back of my dress", the lady admonished, slapping the man's hand away.

"All right, all right, Rose. Only if you promise to meet me here after supper." The man stood to help with the tiny buttons on the back of her frock.

Jimmy grabbed Joe's arm and pulled him quietly back toward the path. When they were far away enough to speak safely, Jimmy said, "Well, I guess you can tell it's just not just a family getaway on Boblo Island, huh Joe?"

Joe wasn't exactly sure what the couple had been doing before the boys had come across the couple's secret spot, but he thought he had an idea. Not wanting Jimmy to think he was immature, he played along. "Yeah, pretty funny. Hope she notices the leaves in her hair before she goes to meet her ma."

"That was nothing. I've caught three different couples this summer. Pretty cheeky, if ya ask me. Their mothers think they are going off to have a sweet old time—get away from the city for a day—and then they meet their boyfriends in the woods and do all kinds of immodest things. This one time I was walking back from the cafeteria and saw two of them stark naked rolling around in the grass like two rabbits."

The two boys walked out of the shade of the trees onto the breezy beach. "Come on, Joe. Let's go down toward the back docks. I found an arrowhead there last week." Running over the sand, they quickly came to a small dock at the back of the island and started searching the sand for Indian relics. Joe took his shoes off and set them in the grass so he could wade in the shallow water.

"Ouch!" Joe yelled, grabbing his bare foot in his hand. "Something bit me!"

"Let me see," said Jimmy coming over to take a look. "You didn't get bit, Joe! You stepped on an arrowhead in the sand. See?" he said, picking up the sharp stone and putting it in Joe's hand. Joe sat down on the grass and looked at the arrowhead. Carved to a point, it was shiny gray in color with jagged edges down the sides.

"That's a really good one, Joe. Your feet make good spotters."

"Ha, very funny. Well, the cut isn't too bad, I'll be all right. Can't wait to show the guys at school. They'll be so jealous." The boys sat looking at the arrowhead together until a small boat pulled up to the back dock.

"That's the *Papoose*," Jimmy said. "She runs from here to Amherstburg."

"How come there's only men getting on?" asked Joe.

"They sneak over to the city to grab a pint of beer or two. They only stay an hour or so, while the women rest at the Women's Cottage. They get back before they're even missed."

Joe watched the men board the *Papoose*. They were laughing and joking, clapping one another on the back as they headed out into the river. Then, a familiar face caught

Joe's eye, and he realized his father was on board. Ojciec recognized his son, too, as the boat pulled away. A startled look crossed his face and then changed to a smile as he winked at Joe and waved goodbye. Joe realized that his father was inducting him into a secret man's world and understood that Ojciec trusted him not to tell his mother.

"Hey, Joe, look at this dead walleye that washed up on the shore." Jimmy had wandered down the beach about twenty yards and Joe ran to catch up. The fish was lying on its side, and one of its eyes had been pulled out by a seagull.

"Ewww . . . disgusting," said Joe as he touched the scales of the smelly fish with his fingertips. Jimmy turned it over with a stick and insects climbed out of the hole where the fish had been bitten. Joe pushed the fish back into the water with the stick and they walked farther down the beach. The boys spent the rest of the afternoon together; they lay on the beach for a while talking about school, family and friends. Later they walked over to the playground and went down the slides and played on the swings. The boys pushed each other so hard on the small merry go-round they fell off laughing into the dirt.

Jimmy lent Joe his bicycle and taught him how to ride. Joe got the hang of it pretty quickly, and they headed over to the bicycle track. The oval track was built to insure a slight angle at the turns and Joe was soon peddling around with the other cyclists. He was too small to give much of a challenge in any of the races, but he enjoyed himself just the same. After a while they walked to a second ball field and joined a game with several boys. Before long, Joe had to say goodbye to Jimmy.

"Hey, Joe, sorry I was such a sourpuss when you were in the garden. I don't want to take your best marble. Here, I wanna give it back to you."

"Keep it, Jimmy. It wasn't my best marble. I just told you that. I always carry a couple of old ones in my pocket just in case." Joe winked and smiled at his new friend. Turning away, he headed off toward supper.

Joe found his family seated at a small wooden table in the sunlit dining room. His father was there, looking no worse for wear; and Matka and Frank were well rested from an afternoon nap at the Women's Cottage. They ordered perch dinners with potatoes and carrots. The menu advertised that the fish had been caught from the Detroit River that morning. While they waited, Joe told his family about his adventures with Jimmy, careful to leave out seeing the *Papoose* ride off to Canada. Matka said she had found a lovely lounge chair to take a rest in on the porch of the Women's Cottage and Frank had taken a nap in one of the baby hammocks that hung in the shade near there.

"Frank slept longer than he ever does at home, Mikołaj. Maybe you could string up a hammock in the backyard for him to take his naps in from now on."

When dinner arrived, the family dug in. The fresh air made them ravenous. Ojciec decided that chocolate ice cream was needed to satisfy his family's appetite. The smooth, cold ice cream tasted delicious, and Joe finished before the others. When supper was over, Matka told Joe that she and his father were going to the dance hall.

Joe took Frank by the hand and walked up the stairs to the gallery, where he found a wooden bench overlooking the large, polished dance floor. The afternoon sun was dimming slightly, making the grand room more magical in the soft light. Matka and Ojciec paid five cents apiece to use the dance pavilion, but the gallery had no cost. Several twosomes of women danced together, not minding an absent male partner. Couples waltzed and two-stepped to music the orchestra played on a small stage underneath the other side of the gallery.

Frank entertained himself with a small wooden replica of the *Columbia* that Matka had bought for him at the souvenir stand, so Joe was able to watch the couples as they twirled around the smooth wood floor. Looking down he saw the couple he and Jimmy had spied on in the trees. They looked decidedly like all the other young couples dancing, and Joe wondered if any other young women had taken their skirts off in the woods or if she was more brazen than the others.

The orchestra began a new song, this one a lively tune, and the couples began to dance with quick half-steps, holding onto each other tightly. A band member stood in front of the stage and played an accordion loud and fast. Joe recognized the polka and searched for his parents. He found them smack dab in the center of the dance floor. Ojciec held Matka's waist tightly as they trotted and bounced around the floor. Other Polish couples joined them, and soon the group was singing along in Polish. Other dancers tried to copy the dance by watching Joe's parents and mimicking their steps. A few of the novices slowly caught on, but most decided the dance was too difficult and moved to the side of the floor. Matka and Ojciec swirled quickly around and around, almost making Joe dizzy trying to follow their movements.

"Look, Frank! Matka and Ojciec are better than all the other dancers! Watch and see!" The boys watched in amazement as their parents made their way athletically around the long dance floor. When the song ended, all the dancers clapped. Ojciec made a deep bow to Matka, and she girlishly curtseyed back to him. Joe and Frank ran down the stairs to the entrance of the dance hall. They found their parents getting a drink at the fountain outside.

"You were wonderful Matka! You too, Ojciec. I didn't know you could dance so well," Joe exclaimed.

"Well, Joe. That's an old song from an old country. Maybe we haven't learned the latest dances here, but we can still polka with the best of them! Right, Blanca?"

Matka just smiled and bent down to grab another drink of water. Grabbing the basket she had left outside the hall she replied, "Better head for the docks and make sure we get a seat on the way back."

Sitting down on the second deck of the *Columbia* for the trip home, the family quietly watched the island disappear as the ship sailed upriver. Joe could see the lighthouse light and wondered if his friend Jimmy had lit the beacon tonight. As the sun set to the west, the boat was bathed in electric light. The Zickels Orchesta played the new popular song "In the Shade of the Old Apple Tree" as the steam boat quietly chugged back to the city. A few passengers softly sang the lyrics along with the band and Joe lay his head on his father's shoulder and fell asleep.

CHAPTER EIGHT

Life returned to normal. Work, school, cleaning and cooking filled the Jopolowskis' days. Joe continued to try to stay out of the nuns' line of sight at school; Mikołaj came home exhausted every night from the plant; Blanca cleaned the house, cooked, baked and supervised a very active Frank. The parishioners of St. Josaphat's planned for the upcoming celebration as the workmen neared the finish of the new school, and the students began to prepare for the dedication.

Aunt Hattie and Matka canned and put up the vegetables from the small garden . The smell of boiling peppers and tomatoes poured out of the kitchen and into the house day after day. Chopped cabbage was set in a large crock in the corner of the small kitchen to ferment for several days until it turned into a tasty kraut.

Hattie and Matka took a streetcar four miles twice a week to harvest potatoes from the last remaining Pingree's Potato Patch in the city. Former mayor Hazen S. Pingree had asked owners of vacant lots to allow the unemployed to grow vegetables during the economic depression of 1893 to 1897. With the economic upturn of the last decade, most owners had rescinded permission to garden on their land and had constructed buildings and houses on their lots. However, one large tract of land remained available, and the women of the Polish community continued to plant and harvest potatoes for their families there.

The neighborhood women met at the church and traveled together to the plot, where they dug the potatoes and put them in wooden bushel baskets, just as they had in the old country. All wore babushkas, dark sensible shoes and long aprons. Aunt Hattie would sometimes complain about the long trek back from the field with the heavy baskets, but Matka said the journey was good exercise and she was happy to get out of the kitchen.

On the days the women visited the potato patch, Joe came directly home from school to help Matka prepare a light dinner of zupa klafiorowa (cauliflower soup) or mushroom omelets. On other days he played stickball in the street or in the alley behind his house. He was trying to improve his skills in preparation for the St. Josaphat's celebration baseball game. Joe felt he was getting better, but he didn't think he could catch as well as the boys who were lucky enough to own a baseball mitt. This was not the time to be hinting for a frivolous item like a mitt either, as Matka had finally realized that Joe's shoes were two sizes too small and had bought a new pair for him.

Two weeks after the outing to Boblo Island, Joe was in the backyard helping to pull the clean laundry off the line with Matka when Ojciec came down the back steps to talk to him.

"Exciting news at work yesterday," he began. Joe and Matka stopped folding and looked at Ojciec. "Mr. Ford built his one millionth automobile yesterday. What an accomplishment! One million cars! To thank the employees for their part he gave some of his best employees two tickets to see the Detroit Tigers play."

"Did you get two tickets, Ojciec?" asked Joe.

"Sure did. You have any plans for tomorrow, Joe?"

"No sir!"

"All right, after Mass tomorrow, you and I will head down to the baseball game."

Mass could not end quickly enough for Joe. As soon as the final prayers were said, he ran out of church and raced home. While he was waiting for his family to walk home he grabbed the Sunday paper and read the summary of the game played the day before. The Tigers defeated the Cleveland Indians 6 to 5, but the win was not enough to keep them in contention for the pennant race against the Boston Red Sox. The game being played today would not help their cause, as Boston had finished the regular season with 101 games in their win column.

As Joe read further he noted that Ty Cobb had shown up at the very last second before the game started, jumping the fence and taking his place in right field. Cobb was famous for skipping games when he felt like it. His teammates felt Cobb played only for himself, and Joe worried the Georgia Peach would not turn out to play today with the pennant race over. Watching Ty Cobb play was one of the major reasons to attend a Tigers game. He had been the hometown hero since 1907, when he helped the team win the first of three straight pennants. He had earned the American League batting title for the last eight years and was batting an average of .369 this year. Although he had averaged above .400 over his previous years, .369 nothing to sneeze at.

"You want to read about baseball or you want to go see a game yourself?" Ojciec said. He startled Joe, who was bent over the paper trying to memorize the statistics. "How about you get your new shoes on and we'll grab a streetcar and take a ride down to Navin Field?"

"Yes sir!" Grabbing his hat off the rack by the front door he raced onto the porch, where Ojciec was waiting for him. The ride to The Corner, as Detroiters sometimes referred to Navin Field, did not take long. As they neared the park, the streetcar became so crowded the conductor had to push people back into the street who were trying to climb on.

"Hold 'em back boys," he yelled to the paying riders. "They'll try to pull us on our side if we pick up any more riders." Joe looked at Ojciec nervously.

"Don't worry, son. This car won't topple. The conductor just wants to keep the freeloaders off his car."

When they reached the park, Ojciec grabbed Joe's hand and pulled him toward the ticket takers. Thousands of people milled about the outside of the park. Signs for tickets dotted the walls of the stadium. The three-year-old stadium was said to have been built upon a sacred Indian burial ground, but what that meant Joe wasn't sure. The large concrete and steel structure could seat twenty-three thousand people, and Joe was sure there were at least that many there today. The sight that met Joe when they entered the stadium would stay in Joe's memory as long as he lived. There, right in the middle of this teeming, loud, concrete city sat the most beautiful baseball field he had ever seen. The green grass looked like velvet carpet, the pitcher's mound stood slightly above the field like a royal throne for the baseball gods.

Ojciec found their seats. Along the outfield walls of the one-story ballpark were billboards for local companies. "Hey there Rooters! Have you seen J.C. Hartz, Co. about your clothing, hats, etc.? 52 Monroe Ave." "Fine Cigars Kept Fine, M.A. LaFonde, Co." There was a funny painting of an old man with a white beard dressed in a top hat with stars represented "Old Farm Springs Whisky brought to you by the Grand Valley Distilling Co Inc." and many others.

"Do you know why the Tigers have that long rope tied along the outfield, Ojciec?" asked Joe pointing to a heavy rope that was tied from one end of the stadium to the other.

"I don't know, Joe," Ojciec said.

The man seated next to Joe on the other side answered. "The rope keeps the standing room fans off the field. A few years ago, when this was Bennett Field, a fan was walking across the outfield to get to his section and ran into a player who was running to catch a pop fly. They knocked heads so hard the player was knocked out for five minutes and they had to delay the game. It's not really a problem anymore with the new stadium but the rope serves as a barrier and as the home run line."

Immediately to the left of the standing room section, a set of rickety wooden bleachers had been erected, complete with a sign that read "colored fans." The view from the segregated section was less than optimal, but to Joe's perception the fans did not appear to mind. Well-dressed Negro men of every shade; from the lightest olive color to the darkest of night, chatted and laughed as they waited for the start of the game.

The crowd cheered as the players took the field. Joe frantically searched for the Tigers' most famous player and began to worry when he couldn't spot him. Just then a loud rumbling of voices and yells arose near the home team's dugout. There he was, the Georgia Peach, tall and thin, baseball cap slightly askew, running onto the field. The crowd stood on their feet and applauded for several minutes. Cobb did not acknowledge the praise as he began to warm up.

Joe watched as the team began their pre-game drills. Bobby Veach and Sam "Wahoo" Crawford lobbed the ball back and forth, then Bobby threw it to Cobb. The Detroit newspapers had named the trio the Greatest Outfield of All Time that summer, and the threesome continued to earn the title. Crawford was hitting .300 and had driven in over a hundred runs. Veach was close to the same, with 112 RBIs. Joe was a fan of all three, but his eyes never left Cobb.

Joe stood with the rest of the stadium and held his hat over his heart when a man walked to the mound and began to sing the Star Spangled Banner. The song was not sung at every game, but because this was the last game of the season, it had been decided that it would be appropriate to finish the year with the national anthem. Ojciec stood proudly next to Joe with his hand over his heart. "Joe, will you teach me the words to America's song?" he asked when the man finished. "I would like to learn my new country's anthem."

"Sure Ojciec. I can teach you tonight after supper. We had to learn all the words at school."

A Cleveland player walked up to home plate and the crowd quieted, settling in for the game. A man in a navy blue uniform walked down the aisle shouting, "Peanuts! Arachidi! Földimogyoró! Orzeski ziemne!" The vendor was announcing his product in different languages; English, Hungarian, Italian and Polish. Ojciec bought a small brown bag of warm peanuts, and they shared the bag, cracking the shells and throwing them on the concrete floor. Ojciec left in the second inning to buy a beer and came back with a Vernors Ginger Ale for Joe.

"Try it, Joe" he said. "It's made right here in Detroit." Joe sipped the spicy smelling amber liquid. His tongue was surprised by the bite of the flavor. As he drank more he began to enjoy the taste.

The stadium was not filled to capacity as Joe had thought. Approximately six thousand fans had come to watch the final game of the season—many, perhaps, with the free tickets given away by Mr. Ford. The day was sunny and the air crisp with the promise of autumn. With no pressure to win the game, the crowd was relaxed and the players seemed to be having a good time playing for the fans.

That is, all the players but Cobb. He played each inning as if the Tigers were in the World Series. He never let up; catching each ball that neared him in the outfield and gunning it back to the shortstop for an out or a double play. Joe watched Cobb as he sat on the steps of the dugout. Cobb looked over angrily at the Indians' bullpen, while he sharpened his cleats till they were like dozens of tiny knives.

Detroit scored five runs in the first three innings. Cobb had one run batted in. Covelskie was pitching, and the Indians could not get a run in. The Tigers looked unstoppable until the fourth inning. Covelskie threw a few fastballs by the first batter for the strikeout, but it was downhill from there. The Indians batted in four runs, and the Tigers were only up by one. The shortstop caught the final out, and the Tigers were up to bat. George "Tioga" Burns was up first. Cobb was on deck. Cobb grabbed three bats and swung over and over again in the batter's circle. Joe stared at Cobb's arms.

"He swings three at once so his bat feels light when he is up," Joe told Ojciec. The boys at school had told Joe that Cobb was the first player to warm up like that, though many players now copied his style. Tioga struck out, and Cobb walked up to the plate. The pitcher seemed nervous as he watched Cobb swing a couple of practice swings. Cobb gave the pitcher an evil stare. He choked up on the bat. The pitcher threw two balls and then Cobb nabbed his first hit of the game, with a ball into right field. He took first base unchallenged, and Veach was up.

Cobb stood ten feet out from first base, taunting the pitcher to throw him out. Turning his back on the Georgia Peach, the pitcher began his delivery. Before the ball left the pitcher's hand Cobb was barreling toward second. The pitch was outside, and the catcher threw to second. Cobb slid into the base with his cleats in the air. The second baseman took a small step back to avoid the sharp blades of his spikes. The umpire called, "Safe!" The crowd stood and applauded. Cobb had just stolen his ninety-sixth base of the season, beating the 1912 record of eighty-eight held by Clyde Milan of the Washington Nationals.

Veach struck out. Harry "Slug'" Heilman hit a pop fly, leaving Cobb stranded on second to end the inning. The next three innings did not produce any runs on the scoreboard. Oldham took the mound in the top of the eighth for the Tigers. The score was tied up, with the Indians good for two hits and the Tigers providing an error in the infield. Burns and Young got to third and second on two singles and a Cleveland error. Dubuc was sent in to bat for Oldham, and he hit a long fly that allowed Burns to score. Dubuc pitched the ninth inning, with three successive strikeouts. The Tigers won the game.

Ojciec and Joe followed the crowd down the aisle onto the baseball field after the game. Joe couldn't believe he was standing right where the Georgia Peach had stood.

"Just a minute, Ojciec, please?" he said. His father nodded his approval as Joe walked to first base. Mimicking Cobb, Joe stood ten feet out and stared at the pitcher" mound. Taking off, he slid into second. Ojciec clapped loudly.

"Safe! Jopolowski steals his ninety-sixth base of the year, tying the Georgia Peach!" Ojciec teased Joe. "Matka won't be happy about the dirt, son, but sometimes a boy has got to be a boy. Let's go."

They headed across the grass to the right field wall, where they exited onto Trumbull.

"Guess you're ready to play at the church baseball game now, huh, Ojciec?"

"Don't know how I couldn't be after watching that fine performance. Don't know if I will be stealing bases like old Cobb, but you never know. I think my catching is getting a lot better. Hopefully I don't embarrass myself when I am up to bat."

"You'll do great; just try to aim the ball where no one is standing. That's how Cobb gets most of his runs. He doesn't hit for the stands, just tries to hit where the other players can't reach it to throw him out."

"Well, I know I can't hit like the Georgia Peach but I'll give it my best."

After the electric streetcar ride and the short walk home, Joe and Ojciec told Matka all about the exciting game over supper. Joe retrieved water from the pump in the backyard and helped Matka with the dishes. Ojciec read Saturday's, *Dziennik Polski*, the Polish newspaper that served twenty-five percent of Detroit's population.

"Maybe, it's time for Joe to get a job as a paperboy," said Ojciec, looking up from his paper. "I helped my father with the fishing before I was his age. I scaled and deboned them when he came in from the sea every night after school."

"Maybe next summer, Mikołaj. He's still young yet. Let him concentrate on his schoolwork for now," Matka replied.

Joe was simultaneously disappointed and relieved. Many of his classmates sold papers in the morning before school to help contribute to their family's income and gain a little pocket change. But Joe had also noted how tired the boys were in school and how the nuns continually rapped them on the back of the head when they fell asleep in class.

The kitchen clean, Joe sat down at the table with Ojciec to teach him the Star-Spangled Banner. First, Joe wrote the words out in Polish and then in English underneath, helping his father with the pronunciation of some of the more difficult words. Ojciec learned quickly.

"There are three more verses, but no one sings them," Joe told Ojciec.

"Why not?"

"Not sure. I don't know them either. The nuns just teach us the first one."

"And he slid into the second baseman, almost stabbing him with his cleats!" Joe was regaling the story of the Tigers game to four of his classmates on the steps of the school the following morning.

"I heard Ty Cobb beat up a man who had no hands a couple of years ago," volunteered an older boy named Paul.

"Uh Uh."

"No way."

The boys argued at once.

Paul said, "Yeah, my father told me. Three years ago there was this fan in the crowd heckling Cobb while he was in the outfield, see? Well, Cobb gets mad as a hornet and jumps the wall and starts waling on the guy. The guy's friends yell, 'He's only got two fingers! Don't hit him.' The loudmouth fan was missing a hand and had only two fingers on the other!" Paul had the undivided attention of the group. "So Cobb stops for a second, looks at the guy and punches him square in the jaw again and says 'I don't care if he has no feet!'"

"No way!"

"My dad says he is off his rocker!"

"Best man that ever played the game though." Everyone agreed with that sentiment.

The chiming of the church bells interrupted the conversation. The boys grabbed their lunch pails and books and headed for the school door. They left their belongings in the classroom and lined up in the hall to walk to morning Mass. Sister Mary Monica roughly pulled Joe aside as he found his place in line.

"Are you planning on running in Our Father's holy church this morning, Joseph? Disrespecting the Lord your God? Maybe defiling a sacred statue of a saint or washing up in the Holy Water Fount?" she whispered viciously under her breath.

"No Sister," Joe replied, startled and scared at the sudden attack.

"I saw you running down the aisle after Mass yesterday like you were in a race against the devil. I will address you after Mass, Joseph."

Joe's little hands trembled as he held them together in prayer at Mass. He ferociously prayed to the Blessed Mother to watch over him and to keep Sister Mary Monica from doling out a severe punishment. But he knew his prayers would likely be in vain. The nuns were not known for their kindnesses on a good day. Running in church would likely mean a paddling in front of the class or worse.

"Go straight to Father Gatowski's office, Joseph. He is expecting you," Sister Mary Monica commanded when the class had returned to their room.

Joe dragged his feet down the small, dark hallway toward the priest's office. Portraits of saints stared down at him in an accusing manner from the walls. He didn't know which saint was the patron of children, and wished he had paid more attention to Sister Mary Monica's lessons so he could pray to him now. Reaching the wooden door at the end of the hallway, Joe held his hand up and knocked lightly.

"Come in!" thundered a deep voice from within. Joe turned the large brass doorknob slowly and opened the door. Peering in around the doorframe, he could see the priest standing at the window looking out onto the construction of the new school.

"Sir, Father . . . It's Joe Jopolowski. Sister Mary Monica sent me to see you," Joe whispered.

"Close the door, Joe."

Joe closed the door softly and turned to face the priest. Father Gatowski walked over to his large wooden desk and sat down behind it.

"Come Joe, stand before me," Father said sternly.

Joe walked to the desk and stood before the priest. He stood on his tiptoes hoping the priest would not notice that he could barely see above the desk. The priest attempted to hide a smirk as the young boy tried to balance his weight on his toes.

"What transgression has brought you to my office, Joe?" asked Father Gatowski.

"Running in church, Father."

"I didn't see you run in church today, son. All the boys and girls filed out very quietly as I recall," he stated.

"Not today, Father, it was yesterday, after Mass," Joe replied, looking down at his feet.

"Ah, yes. I thought I saw a small blur flying out of the church, but I thought it was the Holy Spirit heading for some fresh air," said Father Gatowski. However, Joe was too nervous to notice the priest's gentle voice.

"No Father, I mean, maybe it was, Father, but it was also me. I ran down the aisle after Mass."

"Why were you in such a hurry, Joe? Did you have nothing to pray for? Perhaps the world is at peace and all hunger has ended? Or perhaps you just did not feel like praying?" The priest settled into his chair.

"No, Father. I mean, I prayed hard but I was in a hurry to leave because my Ojciec and I were going to the Tigers game after Mass."

"Well, baseball is not an excuse for impudence, Joe, Eeven when the great Georgia Peach is playing. Do you understand?"

Joe looked up from his feet for the first time and his eyes met the priest's. He was so astonished to hear Cobb's nickname being used by Father Gatowski, he didn't respond at first.

"Joe, do you understand?" Father repeated.

"Yes, Father," Joe responded quickly, stunned to realize the priest was smiling.

"Wish I could have been at that game. Can't let the parishioners see me out on a Sunday at a ballgame, though. Sundays are God's day of rest. Stole his ninety-sixth base of the season, huh? God bless our Tigers. Not the best reputation, Mr. Cobb has. He likes people to think he is mean and ruthless, which he is on the field, and sometimes off for sure. But most don't know he can be a kind man also. He let one of our boys catch fungoes during batting practice, and he gave another a job as a stile boy. Tigers pay him twenty-five cents a game and he gets to watch for free."

Father Gatowski rose from his chair and walked to the front of the desk. He looked down at Joe.

"No man is without sin and no man without good. And neither are small boys, I think." He laughed softly. "Say four Hail Marys and ten Our Fathers, and your crime is forgiven, son. Now return to your classroom and tell Sister Mary Monica you have received your punishment. Don't let on what it is, now. Wouldn't hurt my reputation if you look contrite when you go back, either."

Joe thanked the priest and walked back into the hallway. *Father Gatowski, a baseball fan! What luck!* He had thought being sent down to the priest's office would be a far worse punishment than a paddling before his classmates. That large wooden paddle with holes that hung behind Sister's desk provided a fierce wallop to many a little boy's behind.

Sister Mary Monica was at the front of the classroom discussing the upcoming St. Josaphat's festivities when Joe slipped quietly into his chair. She gave Joe a stern look but continued on without further notice.

"As the class marches in procession we will sing 'Boze, Cos Polske' (God Bless Poland) " she continued. "And our class will learn 'Veni Creator Spiritus.' We will sing this for the bishop before the dedication ceremony on the steps of the church. I expect that every child will sing reverently and with his best voice for his Holiness. We will practice these hymns every day after Mass, allowing more than enough time for them to be learned. Your class is the only one that has been chosen to sing for the bishop, and it is quite an honor."

CHAPTER NINE

Halloween had not been celebrated much in the Upper Peninsula, but Joe was catching on quickly. He and Matka went to Kresge's and bought some witch and pumpkin postcards. They pasted them on the front window of their house. Matka also purchased a black and orange crepe apron decorated with black cats for herself and a similar one with a flying witch for Aunt Hattie. On All Hallow's Eve, Ojciec helped Joe carve a small pumpkin, and Joe placed it on the steps of their porch. Matka gave Joe a candle for it and placed several lit candles on the railing of the porch.

"Can we bob for apples now?" Pauline asked as the two families gathered on the front porch. Beautiful red apples floated in the wooden washtub on the corner of the porch, and the children were impatient for their small party to begin.

"In a minute, Pauline," Aunt Hattie replied, as she came out her front door with a plate of homemade doughnuts in her hand. Uncle Alexy poured a cup of warm apple cider and handed it to Joe. Joe took the warm doughnut, dipped it into his glass, and shoved the entire thing into his mouth.

"Good doughnuts, Aunt Hattie," he mumbled, mouth full.

"Manners, Joe! And thank you," she replied, taking a cup of cider from her husband. "Why don't you light the big winter turnips your father carved and put them in the windows?" Joe grabbed some matches from the kitchen and lit a candle in a large turnip his father had carved with a devilish face. Ojciec said his family had always carved turnips in Poland on All Hallows' Eve to ward off evil spirits.

Uncle Feliks made a rare appearance and brought a roll of Life Savers, a Hershey Milk Chocolate Bar, and a bottle of Faygo soda pop for each of his nieces and nephews. Aunt Hattie grimaced at Matka when the bachelor brother sauntered up the walkway. Matka whispered, "By miły" (Be nice) and told Joe to get Uncle Feliks a beer. Joe's uncle produced two pretty, silver barrettes, one for each of his sisters-in-law, saying, "A small blossom for the two prettiest flowers in the Jopolowski family garden."

Looking at the flowered hair clip, Matka said, "The flower engraved on this barrette reminds me of the red poppies that grew in my village." She removed her babushka, straightened her hair and slipped the clip into place above her left ear. Aunt Hattie didn't don hers but smiled warmly and offered Uncle Feliks a doughnut.

The men sat on Joe's porch and smoked cigars that Uncle Feliks had brought and discussed work. Finally the children were allowed to bob for apples. Pauline, the most determined, soaked her whole head and was sent in the house to towel off. The family laughed good-naturedly at her bravado. Marya assisted Emilia and Frank with the apples, and Joe pretended to help so he could listen to his mother and Aunt discuss his rogue uncle.

Matka said, “It was so nice of Feliks to bring treats for all of us. I wish he would come and live with us. Mikołaj would be so happy, and we have the room.”

“With the baby coming, Blanca? That would be difficult. And besides, Feliks would have to give up drinking in the taverns to dawn and cavorting with all his women.”

“Oh, Hattie, Mikołaj says he doesn’t drink that much—he just likes to gamble. The bars now have a way to wire in the scores of the games, and he just likes to put down a friendly wager.”

“You are completely naïve, Blanca. But let’s not ruin the evening by discussing it further. Joe? Isn’t it your turn to bob for an apple?”

Joe splashed water onto the porch as he bobbed for his apple, and Marya glared at him.

“Joe! Please be careful!” she snapped.

Joe looked up at his blonde cousin and smiled sweetly. “Sorry Marya. Why don’t you take your turn now? I am sure with that mouth of yours you will be able to grab an apple without spilling a drop.”

“Aunt Blanca! Did you hear what Joe said?” Marya pouted at his mother.

“Joe, be nice to your cousin. And your splashing is going to get her pretty costume all wet.”

Joe said, “I’m sorry, Marya,” but inside he was rolling with laughter. Most children didn’t wear costumes on Halloween, but Marya had begged her mother to make her a black witch’s costume out of crepe paper, pointed hat included. Joe felt there had never been an outfit more suited for his bossy cousin. Pauline dressed like the Statue of Liberty in a red, white, and blue dress; and the baby was dressed all in white with a cap of white feathers to signify that she was an angel.

After bobbing for apples with his cousins and eating three doughnuts, Joe asked his parents if he could meet his friends. "Don't get into too much mischief!" Ojciec called after him.

Joe ran down the street and across the two blocks to meet a bunch of his classmates at the schoolyard. Six boys were already sitting on the steps of the cathedral when he arrived. Joe sat on the bottom step next to Sam and listened to tales of previous Halloweens. Ten-year-olds, Franz and Tall Paul, were the last to arrive.

"Well, ninnies . . . what are we going to do?" Franz asked.

"Let's soap some windows!"

"Let's tip an outhouse!"

"Open some barn doors and let their horses out!"

Franz stared down at the boys with a mischievous smile. "All good ideas, my boys, all good. Where should we start?"

"Let's head to Black Bottom!" yelled Tall Paul. The boys whooped and hollered, running down the sidewalk. Red, yellow and brown leaves crunched under their small feet as they headed toward a night of adventure. The sound of laughter from Halloween parties percolated around them and mingled with the sounds of their own merriment. The sun was beginning to set, and an orange glow fell over the city. Candles and glittering pumpkins flickered in the windows of the homes they passed. The evening air was beginning to cool, and the smells of burning firewood and home-cooked meals accompanied the rambunctious group on their short journey out of the safety of their stomping ground.

In a few short blocks they arrived at the neighborhood where the poor Jews and coloreds lived. The houses were run down here. Porches sagged, and garbage littered the alleys. Strange smells drifted into the street. The boys grouped closer and grew quiet. They gathered in a circle in a dark corner of an alley to discuss their plans. Joe's eyes scanned the sidewalks for adversaries. It seemed damp in this forgotten neighborhood, and he shivered under his thin coat.

The name Black Bottom had originally referred to the rich, dark soil that covered the lower east side of the city. Many ethnic groups had established their homes in this area in the late part of the nineteenth century. They had farmed small plots of land on the fertile ground and built stores and houses. But as the years passed, they had moved upward into better neighborhoods and left the ostracized Jewish people and the newly arriving southern Negroes behind, resulting in an altogether different connotation of the phrase Black Bottom.

One of the boys produced a few bars of soap from his pockets and distributed them among the group.

"Let's grab some garbage from back here and dump it in their front yards," suggested a small boy from Joe's class.

"I'm not touching some Jew's leftovers," replied Franz.

The other boys nodded in agreement following the older boys' lead. The boys continued walking quietly down the dark alley looking for a good opportunity for some trouble. Several houses down, Franz spotted an open gate.

"Hey, let's sneak in there and turn over their outhouse!" Paul agreed, eager to show his courage, but the smaller boys were less enthusiastic.

"I don't know, Franz," replied Joe. "If we do that first won't they hear us and chase us out of here before we do any tricks?"

"Yeah, I guess you're right, Joe. We'll do that at the end of the night for our final hurrah," Franz said. Joe was surprised to know that the older boy knew his name. "All right, enough talk, boys . . . let's have some fun."

The boys darted through the streets, soaping car windows and overturning flowerpots. When they reached Hastings Street, the center of the neighborhood, they gathered again. Paul jimmied a lock on a small barn door in the back of a Jewish market. The boys wheeled out a wooden wagon and pulled it around the block. The wagon creaked as they rolled it down the street and Joe looked around nervously. A tall man with a long gray beard and small cap on the back of his head looked over at the group as he locked up his storefront but said nothing. The boys waited till the man turned the corner and pushed the wagon to the entrance of the market, blocking the door. Running and laughing down the street they chanted "Sztuczka! Sztuczka!" (Trick! Trick!)

Pushing deeper into Black Bottom, they entered the area the Negroes inhabited. Here, light was scarce, as there were no gas or electric streetlights. The street was eerily quiet. Only the sound of a crying baby reached their ears.

"Grab some old tires, wood or broken furniture, and meet me at the end of the street," Tall Paul said, pointing to a rundown house a block away. Joe found the remains of what had been a small suitcase and carried it to the designated location. When he neared the side of the house he saw Paul hanging halfway up a wooden trellis, holding a flat tire. Paul shinned up and down the trellis carrying the items the boys had found and piled them comically on the edge of the home's roof. The boys laughed and guffawed until a light appeared in the upper bedroom and they ran for cover.

As the group headed back toward their neighborhood, Franz stopped and grabbed a wooden cart that was sitting on one of the small front yards and began to pull it down the street. When they reached the corner that separated the Polish and Jewish neighborhoods, Franz pulled it into the middle of the street.

"Grab some kindling, boys!" he commanded. The boys ran around to the alley looking for scraps of paper and cloth. Quickly they amassed a large quantity of discarded goods and placed them in the pushcart. Franz produced a box of matches from his jacket pocket. Soon the papers caught and the cart was in flames.

Suddenly in the light of the bonfire, another group of boys appeared on the other side of the street. Joe could not see the faces of the boys, but he could tell by their body language there was going to be trouble. As the enemy group got closer, Joe noticed a few were carrying wooden sticks and clubs. The Polish boys slowly edged backwards, trying to find cover in the darkness of the night. Joe and his friends turned to run but were stopped in their tracks by three older boys blocking their way.

"Not so tough now, are ya?" the tallest questioned.

"Yeah, they're just a bunch of yellow-bellied cowards, huh, Abe?" replied the shortest of the three.

The Polish boys now found themselves surrounded by the older Jewish boys. Franz and Paul stood with their shoulders back to in an attempt to appear larger, but they were no match for the teenagers.

"Uh . . . look, we w-w-was just trying to have a little fun. Didn't m-mean no harm," Franz stuttered.

"Yeah? No harm, huh? Just lighting fires in the middle of my street and blocking my Dad's shoe store with his own wagon?" replied the one named Abe.

"What should we do to them, Abe? Let's clobber the big ones and then we can take the little ones' pants so they gotta run home in their underwear," the short one suggested. His eyes gleamed ferociously in the firelight.

"Shut up, Ray. They're just little kids. What fun would there be in that?" replied Abe. "But Ray is right," he continued, looking at Franz now. "We've gotta get something for you Polacks coming into our neighborhood and playing your dumb pranks. How much dough ya got?"

Joe and his friends emptied their pockets into Franz's hands. Counting quickly he replied, "Forty cents."

"Forty cents?" the older boys slapped each other on the backs and laughed at Joe's group. "Forty cents won't get ya nothing round here! Ha! Forty cents!" Abe laughed along with the others.

"How about forty cents and I don't tell my mother to put a curse on you?" Joe spoke, barely audible.

"What'd you say, midget?" asked Abe, towering over Joe.

"I said, how about we give you our money and I don't tell my mother about any of this?"

"Ya trying to scare us, midget? We don't believe in curses—that's a bunch of old women garbage from the old country. There's no such thing," replied Abe.

"Not normally, no," said Joe, growing slightly in confidence. "But on All Hallows' Eve a curse can cause serious damage if a spirit is called on to deliver it to an enemy. And the old country is where my mother learned how to do it. This old Jewish woman used to watch her when her mother worked in the fields when she was little. She taught my mother how to use evil spirits to get revenge against her enemies."

"Bullshit! No one believes that! You think we're stupid?" Ray chimed in.

"A klog tsu meineh sonim" Joe responded. The older boys laughing silenced. Abe peered down at Joe.

"What did you say?" he asked.

"A klog tsu meineh sonim."

"All right, all right. You boys have had your fun. Now hand over the money and hightail it out of here." Abe looked curiously at Joe while Franz handed over the coins. The boys didn't wait after the coins hit the palm of Abe's hand. They started running toward the safety of their neighborhood.

Breathless, the boys arrived back at St. Josaphat's. "Hey, what did you say to those Jews?" asked Franz.

"It was Yiddish. It means a curse on my enemies. My mother mumbles it under her breath all the time at the market when the butcher tries to cheat her. She learned it from a Jewish neighbor in Poland."

"Fantastic!" Franz said, "Never thought a Jew's curse would save my Catholic ass." The boys laughed again, punching each other's arms and teasing one another about how scared they had looked. The boys laughed and slapped Joe on the back.

"Do widzenia!" (Goodbye!) he called as they neared his block. He wanted to get away before any other tricks were plotted. Joe ran down the lighted street and flew up the steps to his warm home. The lights from the pumpkin and turnips had gone out. The porch was dark and smelled of scorched pumpkin.

Joe stepped into the front room and greeted his parents, who were reading *Dziennik Polski* by gaslight.

"Have a good time, son?" Matka questioned.

"Tak (Yes), Matka," he replied, removing his hat and coat and hanging them on his hook in the hall.

"Not too much fun?" questioned Ojciec. His father looked him over from head to toe.

"No sir."

Ojciec stood and walked over to Joe. Joe looked up at his father as the man circled around his small body.

"Have a bonfire with the boys?" asked Ojciec. "I smell smoke."

"Yes sir. Just a small fire," he replied. Well, it was a small fire, thought Joe, so I am not really lying.

"You were careful not to catch anything else on fire?"

"Yes sir." Nothing else could catch on fire in the middle of a street so he was still telling the truth, right? Joe was getting really nervous now.

"And you made sure the fire was out when you were done, son?" Ojciec kept questioning.

"Uh huh" Joe replied. Now he was lying. Lying to his father. *Breaking one of the Ten Commandments. Honor thy father and thy mother.* He had heard that enough times from the nuns at school. Now he was going to hell and he hadn't even wanted to set fire to the stupid wagon. *Darn that Franz and Paul, always showing off and trying to be tough.*

"Okay son. Fill the big bucket full of water and have a good washing to get the smoke smell off of you. Leave your clothes in the kitchen for Matka to clean tonight," said Ojciec. As Joe turned to follow his father's instructions, Ojciec added, "Make sure to say your prayers before you got to sleep tonight to ward off any lonely spirits wandering the streets."

A few minutes later, Joe climbed into bed, where Frank was already sleeping. Joe lay awake and thought about the destroyed cart . It might have belonged to a poor Negro who collected junk to sell or salvage. Joe knew coloreds had a hard time finding work and had to eke out a living by any means. (Poles were not high on the ladder of society either, but they easily ranked above the Jews and blacks.) Or maybe the cart had been a Jewish boy's toy and his mother pulled him to the park in it on sunny days. He was glad that Franz had forgotten the outhouse prank. Soaping windows, making garbage piles and moving the shoe store wagon weren't destructive. They were just part of All Hallows' Eve as far as Joe was concerned, but igniting the cart made his stomach hurt. Now he wished they had just overturned an outhouse.

He closed his eyes and worried. Would he get caught for being part of the arson? Even worse, would he get caught for lying to his father? Joe was grateful the next day was a holy day of obligation, when the family would go to church to pray for the dead. Maybe if he prayed hard enough, God would forgive his sins. Feeling slightly better and then remembering the spirits that haunted the earth on this night, he drifted into a troubled sleep.

CHAPTER TEN

Mass was a solemn affair, with many women crying into their handkerchiefs as they remembered their loved ones who had died. Many men, including Mikołaj, were not in attendance, as it was a workday and employers did not care if All Saints' Day was a holy day of obligation in the Catholic Church. The priest would hold a Mass that evening for the laborers to remember their dead. The somber atmosphere fit Joe's mood perfectly, and he got caught up in the rituals of the day.

After Mass, the women and children walked the two blocks to Woodward Avenue and caught a ride on a streetcar to Mount Olivet, the Polish Catholic resting place seven miles east of the city. The first Catholic cemetery in Detroit, Mount Elliot, had been established within the city limits in 1841 and had filled very quickly. It expanded twice, but by 1888 the Mount Elliot board of trustees decided to purchase hundreds of acres outside the city to accommodate the flood of immigrants moving to Detroit. The potential for the city to grow and expand was foremost in the minds of the trustees. They developed a grand cemetery outside the city—as they knew had been done outside Paris, France—capable of holding three hundred thousand souls.

At the cemetery Blanca told Joe she wanted to wait for the other members of St. Josaphat's who had driven in their own cars or buggies. Joe wandered over to a large metal sign at the entrance. It read:

Mount Olivet Cemetery

Visitors please remember that these grounds are dedicated to the internment of the dead and a strict observation of all that is proper in a place dedicated will be required of all who visit it. Persons with firearms or accompanied by dogs will not be allowed to enter the grounds.

Why would someone bring a dog to a cemetery? Joe wondered.

Frank picked up a stone that was lying on the dirt road and attempted to throw it over the ornate metal fence. Fortunately Matka was not paying attention because the procession of cars was pulling up to the gates. The sun glanced off the windows of the Model T's and off the shiny black carriages as their wheels crunched over the dead leaves. Matka turned her attention back to her two young charges, calling them over to stand by her.

A beautiful stone building greeted the group as they entered through the gates. Blanca went inside and purchased three small candles, one for each of them to set on a grave. Catholics from many ethnic backgrounds were milling about the grounds. An older woman Blanca knew whispered that they should follow the Jozefatowos to an area where the St. Josaphat parishioners were buried.

The group walked down a dirt lane bordered by trees, shrubs and hanging vines. A small sign directed the visitors not to pick the flowers planted along the paths. The group dispersed upon reaching the Polish sector. A light fog hovered over a few low-lying places, creating an otherworldly feeling, and a peaceful silence descended upon the visitors. Several stately monuments adorned with angels and crosses dotted the meadow. Joe noted two large mausoleums in the distance but didn't see any in this section.

Joe's family did not have any relatives buried here, having just moved to Detroit the year before, so Matka led the boys over to an unvisited gravesite. The simple headstone read "Wizkorski" across the upper portion and listed the names Dewitt, Amboline and Flora underneath; Flora having only lived four years. The deaths had all occurred in the winter of 1890.

"Why would one family all die in the same year?" Joe asked his mother.

"That was the year of the Russian Flu, Joe . . . a terrible illness that raced across continents killing hundreds of thousands. I am sure this poor family all succumbed to it," she said, making the sign of the cross.

Matka set all three candles on the stone and lit the wicks. She instructed the boys to kneel before the memorial and say a prayer for the souls of the young family. Joe kneeled down in the damp grass and said a short prayer for the Wizkorski family and then one for himself.

"Dear God, please don't let my parents find out about setting the wagon on fire" he pleaded. He was brought out of his anxious prayer by the soft voice of his mother speaking out loud. Tears trickled down her face as she prayed for her own mother, who was buried in the village where she had grown up, interred with her ancestors. Matka worried there would be no one to light a candle and pray for her soul. Her father had perished away from her village, fighting in the revolution a decade before. Matka did not know where her father had been buried and had stopped trying to find out when she came to America.

Frank wandered off toward a grove of trees on the outer edge of the cemetery. He was following a squirrel who was burying acorns. Joe chased after his little brother and grabbed his hand. They walked back together among the headstones and statues. Frank wriggled out of Joe's grasp and hid behind a large tomb. He peeked his head out from behind the stone to look at Joe and declared they should play a game of hide and seek. *Sure thing*, thought Joe. *Like I don't have enough trouble right now without adding playing on top of a bunch of graves on All Souls day.*

"Come on, Frank," he said, grabbing his brother's hand again. They headed back to where Matka was still praying.

"Dear Lord, forgive me." Matka was whispering, tears pouring down her face. "Forgive me, forgive me."

"Matka, stop crying," said Joe.

Matka looked up at the boys in a daze. Her light blue eyes tried to focus in on her two small sons. "I'm all right, Joe . . . just missing my mother. Here . . . help me up."

Joe stood stiff, and Matka used his short body to help support herself as she rose."Matka, Ojciec will be mad at you for kneeling out here on this cold ground with the baby inside you. He's always telling you to sit down and rest."

"You are right, my good son. Let's go home and you can heat up some dinner for us. I'll sit by the stove and warm myself. Enough of the dead for today. Let's think of this little one who is yet to arrive." Matka wiped her eyes with the skirt of her dress, straightened her babushka and, holding Frank's hand, started toward the cemetery gates.

They climbed the steps of the streetcar that was sitting at the front of the cemetery. Blanca sat Frank on her lap and settled into the seat. Joe looked up at her, concern in his bright blue eyes. She looked at her handsome son and smiled gently.

"Did I ever tell you about my village in Poland, Joe?" she asked.

"Not really, Matka. Just that you lived by the sea."

"Life in Poland is not like it is here at all, Joe. I was born in Jastarnia, a small town that lies on the edge of the Baltic Sea. It is located on a narrow peninsula. This area is referred to as Kashubia. Our language is slightly different from the other regions of Poland, but we have always considered ourselves as Poles.

"Oh Joe, it is such a beautiful place. I wish you could see it. The sea is so blue. Every morning in the summer I'd open up the front door of our stone cottage and look out at the water. And so many boats, Joe, wide flat boats, sailing back and forth into the marina like busy mice scurrying about. The fisherman would set off at dawn and sail out into the sea to catch cod, herring, whitefish and smelt.

"We had pretty groves of trees growing on the hills behind the town. I'd play there with my older sister, Anna. For hours and hours we'd have tea parties with acorns and leaves on a large tree stump and pretend to invite the animals to join us. Anna would climb the trees and get so dirty. My mother would get so mad and say that Anna came home looking like a forest imp. I was frightened of climbing so high, so I'd climb just high enough for Anna not to tease me. Near suppertime, we would both sit on a thick limb and stare out at the water to see who could spot our father returning from his day of fishing. Then we'd climb down and run back home to greet him." Matka looked thoughtfully out ahead as if she could see her father walking toward the cottage with the sea behind him.

"Did you eat fish every day?" Joe asked.

"Almost. Sometimes we had to eat seagulls in the winter, when the sea would freeze and he couldn't catch any fish. Father would lay a seagull trap behind the house with a piece of bread lying on it. When a bird flew down to scavenge a bite, the brass trap would snap shut, killing it. My mother would soak it in salt water for two days; this would help remove some of the fish taste. Sometimes Anna and I would hunt the beach for seagull eggs, and she would bake cakes with them. Food could be scarce, but we had buttermilk to drink every day, and I never remember going hungry as a child."

The streetcar was quiet as the few riders were reflecting on lost loved ones; busy with their inner thoughts, they were not listening to Blanca. Frank was unusually quiet, and Matka continued her story.

"The church in my village was also very beautiful. Not as large as St Josaphat's but just as pretty. The pulpit where our priest would speak his sermons was made to look like a ship riding the waves. Imagine Father Gatowski preaching from an elaborate brown ship just above your pew! Two sculpted angels looked down from above to symbolize God protecting our fishermen. Each end of the wooden pews was carved into the shape of a rolling wave. The towering walls were painted the same blue as a calm sea with gold trimmings embellishing the arches and domes of the ceilings.

And the organ! Such melodious songs it would play. Hundreds of organ pipes driving out thunderous notes; the melody could be deafening. Then, when your ears felt they were going to bleed, the organist suddenly softened the music and played so sweetly and delicately tears would gather in my eyes.

When there was a wedding in our village everyone would attend. The kapela—that's a group of musicians, Joe—would bring their instruments and play long into the night. Anna and I would wear bright red costumes adorned with a pretty white apron that our mother had embroidered. We would braid colorful ribbons into our hair and dance to the Maruszka and Krzyznik songs of the kapela for hours.

There were violins, clarinets and accordions along with special instruments that only Kashubes play. One was called a burczybas. It's a sort of double bass wooden barrel without a bottom. Horsehair is attached to it and wetted down by one player as another pulls it to make a low rumbling sound. And they played devil's violins, which are not really violins at all but a percussion instrument in the form of a long stick with un-tuned strings and jingles attached. It's decorated with the mask of a devil and many ribbons at the top. And the strongest man in the kapela would play the bazuna, a trumpet three feet in length, made of maple."

A few small farms dotted the scenery as the streetcar drove back toward the city. The rocking of the car had lulled Frank to sleep, and Matka laid his head on her lap. Thick gray clouds rolled in and hid the sun. Joe listened intently to the tale of his mother's childhood.

"But life for the people of my village was not as peaceful as the scenery. Prussia took over our land almost two hundred years ago, and Poland was not even a country anymore. The Prussians tried to erase our culture and traditions. Decrees were passed outlawing the use of the Polish language in our schools and in public life. Poles could not hold political office, and any one resisting the laws was arrested and imprisoned. A Prussian bishop was even installed to be the leader of all the Polish Catholics!

"Such indignities were far too much for my father. The Polish language was as important to him as was his faith in God. When I was twelve years old, he left with a group of men from Jastarnia who wanted to rebel and fight for our right to live as our ancestors had. He never returned. We heard reports from a few of the men who came back that he had been jailed, and then later we heard he was dead. We never received notification from the Prussian government."

Tears welled in Blanca's eye's and she squeezed Joe's hand. Taking a deep breath she continued.

"After my father was gone we had trouble getting by. My mother would make Kashubian embroidery and give it the men who were going into the interior of the country to try to sell. She was very talented. Her embroidery was quite extraordinary. Kashubian embroidery uses just five colors—green, red, yellow, black and blue. Green represents the forests, yellow the sun, black the earth, red the fire and blood that has been shed in defense of our homeland and three shades of blue to represent the sky, the lakes and the sea. But no one had money to buy her beautiful work. All the Poles that were being persecuted were dirt poor, and the Prussians wouldn't buy any Polish goods.

"Then the Prussian army decided they needed to have power over the Baltic Sea to control trade routes and take new territories. They came in great numbers and occupied our village. They threw out families who had lived in their homes for hundreds of years. Luckily, the soldiers were not interested in our small cottage, and we were left alone at first.

"My mother tried everything she could think of to help us get by. But without the living my father had provided, we were going hungry. Anna went to work as a maid for a lieutenant in the Prussian army. My mother cried and begged her not to take the position, but we were starving and Anna felt she had to. She was always headstrong, my sister. Shortly after she began working at his home, the lieutenant fell in love with Anna. I was not surprised. She was very beautiful. Tall and strong with wide blue eyes. You have her eyes Joe; did I ever tell you that?"

Joe shook his head. His mother rarely spoke of her life in Poland because the memories always upset her. He tried to remember her mentioning her older sister and could not.

"The lieutenant was becoming angry at Anna's refusals and became more persistent every day. She decided she had to run away to escape his advances. She left in the middle of the night, stealing one of the fishermen's boats, but the lieutenant ordered his men to sail after her and bring her back. When she was brought before him, he told Anna he would have her tried for treason unless she married him. She knew that she would be found guilty and imprisoned or put to death as our father had been. Despondently, she agreed. My mother died of a broken heart on the day of Anna's wedding. There was nowhere for me to go to live. I could not live with Anna, because the lieutenant had too many soldier comrades that were eager to force their hand with the life of a young girl, just as he had done to Anna."

The houses outside the streetcar windows were closer together now, as they came upon the outer edge of the city. Joe inhaled, and the smell of hot tar and burning rubber made his eyes water. He coughed into his hands and felt better. "Are you all right, Joe?" Matka asked.

"Yes, I'm fine. Please tell me the story," he replied.

"This is where your Ojciec comes in, Joe. He'd been a neighbor of ours, and our families had been friendly. I was too young to pay attention to him before the soldiers occupied our land. After they came, all we did was try to find ways to survive. He came to my cottage the night I buried my mother. He knew my impossible situation. He felt my fate would be similar to Anna's, and he was worried. I was fifteen and very vulnerable. He was leaving on a ship for America the next day and wanted to give me his ticket. His family had saved for many years and finally had enough for the passage for him and his two brothers.

"I refused his offer. I could not take such a gift. There would be no way for me to repay his family. He insisted, telling me he had spoken to the sailors on the ship, and they had agreed to let him sail in exchange for working on the boat during the passage. Finally, I agreed, as there were no other options for me and he wouldn't leave until I took his ticket. I didn't not know until I boarded that he'd lied about the agreement with the ship's sailors and had actually agreed to become an indentured servant to work off his passage to America. Ojciec would have to work in the copper mines in the Upper Peninsula of Michigan for five years to pay off his debt.

"During our two week voyage, I stayed near him on a bunk in the bowels of the ship. He protected me from the thieves and thugs on board. Before we arrived in America, I asked if I could accompany him to the Upper Peninsula. Uncle Alexy and Uncle Feliks were going with him and were going to find work there also. It was bold of me to ask such a favor, but I knew no one in the new country and I was falling in love with your father. He asked instead if I would marry him and I agreed. The captain married us before we reached Ellis Island. The passengers on the ship were our wedding guests. They all laughed and clapped when we kissed and said it was fitting for us to start a new life together as we came to our new country."

Matka had been looking off into the distance as she'd been telling her story to Joe. She paused now and looked down at his face.

"When you saw me asking for forgiveness in the cemetery, it's because I left Anna. She's there without her family and cannot even speak our language in her own home. I miss her so much every day, but am powerless to help. I write to her but never get a reply. I am sure the lieutenant destroys my letters before she sees them."

The streetcar stopped on the corner of Woodward near their house. They paid their fare and walked home. Joe put wood in the kitchen stove, and Matka put Frank to bed upstairs. Then she sat on a small wooden chair near the stove, warming herself. Joe put the warmed up supper on the table and sat down. He looked over at his mother as he took a bite of kielbasa. Again she was looking not at him but out the window of the kitchen. A tear rolled slowly down her cheek. Joe walked around the table and gave her a hug. Surprised, she looked down at Joe and hugged him back.

"Perhaps now that Germany and Russia are fighting on our land the lieutenant will become distracted with the war and my letters will reach her. Or maybe he has joined the fighting. But I don't know if she will be able to write back. Every day I read how horrible the battles are in the newspaper. So much human loss and destruction of our lands . . . I worry how my village is faring. It is in such a remote part of the country, and it seems there are no reports about the Kashubian region. Both Germany and Russia have offered pledges of an independent Poland in exchange for loyalty and army recruits. Every day my hope increases that I will hear from her, now that Poland has a fighting chance of becoming its own country again. And every day I hope she will forgive me for leaving her and not saying goodbye."

"I hope Aunt Anna can get a letter to you real soon, Matka," Joe said.

"I hope so too, Joe. That is my perpetual prayer," she replied, another tear rolling down her soft cheek.

CHAPTER ELEVEN

Two weeks flew by. The Feast of St. Josaphat was upon them. The children had practiced singing "Veni Creator Spiritus" for hours and hours, until the Latin words rolled off their tongues. Joe knew he would never forget the lyrics for as long as he lived. Unfortunately, he had no idea of their meaning, as Sister Mary Monica had not felt it necessary to translate the song for the class. The class would sing this song for the bishop at the end of the dedication ceremony.

Matka and Aunt Hattie spent hours cooking for the festival. Ojciec and Uncle Alexy wouldn't be able to attend the festivities until Saturday because of work, but Ojciec took Joe aside before heading out the door that morning.

"I'm going to skip dinner today and practice my curve ball, Joe. Hope I get a chance to pitch in the game." Joe laughed and was about to reply when he had a small coughing spell.

"You all right, Joe?" Ojciec asked.

"Yes, Ojciec, just a little cough. I feel fine."

"All right son, drink some water then and I'll see you tonight." Ojciec grabbed his hat and walked out the front door.

Joe got a drink from the kitchen and said goodbye to Matka. "I will see you at the church," she said, kissing him lightly on the top of his head. "Walk with your cousins to the corner of Canfield and Dequindre and look out for them," she called as he was heading for the door.

Great, he thought. *Now I will be late waiting for those ninnies, and then Sister probably won't even let me play in the game tomorrow.*

But he was wrong. Marya and Pauline were waiting for Joe at the end of the walkway leading to their house.

"Well, hurry up Joe!" said Marya, bossy as usual.

"I'm here, Marya. You in a hurry to meet your boyfriend, Tall Paul?"

Marya's faced turned a bright red. "Joe, you are a despicable boy! If I didn't want to be tardy I would turn around and go tell your mother what a horrible son she has!"

"And I would turn around and tell *your* mother how I heard you skipped confession yesterday to sneak off behind the church and kiss Tall Paul!"

Pauline's eyes grew wide as saucers as she stared at her sister, then at Joe, and then turned to look at Marya again.

"Joe! What a loathsome lie," Marya replied, but quieter now and less forceful. Marya's face became a darker shade of scarlet. Joe could see he had the upper hand and decided to back off for the present. He knew Marya would try to stay far away from him all weekend now (that being the exact reason he'd revealed his information). He'd planned on telling her after morning Mass, but she'd pressed it out of him.

"Listen, Marya. Just stay out of my way this weekend, and your secret is safe with me, okay?" he said.

"What secret, Joe? I don't know what you are talking about," she replied. She grabbed Pauline's hand, pulling her quickly down the sidewalk ahead of Joe. "Come on, Pauline. We don't want to walk with Joe. We don't associate with liars!"

Joe laughed to himself as his cousins trotted off ahead. Boy, he'd have to thank Franz for sharing that golden piece of information with him. Yesterday, Franz, like Tall Paul and Marya, had snuck away during confession. His purpose, however, was to find a place to smoke a cigarette he had pilfered off his big brother. Standing in the shadows behind the priest's rectory, he'd heard two voices whispering near the church. Believing he was about to get caught by one of the sisters, he quickly stubbed out his cigarette and headed for one of the church's side entrances to avoid being noticed. As he guardedly turned the corner of the rectory, he saw instead Tall Paul and Marya smooching behind the church.

Franz and Tall Paul had been friends since first grade, but Franz always played the sidekick. Paul was better looking, more courageous, more adventurous, and of course, taller than Franz. Paul was good to Franz, but he never seemed to notice that his large personality overshadowed the smaller boy. Franz wrestled with his conscience on whether to divulge his secret, but his need to be in the spotlight won over his loyalty to Paul. Franz approached Joe immediately after Thursday's Mass and divulged his knowledge of the kissing couple. Franz had been impressed with Joe's quick thinking on Halloween and thought he would make a good ally. He also felt he owed Joe for getting him out of a beating with the Jewish boys.

Joe and Franz laughed and poked fun at the couple. Franz said, "I guess Tall Paul will be your relation when they get married." Joe said girls were disgusting, especially Marya, and he was sure Tall Paul could never really like his cousin because she was snooty and bossy. Franz made Joe promise not to tell Tall Paul, but he hadn't said anything about not telling Marya. Recalling how red Marya's face got, Joe laughed again and ran toward the procession's starting location.

The Felician Sisters were organizing the classes in order of grade when Joe arrived. Father Gatowski and the altar boys would lead the school down the streets, and each nun would then lead her class in the procession. A child from each class was placed in front of their class and held a banner bearing an image of the Blessed Mother, Christ, or St. Josaphat. Sister Mary Monica directed Joe's class to line up in rows of two. All the children were wearing their Sunday best; some were dressed in traditional costumes representing the region of Poland their family had immigrated from.

The November sun shone weakly down on the brick street. Although the air was chilly, Joe felt flushed.

Father Gatowski took his place at front of the procession, and everyone began to march down the street. At the nuns' direction, the children began to sing "Bo e, co Polsk " (God Save Poland) as they headed toward St. Josaphat's three towering steeples. People came out of stores and homes when they heard the children singing. Women waved small Polish and American flags from their porches and sidewalks. Several men came out of a barbershop on the corner and joined in singing the Polish national anthem. Soon others joined in, and the street was filled with the harmony of men's, women's, and children's voices proudly singing of their homeland. All three church communities—Jozefatowo, W*ojciec*howo, and Sercowo—came together for a moment, and the song rose in volume as the children made their way to the new school.

As the procession reached the cathedral, the singing died down and the parishioners entered the church. Joe's class made their way to the front and took their seats. The organ struck the chords of the opening hymn, and the congregation rose from their seats. Joe and his classmates genuflected, knelt, rose, and genuflected again throughout the two hours while Bishop Foley, with the assistance of eight other clergymen, celebrated the Mass. At one point, Joe felt a tickle rising up in his throat that threatened to produce a loud coughing spell. Luckily, he had remembered to put a few peppermint Chiclets in his pocket; the sensation was quelled.

Finally it was the moment for Joe's class to sing before the bishop. They stood in their pews as the priests prepared for the final hymn. Sister Mary Monica stood in front of the first pew and held both hands high as if she were conducting an orchestra. Looking at the nun's face, Joe realized that his teacher was nervous. Her black veil had slipped slightly, and he could see a strand of blonde hair peeking out from underneath. Funny, he hadn't thought of Sister Mary Monica as having hair. And he had *never* thought about what color it would be.

Straightening herself, Sister Mary Monica began waving her arms, signaling the children to begin the hymn.

"Veni, Creator Spiritus, Mentes tuorum visita, Imple superna gratia, Quae tu creasi pectora."

The class sang together, emphasizing the lyrics as Sister Mary Monica had taught them. Joe looked up at the altar as they began the second verse. Judging by Bishop Foley's reaction, Joe was sure the song wasn't resonating the feeling of reverence that Sister had hoped for. Bishop Foley had started his way down the altar steps when the organist played the first stanza. As the altar boys and priests of the church continued down the main aisle, the bishop stopped suddenly and looked over at Sister Mary Monica's second grade class. Astonished by the priests' departure from tradition, Joe stopped singing.

Perhaps the bishop was surprised by children singing at such a solemn occasion as a Pontifical High Mass. Or perhaps the children's Polish accents, combined with their new American accents, made the Latin lyrics incomprehensible to the Irish bishop. Or most likely, the bishop was shocked to see Sister Mary Monica's' small frame vigorously swaying back and forth, habit rocking side to side as she directed her charges through the ancient hymn. Joe's teacher was enthusiastically waving her arms about her, encouraging the children to sing loudly and in unison and never looked in the direction of the bishop. Gratefully, Bishop Foley gathered his senses and with a look of discernment continued down the aisle and exited the church.

Joe smiled to himself as his class left the building. Everything seemed to be going his way, and tonight he'd attend his first dance! Tomorrow would bring the long awaited baseball games.

Joe's class walked to the basement of the school, where the luncheon was being set up. He found a seat next to Sam. The parishioners bowed their heads to say a prayer over the food. The aroma from the banquet was mouthwatering. Tureens of mushroom soup and borscht, together with platters of boiled pike, fried carp, cheese and potato pierogi, cucumber salad and sour cream, sauerkraut, and homemade bread covered the tables. The women of the Ladies' Catholic Benevolent Association, a society club to which Joe's mother belonged, piled food on the children's plates. There were eleven such societies belonging to St. Josaphat's, and all had worked tirelessly to prepare for the feast day.

Sam dug into the mountain of food on his plate as soon as it was set in front of him. Joe took a bite of a warm cheese pierogi and then gulped down his milk. Whichever lady had made this dumpling was not as good of a cook as his mother. Joe ate a few more bites and then pushed his plate away.

"You're not going to eat any more?" asked Sam.

"Nah. I'm not very hungry," he replied. "You can have it if you want."

"Thanks. Here, trade plates with me so the nuns don't notice and start nagging I'm committing the sin of gluttony." Sam said.

After the luncheon the boys were free for the afternoon. Their female classmates and the women had to stay to wash the dishes and clean the basement hall, but the boys had an entire Friday afternoon to themselves. Walking up the couple blocks to Woodward Avenue, Sam and Joe discussed their options.

"You have any money?" Sam asked Joe.

"A couple pennies, How about you?"

"Yeah, my mother gave me fifty cents this morning for helping her cook breakfast for the boarders," said Sam.

"Fifty Cents! Whatcha gonna do with all that money?" Joe questioned.

"Spend it! Come on. We've got a whole afternoon with no one breathing down our necks . . . no mothers, no priests, and *especially no nagging nuns*! Let's go!" Joe bounded after Sam, not believing their luck. Fifty cents for just two boys to spend? He wasn't sure they'd be able to find enough things to spend it on.

CHAPTER TWELVE

The crowds grew as Sam and Joe neared the large avenue. Joe hadn't been on Woodward without his parents before, and he stayed close to Sam. They walked a couple blocks east, trying to decide where to spend their treasure. Sam wanted to take a ferry ride to Belle Isle and see the zoo, but Joe said he thought was too cold for the animals and they would all be sleeping. Truthfully, Joe was feeling the chill of the air. He didn't think a boat ride would help his constitution.

"Okay, you want to go to Grinnel Brothers Music House?" asked Sam.

"Sure, what's there?" Joe inquired.

"They have tons of sheet music, pianos and . . ."

Joe interrupted, "Neither one of us can play an instrument, and fifty cents isn't going to buy us a piano."

"Let me finish, Joe. They have really good piano players in there that play the latest songs while people walk around and shop. And I heard they got a gramophone player last week and they play records a few times an hour. Have you heard a record yet, Joe?"

"No, but I heard about 'em." In fact, Joe had heard very little about records, but he didn't want to sound like a country bumpkin. "Well, let's go have a look Sam."

The boys waited for a signal to cross the street from a policeman stationed in a crow's nest. This was the city's busiest intersection; the nation's first traffic tower had been built here to provide additional visibility for police officers. The traffic cop stood six feet above the heavy traffic on a small enclosed pedestal. The Traffic Division had erected several semaphores two years before, but automobile traffic seemed to double on a daily basis thanks to Henry Ford's assembly line, causing the police department to continually think of new ways to deal with congestion.

The policeman signaled for the boys to cross the street. They stepped onto the cement avenue and immediately had to dodge a bicyclist that was swerving through a bottleneck of horses, carriages, and motorcycles. Joe almost tripped on an iron streetcar rail, but Sam grabbed his arm and pulled him onto the safety of the sidewalk.

Joe could hear notes drifting onto the walkway before they reached the protection of the music store. Sam pulled open the heavy wooden door and Joe slipped inside. The raucous noise from the street immediately diminished as the oak door shut behind them. A middle-aged man with light olive skin was playing a piano near the entrance. Two darker men were leaning on the upright, listening and tapping their hands and feet with the rhythm. The melody was rapid and boisterous. Joe had never heard anything quite like it.

"What kind of music is that, Sam?" he asked.

"Ragtime! Isn't it great?"

"Sure is" said Joe, his eyes and ears taking it all in.

The trio at the piano were swaying side to side and one was pounding out the beat on the top of the upright. The boys listened in awe to the lively broken rhythm. The young men finished the song with a flourish. Joe and Sam clapped their hands in appreciation. The pianist looked over at the two young boys and smiled.

"Thanks boys. Happy to have an audience. Been quiet as a convent in here today," he said. "Can I help you boys find something?"

"What was the name of that song you just played, sir?" Joe asked, encouraged by the piano player's friendly expression.

"That old song? That's 'Maple Leaf Rag,' by good old Scott Joplin. He was one of the best ragtime composers ever born. First Negro that ever had a piece of music published, I think. Wrote 'The Entertainer' a few years after that . . . 1902, I believe." The piano player started plunking down a few notes of the aforementioned and stopped after a small riff, then looked up at the boys again with a broad grin.

"What do you mean, *was* the best composer?" asked Joe.

"Ragtime's on its way out the door, boys. You just hearing it now? Ha! Sorry to say, but that syncopation been put up on the shelf. People want to hear lyrics, words, love songs. Marches are the thing now, boys!" The man began to play a slow melody.

The two men near the piano harmonized a practice note and sang:

In the good old summer time,
In the good old summer time,

Strolling thru' a shady lane
With your baby mine.
You hold her hand and she holds yours,
And that's a very good sign
That she's your tootsie wootsie
In the good, old summer time.[1]

"Why would anyone want to listen to that mushy nonsense instead of ragtime?" Joe asked.

The piano player laughed. "Easier to dance slow to, my boy, and the ladies like it. But you two won't care about that for a few years yet. Here, I'll play you another rag. This one's called 'Echoes from the Snowball Club.'" The man turned toward the ivory keys and began to play another spirited tune.

"That's the best song I've ever heard," said Sam when the player had finished.

"Uh huh!" added Joe.

"Well, thank ya kindly small gentlemen . . . you're looking at the composer of that rag. Harry P. Guy, at your service." Harry P. Guy tipped his imaginary cap.

"You? You wrote that?" asked Joe.

"Sure did, boy. Almost twenty years ago. Probably played it a thousand times since then. Still love it. I could play that rag every day and never get tired of it," said Harry.

"Wow, a thousand times? And never get tired of it?" asked Sam.

"No, and I'll tell you why. Come here closer boys. I'll let you in on a little secret . . . 'Echoes from the Snowball Club' is a musical story of sorts. Ya see, when I came here to Detroit over twenty years ago there was only one or two small Negro bands. All the white folk listened to classical music and such; ragtime had just come out a year or two before at the Chicago World's Fair."

Joe interrupted for a moment. "Were you at the World's Fair?"

"No boy, now be quiet and let me tell you this story, ya wanna hear it, right?"

"Yes sir! Sorry." Joe sat on a stool near the piano to listen to the piano player's tale.

"Now, I been playing piano since I was a boy. Some said I had a knack for tickling the ivories. Didn't much care what others said . . . just loved playing. Even got a scholarship to the National Conservatory of Music in New York! Can you imagine? A scholarship for a mulatto piano player! Family was so proud. Had myself a grand old time in New York. Even played at Carnegie Hall one time. I suppose you boys never heard of Carnegie Hall."

"No sir, is it famous?" asked Joe.

"Is it famous?" Harry laughed. "You could say that. Well, I meet this beautiful angel named Julia, and I follow her here to Detroit because she puts some kinda voodoo love spell over me and I gotta have her for my wife. So I look around and find me a job playing in a Vaudeville theater while I am trying to convince Julia to marry me. Soon I hear about an opening in an all-Negro orchestra called Finney's and I audition. Before I know it, I'm playing with the best musical group in the city, and we can't find enough nights in the week to play for all the requests we're getting; on account of the white folk are loving ragtime music and want us to play for all their dances and parties.

"Woo Hoo! And did we have a good time playing. We played day and night! Played for the Detroit City Band afternoons on the steam ships on the river and for Finney at night! Rolling in dough we were."

Joe and Sam stood next to the upright piano listening. Harry's arms and hands emphasized words and sentences for effect.

"Well, good money for a colored man, anyway. We spent all of it too, but that's a story for another day. Did one thing right though, joined the Black Musicians Union. That's leading me to the point of the Snowball Club. The Negro bands and orchestras got so popular, the white musicians couldn't get any work. So the white boys decided they wanted to get a piece of the pie and they petitioned to join our union."

Harry started laughing so hard at this point that a tear streamed down his light bronze cheek. "White boys tryin' to join a colored union! Whites were putting us down for two hundred years . . . we finally got a leg up, and they thought we were going to help them out?" Harry guffawed and slapped his knee. "So I was so tickled by this. I sat down and wrote a song about it. Called it 'Echoes from the Snowball Club' because that's what they called the union when we blackballed the white musicians."

One of the other men picked up the story. "Best part is Harry's song's so popular, the white boys gotta play it when they *do* get a job!" The men laughed and laughed, smiling and playfully punching each other in the arm. The boys smiled at the men and waited for their amusement to subside.

"Sorry boys, we get carried away with that story sometimes," Harry said, wiping his eyes. "You boys looking for something in particular?"

"No sir," replied Sam. "Just having a look around."

"You don't happen to be wanting to hear the gramophone, do you?"

"Yes sir! I mean, if we can; that'd be terrific sir," replied Sam.

"Come on boys. Let's show these young lads our new piece of musical machinery, shall we?" Harry said. The boys followed him to the other side of the store, where the gramophone was. Joe looked at the tall wooden cabinet with the horn attached and wondered how it could play music.

"You mind if I choose the record?" he asked.

Joe and Sam looked at each other unsure how to reply. "No sir," said Sam.

Harry walked behind the gramophone and pulled a long thick envelope from one of fifty wooden slots on the wall behind it. He glanced at the title and put it back. "Too slow," he said. Pulling another he also returned it to its place. "Too lovey dovey." Pulling a third envelope out he announced that he had found the right record.

"Here we go boys. This one'll tickle your funny bones." Harry took the record out of the envelope, placed it on the Victrola and set the needle on it. After a few bars of music, a man's comedic voice began to sing "The Little Ford Rambled Right Along." Harry knew a few things about young boys, because he couldn't have chosen a better tune. The singer crooned about a Ford automobile beating out a limousine. The little Ford could run over glass, smash up fences and telegraph poles, run into ditches, and speed out of sight of cops. The boys giggled at the verses, enjoying the antics of the car. When the singer sang "he ran into a mule and the darned old jackass kicked like a fool," the boys laughed out loud.

When the record was over, Harry stopped the gramophone and placed the record back in its slot. "Well, boys . . . whatcha think?"

"That was great, Mr. Guy," said Joe.

"Now, don't be calling me that, boys. Harry will do just fine. I gotta get moving on out now. I'm filling in for one of the boys at the Pier Ballroom tonight. Hey, why don't you come down and watch a set? Just stand by the back door where it says colored employee entrance and I'll find you."

"We're going to go to a dance at the Polonia Hall, but thanks anyway Harry. Maybe another day!" replied Joe. Joe and Sam looked around the store for a few more minutes after Harry left. Sam pointed out the player pianos to Joe and explained how they operated. Joe wanted to try working the pedals and make music on his own, but Sam was anxious to move onto to their next adventure.

A cold wind swept down the avenue as the boys exited the store. Joe pulled his cap down over his ears and felt a chill go down his back.

"Come on, Joe" said Sam excitedly. "Let's check out a real live show!" Sam took off down the busy sidewalk toward Campus Martius Park and turned right on Monroe Street. Large gaudy signs covered the buildings here and extended above them. This street was known as the Theater District, a broad term to describe the entertainment available there. Flashing lights advertised vaudeville, burlesque, and moving picture films. Nickelodeons and arcades sandwiched in-between larger theaters. Joe stopped to gawk at the bright lights.

"We've gotta come here at night and take a look at these lights, Sam" Joe said. "It must look incredible."

"Yeah, sure, come on Joe. Let's go buy a ticket for a show. What do you want to see?"

"Your pick, Sam, I wouldn't know where to start."

Sam appeared unsure himself as he looked up the bustling street. How to choose their afternoon entertainment with so many choices on one street? All within two blocks; the Palace, the Temple, the Liberty, the Columbia, the Royale, and the National Theatre all beckoned to acquire the boys' coins. Joe thought the National Theatre looked the best, with its two dazzling domed towers straddling an arched entranceway. But it was Sam's money and his choice, so Joe remained silent.

"Here! Let's go in this one," Sam said, pointing at the Palace Theatre, next door to the one Joe wanted to attend. "Shows are only ten cents, and they are showing Charlie Chaplin in 'Shanghaied.' Sam paid their twenty cents to the ticket attendant in the booth on the sidewalk, and they walked into the theater. The lobby was small and dark, with posters of upcoming films haphazardly pasted on the walls. A uniformed man took the boys' tickets and opened the door to the theater. Joe and Sam walked down the narrow aisle and found a seat near the front of the stage.

"Hey, look! See the organ?" Joe asked Sam.

"Yeah, they play the music for the movies on it. Some bigger theaters have a whole orchestra that sits down near the stage and plays."

Joe settled into his wooden seat, enjoying the warmth of the theater and the excitement of a new experience. The organ began to play a light tune. A couple appeared on the stage, which was thirty feet in length. They were introduced as Mr. Bee Ho Gray and his wife, Ada Sommerville.

Bee Ho was dressed in cowboy chaps, neck bandana, and Stetson hat. Ada was in similar attire but wearing a tasseled leather skirt. Holding hands, they smiled at the crowd and moved to separate sides of the stage. Bee Ho began twirling a lasso above his head, and Ada mimicked the maneuver. They dipped and twirled their ropes in perfect synchrony. Bee Ho spun his lariat and began to jump through it and back.

Then Ada brought out several objects onto the stage, a small beer keg, a Coca-Cola bottle, and a thimble. She placed the keg on a stool and stood back. Bee Ho easily lassoed the keg and caught it with his left hand. The audience clapped and stomped their feet. Next she placed the glass bottle on the stool and Bee Ho caught it as easily as the first. The audience responded with whistles and applause. When Ada place the thimble on the stool the crowd began to cheer in anticipation. But Bee Ho tricked them and just knocked off the thimble with the rope. The crowd laughed and Ada moved the props off stage.

Ada threw another rope at Bee Ho and he began to twirl one above his head and the other at his feet. As he jumped into the second rope at his feet while twirling the first around his body the crowd stood on their feet. Joe and Sam had to stand on their chairs to see. A white horse walked onto the stage from the left, with Ada was sitting astride her. As they reached center stage, Ada whispered in the horse's ear, commanding her to bow before the audience. The audience roared, and Ada directed the horse to stand again and dance along with the organ. Joe had seen horses do many tasks but never dancing! He was delighted. The act ended with Bee Ho spinning three lariats and lassoing the horse by its neck and feet and his wife by the neck. Ada laughed; lifting off the lasso and jumped from her mount as they both took a bow.

The theatre manager came onto the stage and announced that the couple had been secured by the Palace for a one-time engagement only and that they could be seen all weekend performing at the Orpheum Theatre on Lafayette, with their entire entourage of cowboys, Indians, rodeo clowns, and horses.

Joe wiggled in his seat as a large white screen was pulled down by two ushers in matching uniforms. The lights dimmed. For a minute the screen remained black, and then it came alive with scenes of soldiers fighting in Europe. The newsreel had subtitles in English informing the audience of the latest battles that had occurred. Images of young men in muddy fields operating cannons and men in trenches shooting at the enemy flashed before Joe's eyes. The men looked crowded and dirty as they went about digging and fighting. Typed updates flashed at the bottom describing the progress of the war and reminding the audience of the continued state of neutrality of the United States.

When the newsreel showed several young soldiers lying dead in a shallow grave, the audience began to murmur loudly. A man a few rows behind the boys spoke loudly to his companion. "America needs to join the war." His companion disagreed, and others chimed in with their opinions.

"We need to stay out of their war. Europe is always fighting!" one yelled.

"My family is over there! We need to join in and help the Allies!" shouted another.

"Germany needs to be stopped! Remember the Lusitania!" shouted yet another, referring to the passenger liner that had been sunk by the Germans the year before, with many Americans aboard. Several men stood up and began arguing and pushing each other.

The organist began to play a lighthearted tune to change the mood of the audience, and the theater manager quickly started the feature film. The crowd quieted and settled in to watch the show. A funny sort of Gypsy music floated from the organ as the opening credits played on the screen.

Joe and Sam laughed uproariously as Charlie Chaplin kicked, punched and tripped about the ship he was on, never losing the small bowler hat he always wore. He rambled and danced on the screen. The crowd went wild when he tried to eat his dinner on the rocking ship. They clapped and whistled when he sailed into the sunset with his girl.

The boys left the theater completely satisfied that they'd spent their twenty cents correctly. It was only four-thirty, but the sun was beginning to set. November sunsets come early in Detroit, and the air was cold and damp.

"Come on Joe! Let's go to one more place!"

"We'd better not, Sam. I don't want to get into trouble."

"Aw, come on. It's on the way home." Sam started running down the sidewalk, dodging baby carriages and shoppers. Joe hurried to keep up but could not. His lungs were burning. He had to slow down to a walk. Sam was out of sight in five seconds. Wandering down the crowded sidewalk, he searched for a familiar landmark. Suddenly someone grabbed him by the back of his collar and pulled him off the sidewalk into a store.

"Hey!" he yelled turning to knuckle his abductor, stopping when he saw it was Sam.

"How you gonna run around the bases tomorrow at the game if you can't keep up with me for a block?"

"Don't worry about me. I can beat you in baseball any day of the week. Hey, where are we?" Joe asked looking around.

"The palace of sweets—Sanders Confectionery!"

Joe looked around and grabbed a chair at a small rectangular wooden table near the front door while Sam went to the counter to order.

"Pretty nice in here," Joe commented when Sam returned.

"Yeah, my mom told me that the fountain over there on the back wall won a prize or something at the World's Fair in Chicago in 1893."

"Boy, that thing is really old," Joe said.

A waiter in a red-and-white-striped apron brought over two tall glasses and set them on the table with cloth napkins and spoons. "Anything else, young men?" he said, smiling down at the two boys.

"No sir," they replied in unison.

"What is this?" asked Joe.

"Ice cream soda—you never heard of it? Mr. Sanders invented it right here in Detroit. Best thing you ever tasted. Dig in, Joe!"

Joe picked up his spoon and took a bite. Sam was right. It was the best thing he had ever tasted. Sweet and tingly and spicy all at the same time. The boys ate every bite and thought about ordering another to share, but Joe wanted to get home. As they parted on their block Joe called out, "Thanks for the movie and ice cream soda, Sam!"

"No problem, Joe! See you at the dance!"

CHAPTER THIRTEEN

Joe's mother was getting dressed upstairs when he entered the house. His father was sitting in the living room waiting for her to finish getting ready. The smell of onions hung in the air from the supper that Joe had missed.

"Getting home kinda late, Joe?" his father said, as Joe hung up his coat and hat in the front hallway.

"Yes sir. Sorry I missed supper."

"Matka left some for you in the icebox. Go and eat."

"Thank you sir, I'm not hungry. I'll eat later."

"Well, go on and get cleaned up for the dance. Matka was worried you wouldn't be back in time to go with us."

Joe climbed the stairs to his bedroom to change his shirt. Matka met him at the top of the stairs. "Joe! You're so flushed. Come let me feel your head." Joe obliged his mother and let her take his temperature with the back of her hand.

"You are very warm! Are you feeling ill?" she questioned.

"Just a little tired. Sam and I ran around a lot."

"But your eyes are glassy. I don't think you should go to the dance. Come downstairs and I'll get you a cold cloth for your head and a drink of water."

The kitchen was warm from the stove. Joe was sweating. He drank the water and sat at the table with the cool cloth covering his forehead.

"I feel fine, Matka. Please let me go to the dance."

"I don't think so, Joe. I think you might be coming down with something. If you want to play in that baseball game tomorrow, you had better stay home and get some rest."

"Yes, Ma'am." Joe was disappointed to miss the dance, but honestly he was extremely tired from the excitement of the day and a silly dance was not worth missing the baseball game.

"Eat your supper and you'll feel better," she said, putting a plate of pork and onions in front of him. Joe knew if he told his mother he was not hungry she would worry more, so he feebly took a few bites to appease her.

"See? I am fine, Matka. Go to the dance and leave Frank here with me so you can have a good time. I'll put him to bed and go to sleep." Joe's mother was so excited she didn't have to drag Frank to the dance that there was no further talk of Joe's fever. An hour after his parents had bustled out the door, Joe took Frank up to their room and read him a short children's story from the newspaper. The paper published a one-page story every Saturday, and Joe had kept the paper under his mattress to read at night. Frank liked the story and quickly fell asleep, as did Joe. He awoke a couple hours later extremely thirsty. He was surprised to find his parents were still not home when he went to the kitchen for a drink. *They must be having a good time*, he thought, climbing the stairs back to bed. Joe quickly fell back asleep dreaming of fly balls and running the bases.

When Joe awoke the next morning, he felt better and he hurriedly got dressed and ran downstairs to the kitchen. His parents were still sleeping, so he decided to whip up breakfast, hoping to prove that his illness of the night before had run its course. There was a definite chill in the air as he stepped off the back porch toward the water pump. But the sky was blue and clear and had the promise of a nice day. As he finished filling his bucket, his cousin Marya walked down her family's steps to use the pump.

"Morning, Marya," Joe said, trying to stay on her good side today.

"Good morning, Joe. Missed you at the dance last night. Aunt Blanca said you were ill. Are you sick or were you too scared to go because you don't know how to dance?"

"Neither. Just didn't feel like watching you fawn all over Tall Paul all night," he replied as he grabbed her bucket and began to fill it for her.

"Joe Jopolowski! You had better stop spreading false rumors. And Paul is a nice Polish boy. He'd better not hear about you talking like that about me. He will beat your brains out."

"Sure, Marya. Here's your water. Are you coming to the baseball game? I think Paul is playing."

"I hope to, but I have to help my mother make the picnic lunch and watch Emilia."

"You want to watch baseball? You hate baseball. Boy, you must *love* Tall Paul."

Marya grabbed her bucket of water and turned to walk back into the house. When she reached the first step she turned and looked at Joe. "No, I really like watching strikeouts, and with you playing there should be about a hundred!" With that, Marya walked up the stairs into her house. Joe wondered why he ever tried to be civil to his cousin.

He grabbed some wood by the shed. Balancing the wood and the water bucket wasn't easy, but he managed to get both into the kitchen. He lit a fire in the stove. While the stove was warming up, he gathered the eggs from the chicken coop. Mikołaj and Blanca came to the kitchen as Joe was finishing scrambling the eggs

"Joe, you made breakfast!" Matka said. "You must be feeling better. Thank you, kochanie (my baby). Let me feel your forehead."

"I'm fine, Matka. I was just a little tired yesterday. You were right. I just needed some rest." Joe knew that by telling his mother she was right, he could avoid having her check his temperature.

Frank wandered down the stairs still looking sleepy, his bright blond hair sticking up like a porcupine's quills. "Hungry," was all he said. Ojciec picked up Frank and set him at the table. Matka buttered the toast that Joe had made on the stove and gave him a piece. They bowed their heads to bless the food before them and dug in.

"Did you have a good time last night?" Joe asked his parents.

"Oh yes!" Matka replied. "It was a lovely dance. The band played wonderfully. I haven't heard such good polkas since we left Poland. Ojciec and I danced for hours! I'm not sure what time we even got home."

"After one o'clock. Your mother was like a teenager again. 'Just one more dance, Mikołaj, one more.' The only reason I got her home was the band packed up and left. My legs are going to be aching for a week!" He laughed. "Not sure I am in any shape to play baseball this afternoon."

"Sure you will, Ojciec! You are the strongest man I know," replied Joe.

"Thanks for the assurance, Joe. Well, I'm not as old as your Uncle Alexy, and he's playing today too. When your mother finally gave me a break from the dance floor I talked him into to it."

Matka said, "I'll get the dishes, Joe. Why don't you run off and get ready for your game. Thanks for getting up and making breakfast. It's quite a treat for me to sleep in. Good luck at your game. I will bring Frank later with the picnic lunch and watch the end of it."

Joe didn't need any further encouragement to leave for the ball field. Grabbing his coat and hat, he ran out the door and down the sidewalk toward the park. The sun was beginning to warm the air, and he could no longer see his breath. Halfway to the park, he began to feel winded and slowed down to a fast walk. *Must still be a little tired*, he told himself. When he got to the corner park, several boys were already tossing a ball around and warming up.

"Hey Joe!" one his friends called. Joe joined them and quickly forgot about being tired, as he threw the ball and took some warm-up swings with a borrowed bat. Father Gatowski pulled up in his horse and carriage half an hour later. The round priest was dressed all in black except for a Tigers baseball cap perched on his head. The boys giggled to themselves at the sight of the monsignor in a baseball cap.

"Let's play ball!" He sorted the boys out into two even teams of nine. Joe's team was first up to bat, and he sat down on the sideline to cheer on his friends. Tall Paul was pitching for the other team, and his throwing arm was in excellent shape today. The first boy got on base, but he was left stranded after the next three batters struck out.

Joe's team took to the field. Joe, being one of the younger players, was stuck in the outfield. The first two batters were tagged out at first, and the third struck out. Joe's team ran off the field laughing. Joe yelled, "We hardly had time to get into position."

Joe was first up to bat. Standing at home plate, he looked small and unintimidating. Tall Paul's first pitch sailed by him. The catcher on the other team called, "Move in! He can't hit." Joe dug his feet into the dirt and grabbed the bat, hands apart like he'd seen the Georgia Peach do. The next pitch came high, and Father Gatowski called a ball. Tall Paul threw a low slider and Joe swung the bat at the right moment. The ball went over the first baseman's head and stayed fair. He sped off toward first base and was safe. His team cheered. Tall Paul looked impressed. Sam was up next and hit a ground ball back to Paul. He was out at first base, but Joe slid safely into second.

Joe pondered stealing third. He stepped off the base to get a lead. Tall Paul threw to second, and Joe slid back just in time. Leading off closer to the base this time, he watched a boy a couple years older take a couple of practice swings. Tall Paul threw a fastball, and the boy hit it over Joe's head. Joe took off toward third. He rounded the base and headed home. Feet first, Joe slid into home and his team took the lead. The runner was batted in and Joe's team was up 2–0.

Joe was sweating as he jogged to the outfield for the bottom of the second inning. The sun was beaming down, and he wiped his brow with his cap. Tall Paul's team scored one run and the game was getting off to a competitive start.

Joes' family came to watch as the game entered the bottom of the eighth inning. Tall Paul's team had pushed ahead 4–2. Blanca laid a blanket down and began to set up the picnic lunch as she observed the game. Frank ran off toward the swings and Mikołaj joined a group of men who were already watching the game. The crowd was growing, and the excitement and cheering were rising in the park. The boys' intensity increased as Father Gatowski called out three strikes for Tall Paul's team and the ninth inning got under way.

Joe was up to bat. He walked nervously toward home plate. The other team backed up slightly, and Joe suppressed a grin. Tall Paul threw a spitball, and Joe let it fly by.

"Strike!" Father called. Joe looked at Ojciec, who winked back at him. Tall Paul threw a low ball enticing Joe to pop up, but Joe knew that was the pitcher's plan. He swung the bat around grabbing it with both hands and lightly bunted it toward the pitcher's mound. Joe took off down the baseline and was safe before Paul had retrieved the ball. The crowd cheered. Joe panted and smiled at his father. Sam was up next and hit a low ball toward the shortstop. Joe ran toward second. Halfway down the base line he felt his lungs suddenly seize up and he had to slow down. Father Gatowski called him out. Joe walked back toward the first base line and sat down hard on the grass.

Joe's teammates patted him on the shoulder and head, saying "It's okay, Joe," and "Nice try, Joe." Joe was angry he hadn't run faster but brushed it off to watch the end of the game. Sam made it home from a grounder to right field, but the game ended 4–3.

Tall Paul and his team ran around the bases, whooping and hollering. Father Gatowski declared them the champions of the St. Josaphat Boys' Baseball Game and gave each a baseball as an award. Joe hadn't known there would be a prize. He was even more dejected as he watched the team congratulate themselves and throw their new balls in the air.

Joe sat down to eat the picnic lunch with his family.

"Don't worry, son," Ojciec said. "That was a great bunt you had. Tall Paul had no idea you were planning that! You should have seen the surprised look on his face."

"Thanks, Ojciec." Joe took the ham sandwich Matka offered him and sat on the blanket.

"You are all flushed again, Joe," Matka commented, her eyes wrinkled in worry.

"Leave him, Blanca. He just got done playing a game. If he wasn't sweaty he wouldn't be trying," his father admonished.

Father Gatowski walked through the picnickers visiting and laughing. He accepted sandwiches and cookies from his parishioners as he mingled among them. Reaching Joe's blanket, he greeted the Jopolowski clan heartily.

"Great day for a ball game, huh, Mikołaj?"

"Yes, Father. Can't wait to get out there myself. First time for me."

"If you play half as smart as your son does, I'm sure your team will come out on top."

"Well, I don't know if I'll do that well, but Joe has been giving me some pointers. Um . . . Father?"

"Yes Mikołaj?"

"Is the American anthem going to be sung before the game?"

"Well, I hadn't thought about it. Guess it would be a good idea. I'll have to find someone to sing it for us."

"I could," Mikołaj responded quietly.

"You could,Mikołaj? You know the anthem?"

"Yes, Father. Joe had Sister Mary Monica write down all the verses and he brought it home for me to learn."

"All the verses? I was only aware of the one! How many are there?"

"Four in total, Father. But I'll only sing the first one—the one everyone knows."

"Sounds terrific, Mikołaj! I'll call you up after I say a prayer before the start of the game."

Joe was surprised at Ojciec's bravery in volunteering to sing the national anthem, but Matka was not. "Your father has a lovely voice, Joe. He used to sing in the boys' choir in church in Jastarnia.

As Father Gatowski walked away from their picnic area, Joe looked up at his father and said, "Ojciec, do you want me to go over the words of the anthem with you before the game?"

"No thanks, Joe. I have been singing it every morning on my way to work since you taught it to me."

Joe took another bite of his sandwich and thought about what his father had said. He knew his father greatly valued his heritage and missed his home country every day. But he must be very proud and thankful for his adopted country to want to learn the national anthem so badly.

Joe wondered if all immigrants felt like his father. His father had recently been notified by Henry Ford's administrative offices that he had to begin English classes twice a week in the evenings at the plant. Mr. Ford was requiring all his employees to learn English or they would lose their position. Some men at the plant felt Henry Ford didn't have the right to force them to assimilate into American culture; but Joe's father, like most others, did not feel that way. He felt he should learn the language of a country who had welcomed him and his family. He felt he could adopt many of the American customs and still keep his Polish identity.

Father Gatowski walked onto the pitcher's mound and began to thank all the parishioners for their hard work in building and donating to the new school. He said a short prayer thanking God for the talent and contributions of all the good people of St. Josaphat's and a prayer for the future of the great cathedral, that generations to come would learn the good news of the Lord within its holy walls. Then he called Mikołaj over to the mound to sing the national anthem.

Ojciec walked slowly over to Father Gatowski. Joe watched as he shook the priest's hand and turned to face the crowd. Ojciec stood tall. He removed his hat and placed it over his heart. Then he began to sing. The first two notes were so quiet that Joe worried his father would whisper the song and everyone would ridicule him. But his father stopped suddenly and held up his hand for attention. Clearing his throat, he smiled and began again, this time in a loud, beautiful baritone voice. His voice thundered musically above the crowd. They stopped their picnicking to look at where the melodious sound was coming from.

Sister Mary Monica stood up from her picnic blanket and joined Joe's father with her soprano voice. A few others scrambled to their feet and joined in. Joe looked around the park and saw boys and girls from his class tentatively stand up and join in. Soon, most of the spectators had taken to their feet, uniting their voices in a show of loyalty to their new country. Joe stood up, and his mother followed her son's lead. Removing his cap, he sang the last few lines of the song. Matka's light blue eyes glittered proudly as she listend to her husband finish with a magnificent crescendo.

The bystanders all clapped, whooped, and hollered when the song was over. A couple of men walked over to Mikołaj and clapped him on the back. Father Gatowski shook his hand again, turned to the crowd, and yelled, "Play ball!"

The men took to the field and everyone sat down to enjoy the afternoon's entertainment. The sun had warmed the air, making for a gorgeous fall day. November could bring snow or sun in Michigan, and the parishioners thanked God for providing a warm day for their festival. Joe's father jogged to third base, and the opposing team's batter walked to home plate. Joe took his seat on the blanket and settled in to watch the game.

As the batter tried a couple practice swings, a coughing spell came over Joe. Holding his hands over his mouth as the nuns had taught him he doubled over gasping for breath. Matka kneeled at his side, softly encouraging him to try and relax his muscles and rubbing his back. Finally, he regained his composure and the fit subsided. Red-faced and sweating, he lay back on the blanket to grab some deep breaths.

"You do have a fever, Joe!" Matka exclaimed, placing her cool hand on his forehead.

"No, I'm fine, Matka. Just a little cough. I just need a drink of wat—" another coughing spell overtaking his sentence.

"We're going home and putting you straight to bed. You are very ill," she replied. Worry crinkled her forehead as she started putting the picnic items in her basket.

"No Matka, please. I want to watch Ojciec play in the game. Really, I am fine."

"Absolutely not! We are going home right now." She looked around to find a neighbor to relay the message to Joe's father that they were leaving and why.

Gathering their picnic items, she spotted Sam's mother, Mrs. Ludwicka, who was watching the game from beneath a large maple at the edge of the park.

"Please, Mrs. Ludwicka, tell Mikołaj that my Joe is ill and we had to leave. Have him bring our basket and blanket when the game is over. May I leave them with you?"

"Certainly," Mrs. Ludwicka said. "And I hope Joe feels better soon."

CHAPTER FOURTEEN

Matka picked up Frank and grabbed Joe's hand. They started down the wooden sidewalk toward their house. Joe was still trying to convince his mother that he wasn't sick when another coughing spell overtook him. They stopped on the sidewalk while the attack racked his little body. As he coughed into his hands, blood spattered his palms. Surprised and scared he held out his hands for his mother to see. Wiping the blood with the hem of her dress she told him not to worry—that he was going to be all right. Her face however, indicated extreme apprehension. This spell was worse than the two before, and Joe had to sit on the sidewalk to recover. After a minute, Joe stood up to walk the rest of the way home, but when he took the first step his knees buckled and he fell face first onto the wooden planks.

There was no one on the street. Everyone was at the park for the baseball game and picnic. Matka looked around desperately for help. She couldn't carry both children for two blocks. But for once, the streets were empty.

"Frank, you're a big boy, aren't you?" she asked his little brother. Frank nodded that he was. "You are going to walk next to me and I will carry your brother. Can you do that like a big boy?" Frank nodded again, his eyes wide with worry as he looked up at their mother. Matka picked up Joe's hot tired body and lifted him onto one shoulder. Avoiding the cracks in the sidewalk with the tiny heels of her shoes, she began to make her way toward their home, little Frank toddling behind her.

Matka set Joe down on the front step when they reached home. "Can you walk up the steps, Joe?" she asked.

"Yes, Matka," he said attempting to stand up. With his mother's assistance he made it to the top of the steps. He was so fatigued he felt like he had run several miles. His mother helped him into the house and into the rocking chair by the empty fireplace in the living room. She covered him with the quilt from her bed and brought him a cold drink of water. Joe took a couple sips and began to cough again. Pushing the quilt off, he knelt on the floor as the spell overtook him. Matka wanted to get Joe up to bed but she couldn't carry him up the stairs, and she didn't think he could make it himself.

"Joe, if I help you can you walk up the stairs to your room?"

"I think so, Matka," he replied. He couldn't understand how he could play ball that morning but now he could barely walk up a flight of stairs without help. He only knew his body was burning up and his muscles felt like jelly. Together they managed to get him up the stairs and into his bed. Matka pulled his sweaty clothing off him and covered him with a light blanket. She pulled up the shade and opened the window to let in some fresh air.

"Can you ask Ojciec to come up to my room and tell me what happened at the baseball game as soon as he gets home?"

"Yes, Joe. Now, just rest please." She smoothed the cool sheets on the bed. Her hair had fallen out of its upward arrangement and Joe realized how taxing carrying him had been on his small mother. His bright eyes widened in anxiety as he remembered the baby she was carrying inside her.

"Oh, Matka! The baby . . . I forgot. I'm so sorry."

"Don't worry about the baby, my Joe. Your Matka is much stronger than you think. And you are not quite as big as you think you are." She pushed his damp hair back off his forehead tenderly. "Now close your eyes and rest, and concentrate on getting better." Joe immediately drifted into a heavy sleep.

When Joe awoke the sky was dark outside his window. Cold air was drifting into the room, chilling his skin. He slowly sat up, trying to reach the glass of water by the side of his bed.

"Whoa, son. Hold on there," Ojciec said. He'd brought up a chair from the kitchen and had been watching Joe as he slept. "I'll get it for you." He handed Joe the glass. Joe took a long drink and handed it back to his father. Ojciec turned on the small gas lamp on the dresser, and the room was bathed in warm, yellow light.

"Thank you, Ojciec," he said quietly. "How was the baseball game? Did your team win? Before his father could answer, another coughing fit overtook him and he lay back down, giving into it. Speckles of blood sprinkled the light blue blanket he covered his mouth with. "Am I going to die, Ojciec? Why am I coughing blood?" he asked.

"No! You are not going to die, Joe. We've sent for the doctor and he's on his way. You are going to be just fine. Don't worry." He started to give Joe a small grin to show his confidence, but the grin stopped halfway from completion. Joe was overtaken by yet another cough.

"Blanca, come quick!" he yelled out the doorway. Joe's mother bustled into the room carrying a bowl of hot water and a towel. Setting the items on the small bedside stand she sat on Joe's bed.

"Are you having trouble breathing, Joe?" she asked.

"Only when I cough, Matka. Why am I coughing blood? What's the matter with me?"

"I don't know, Joe," she said. "Mikołaj, go and see what is keeping the doctor, please." Joe could hear his father running down the stairs and out the front door. His mother removed his undershirt and washed his perspiring body with the warm water and towel, then dressed him in a dry undershirt.

"Lie down, Joe, and don't worry. The doctor will be here soon." She brushed his light hair with her hand. He closed his eyes again and fell asleep.

Joe was awakened by a strange voice outside his room. A German-accented man was speaking to his parents.

"How long have you noticed the cough?" Ojciec translated the man's words for his mother, and she responded in Polish.

"Just yesterday," Ojciec repeated to the doctor..

"The boy has been tired, ja?" Again Mikołaj translated.

"My wife says she just noticed yesterday and made him stay home from our festival. She thought it was funny that he agreed without much argument."

"Ahh . . . well it is difficult with young boys. They are so full of energy—spinning like a top around and around until they drop—it is difficult to tell with them," the voice replied reassuringly. "Let's go have a look at the patient, shall we?"

Joe was stunned to see his parents accompanied by an elderly Jewish man. He wore a traditional yarmulke and had long sideburns and a beard.

"Kochanie, this is Dr. Levy. Your father found his office over on Hastings Street. Ojciec has brought him to look at you."

"Come, young man, sit up for me." Joe sat up and the doctor put his stethoscope on Joe's back. "All right, now can you cough for me, Joe?"

Joe tried a small cough but it quickly turned into a two-minute ordeal, leaving him again exhausted with speckles of blood on his hands.

"All right, lie down, son." The physician continued his examination, listening to Joe's chest and feeling his abdomen. "Are you having trouble breathing?"

"Just when I'm coughing," Joe said. His voice was raspy.

"How long have you not been feeling well?"

"A few days." he replied quietly, avoiding his mother's eyes.

"Ahh . . . well it might be too early to tell but I am sorry to say that I think he has acquired tuberculosis. He will have to be sent to the sanitarium so as not to infect anyone else."

Ojciec translated the doctor's words to Matka.

"No," she told Ojciec. "I will care for him. He is my son. I will not send him away when he is sick. Just last week I saw a cure for tuberculosis in the Polish newspaper. It was called . . . Eckmans Alternative. Yes, the advertisement said calcium deficiency was responsible for the disease, and Eckmans contains lime salt that can cure it. Mikołaj, you can go to the druggists now and buy it. Joe will get better and he can stay here with us."

Mikołaj translated for Dr. Levy, although Joe was sure the doctor already understood Matka's argument.

Dr. Levy smiled at Matka. "Those medicines don't work; Mr. Jopolowski. They are made by quacks and charlatans. The boy needs to be treated away from the community. Tell your wife that he is highly contagious and she needs to think of your other son and her neighbors. I can recommend a very good place for you to send him."

As Ojciec turned to explain the doctor's words to his mother, Joe pulled on the bottom of the elderly man's suit coat. "Please sir," he whispered, "my mother is carrying a baby. Tell them I will go away to this place. I don't want anything to happen to the baby because of me."

"You are a brave boy and a good son." The doctor interrupted Joe's parents to repeat what the boy had whispered to him. "Now, I cannot force you to send Joe away, but I cannot emphasize enough how important it is for him to get treatment and for you not to expose your young son and mother and baby to the disease. If you will let me, I can take him to the sanitarium tomorrow. I have business there I have to attend to, and he can ride with me in my car. It is not far from here, but I would prefer the boy doesn't go by streetcar as I don't wish him to expose anyone else."

"Where is this place, Dr. Levy? What are the costs? It must be expensive for him to stay there?" Mikołaj asked.

"The Children's Free Hospital is on St. Antoine, not far from here by streetcar. You can come visit him in a few weeks when he is feeling better. The hospital was built on donations and is subsidized, so just pay what you are able, Mr. Jopolowski. Joe will get very good care there, don't worry. And I will check on him once a week to monitor his progress and treatment."

"Please, Matka? Let me go with the doctor. I don't want you or Frank to get sick because of me. I'll be fine—I promise. And Ojciec can come and see me soon."

"Yes. Yes. And Joe can get paper and write letters to you every day. You can write, Joe?" the doctor asked.

"Yes sir." His voice cracked.

"Now, see? He will be fine. He is a brave young man. Now let's go downstairs and discuss the arrangements and let this boy rest. Goodbye, Joe. I will see you tomorrow." The adults left Joe alone in his bedroom and made their way downstairs.

Joe was too tired to worry about going to the sanitarium. He was happy there was a place that would take care of him and not bankrupt his father. A worried Frank tried to sneak in the bedroom while the doctor was talking to his parents in the living room, but Joe sternly told him to go play in their parents' room and stay out. Frank pouted but obeyed his older brother. Joe fell back asleep before Dr. Levy left.

The next morning he was awakened by his mother. She was packing a small leather case with his few items of clothing. Her pretty blonde hair peeked from underneath the blue babushka she wore. Her hands moved quickly, folding his clothes and placing them neatly in the case. She turned and saw he was sitting up in bed staring at her.

"Joe, kochanie, are you hungry?" she said, startled that he was awake.

"Yes Matka, a little."

"I will bring you some broth. I made some this morning. But first let me help you wash up." Matka washed him with warm water and dried his skin softly with a towel. She helped him get dressed in his brown knickers and ivory shirt. "Now sit here while I get you some broth."

Frank peered behind the doorway as their mother's skirts bustled out. "Don't you come in here, Frank. I mean it," Joe said.

"Joe go?" Frank asked.

"Yes, I'm leaving, but I'll be back soon. And you will get the bedroom all to yourself while I'm gone."

"Don't want Joe to go," Frank had tears in his eyes.

"I won't be gone long, Frank. Listen, Frank. Can you do something very important for me while I am gone?"

Frank nodded yes, his dark blue eyes staring at his brother.

"Will you take care of Matka while I'm gone and help her by being a very good boy?"

"Okay!" Frank toddled off down the hall in search of some new entertainment or a snack.

Matka came in and gave Joe a bowl of steaming broth. Joe drank the broth, but the steam caused him to start coughing and his mother took the bowl from him.

"Oh, Joe, how can I let you go? I will miss you so much. I will tell the doctor we have changed our minds, and I'll take care of you here at home."

"No, Matka. I need to go to the Children's Hospital. Please don't worry. I'll write you a letter every day to let you know how I'm doing. I'll be home before you know it, and you will be yelling at me to come in from playing street ball and complaining that boys bring in more dirt than horses to a barn."

Matka smiled and patted Joe's head. She squeezed his hand. There was a knock on the door. Ojciec let the doctor in. His father wrapped Joe in Matka's quilt and carried him to the doctor's Model T that was idling in front of the house. The doctor opened the door, and Ojciec gently placed Joe in the front seat.

"Get well, son. I'll come see you as soon as Dr. Levy says I can." Blinking away a tear, he closed the door and walked up the steps and into the house.

"Well, let's get going," said the doctor. He put the car in gear and pulled away from the curb. Joe wished he felt better so he could enjoy his first automobile ride. The air was chilly in the car, and Joe pulled the quilt tighter around his body. The car bumped down the cobblestone street till the doctor turned onto Woodward Avenue, where the street was paved with concrete. The ride immediately became smoother. Joe looked out the window at the people walking to Sunday Mass.

Joe apologized to the doctor. "Sorry you can't go to church today because you are taking me to the hospital."

"My Sabbath is on Friday night, Joe. All Jewish services are held then." The doctor chuckled.

"Oh, right," Joe replied, embarrassed. "I forgot."

"That's all right, son. Just rest and we will be at the hospital soon."

After a few minutes, Joe's curiosity got the better of him and he had to ask, "Why is the hospital free for children?"

"Well, Mr. Hiram Walker gave one hundred twenty-five thousand dollars to build it about twenty years ago, when his thirteen-year-old daughter Jennie Melissa died. Mr. Walker owned the Canadian Club whisky distillery in Canada, and he was extremely wealthy. He was an American who lived here in Detroit. When his little girl died he wanted to do something for all the sick children, so he built this hospital and left money to help with the cost to run it."

"Was she his only child?" Joe asked.

"No, no, he had three older sons who run the company now. Not sure how long they will fund the hospital though, with the temperance movement in full swing over here."

"Temperance?" Joe asked.

"Yes. A lot of people over here have been fighting to make liquor and beer illegal to sell or drink."

"Why would they want to do that?" Joe inquired. His father drank beer almost every day and the idea that people would make a law banning it puzzled him.

"Temperance supporters believe society would be better if men did not consume alcohol. Oh, they all have their own ideas mind you. The Anti-Saloon League preach total abstinence, while others are only against liquor and still others believe in moderation in regards to drink. I am of the latter opinion. But I understand why some feel abstinence is the only solution. Too many husbands getting drunk in this country and beat their wives and children. If passing a law to ban alcohol meant not one more wife or child would be hit in drunken anger; I would be behind it one hundred percent. But human nature being what it is; I don't think banning liquor will bring about the results the temperance movement is looking for."

Dr. Levy looked down at Joe and smiled. "My turn to apologize to you, son. What you need now is a doctor and not a man on a soapbox. My point is that I'm not sure how much longer Mr. Walker's money will be able to fund the hospital if the government bans the sale of liquor. Well, here we are now, young man."

Dr. Levy pulled into a curved driveway and parked the car under an arched tower that led to the entrance of the stone-walled hospital. Two nurses in white uniforms and large caps came out and put Joe in a small wooden chair with wheels.

"Goodbye, Joe. I will check on you after I go on my rounds. You are in good hands." Dr. Levy climbed back into his car and drove off to the back of the hospital.

The nurses wheeled Joe inside and went through the process of admitting him to the sanitarium portion of the hospital, where all the children diagnosed with tuberculosis were housed. They gave him a bed in a long room with nine other beds. Boys between five and twelve years old lay in the small metal beds with white sheets. Each bed was placed in front of a window that was open to the air as the doctors believed sunlight and fresh air could cure their disease.

CHAPTER FIFTEEN

1916

The following six months were a haze to Joe. He read books and played board games with his ward mates, but mostly he slept. Exhaustion overtook his small body and he felt cold all the time. The windows of his ward were always open, even when the temperatures dipped below zero. Once a day the boys were wrapped up in blankets and taken outside to sit in the sun for two hours. They were expected to silently rest on chaise lounges to encourage the sun to heal their lungs. Most days the goal of quiet rest was not achieved, because the boys' teeth chattered so violently.

The nurses were kind but strict. Often Joe fell asleep to the sound of one of his ward mates crying. Doctor Levy kept his promise to check on Joe's progress every week. Towards the spring, Joe's father was allowed to visit him. The nurses would wheel Joe outside to a small covered patio behind the hospital, where he and his father would visit for an hour. Ojciec brought with him the children's section of the *Detroit News* and a copy of the *Dziennik Polski*. Joe enjoyed reading in his childhood language; it helped lessen his feeling of homesickness. His mother sent cookies and candy for him to share with the other boys. The sugary sweets would momentarily lift the melancholy atmosphere of the ward. Joe missed home but was so tired and weak his homesickness was secondary to his desire to feel better.

His health improved in the spring, and Dr. Levy began discussing his discharge, but he experienced a severe setback at the end of June. Again, his father was not allowed to visit. Joe felt like he was never going to leave the sanitarium. Long, cold, lonely hours encompassed his nights, and grueling coughing spasms his days. The relapse lasted two weeks and left him weaker than before. He couldn't get out of bed without assistance. The nurses worried that he wouldn't regain his strength and the disease would cause him to be an invalid.

Joe overheard the nurses discussing his condition one evening at the end of the ward when they thought the boys were all asleep. The women whispered to each other, occasionally glancing down the ward to where they thought Joe was asleep in his bed. That morning the doctors had determined that one of Joe's lungs did not work and it never would. "How will the poor child recover now with only one functioning lung?" one asked. The others only responded, "It's a pity" and "It's in God's hands now."

Joe rolled over in bed and put his small hands together in prayer. He prayed, "God, give me strength."

Suddenly he felt a heavenly warmth surround his lungs and then his entire body. For the first time since being in the sanitarium, Joe felt at peace. He knew he'd received an answer to his prayer. He reached inside himself, grabbed onto the fighting side of his soul, and decided to battle his illness.

Every day Joe used will power to perform the exercises prescribed by his physicians. The nurses told him to stop when they saw sweat pouring down his pale brow and forced him back to bed, but Joe continued flexing and moving and deep breathing under the covers after they left. It took several weeks for his condition to improve enough for the doctors to allow his father to visit him again. The first time he saw his father after his relapse, Ojciec had tears pouring down his face.

"Joe, I thought I'd never see you again. My son, we were so worried and frightened. Your mother cries every day, and the entire family has been lighting a prayer candle every week in church for your recovery. Marya and Pauline light one at every morning Mass before school too."

"Boy, the doctors must've made it sound real bad if Marya is lighting candles for me!" Joe attempted to laugh but broke into a ragged cough.

"Don't tax yourself, son. I need you to rest so you can come home soon. Joe, the doctors told me some bad news. I want to be honest with you and tell you what they're saying."

"What, Ojciec?" Joe wondered what other bad news awaited him. He squared up his small bony shoulders and waited.

"Well, the doctors say. . . . Well son, you only have one lung that works now. They say the other one will never work again. I'm sorry Joe. They say you won't be able to run and play anymore. Dr. Levy says you'll have to find a quiet office job when you grow up and that colds and influenza will affect you worse than others. " Ojciec looked down at his feet, not able to look into Joe's eyes.

Relieved, he replied, "I already knew that, Ojciec. I listen to the nurses when they think I'm asleep. I'll be able to run and play . . . don't worry. My other lung is as strong as most boys with two good lungs. I'm not going to let this illness beat me. Every time I feel weak and tired, I think of this boy I saw last summer at the park. He'd tripped and fallen and the train had run over his arm. But he still played and ran with all of us at the park. That's how I am going to think of my lung. I lost one but I'll still be able to throw balls and run and play."

"Of course you will, Joe. You are a Jopolowski and we are fighters! How proud you make me. The doctors think if you continue to gain strength they will discharge you in time for Christmas. Please keep working to get stronger."

"Sure, Ojciec, I definitely want to be home for Christmas. I missed it last year."

"We'll have an enormous celebration this year when you come home. We'll get a Christmas tree and have a feast! You just get better, son."

Autumn passed slowly, but each day Joe felt sturdier. Every day the nurses worked his atrophied muscles, encouraging his legs and arms to grow stronger. Joe worked arduously, and he continued to pray to God for strength before falling into an exhausted sleep. Eventually he was able to walk around the hospital grounds without assistance.

The first week of December came, and Dr. Levy visited Joe in the boys ward.

"Well Joe, looks to me like you are fully recovered. The hospital is discharging you tomorrow, but you will not be able to go to school for a while. You must continue to rest and get stronger at home. If you push yourself too far you will just end up back here, do you understand?"

"Yes sir, is my father coming for me tomorrow?"

"No, I told your father I would come for you and drive you home. I thought you might enjoy a nice ride now that you are better. Does that sound good to you?"

"Yes sir! Thank you, Doctor Levy . . . for everything."

"Well, we weren't sure you were going to make it, Joe. You sure gave us all a scare. I've never seen a boy as ill as you recover. You have a strong drive inside of you. That will come in handy for the rest of your life. You keep that inner strength and you won't have any problems surviving. God must have great plans for you," Doctor Levy said, patting Joe on the shoulder. "Now you just need to gain a little weight and we can send you back to school so you can be a normal little boy. I'm sure your mother can take care of that part on her end. She's been sending baked goods and her good Polish food to my office every week to thank me for taking care of you. I'm glad you're better . . . maybe I can lose a few pounds now." He patted his expanding abdomen and laughed.

The following day the nurses wheeled Joe out to the portico at the hospital entrance, where Dr. Levy was waiting in his shiny Model T. Joe got out of the wheelchair and turned to face the nurses. He thanked them for helping him in his recovery. Glancing at the wheelchair, he made a promise to himself that he'd never again be confined to a bed or chair. Joe opened the door to the Model T, sat down, and waved at the nurses as Dr. Levy drove off.

"Thanks for driving me home, Dr. Levy," Joe began. "It really wasn't necessary. My father could have come for me."

"It's my pleasure, Joe. Now, I know you are anxious to get home, but I was hoping we could go for a short drive?"

"If my parents won't be upset . . . aren't they expecting me?"

"I informed them of my plans and they agreed. Now, if you are also in agreement . . ."

Joe nodded his assent, and the physician drove down Woodward Avenue. Pointing to the left he said, "This is Grand Boulevard, Joe. It was designed to be a park around the city limits, but it's not really the park they envisioned; there are hospitals, orphanages, and factories here now. Henry Ford completed his hospital on Grand Boulevard just two years ago. Now all of Detroit's finest are making their homes beyond it, so the politicians moved the city limits outward again."

He drove a few blocks further, where he turned off the busy boulevard onto Longfellow Avenue and headed west. Large homes dotted the quiet street, each different in appearance. Between vacant lots of land brand new homes stood two and three stories high, with decorative facades and short front yards. Several had towers with pointed steeples grandly facing the street. The trees were bare, as it was December; but it was easy to imagine the shaded canopy the elm trees would provide in warmer months. Ornamental shrubbery enhanced the landscape of every yard.

"This house is the home to Frank Navin. Do you know who he is?" The doctor pointed to one of the smaller homes on the street.

"Yes sir! My father and I went to his stadium last year to see the Tigers play! He lives there? Wow." Joe thought that a man who had the money to build an enormous stadium would live in one of the large mansions on the avenue and not a simple two story home. "Who lives in the bigger houses?"

"The founders of the big stores downtown, attorneys, real estate brokers, judges, even a few physicians. Not myself of course. But mostly the auto barons."

"Like Mr. Ford?"

"Yes and Mr. James Couzens. He was Mr. Ford's general manager. That stone mansion with the large chimney over there is his. He invested twenty-four hundred dollars with Ford back in the early 1900s, and it sure paid off for him—in the millions. Earlier this year he left Ford and now he is the police commissioner for the city."

Driving one block south, they turned onto Edison Avenue and passed a Cadillac driving in the other direction. "That was William Fisher in that automobile. He's building a house on this street. He and his brothers own Fisher Body Company; they make the auto bodies for several auto companies. Let's see . . . they manufacture for Cadillac, Ford, and . . . oh yes, Studebaker. I think there are seven brothers who own the company."

Joe studied the stone workers constructing the elaborate home. Men perched on scaffolding were assisting a complicated lever system to haul large stones up to the second floor and place them on the exterior of the house. Others stood and yelled directions, their faces bright red from the biting cold wind.

"They're building these enormous homes all over this area—they call it the Boston-Edison District. The Rabbi for my synagogue, Temple Beth El, lives here on the corner.

The doctor indicated a smaller two-story brick home with a large porch and white painted steps. The pretty porch had a peculiar arched window carved into the brick under siding. "Not a very large house. I guess the synagogue's not paying him too much." He laughed.

After traveling a bit farther down the avenue, Dr. Levy pulled over the Model T and parked at the curb. "This was Mr. Ford's home till last year. Above the garage is a machine shop he had built for his son Edsel," he said, pointing to a stately home that sat on at least three lots. Joe knelt on the fabric seat to get a better view. The house had a charmingly classic design and reminded him of a large fairy tale cottage. Perhaps his imaginative perception was due to the elaborate gardens that surrounded the home. Vines hung from a long wooden arbor on the side of the home, which was surrounded by ornamental trees and shrubbery.

"I can see why Mrs. Ford wanted to move out to the country. She sure must love flowers," Joe said.

"Yes, and bird watching. Not so many birds around here with all the construction and factories." Immediately to the west of the home was a park the width of an entire block which beckoned the residents to picnic, play, and stroll. Ancient trees rose above the park, intermingled with benches and picnic tables.

A couple minutes later the doctor put the car in gear and turned onto Second Avenue. "I'm going to double back so I can show you some of the mansions that the clothiers have built. They drove up a few blocks and turned onto Boston Boulevard. A large landscaped island separated the two sides of the street. "This neighborhood has been like a beehive of activity the last couple years. Building these huge homes takes a lot of men and material that have to be trucked in every day. This first home on your right belongs to Wolf Himelhoch. He attends the same synagogue I do. Mr. Himelhoch owns a woman's clothing store on Woodward Avenue. Have you been there, Joe?

"No, but I've seen it."

"Benjamin Siegel lives on this street too. His store, B. Siegel Company, sits right across the street from Himelhoch's and is a fierce competitor. Funny, they make their homes across the street from each other just like their businesses, huh, Joe?"

Joe nodded in agreement but had to admit that he might live next door to the devil if he could live his life in such luxurious style. The fronts of some of the great homes were festooned with evergreens in preparation for the Christmas holiday. Lights glittered inside, and an occasional Christmas tree could be seen twinkling in a large front window. Snowflakes lazily drifted through the air and landed on the eaves and roofs as if the wealthy owners had ordered the white trimmings from above.

Dr. Levy was still listing the homes of Detroit's leading citizens as they drove further down the street, " . . . and Mr. Kresge lives at the end of the street and Mr. Ira Grinnel right here."

"I've been to both those stores! I heard a record played at Grinnel Brothers' store right before I got sick. And there was a mulatto pianist there who played this neat music . . . umm . . . ragtime!"

"Don't be surprised when you see more mulattos and blacks around the city now. Since you've been in the hospital they've been arriving by droves to try to get work in the auto factories. I would guess more than thirty thousand have come since you took ill. They even started a committee this summer to help them get acclimated—it's called the Detroit Urban League. Volunteers for the league go to the Michigan Central Depot station every day and meet them when they get off the train. The League tries to find a place for families to stay for a little while, helps them acculturate to city life, and shows them how to dress for our northern environment."

"Do you mean because they're from down south that group tells them it's cold in the winter and they'll need coats?" asked Joe.

"Well yes, I'm sure that's part of it, but they also pass out pamphlets titled the 'Dress Well Club.' The Urban League members believe that segregation of the Negroes is partially due to southerners who dress like Mother Hubbards—wearing worn, thin clothing that people should only dress in to clean houses. They distribute these pamphlets to newcomers when they get off the train so they should know how to dress and how to behave, and then they invite them to learn about what the Urban League can offer—help with food, a place to live, finding work, and so on."

"That's nice of them. I wonder if my parents got a 'Dress Well' pamphlet when they came through Ellis Island."

"I don't know, Joe. I came over many years ago through Canada, so the procedures have been different." Dr. Levy's tire ran over a large rock in the road that had fallen off a construction truck and Joe bounced high in his seat, his head almost touching the roof. He looked over at the physician, worried the Model T's tire or chassis was damaged but Dr. Levy smiled at Joe and continued down the street.

"These seats have some spring to them don't they, Joe? It's one of my favorite things about driving this thing around. My wife complains, but I like a little bounce in my buggy." He laughed. "Now look over there . . . that enormous estate is called Stonehedge. Walter Briggs built it last year. He's one of those men who like to show off his income. Do you know who Briggs is?" he asked.

"No sir." Joe looked at the enormous mansion with multicolored stonework. Four chimneys rose up above the three-story roof, and a gated portico stood covered at the side of the great home. To have so much wealth was incomprehensible to Joe. In his eyes, the home was as large as the hospital he had just left. "I've never seen anything like it . . . even when I took the boat to Boblo Island with my family and saw the mansions sitting on the river. How could anyone have that much money?"

"Sometimes it's just good timing, Joe. Mr. Walter Briggs worked for Everitt Carriage Works in the late eighteen hundreds, just about the time your Mr. Ford was building his Quadracycle in his garage. Briggs bought the carriage house and started making car bodies for Ford in 1909. Now his company manufactures bodies for Ford and Hudson. Looking at the size of Stonehedge and that house William Fisher is building, there must be a lot of money in making automobile bodies. Of course, timing combined with a good gut sense works, too.

Joe stared out the window onto Boston Boulevard. The expansive lawns, the homes, and the trees created a tranquil atmosphere, but there was an undercurrent of industriousness throughout the district. Perhaps the feeling derived from the immigrant workers erecting the giant estates, or maybe it came from the servants cleaning and cooking inside the homes. Possibly, he sensed the determination of a Negro maid traversing the sidewalk nearby, as she carried a basket of groceries on her head. Or perhaps the feeling arose from the power of inspired minds from the men who resided in those mansions—the men who were constructing a new economy for Detroit, the men whose ideas were forging new ways of travel, of life really, and in that, a new means of freedom.

Dr. Levy pointed at homes on the block as the Model T rumbled down the street. "Cash Talbot's house is over here. He owns Talbot Coal Company, and by the looks of his house the rising price of coal hasn't affected his pocketbook the way it has mine. There's a shortage now because of the war. There's a shortage on many things now—wheat, fuel, sugar—and the government has informally decreed 'less' days"

"What are 'less' days? Have they shortened the week?" asked Joe.

"No son," the physician chuckled, "I meant days of the week where one goes without, like meatless Mondays or wheatless Wednesdays. This week Uncle Sam advised all Americans to have porkless Saturdays; of course all my days are *already* porkless." He smiled. "You'll see. The Great War hasn't affected the Children's Hospital yet, but I should think the time will come soon. You should see the ladies' section of the *Detroit News*, abounding with recipes to help the women cope with shortages."

Joe was aware the United States had joined the war in the spring, but not much information had been passed onto the children at the hospital. The medical staff felt if the children had knowledge of their families' daily adversities and struggles or were continually apprised of the tragedies occurring in Europe, the young boys' health would be further impeded. However, none of the nurses caring for his ward had been Polish, and they had not thought to confiscate the Polish newspaper his father brought him every week. So Joe gained quite a bit of knowledge regarding the war. Being a child, he hadn't perused the articles regarding shortages and make-do recipes in much detail, his interests lying in U-boats and the aeronautical adventures of the pilots flying SJ-1s and DH.4s.

"Does Henry Ford's son, Edsel, live on this street too?" asked Joe.

"No, he has an estate north of here near Belle Isle, in a neighborhood called Indian Village. Edsel just bought a home there this year and that brewer . . . hmm . . . ah, Goebel; he lives over there too. I wonder what *he'll* do if the temperance movement passes into law. And Goebel's competitor, Mr. Stroh, lives north of the city in an enormous mansion on Lake St. Claire. But enough of these rich brewers and capitalists for today. If one spends too much time touring areas like this, he can find himself feeling as if everyone is more affluent than he. It's time we headed home, but I have one more house to show you before we do. It was actually the reason I drove you here."

Turning back on Second Street they drove in companionable silence, and Joe thought about all the wealth he'd seen. He decided at that moment that he wouldn't live a life eking out a living in a hot factory like his father. He was proud of Ojciec, but Joe wanted what these men had: fancy new cars, clothes, servants, and power. He just wasn't sure how he was going to get it.

"I can tell you're thinking of your future, Joe." Dr. Levy interrupted his thoughts. "Be careful what you wish for, Joe; great wealth provides luxury and power, but it can also lead to great anguish."

Before Joe could ask how a man with enough money to build a castle to live in could be unhappy, the physician pulled over to a small house on the corner of Atkinson Street. "Here it is, Joe. Eight hundred Atkinson Street." Joe looked at the brick home perched on the corner. This was the smallest of all the homes they'd driven by that morning. Its small yard was prettily landscaped, but there were no discerning characteristics appearing on its fascia that could explain why the physician was peering at the front of the house and then back down at Joe with such excitement in his eyes. Joe looked at the house again and questioningly back at Dr. Levy.

"This, Joe, is the home of the prodigious Georgia Peach, Ty Cobb!" the doctor exclaimed. "A friend of mine told me his house was in this neighborhood, and I thought you would like see where your great hero lives."

"Wow! Ty Cobb's house!" Joe searched for a sign of the baseball phenomenon in the front windows of the modest house. The drapes were drawn and the home appeared to be empty. "I wish he'd walk out the door so I could see him."

"I don't think he is there, Joe. Mr. Cobb goes back home to Georgia in the winter."

"Oh right . . . that would make sense. But thanks for showing me just the same, Dr. Levy." Joe looked over again at the simple brick home and smiled. "Wow!" he repeated softly. "Ty Cobb's house."

"Well, we should be getting you home. Your parents will be waiting, and you have to meet your little brother, right?"

CHAPTER SIXTEEN

The birth of Joe's new brother, Stephan, had coincided with President Wilson's announcement that the United States was declaring war. That had been over ten months ago, and Joe was anxious to see the new addition to the Jopolowski family. On the drive to his Polish neighborhood, Joe noted many brand new buildings, businesses, and homes. He was surprised how much the landscape had changed in his absence. New skyscrapers peppered the skyline as they drove back into the bustling metropolis. The city felt like it was bursting with structures and humans. People of every color, in every sort of dress, walked, rode, peddled, meandered, and sashayed down the streets and sidewalks. Sometimes it felt as if Dr. Levy's car was idling more than it was moving forward due to the traffic, but eventually they arrived in Polonia and turned onto Joe's street.

Joe immediately noticed how meager his surroundings were compared to the Boston-Edison District. Dogs and chickens wandered down the street in search of scraps. Children, some without coats, ran across the roadway without bothering to look for approaching cars or carriages. Laundry hung from the front porches of homes, and the smell of cabbage wafted into the car. But Joe didn't care. He was home. He had recovered and he was home. And on one of the porches a red and white Polish flag flew next to the red, white, and blue of his adopted country and made him feel he was where he belonged.

"Joe, my Joe!" his mother yelled, running down the front steps of their home as the car pulled up to the curb. Matka opened the door herself and pulled Joe out of the car and into her arms, squeezing him so hard he thought she was going to damage his healthy lung.

"Matka, put me down . . . the neighbors," Joe said, looking at the children from the block who had gathered to watch the homecoming scene. Matka set Joe back on his feet and grabbed his small suitcase from the hands of Dr. Levy.

"Dr. Levy, please, won't you come inside?" she asked.

"I can't today, Mrs. Jopolowski. I must return to my office; I have patients waiting. But thank you."

"Then please wait a minute, doctor." She ran up the stairs into the house. Joe watched his mother bound up the stairs like a young girl and then suddenly realized something.

"My mother was speaking English to you—good English! She learned English while I was gone?" Joe asked the physician.

"Your father had to take those English classes Mr. Ford is requiring of his workers, and your mother decided she would have him teach her while he was learning. She sure is a quick learner. Don't tell your father, but I think she is sounding better than he is." Dr. Levy laughed.

Joe's mother returned to the side of the Model T carrying a dish covered with a clean cloth. "I made cheese pierogi for Joe's homecoming, Dr. Levy. No meat for Uncle Sam and no pork for my son's Jewish savior doctor. Tell your wife to warm them up in butter in the skillet for five minutes and eat them with sour cream."

"Please Mrs. Jopolowki, there is no need to give me anything more. You have fattened me up enough for the last year. My wife has had to let out my pants two times."

"You were too skinny before. Now take this food and let me thank you again for saving my Joe."

Knowing better than to argue with a Polish woman pushing food, the physician took the plate and placed it on the front seat of the car. "Well, goodbye Joe. Come and see me in a month so I can check on your progress."

Blanca put her arm around Joe's shoulders, and they headed into the house as the Model T drove down the street. The smell of onions and sounds of laughter greeted Joe as she opened the front door.

"Welcome home, Joe!" cried Aunt Hattie as she rushed over and pulled his small frame into her soft plump one. As she released him, Ojciec grabbed him up and gave him a bear hug. Uncle Alexy and Uncle Feliks patted him on the back, saying how happy they were that he'd recovered and was finally home. Emilia, who looked like she had grown a foot, shyly handed him a stick figure drawing she'd made of a boy playing baseball on a grassy field.

"Thank you, Emilia. It looks just like me," Joe said. Emilia smiled proudly. Turning to his mother, Joe asked, "Where are my brothers?"

"Marya and Pauline are watching them next door. We had them get out from under foot so we could cook you a welcome home feast. Emilia, go get your sisters and cousins," she said, reverting to her native Polish. "Joe wants to meet his baby brother."

A beautiful Christmas crèche carved by Blanca's father sat on the mantle. It was one of the few things Matka had been able to bring with her from Jastarnia. Joe walked over to the nativity scene and stared at the charming figures. The manger was empty to signify that the Christ child had not arrived yet, and the other small wooden statues stood in their places, waiting patiently. Mary was sitting on a bed of straw, and Joseph stood at attention near her. A donkey, ox, and camel were positioned next to the three magi kneeling in front of the empty manger. Two young shepherds toting staffs guarded several sheep.

Joe picked up the intricately carved Mary figure and looked into her face. He thanked her silently for her role in Jesus' birth and any help she might have had in his recovery. Boisterous voices interrupted his prayer as his cousins and brothers swept into the room in a chaotic flurry. He placed the saint back on the mantel before Frank tackled him with a hug. Frank had grown. and in his loving fervor he knocked Joe to the floor.

"Frank! Be careful. Joe, are you all right?" Matka looked worried.

"Yes, I'm fine. I see that I have a lot of eating to do to get as strong as Frank." Matka ran her hands over his arms and back; satisfied Joe was unharmed, she took the baby out of Marya's arms and presented him to Joe.

"Here is your baby brother, Stephan," she said. Stephan was much bigger than Joe had anticipated, but he had to remind himself that his brother was close to ten months old. Stephan wiggled in Joe's arms and tried to get down. "Oh, put him down Joe. All he wants to do is crawl all over the house and grab onto the furniture to stand up. He's trying to walk so he can keep up with Frank."

Joe put his brother down on the wood floor and said hello to Marya and Pauline. "I'm glad you're better, Joe," his eldest cousin ventured.

"Thanks, Marya. And thanks for lighting the candles at church for me" he replied.

"Well, I had to help your mother and mine after Stephan was born, so I needed you to get better. I was tired of having to do your chores *and* mine. Glad you're home now."

"I knew there had to be something in it for you, Marya." He winked at her and smiled.

"I'm glad you're home too, Joe," said Pauline. "Nothing was the same without you around." Pauline had grown taller than Joe in his time away, but Marya had experienced the most drastic change. Her face was thinner, and she wore her blonde hair up, like his mother did. Her figure had developed into one of a young woman, and she carried herself differently. Joe felt awkward at noticing his cousin's new shape. He turned away to ask his mother if he could help with dinner.

"No Joe. Sit down and rest, and we'll finish getting dinner ready. I can't wait to feed you some of my cooking. I am going to fatten you up and get you strong as an ox. If they'd let me send you real food at that hospital instead of just sugary sweets, you'd have been home six months ago." Her eyes teared up and she wiped them with her apron.

"Come on, Blanca . . . he's home now," his Aunt Hattie said, grabbing her elbow and steering her toward the kitchen. "Let's get this feast finished so we can eat." Marya and Pauline dutifully followed the women into the kitchen, and the men sat down in the living room and watched Stephan as he tried to balance on his chubby legs. Joe looked around the small living room and smiled. A log crackled and popped in the fireplace as the men lounged on the meager furniture discussing the factory and the war. He could hardly believe he was finally home.

Aunt Hattie and Matka had prepared stuffed roast mutton, pierogi, mushroom cutlets, wikła (a beet root salad made with horseradish), and a chocolate cake with marzipan spread between the layers. And of course, his mother had made dozens of sugary cookies, which were piled high on a round platter. The women had been cooking for several days, and the spread was extensive. Joe felt humbled they had prepared so much food in honor of his homecoming. After a prayer of thanks by Ojciec, the family heartily dug in. The mood was fun and playful and the evening passed quickly. Joe fell asleep in the chair next to the fireplace, and his father carried him up to his bed. He didn't notice till the next morning that an additional bed had been placed in the room for Frank. Getting ill had one advantage; a good night's sleep without Franks' knees in his back.

CHAPTER SEVENTEEN

Later in the week, on the eve of Saint Nicholas feast, the boys put their shoes outside of their rooms for Saint Nicholas to fill. Frank woke early and ran out of their room into the hall.

"Joe! Joe!" he called. "Get up! St. Nicholas was here!" Joe pushed himself up on his hands and looked out into the dark hall.

"Go get Stephan from Matka's room," he called from the darkness. "It's only fair that we look in our shoes at the same time." He was hoping to grab two more minutes of sleep. But Frank returned in what seemed like a few seconds and pleaded with Joe to get up. Joe threw on his robe to fight the cold of the morning and walked into the hall. Lincoln Logs lined all six of the boys' small shoes, and a cardboard box containing the rest lay underneath. Joe picked up Stephan and Frank carried the box down the stairs to the living room. Joe showed his brothers how to connect the wooden logs to make different structures. They tried to build one of the new skyscrapers on Woodward Avenue. It didn't have the same characteristics, as the logs were wood and the large buildings were built of steel and concrete. But they immensely enjoyed knocking it down.

The weeks before Christmas passed quickly as Joe continued to rest and recover. Dr. Levy would not allow him to return to school, but the nuns had sent some work home for him so he could try to catch up. A year away from school was a long time, and Joe was worried the nuns would keep him in the third grade. He concentrated on the reading primers Sister Mary Monica had sent, because he'd always enjoyed reading and the work taxed him less than arithmetic. After only a week, Sister Mary Monica sent home a fourth grade primer and he worried a little less. He supplemented his reading with the *Detroit News*, showing Frank the Christmas ads from Hudson's that proclaimed that within its empire a three story child's wonderland of toys had been erected for the children of Detroit.

The scent of pine needles permeated the air as Joe walked into his Aunt Hattie's living room on Christmas Eve. A roaring fire was burning in the fireplace, and a Christmas tree waiting to be decorated with fruit, cookies, candy, and candles sat near the front window. Cheerily wrapped presents lay on the floor near the tree. Marya and the women gathered in the kitchen to finish preparing the Christmas Eve feast. They'd been cooking and baking for days, but their work was not finished.

"Time to decorate the tree, children," Uncle Feliks called. Joe and Pauline ran over to the tree and looked eagerly at the feast of treats that lay on the front windowsill. "Grab that long string, Pauline," Uncle Feliks instructed. Pauline began to thread cookies and small fruits onto the string, and Joe's uncle showed him how to thread popcorn.

Frank tried to help string the treats but he mostly snuck pieces of candy into his mouth when he thought no one was looking. When the long garlands were hung on the fir tree, Uncle Feliks attached small white candles to the ends of the branches.

Dusk arrived and the family gathered in the living room as the first evening star appeared in the sky. Uncle Alexy divided the opłatek among the family members with the exception of Stephan. The wafer was multi-colored and decorated with embossed patterns of the nativity scene. Walking toward his mother, Joe held out his wafer to her. “Merry Christmas,” he said. He broke a small section of her wafer and placed it on his tongue. Matka repeated his actions, taking a small piece from Joe's wafer and placing it on her own tongue, and smiled down lovingly at her small son. “Merry Christmas, my Joe.” She leaned down and kissed his cheeks and hugged him. Next he approached his father and they performed the same ritual. This continued until he had exchanged bread with every member of the family. His Uncle Feliks broke half of Joe's wafer and shoved it in his mouth when it was their turn, and Joe laughed; teasing was also part of the custom.

The lights gleaming from Aunt Hattie's small tree and glittering candles washed the room in a warm yellow glow. Sheaves of wheat hung in the four corners of the room and lay on the table, an old practice that signified the wish for animals of the farm to ensure good health and strong offspring. Part of the tradition included the belief that animals could speak with a human voice at midnight on Christmas Eve. To hear them speak meant bad luck, but Joe always left his window open a small crack every year in case the chickens in the backyard decided to have an interesting conversation.

The family sat down to eat in the living room. The men had set up a couple of long tables, and the women had spread beautifully embroidered tablecloths—one new and two they had brought from Poland that had been sewn by their grandmothers. Marya sat next to an empty chair and place setting that had been set for "the absent." A small piece of each course would be placed in the plate in remembrance of the dead. Uncle Alexy led a prayer of thanks. He included Joe's health in his litany. Joe silently said his own prayer of thanks

"All right!" Matka said as soon as the prayer was delivered. "Time to eat!" Aunt Hattie and she rose from the table and brought dish after dish out to the waiting family. Aunt Hattie ladled out red borscht with kluski into everyone's bowls. In a matter of minutes the tables were laden with soft, warm bread, boiled perch, fried carp, horseradish, and cabbage with mushrooms and nut croquettes. Joe dug into the aromatic cabbage and smiled.

"A fabulous feast you have prepared, Hattie and Blanca" Uncle Feliks praised the women, holding up an enormous stein of beer and toasting the meal. The women, in turn, raised their small glasses of wine and the children their thick glasses of milk.

"A fine meal," Mikołaj agreed, as he put his beer down and speared another piece of the perch. "Did you perhaps save a scale from the carp for my wallet?" he asked.

"Of course we did! I'll give it to you after we have dessert." When the children heard the magical word dessert, they offered to clear the table and wash the dishes. They worked quickly through the mounds of plates, bowls, platters, pots, and silverware together. Joe dried the dishes that Marya washed, and Pauline returned them to their proper places. Marya carried a stack of small plates to the living room, and Pauline brought the freshly washed silverware. Their eyes opened wide in eager anticipation when they looked upon the array of sweets lining the middle of the tables.

A large bowl filled with poppy seed paste and a platter of waffles commanded the center of the table. Gingerbread, pastries, and cakes flanked the bowl, and a pot of steaming hot coffee gave off an aromatic scent throughout the room. The men poured vodka into shot glasses. Raising their drinks, they clinked their glasses together. Joe took a waffle and spread the thick poppy seed paste on top with a knife. The taste of honey, vanilla, and raisins filled his mouth.

Everyone satiated beyond comfort, the children returned to the kitchen to rinse the dessert dishes and cover the leftovers. Aunt Hattie retrieved the royal carp scales for the men's wallets. Just then they heard singing on the front porch. "Come, children," she said. "Leave the rest. I believe we have carolers!" The children ran to the front window and looked out on the porch. A group of twenty singers had gathered on the small lawn. A tall, robust man was carrying a large colorful lighted star on a stick. The carolers began to sing "Lulaj e Jezuniu" (Sleep, Infant Jesus"), a sweet melody by Frederic Chopin. "Oh, I love this song!" Matka clapped her hands together in delight. Uncle Alexy opened the front door and picked up Emilia in his arms. Joe walked over to his baby brother, who was playing with two spoons on the floor. Joe picked Stephan up and carried him to the window so he could see. The baby looked surprised to be in his arms, but his apprehension was allayed by the harmonious voices of the carolers.

Ojciec joined in with the carolers as they launched into another beloved Christmas hymn, *"Gdy sie Chrystus rodzi"* (When Christ is Born), a traditional Polish favorite. As the carolers began their final song, *"Dzisiaj W Betlejem"* (Today in Bethlehem), the women rushed into the kitchen to wrap up sweets to give to the singers. The entire family joined in the jovial song and applauded them when it was over. Matka and Aunt Hattie passed out the treats on the front porch, and the family gathered in the living room to open gifts.

The children received small puzzles and candy from their aunts and uncles. Uncle Feliks, in his usual fashion, had bought more elaborate gifts. From behind the couch he pulled out four shiny silver sleds and presented them to Marya, Pauline, Emilia, and Frank. Frank jumped onto the couch and onto his Uncle's back to thank him.

"Whoa, Frank! You're going to break my neck!" Uncle Feliks laughed. "Or should I say . . . don't break yours on that sled?"

"Thank you, Uncle Feliks," each of the cousins said, as they kissed their blushing uncle on his cheek. The children gathered together with their sleds at the back of the room and debated where the best sledding hill was located. Feliks reached under the couch and brought out a funny wooden duck on a string that bobbed up and down when it was pulled across the floor. He gave it to Stephan.

Uncle Feliks handed Joe a rectangular box wrapped in brown paper and tied with a simple white string. "Didn't think your Matka would let you go sledding this year, Joe, so I had to think up something a little different for you." Joe slid the string off, ripped off the paper, and stared at the box. He couldn't believe his eyes! In large print across the top of the box were the words Empire Express. Underneath was an image of a powerful black locomotive chugging fiercely down the tracks, a trail of black smoke pouring out its stack. Joe stared at the picture of the bright headlight illuminating the darkness as the train made its way to far off places. Joe's face beamed up at Uncle Feliks from where he sat on the wood floor.

"A train? You bought me a train?"

"Well, open up the box and find out, Joe."

Joe carefully lifted up the cardboard lid and peered inside the box. He pulled out the shiny black engine and examined it, noting the silver wheels and smoke stack. A small coal tender with the words American Flyer Line rode behind the engine, followed by a light brown passenger car with windows. Joe jumped up to shake his uncle's hand but excitement got the better of him and he gave him a hug, thanking him over and over.

"All right, Joe, you thanked me enough." he said, pulling Joe off him and laughing. "Just keep getting better, and that'll be good enough for me, all right?"

"Yes sir, I will!"

Joe pulled the four curved track sections out of the box and connected them into a circle. He gently placed the engines wheels on the rails.

Uncle Feliks sat down on the floor next to him and picked the engine off the track. He pulled out a shiny metal key from the empty box and inserted it into the side of the train and wound it up. When the key could move no more,

Uncle Feliks set it back on the track. "Just push that lever on top of the engine Joe and it should go."

Joe pushed the small lever, and the train took off, speeding around and around the small track until it was spent. No smoke came from the stack ,and there was no light from the front of the engine as the box had portrayed. But to Joe, it was the most magical gift he had ever received. He could imagine himself standing in the front of the little engine, driving the train, feeling the heat of the hot coal as it burned in the firebox, powering the engine faster down the line.

"Let's hook up the other cars to the engine and see if it still goes as fast," he said to his uncle.

""Joe you need to put the train back in the box and carry it home now," Matka said, stopping him.

"Oh, Matka. . . ."he said, looking up pleadingly.

"Sorry Joe. It's time to get ready for midnight Mass." "Merry Christmas, everyone! We will see you at church." Ojciec picked up Stephan, and they gathered their things and went next door to get their coats and hats.

CHAPTER EIGHTEEN

Blanca worried about allowing Joe out of the house and exposing him to so many people, but her devotion to God conquered her worry and she relented. Joe was eager to go to church just to be able to be somewhere besides his house, and also to see his friends.

"Joe, go upstairs and get dressed for Mass," Matka said when they returned home. "Wear your long-sleeved shirt and sweater. And two pairs of stockings—it's very cold out tonight," she called as he ran up the stairs to his room. Joe quickly changed and ran back down the stairs to the front hall. He shrugged his coat on over the heavy sweater. His arms felt tight and uncomfortable.

"Ready, Joe?" Matka asked as she came out of the kitchen into the hall. "Don't forget your hat and scarf." Joe knew he'd be sweating within five minutes of arriving at the cathedral, but he knew better than to complain or argue.

The air was cold. Several inches of snow lay on the ground, but the sidewalks had been shoveled. Joe enjoyed the fresh air as he inhaled it into his one good lung. They walked quickly down the wooden sidewalk, Ojciec carrying

Stephan and Matka holding his other arm to steady herself as they traversed icy patches. Joe listened to Frank jabbering about his sled and how he'd be faster than their girl cousins when they went sledding. Joe looked in the brightly lit windows of the homes they passed and waved at classmates on their way. The sound of jingle bells rang down the street as an elegant sled pulled by a large chestnut horse pulled its occupants down the lane.

"If you're tired-let me know, Joe," Matka told him as they approached the great cathedral.

"I feel fine, Matka," he replied, and he did. Joe had done his best to continue the exercises the doctors had taught him, and he was regaining his strength every day. Earlier in the week Joe had visited Dr. Levy. The physician had been extremely pleased with his progress and had cleared him to return to school after the Christmas holiday. He was still under strict orders not to overexert himself by running and playing with the neighborhood boys, but he was hopeful his mother would lift his house arrest now with the consent of Dr. Levy.

Joe enjoyed the Christmas Eve ceremony despite the two-hour duration and the sweaty discomfort of his layered outfit. The congregation was in a jocular mood and sang loudly and harmoniously to all the traditional Polish Christmas hymns. Several times Joe heard a parishioner coughing and watched as they got up and walked to the back of the church to avoid interrupting the Mass. He hoped they didn't have tuberculosis, and he prayed he couldn't catch it again. He was pretty sure he needed at least one lung to breathe.

The worshipers greeted each other after Mass, kissing and hugging and wishing each other a Merry Christmas. Joe was tired when they arrived back home and went directly upstairs to change out of his sweaty clothes. "Joe?" asked Frank as they lay in bed.

"Yes Frank?"

"Will wi ty Mikołaj(Santa Clause) visit a boy if he's been bad?"

"Why? Have you been bad, Frank?"

"I took Emilia's Crayola Crayons. I took them and I buried them in the backyard."

"Why would you bury them in the backyard?"

"Because I was mad at her. She got eight of them for her birthday and she wouldn't let me color with them. I saw them a couple of days later lying on the front porch. I was just going to color with them a little so I brought them to our room but when I got here I couldn't find any paper to color on."

"So you buried them?" Joe's eyebrows rose.

"Well by then I heard her looking for them and I didn't want to get caught so I figured no one would find it there. Do you think wi ty Mikołaj knows?"

"Yes, yes I do," replied Joe. Frank started to cry, and Joe felt bad for his brother, but he thought it was a lesson he had to learn. Frank had to know stealing was wrong, but Joe didn't want to ruin Frank's Christmas.

"I know how you can fix it before wi ty Mikołaj comes tonight."

"How?"

"Do you remember where you buried them?" he asked.

"Sure, right behind the outhouse. I was going to dig them up when I found some paper."

"All right, come on. Our parents are still next door visiting. I'll help you dig up the crayons, and you can put them back on the front porch before wi ty gets to our house," Joe said, already sitting on the side of the bed and tying his shoes.

Frank jumped out of bed and threw his shoes and clothes on. The two boys quietly sneaked down the dark stairwell, and Frank headed for the back door. "Wait," said Joe, and he went into the kitchen and came out with a large spoon. "We need something to dig with." They walked to the back door and opened it quietly so no one would hear them next door. They needn't have worried; conversation and laughter from the adults in the adjacent house could have drowned out a train. Apparently, his parents and aunt and uncles were still exuberantly celebrating the holiday. Avoiding the light from his aunt's back door, they stealthily walked to the outhouse. Frank pointed to the spot where he had buried Emilia's crayons. Joe handed his brother the spoon and Frank started digging. There were several inches of snow on the ground and Joe was worried the ground would be too frozen to penetrate. Frank had only buried the crayons under a couple of inches of dirt, though, and he recovered the box after a few minutes.

"I've got it!" Frank had wrapped the small green box containing the eight crayons in an old sock, so it wasn't covered in dirt.

"Shhh . . . be quiet, Frank!" Joe whispered. Joe wiped the dirt off the spoon on the leg of his pants as they walked back toward the house. They crept up the stairs amid the raucous laughter pouring out of Aunt Hattie's house and went inside. Joe motioned to Frank to put the stolen crayons on the front porch, and when he returned they ran up the stairs to their room. Careful not to wake Stephan, they climbed back into bed, giggling quietly with the victory of not getting caught.

"Will wi ty Mikołaj bring me a present now?" asked Frank.

"I'm sure he will, but don't ever steal again, OK?"

"OK Joe. Thanks for helping me." With his worries over he pulled the covers up and fell asleep.

Frank awoke early the following morning and shook Joe awake. "Come on, it's Christmas morning Joe!" Then he ran to their parents' bedroom to wake them. Joe grabbed Stephan out of his crib and followed him down the hallway. They woke their parents and Matka and Ojciec sleepily followed them down the stairs.

Joe would remember that peaceful Christmas morning as his favorite for the rest of his life. The image remained like a postcard on his heart. Ojciec and Matka sitting by the crackling fireplace, watching the boys open their meager gifts. Joe, opening a box with a sweater Matka had knitted and a pop gun from his father. Stephan sitting on his mother's lap or crawling on the floor playing with the wrappings. Frank, tearing open his gifts of small metal planes and cars. Ojciec, proudly carrying in a large Victrola he'd hidden at Aunt Hattie's. Matka exclaiming at the extravagance of the gift and her excitement as he placed the first record on the machine and played a lively polka. Joe, savoring the breakfast of warm omelet, cake, stuffed mushrooms, and slices of oranges as he watched his parents dance the polka around the living room floor with the tree shining in the background.

CHAPTER NINETEEN

1917

One year later and Joe was stronger than he had been before his hospitalization. His cough had subsided and he'd been without one remission so his mother had finally relented her strict rule of school and home only. Able to explore the city again with his neighbor Sam, he noticed a different atmosphere on the city streets. Black bunting hung on doors and porches on his block in remembrance of soldiers who had died. A big black cauldron sat in the front window at Dom Polski, the Polish club in his neighborhood, into which people could drop their jewelry to donate toward the war efforts. Flyers hung on the walls of the club, calling men to join the United States Army and help the allies in the Great War. There were smaller signs for women, asking them to join the nursing service with the Polish Army in France.

Every day the newspaper listed the Detroit soldiers who had died, almost half to the Spanish Influenza that ravaged the world that year and killed millions. Living in isolation in the hospital and at home for the last year and a half likely saved Joe's life. During his confinement in the fall of 1918, the Spanish Influenza raced across the country like an evil cloud of destruction. Spurred on by the movement of American soldiers traveling on trains and ships, it quickly spread to citizens of every age. People on the street wore gauze masks to keep from getting ill. Every policeman and soldier was issued one.

Blanca told Joe that during his hospital stay the school and church had been closed for the months of October and November to stop the illness from spreading. Red Cross workers had made daily rounds through the neighborhoods in trucks to pick up the dead. His father had worn a gauze mask to work and had stayed with Uncle Feliks to avoid getting his mother and brothers sick. The illness rushed through the city, and although pockets of new cases appeared now and then, it seemed that it had run its course in Detroit. Ojciec had been lucky and had somehow avoided the epidemic, although thousands of his fellow employees had succumbed.

Ojciec had registered for the draft when the U.S. entered the war. All men ages twenty-one to forty-five were required to sign up no matter what their citizenship. If drafted, an immigrant would automatically become a U.S. citizen upon completion of his tour, as would his spouse. Joe's father had prayed at church every Sunday that he wouldn't be called for the draft while Joe was recovering from his illness. God had listened to Mikołaj's prayers and kept him near his family. Now that Joe had recovered and Stephan was almost two years old, Ojciec went down to the recruitment station and volunteered to fight.

Matka had begged him not to. She was terrified he'd be killed or maimed, but he wouldn't listen. He believed God had generously listened to his prayers, and he felt that he owed his new country loyalty and service. America had been good to his family, and he wanted to repay her. He still had distant relatives living in Poland, and his enrollment would benefit his birth country also. Ojciec was called to duty on March twenty-eighth. He had one week to get his affairs in order before reporting to Fort Wayne on the south side of the city. Ojciec told Matka the factory would hold his position for him until he returned, but he hoped he'd be able to learn mechanics by working on trucks or planes in the army so he'd be able to obtain a skilled position when the war was over. Matka and Aunt Hattie got busy knitting khaki sweaters and scarves so he would stay warm. At the end of the week, he kissed his wife and sons goodbye and walked to the streetcar to report for duty. When Ojciec was halfway down the block, Joe jumped off the steps of the front porch and ran after him calling his name.

"Ojciec! Ojciec! Wait!" he yelled as he ran. His father stopped and turned as he ran the last few yards to catch up to him. Breathing heavily, he said, "Please Ojciec, wait."

"Now Joe, I have to go. We've discussed this. You are to be the man of the house while I'm gone."

"Yes, Ojciec, I know. I just have to ask you something before you leave."

"Yes, Joe?"

"Why? Why do you have to go? I know you told Matka that you wanted to help your new country, but can't you help some other way? There are lots of men without families who can go and fight, and we need you here. I feel like I just got back from being away for so long and now you're leaving." Joe looked up at his father's face, with one small tear falling down his cheek.

"Joe," his father replied kindly, kneeling down on one knee on the sidewalk to bring himself to his eye level. "You are truly an American. Yes, you're Polish, but you were born here. That's why Matka and I named you Joe and not Joseph or Josephat. You have the fighting spirit of an American and no one can ever take your citizenship from you. I want to be a true American like you. When I come back from fighting for this country, everyone will see that I am a real patriot and I will be a true American. Do you understand?"

Joe slowly nodded that he understood. Ojciec stood up again. "Now take care of our family, and don't let Matka be too sad while I'm gone, OK?"

"Yes Ojciec. You can count on me." Joe wiped away a tear.

Joe watched his father's figure grow smaller as he walked away, but he knew he'd be able to see him again before he left for Europe. Ojciec had to train for a month at Fort Wayne before deployment.

Marya stitched a star flag for Matka to hang in their front window. Mothers, sisters, and daughters of men serving in the war were lovingly sewing little red and white striped flags with a blue star and hanging them on their doors or windows to let their neighbors know a soldier's family lived there. Uncle Sam started a campaign for children that week with a plea to the youth of the city to buy at least one twenty-five cent thrift stamp for the War Savings campaign. With the price of food skyrocketing due to shortages from the war and his father's cut in pay, Joe decided he should earn the money himself. He went door to door, asking the ladies in the neighborhood if they had any small jobs they needed done to earn the twenty-five cents. He cleaned out a chicken coop, cut wood, cleaned windows, and ran to the market for grocery items. He really didn't mind the work (except for the filthy chickens), and within four days he had more than the required amount. Joe bought his stamp and proudly brought it home, where he put it in his nightstand drawer.

With so many in the army or dead, few men were left in the city, and Joe had stumbled upon a way to help make ends meet at home. He wouldn't clean out any more chicken coops, but he continued to do odd jobs for the soldiers' wives and war widows after school. Joe built a small wagon in the backyard to carry wood and groceries for his customers. Soon, he was a regular sight walking down the sidewalks, pulling his little wagon. Shopkeepers and foot patrolman called out greetings to the small boy as he wound his way through the market gathering groceries. Between school and his new occupation, the days flew by.

The time for his father's deployment arrived. Joe was allowed to miss school so he could attend the deployment parade. The parade down Woodward Avenue had changed over the last year. In the beginning, great crowds would gather on the sidewalks, and traffic would be stopped for hours to allow the throngs to cheer for the men and wave their goodbyes and well wishes. During the height of the flu epidemic, the government forbade the public to congregate; soldiers marched quietly to the train station with their mouths and noses covered in gauze masks, with no send-off from family and friends. Now the crowds had returned, if perhaps with less enthusiasm than a year earlier.

When Joe and his family reached Woodward, they walked towards Campus Martius Park to find a place to sit and wait for the soldiers. There were other families already waiting when they arrived, but Joe found Matka a place to sit on a concrete ledge near the Michigan Soldiers' and Sailors' Monument in the center of the square. Throngs of people passed by as the family waited. Matka saw Mrs. Stanislewski walking toward them from across the crowded street. "Dzie dobry, Mrs. Stanislewski! Hello!" she called.

Mrs. Stanislewski waved at Matka. "Hello, Blanca," she said as she and Walter neared the Jopolowski family. "How are you?"

"Fine, fine . . . I was so sorry to hear about Mr. Stanislewki. How are you faring?" Walter's father had died in combat in France at the beginning of the war. He, like Ojciec, had volunteered for the army so he could become a citizen.

"As well as we can. Walter had to drop out of school to help us stay afloat. He's working down at the boat docks and gives me all his pay to help with the bills and groceries. I don't know how I would survive without him."

"Yes, Walter had always been a good boy," Matka responded, patting Joe's red-faced friend on the head. Walter hardly looked like a boy to Joe. He must have grown six inches since they had least seen each other and sported a soft blonde mustache on his upper lip.

"How's it going, Joe?" Walter asked. "Glad to hear you're all better."

"Thanks, Walt. It's going good. Doing some odd jobs in the neighborhood to help out, and I've been back at school for over a year now.. How's work at the docks?" But before

Walter could respond, the sound of trumpets and bugles could be heard, and the traffic driving on Woodward was directed onto the side streets. The shoppers and businessmen, who had been going about their errands, stopped and lined up on the sidewalks to watch the soldiers march by. The people of the city had grown accustomed to this monthly or sometimes weekly event but always stopped to cheer for the rows of men going off to fight.

Joe grabbed the hands of his mother and Frank and pulled them to the edge of the sidewalk. They stood there waving and searching for Ojciec as the uniformed men marched in unison. Frank saw him first, "There's Papa! There he is, in the middle," he yelled. Joe squinted into the sunshine and saw the familiar frame of his father approaching amidst his fellow troops.

"Po egnanie, Ojciec! Goodbye!" Joe yelled as his father neared. Ojciec turned his head slightly, and seeing his family waving, he smiled and gave a wink and continued down the street. Hundreds more men followed after Ojciec passed. Mrs. Stanislewski, Walter, and the Jopolowskis waved and cheered for the men. A large regiment of black men proudly marched at the end of the parade, and their women and children tried to fight their way to the edge of the sidewalks so they could say their goodbyes. Some let the black families make their way to the street, while others blocked their way in a show of superiority. Joe became upset when an obese man standing next to him purposefully obstructed the path of a thin Negro woman.

"Hey, mister! Her family's leaving same as mine and yours, and she has just as much right to wave goodbye as we do." The man looked down at Joe with a look of disdain and turned his attention back to the avenue. "Here lady," Joe said, grabbing her hand. "You can take my spot. My father's gone by already." He gently pulled her over to him and stood behind her so she could see. She smiled her thanks at him and searched the rows of soldiers to find her man. Joe looked over at his mother to see her reaction, but she hadn't noticed his act of kindness. She was holding Stephan tightly in her arms and trying to pick up Frank, who was crying. Joe pushed through the crowd and picked up Frank. "Stop crying, Frank," he whispered in his ear. "It's not patriotic."

"I'm only crying cause Matka was," he told his big brother. Joe looked up at his mother and saw her eyes were red and weeping.

"Matka," he said. "Be brave. Ojciec wouldn't want you to be standing here crying on the street." Joe was slightly embarrassed his mother had shown such weakness in public. He'd felt tears gather in his eyes when Ojciec had passed by but had quickly blinked them away before anyone could notice. His mother wiped her eyes with her handkerchief, and they made their way down the sidewalk as the crowds began to disperse. "I know. Let's go get something to eat. That'll take our minds off of Ojciec leaving," Joe said.

"I didn't bring my purse, Joe. I wasn't planning on buying anything today. I have cold ham in the icebox if you're hungry."

"I have money. Come on Matka. It'll be fun. I know just the place, and it's not far from here." Matka looked down at her boys and composed herself. Three sweet faces beseeching her for a distraction from their own sadness helped her overcome her own sorrow.

"You're right, Joe," she said, "and if you want to treat your family to lunch, who am I to stop you?" The family walked a few blocks toward the river and turned onto Lafayette Boulevard. "Where are you taking us, Joe?" she asked.

"The All American restaurant," he replied. "I read about it in the paper. It opened last year and they have sausage sandwiches and chili. I thought since you and Ojciec will be officially all-American when he gets back, it'd be a good place for us to go."

Matka laughed and said that Joe was sweet and very smart and that the All American sounded like a perfect place to eat. The restaurant was small and narrow. A white marble counter ran along the back wall, with metal stools screwed into the floor in front of it. They found a small empty table near the far wall and sat down. The eatery was packed with businessmen grabbing a quick bite to eat. Short Greek waiters hopped through the horde carrying trays of food, yelling orders to the small kitchen in the back.

They were approached by a handsome Greek man, wearing a white apron and pointed paper hat. "Hello, I'm Gus" he said, "What can I get for you folks?"

Joe quickly scanned the menu hanging over the counter. "We'll have three bowls of chili, three wieners, and three Coca-Colas," he said.

"All right. Coming right up, young man. How's about some crackers for your little brother?" Joe nodded his assent, and the man was gone. Joe translated the order to his mother, and she asked what a wiener was. He told her it was a mild sausage on a bun. She looked relieved. Three minutes later, Gus returned with their order.

"Wow that was fast!" Joe said, looking at the food on the table. "But we didn't order any potato chips."

"Comes with the wiener, son. I decided I had to have a little extra something to go with the hotdog when I opened this place. Potato chips are about as cheap as you can get, and people seem to enjoy them. So eat up," Gus said with a smile.

Joe and Frank bit into their wieners and smiled at each other. "Try it, Matka," Frank implored. "They're good."

Blanca tentatively took a bite and smiled back at her boys. "It sort of tastes like a German sausage." She quickly looked around to see if anyone had heard her. Since the start of the war, the government had been distributing anti-German propaganda in newsreels and papers. Sauerkraut had been renamed liberty cabbage, and a month before a man had been lynched in the South just for speaking German. Luckily, no one had heard her in the noisy restaurant. Joe ate his bowl of chili quickly. His appetite had finally returned that spring. Sometimes he felt like he'd never be full—even eating his mother's cooking.

Matka took turns giving Stephan a cracker or bit of bun and taking bites of her hot dog. Joe watched a man hurriedly pour the remains of his chili bowl onto his hot dog, finish it off and head out the door. *Funny*, he thought. He told Matka and Frank what he'd seen. Matka shook her head, laughed, and said that eating too fast could only hurt a person's digestive system. Joe walked to the cash register and paid for their meal: five cents each for the wieners, ten cents a bowl of chili, and two cents each for the drinks. He counted out fifty one cents and left a dime on the table for Gus.

The house seemed empty when they walked into the kitchen, silent and lonely. Aunt Hattie had made some pra onki, a potato and sausage casserole, and left it on the kitchen table.

"Well, thank the Lord for family," Matka said. "At least I won't have to cook supper today."

Matka walked into the living room, sat down in Ojciec's chair and put her face in her hands. Joe took Stephan upstairs, laid him in his crib for a nap, came downstairs, and knelt next to his mother's feet. Matka laid her hand on the top of Joe's head and smiled.

"Don't worry, my son," she said. "No more tears from your mother today. We'll be fine. Look, already you have provided your first meal for the family, and your father probably hasn't even got on the train yet! Now go play outside with your friends. It's a nice day and you could use some fun." Joe kissed his mother on the hand, looking back just once as he headed out the door. He smiled at her and ran down the front steps.

CHAPTER TWENTY

"They'll never pass it!"

"They can't do that. It's a crime against our rights!"

"My family will starve. How am I supposed to make a living?"

Talk was unending, angry, and loud as Joe made his way through the city with his little wagon performing his odd jobs and errands. It seemed to Joe that the news of the war had suddenly been superseded by the subject of Prohibition. Several states had already outlawed liquor or beer or both, and many counties in Michigan had voted themselves dry. Now the voters of the State of Michigan had approved a prohibition amendment to be added to the state constitution, and Detroit was to become the largest city in the nation to fall under the Great Experiment. The law would not be enforced for another year, but the city was already in an uproar. Tavern owners were furious, and most immigrants felt that wine and beer were part of their heritage. Of course, no one could deny the negative effect liquor had on some of the city's lesser citizens. Drunks sleeping on sidewalks, in parks, or the stoop of a store or church were almost a daily sight.

Real men drank, be it liquor or beer. But when they drank so much that they couldn't take care of their families, they were not real men. It had been like that for a hundred years, and the effects were starting to cause the nation's work and morals to decline; or so said the temperance groups, the Anti-Saloon League chief among them. The nation's brewers had tried to counteract the movement with positive propaganda promoting beer. Pictures of babies holding a beer, nursing mothers sipping from a stein, and elderly men drinking from a bottle with the slogan "Beer—It's the Health Drink" were posted on the windows of saloons and on street corners.

How can everyone care so much about beer when our fathers are over there, fighting and dying? Joe thought. *Boy, people can be so stupid . . . just let them drink their old beer. It's their choice and then maybe we can get back to fighting the war and getting the soldiers home.*

Of course, the anticipation of Prohibition hadn't hurt his business. Two of his elderly widowed customers had him making weekly trips to the druggists for their "special medicine" so they would be well stocked when the law came into effect. Joe could tell from the effects the medicine had on them that there had to be quite a bit of liquor in the bottles labeled Doc Schwietz's Miracle Cure and Humphreys 77 for grippe, influenza, and colds.

CHAPTER TWENTY ONE

The weather was turning warmer. Hyacinths, tulips, and daffodils sprung up in the small yards of Joe's neighborhood as a sign of God's promise that Easter would arrive soon. Every time he noticed a new flower shoot out of the ground during his daily trek he would smile to himself; grateful that Lent was soon to be over. His mother in her devout Catholicism had implemented a strict rule of fasting for the family during the last forty days. She believed if their family fasted as the Catholic Church decreed, their sacrifice would assist in Ojciec's safe return. She had prepared only fish, cabbage, kasha, and potato dishes for the last month, and Joe was craving meat. The delicious smells of smoked kielbasa and ham that poured out of less devout homes made his mouth water. But he didn't succumb to his taste buds, believing that God would take special watch over Ojciec in exchange for his sacrifice.

Matka and Aunt Hattie began to prepare the traditional fluffy baba and nut mazurek cakes. Uncle Alexy bought kielbasa and ham for Easter breakfast. Joe collected the eggs from the chickens and kept them in the icebox. Marya and Pauline had the chore of laundering the sheets, curtains, tablecloths, and napkins to prepare for the holiday. The only thing that was missing was Ojciec, but the family would say many prayers for his quick return at Easter Mass.

On Holy Thursday, Joe and Frank were in the kitchen trying to wash the walls and the floor, while Stephan was doing his best to tip the bucket of water over, when they heard a scream come from Aunt Hattie's house. Joe told Frank to watch their little brother and ran next door. Joe pushed past two tall men in the doorway towards where his Aunt Hattie was kneeling on the floor of the foyer. Her skirt had risen above her knees and her knees and thighs were exposed revealing her pasty white cellulite skin. *Did these men hurt my aunt?* he thought. He turned from her to face the men and prepared to defend his ground. Fists clenched he reeled up and suddenly stopped mid-flight. Both men were dressed in army uniforms.

"It's ok, young man," said the taller one, who had lieutenant bars. "She's just had a bit of a shock. Why don't you fetch her a glass of water?" Joe went to the kitchen and retrieved a small glass of water and handed it to his aunt, who was still kneeling on the floor and sobbing. "Oh Joe," she cried, as she grasped the glass with shaking hands.

"What is it, Aunt Hattie? Why are these soldiers here?"

"Oh Joe . . ." but she couldn't finish. She began to moan and cry again. She accidently tipped the glass of water onto the floor at her knees.

"What is it?" he asked, looking up at the army lieutenant. "Why is my Aunt Hattie crying?"

"I'm sorry to tell you son but your uncle has died. Your aunt is obviously quite devastated. Can you go get your mother? We could use her help in calming her down."

"My mother's not home. She went to Eastern Market to buy some lamb butter for Easter. I don't understand . . . Did Uncle Alexy get hurt at the factory?"

"At the factory? No," he said with a puzzled look on his face, "he died of pneumonia in France." Aunt Hattie let out a loud wail. Her upper body fell over her knees and her forehead touched the floor as she moaned and cried. Joe looked at his aunt and back at the soldiers. Uncle Alexy wasn't in France. His father was. All the blood poured from his face as he came to the realization of what had occurred.

"Oh damn. We got the wrong house" was the last thing he heard as the shorter man, a sergeant, rushed to grab Joe before his body fell to the floor.

Joe regained consciousness a couple minutes later. He was lying on Aunt Hattie's couch with a cold rag on his forehead. Aunt Hattie's mothering instincts had finally beat out her grief, and she was patting his cheeks trying to bring him around. The two officers were standing in the hallway nervously whispering and looking over at Joe and his aunt.

"Joe, do you think you can speak?" Aunt Hattie asked in Polish. Joe nodded and weakly said yes.

"How long has your mother been gone?" Joe didn't answer. Aunt Hattie slightly shook his shoulders and pleaded, "Please Joe, how long has she been gone?"

"About an hour," he whispered. Joe looked over his aunt's shoulder and saw Marya, Pauline, and Emilia shrunk together in the corner of the room. They'd been in the alley when they heard their mother scream and had rushed into the hall as Joe's body plummeted to the wood floor.

"Quick, Marya. Go get Frank and Stephan and bring them over here. Don't tell them anything. You men will follow me and we will wait for Blanca in her parlor. Hurry now! You've already caused enough harm with your ignorance. Follow me." Aunt Hattie's broken English was difficult to understand but the officers comprehended her meaning and followed the husky woman out the door.

Pauline grabbed Emilia's hand and sat on the worn couch next to Joe. She reached her small hand over and silently grabbed Joe's. Marya came in trying to balance a very large Stephan on her hip while arguing with Frank. "Why do I have to come to your dumb house?" He was badgering her. "Who are those soldiers and why do they get to stay there and I have to come over here?"

"Shh! Frank. Just sit here and I'll read the comics to you and Stephan." Marya grabbed the newspaper and sat in the rocking chair with Stephan on her lap. "OK Frank, which one do you like best?"

"I like 'Mutt and Jeff.'"

"All right, I'll start with that one." Marya read all the comics and then she went on to the children's story on page eight. Then she read about the Easter preparations around the city and even an article about the tavern owners protesting Prohibition. Decidedly absent was any news of the war in her recitation. When she was reading the society news, Joe heard footsteps coming up the front steps of his porch. Quick and lively, his mother was eager to show the boys the lamb butter she had purchased for their Easter festivities. Marya stopped reading and looked sadly over at Joe. Joe looked at her and looked away. He couldn't take the look on her face.

"Are we done reading now, Marya?" Frank asked. "Can we go home now? I want to play with my Lincoln logs."

"I bet Stephan is hungry." she replied. "Are you hungry, Frank? Would you like a ham sandwich?"

"Sure, but what about fasting?" he asked.

"God won't mind," she replied. "it's close enough to Easter now." She led Joe's brothers into the kitchen, and Emilia followed her, unsure of what was going on but aware enough to know that she wanted to get out of the room. Joe realized he was still holding his cousin's hand and let go. Pauline clasped her hands together on her lap, and she sat still and silent as if she were a small rock he could lean on if needed.

To Joe's surprise he didn't hear any screams or moans from next door. He kept waiting for the other shoe to drop. He and Pauline must have sat like that for a half an hour, not moving or speaking, and still no noise came from the other house. Eventually, he heard the sound of the soldiers' footsteps walking slowly down the stairs. But still, no one opened Aunt Hattie's front door. Pauline got up, went into the kitchen, and brought Joe a glass of milk and a ham sandwich. She put it on the table next to him and sat back down on the couch. Joe couldn't eat. He couldn't move. "What was going on next door? Was his mother all right?" He couldn't think about Ojciec right now, so he focused his attention on his mother. Maybe he should just get up and go next door. Maybe Aunt Hattie needed help. But he couldn't get his arms to push himself off the couch, and he honestly wasn't sure if his legs were still attached to his hips.

Marya came out of the kitchen followed by Emilia and the boys. Joe took one look at his brothers and found the will to get up. He stood at the edge of the couch and forced his right leg to take a step. The left followed. "Pauline," he said, "watch the little ones. Marya and I are going next door." Marya looked at Joe and nodded in agreement.

"Pauline, there is some dough rising in a bowl on the counter. Give it to Emilia and your cousins to play with at the table," Marya said to her sister. Marya opened the front door and stepped out onto the porch. Joe followed. A happy whistling melody greeted their ears; Uncle Alexy was coming up the walk, swinging his metal lunchbox, happy to be home from the factory and looking forward to a three-day weekend. His bouncy step stopped mid bounce as he looked up at his daughter and nephew's faces.

"What is it? What's wrong?" he asked.

"Uncle Mikołaj" Marya replied softly. Uncle Alexy ran up the steps and swung open the door to Joe's house.

"Hattie! Blanca!" he yelled as he tore through the house looking for the women. "Where are they?" he asked Marya.

"I don't know. Mother asked me to stay next door with all the children while she told Aunt Blanca about . . ." she couldn't finish.

"Why didn't the army come and tell her themselves? Why did they tell Hattie?" His tone was worried and desperate. He looked over at Joe and put his large hand on his small shoulder.

"I guess they came to the wrong house," she replied. "I was outside. I think Joe heard her scream and ran to our house. I heard her scream too, but we were in the alley and it took me longer to get there. When I ran into the hall,

Joe was out cold on the floor and mother was trying to wake him."

"Holy Mary, Mother of Jesus! The wrong house! Hattie! Blanca!" he yelled again.

"We're upstairs, Alexy," Aunt Hattie called down softly. "Tell Marya to watch the little ones and bring Joe up with you. It's OK."

Joe climbed the narrow stairway behind his Uncle Alexy. When they reached the top of the stairs his uncle took his shoulder again and said, "Come on, Joe. It'll be OK." Joe looked in the door of his parents' bedroom and saw his mother and aunt sitting on the side of the bed. Joe walked across the worn floor slowly until he was standing in front of his mother. He looked at her face and was surprised to see no tears had fallen. Her light blue eyes were as clear as they had been that morning.

"Matka, are you all right?" he asked. His mother didn't respond. She just kept staring out into the space that was between Joe and herself—or perhaps the space that was behind Joe. "Matka, please, are you OK?"

"She hasn't spoken in an hour, Joe. After the soldiers told her about your father she said, 'I won't cry.' She said, 'My Joe says I have to be brave and not cry,' and she hasn't said a word since. I didn't want to leave her so I've been sitting here waiting for you or Marya to come. Did you tell her not to cry Joe?"

Cry, thought Joe. *What's cry?* He stood there numbly for a minute. Aunt Hattie gave her husband a look as if to say, Now they're both going to be catatonic? Uncle Alexy shook Joe's shoulders and said, "Joe! Joe! Wake up. Snap out of it! Are you all right?"

Joe heard his uncle's voice in the recesses of his brain. Then he heard his father's last words to him as if he were standing right there in the room: "Now, take care of our family and don't let Matka be too sad while I'm gone, OK?"

Joe blinked and looked up at his uncle. "Yes, Uncle Alexy, I'm all right. Matka, come on now. Listen, it's Joe. Everything will be all right. I'll help you take care of Frank and Stephan. And we have family here—Uncle Alexy, Aunt Hattie, Uncle Feliks, and the cousins. We'll be all right, Matka. Please go ahead and cry. It's OK, Matka. You can cry now. Ojciec won't be disappointed if you cry. You can't always be brave. Please, Matka, please for me?"

His mother's eyes did not focus on him. He was worried it was hopeless. He looked up at his aunt and uncle questioning what he should do, when he saw Aunt Hattie breathe in slightly and let several tears pour down her round cheeks. Joe turned back toward his mother and saw that one lone tear had fallen.

Blanca reached out and gathered her eldest son in her arms. She sobbed and sobbed.

The army shipped Mikołaj's body home with an American flag draped over a plain wood coffin. The government paid for a plot at Mount Olivet Cemetery, and the funeral, at St. Josephat's, was held a few days after Joe's father took his last ride across the ocean to rest in his adopted country. Fifty or so neighbors, friends, and parishioners attended. The city had endured many funerals during the long winter, and this fact accounted for the small attendance. It was only natural that a person only slightly acquainted with the Jopolowkis would choose not to attend, to avoid reliving his own recent losses. However, a few men that had worked with Mikołaj came, as did many neighbors from their block. Even Dr. Levy came, which surprised Joe, because he didn't think a Jewish person was allowed in a Catholic Church. After the Mass, Dr. Levy took Joe aside on the sidewalk as they waited for a streetcar to take them to Mount Olivet.

"Joe, I want you to know something, and I think you are old enough to hear it, OK?" Joe nodded. "The death certificate for your father said pneumonia?" Joe nodded again. "I want you to know that I have examined these pneumonia cases a hundred times this year—even after their deaths. Do you understand what I mean?" he asked. Joe affirmed that he did, and the doctor continued. "The doctors are calling the cause of death pneumonia because they don't know what else to call it. The tissues in the lungs are scarred and blue. Pneumonia doesn't make tissue turn blue. Nothing does that we know of. It's the Spanish Influenza that is doing that. I don't know why it does or what it means, but it's that damn Spanish plague. Anyway, not that it makes a difference but I thought you should know." Dr. Levy patted Joe on the back and wished him good luck and said his condolences. Joe boarded the streetcar with his family and waved goodbye to the doctor.

When they returned from the cemetery, Joe went to his room while friends and family gathered downstairs for the wake. He didn't want to talk to anybody, and he was tired of everyone telling him how sorry they were. He knew they were sorry, but what did it mean? Were they going to help pay for the food and rent for the house? Would they help Matka find a job? Her English was much better, but who would hire her and how much could she earn? And who would watch his brothers while she was at work? Joe's little errand job seemed foolish now, and he had to decide how to earn more money to support them. He'd promised Ojciec that he would take care of their family—and he would. He just had to figure out how.

CHAPTER TWENTY TWO

1919

The train gathered speed as it headed out of the city. The surroundings changed from towering buildings and dark, smoky factories into a tranquil countryside. Joe leaned back into the plush passenger seat and gazed out the window, his hand never leaving its tight grasp on the stack of twenties in his pants pocket. He was headed south on the Michigan Central Railroad toward Grosse Ile. He closed his eyes and thought about the last time he had seen the island. Only four years earlier, he and his family had made the trek aboard the *Columbia* for a day's outing on Boblo and had passed by the large island summer homes of the wealthy.

Now twelve years old, he was traveling alone—and not for pleasure. The conductor and the passengers would not realize that, of course. To them he was a young boy traveling to visit a relative in the country. They wouldn't know he had five hundred dollars in his pocket to purchase liquor and transport it back to the city.

The year or so after his fathers' death had been difficult. Matka had found a job at a cigar factory but already the burden of watching Frank and Stephan had taken its toll on Aunt Hattie. She didn't complain, but Joe could see the beginnings of resentment creep into their family life. And even with Matka working they were not getting by very well. His mother's paycheck was half of what Ojciec had earned, and she struggled to put food on the table. The neighbors had helped in the beginning, but they had their own troubles. The church contributed a weekly basket of food and had paid for Joe's school tuition. But in the end it wasn't enough for a young family of four. Matka had grown thinner and Joe's brothers hadn't grown much at all. Joe continued his errands and odd jobs, but the family couldn't seem to make ends meet.

The winter had been very cold, and when the price of coal skyrocketed Matka was unable to heat the house very often. Stephan slept with their mother to share her body heat. Frank returned to Joe's bed, and this time Joe didn't complain about his brother's hot little body sidling up to him all night long. Joe ran to the railroad tracks every morning before school looking for coal that had dropped from the coal tenders passing through the city at night, but he competed for the black rocks with hundreds of children, and often he came home empty handed.

Most of the time he was hungry, but there was no use in complaining. Many children were hungry and poor. The Spanish Flu targeted young adults in their prime, and many families lost the men who provided for them during the war. Piles of furniture and clothes thrown into alleys were a common sight as landlords evicted immigrant family after family. Joe was thankful they had enough to pay the rent but feared for the future. A dark cloud seemed to hang over the city, and the poor were becoming more and more desperate.

Every day the newspapers were filled with stories of theft, burglary, and hangings. A man living a few blocks from the Jopolowski's who had been out of work went missing for several days and was found hanging from the clothesline in his backyard. Another story reported that a man who lost his wife during the flu outbreak was forced to leave his three children alone in their eighth story apartment while he was at work. His three-year-old daughter had been watching a puppy play in the street and had fallen out the window to her death. Reading the daily accounts of the destitute, hopeless, and starving only motivated Joe to work harder to help support his mother and brothers.

Joe was sitting on a bench in the park near his house racking his brain, trying to think of a way to bring home some meat for supper when a well-dressed man sat down next to him. Joe turned and instantly recognized the man. The hair on the back of his neck stood up. It was "Let's make them run home in their underwear" Ray from that long ago Halloween night. Joe had tried to steer clear of the Jewish neighborhood since that night, but the Bernstein brothers and their juvenile street gang were infamous throughout the north side of Detroit. Their gang looted boxcars, pick pocketed, shoplifted, extorted, gambled, rumbled with other gangs, and engaged in any other illegal or violent behavior imaginable. Joe had seen Ray a few times around the city, but he'd always pulled his cap down or ducked into the nearest store to avoid him.

Joe would have stood up and run away, but he didn't want to leave his wagon. And he was pretty sure Ray wouldn't pummel him in the middle of a park.

Ray looked off across the grass to a pair of swings that two little girls where playing on. "I been looking for you, Joe. I heard you've been making the rounds doing errands for old ladies, and I thought you might be interested in making some extra cash. Me and my brothers got a stake in a wholesale sugar business and we could use someone to do some errands for us."

"Why me?" Joe asked.

"We need a boy 'cause no one pays no attention to kids," Ray said. "We've been watching you for a little while. You're a hard worker, and we know your family's going thru a hard time. Your dad died in the war, right?" Joe nodded and looked down at his shoes. "So we figured you could use some dough. Everyone around here is used to seeing you pull that wagon around, so no one's gonna think any different if you do some errands for us. Plus my brother Abe remembered you from that Halloween night. He said you were a pretty smart kid to keep us from pummeling you, so you might be the one for the job."

Joe already knew the Bernstein brothers had a part in a wholesale sugar company that dealt in brewing products. Under the Prohibition law, home brewing of liquor and beer was allowed for personal consumption and the Oakland Sugar House was a legitimate business that furnished corn sugar to home brewers. However, Joe also knew that the Oakland Sugar House illegally distributed the sugar to larger-scale operations. He was not singular in having this information. Practically anyone who lived in the area knew it, even the cops. He was also aware that the men who ran the Sugar House were mean, ruthless, and the source of perpetrators of kidnappings and murders.

"What kind of errands?" was all Joe asked. Whatever answer Ray gave, he felt his fate was already mapped out. Ray looked at Joe with his wide set eyes, and when he smiled Joe noted a couple broken teeth. Never backing down from a fight had not improved Ray's dental work, but his handsome baby face combined with a strange charisma, magnetism, and violent temper had convinced many a man to consent to the gang's extortion tactics.

"Oh, just grabbing some lunch for the guys or picking up an envelope or delivering a package in your wagon . . . nothing too heavy or anything. Pays thirty bucks a week to start. You're still in school, right?" Joe nodded. "Well, we'll need you during the day so I guess you'll have to figure that out. I was never much for schooling. Got sent to that Old Bishop School where they send delinquents."

Ray Bernstein's eyes never stopped moving as he spoke to Joe. Ray would look him in the eye for a mere second and then glance to the left or behind him as he spoke. Joe didn't trust Ray and was frightened of the brutal reputation he and his brothers had. But he knew one other thing. He'd seen the money that had started to flow through Detroit within days of Michigan's new Dry Law, and getting in on the ground floor was his family's only chance at a decent life. Joe made up his mind right there on that park bench.

"You've got yourself an errand boy, Mr. Bernstein," he said. Joe stuck out his hand.

"Mr. Bernstein," Ray laughed as he walked away, shaking his head.

Matka was distraught when Joe sat down with her in the kitchen and told her he was quitting school. But her spirit had weakened over the last eighteen months, and she conceded when he told her how much money he'd be bringing home. Frank had started school that fall. This was another financial hardship, as St. Josaphat could not sponsor two boys' tuition. Frank could take over Joe's scholarship, resulting in one less bill for the family. Matka had quit her job at the cigar factory to stay home with Stephan. She took in sewing, and with Joe's contribution the family would be making more than Ojciec had at the Ford factory.

A lot of Joe's time working for the Sugar House was just spent sitting around and waiting. He arrived in the mornings at eight and made coffee and ran over to the bakery for pastries or donuts and then waited for the men to arrive, usually around nine. To his surprise, Ray wasn't usually around; apparently Ray was only a rung or two above Joe's position as errand boy. The men who worked daily in the office were older, and Ray was definitely not their equal in the pecking order.

At first Joe's responsibilities were to fetch food for the men and occasionally deliver a note to a blind pig—that's what they called an illegal gambling den—in the area. The men told him to always take his wagon, even if he was just delivering a message. He got to know the streets of the city like the back of his hand, and the bosses were usually nice to him. Charles Leiter was a stout man who dressed to the nines. His sharp eyes never missed a thing. Henry Shorr was a quiet man who didn't make small talk. He didn't dress well and had little personality as far as Joe was concerned. In the morning, Henry would tell Joe what his errands were and then ignore him for the rest of the day.

"Morning, Joe. Run out and grab me a paper from the corner," Leiter said one morning as he walked into the office and hung his long overcoat and bowler hat on a hook near the door. Joe ran to the corner and back in two minutes. Leiter was just sitting down at his desk with a cup of coffee as he came bounding up the steps. "Pretty quick, Joe. But not as quick as the dame I was with last night." Charles Leiter and Henry Shorr headed the Oakland Sugar House operation.

Eventually, his tasks expanded to include collecting profits from the gambling houses. Leiter took him to the places they owned and introduced Joe to the men who ran them. Monday through Friday, he'd walk the streets, visiting taverns, dives, gambling dens, and storefronts that hid bootlegging operations, where he would collect the receipts —small envelopes, big envelopes, cash wrapped in brown paper, and rolls of money stuffed into socks, tin cans, or empty cigar boxes. He'd throw it into a false bottom he'd built into his wagon and cover it with an old burlap bag and several empty tin cans so it appeared he was collecting metal to sell for scrap. The ruse was unnecessary, as the Sugar House Gang's fierce reputation protected young Joe like an invisible phalanx.

He still played ball on the weekends with the kids in the neighborhood and attended mass at St. Josaphat on Sunday mornings. He'd made his first reconciliation and communion the spring his father died, and he felt grown up when he knelt at the altar to receive communion. Sunday dinners were once again filled with the aroma of delicious foods and desserts thanks to Joe's generous paycheck. Matka began to smile more as she cooked and cared for him and his brothers.

Nearly a year passed this way until his bosses decided that Joe should be used in a better way than just collecting money and grabbing meals. One morning, Leiter called him into the office as he was making coffee in the break area.

"Morning, Joe. Thanks," he said as Joe handed him a cup of steaming coffee. "I can use this after the night I had last night. Shorr tried to drink me under the table at the club." Charles's eyes were bloodshot, and the smell of whiskey lightly emanated on his breath from the night before. "We came up with an idea though, so the hangover might be worth it." Joe looked around the room, trying to decide if Leiter wanted him to sit down for this conversation or just stand in front of the desk.

"The cops are getting tougher on us lately, and they're gonna pull a sting on our transport route from Ohio." Charles said, pointing to the wood chair behind Joe. Joe sat down. "Did you hear anything on the street about it?" Ohio had not passed the Temperance Law yet, and the gang had simply been driving the forty-five miles south and picking up liquor and driving it back to the city.

"Yeah, I heard something about it, but it seemed more talk than anything. Cops don't really care about booze smuggling, as far as I can see. I see them bellied up to the bar in full uniform when I'm out collecting." Joe tried to make his voice sound like the toughs that came and went at the Sugar House.

"You're right, Joe. They don't give a horse's patoot about stopping booze from being funneled into the city unless one of them gets high ambitions and is trying to get promoted."

Charles paused and took a sip of his coffee. "Meanwhile, they collect hush money from us every week. You can't trust people to keep their traps shut; even when you're paying them to look the other way." Charles looked Joe up and down at this point and said, "Can I trust you, Joe?"

"Yes sir," he replied. Joe sat straight and erect in the chair, trying to look taller than he was. He'd grown a lot over the last year, but puberty remained ahead of him.

"You've done a good job for us for almost a year now, Joe. Not a penny missing from the kitty every week. So Henry and I got to talking and decided we'd have you go down to Grosse Ile on the train and meet one of our boys to help acquire a little whiskey for us. We're figuring no one's gonna pay any attention to a little boy, and you can meet our man down there and hand off the dough for the booze. He'll make the deal, and you help him get it back here. Ha! Those stupid cops'll never think a father and son are smuggling across the river." Charles guffawed.

Joe however, didn't find it so amusing. "What if the cops did notice?" Joe would probably be sent to a children's home for the wayward or locked up. He wasn't really sure what they did with kids who broke the law, but he knew there'd be trouble.

"Don't look so worried, Joe. We've got a designated spot south of here to drop the load if someone's on your tail. Another guy can grab it and bring it into the city."

"What if somebody finds it?" he asked, thoroughly confused now.

"Just wait and see, it'll work out; don't worry so much, boy." Charles winked at him.

CHAPTER TWENTY THREE

The train was slowing down. Joe opened his eyes to look around. They were approaching a small wooden platform with a neat, hand-painted sign with black lettering stating that the train had arrived in Trenton. Charles had told Joe he should stay on the train and cross the river to Grosse Ile. Several passengers exited the train, and he saw only one pretty young lady get on. Her hair was cut just below her ears, and she had on the shortest dress Joe had ever seen a woman wear. Long strands of pearls fell to her waist. She laughed loudly as she greeted a male companion at the front of the car. He grabbed her waist and kissed her straight on the mouth. Joe was shocked at their behavior, but the couple didn't seem worried about the scandal they were causing. The conductor walked down the aisle toward the couple, but Joe was unable to hear what admonishments he was throwing their way. The woman didn't appear to be concerned. She laughed even louder and waved the embarrassed trainman away.

The train chugged toward the river and crossed the precariously high trestle that traversed the fast moving water. Joe was getting more and more nervous. He was carrying an immense amount of money, and he was just supposed to hand it off to some man he'd never seen and pretend he was his son? "What if the man took the money and ran off? Would Leiter believe him? Probably not. Then what—a beating? Or worse?" As the train hit land on the other side, Joe crossed himself and said a quick prayer to Saint Mary to watch over him. The engine chugged to a slow stop, and Joe grabbed the empty suitcase that Leiter had given him to carry so it would appear as if he was visiting family. He stepped off the train and found a bench by the small stone depot.

The day was gray and windy. Low clouds traveled swiftly toward Canada as Canadian geese headed in the opposite direction. Joe looked around but saw no one who appeared to be alone or searching for him. The train was boarding passengers for the return trip and soon pulled out of the small station. He sat there for half an hour thinking about the train ride and remembering how he'd dreamed of steering a mighty locomotive down the tracks the Christmas his Uncle Feliks had given him the wind-up train. Feeling conspicuous, he headed down the embankment to sit by the water and think of his next move. The grass was tall here, and an old tree lay where it had fallen, providing a seat for him. The embankment gave some relief from the gusty day.

"Thought you'd never walk down here." A thick Hungarian-accented voice startled him. A man, broad and tall, walked over to where Joe was sitting on the old tree. His cap was pulled down low, almost covering his eyes, and a thick brown beard hung raggedly off the sides of his face. Instinctively, Joe put his hand on his pocket where the cash was and then, realizing his mistake, quickly removed it. "What are you so nervous for?" the man continued stepping closer. "You're Joe, aren't ya? My little boy that's come to visit?" He laughed at Joe's frightened face.

"Yes sir, I'm Joe." His shoulders relaxed slightly as he watched the large, bearded man step over a branch and over several dead fish as he approached.

"Didn't want to meet you at the station—just in case the ticket agent was paying any mind to the passengers. Figured if I was a boy I'd wander down here by the water, so I've been just waiting here for you to do that very thing. And here you are. You're a little taller than I pictured, but you'll do I guess. Ready for a boat ride, Joe?"

"All right, but first I'd like to know one thing. What's your name?" Joe said, standing up, reaching his hand out to shake.

"You can call me Cappie." The man shook Joe's hand. "Well, now that we've been properly introduced," he said with a smirk, "grab your case. We've got a little walk ahead of us." Joe picked up the old suitcase from the dirt and followed Cappie up the embankment.

"Where we going?" he asked.

"I've got the boat tied up at the south end of the island. It's about a mile and a half from here. A little windy but whatcha gonna do?"

They climbed to the top of the embankment and headed down the dirt road next to the river. Joe walked beside Cappie, trying to calm his frayed nerves. He didn't think the combination of the wind and waves made for good boating weather, but he didn't say anything to Cappie.

"Trees sure are pretty this time of year," Joe said, making small talk to get his mind off the flips his stomach was performing.

"Yep, all sorts of colors—red, yellow, orange, purple; you should see them on a sunny day. And the squirrels and chipmunks playing in the trees and deer walking right on by you like they ain't afraid of nothing. It's a pretty island in the daylight, but it's a whole different story at night."

"Why? Are there bears or cougars?" Joe asked.

"Well, they say there were at one time—some say there still are, but I've never heard or seen one. I just meant you never know who you'll have the luck of running into in the dark," Cappie replied.

Joe wasn't concerned about who wandered around the island at night. By that time he would be safely back in his bed in the city.

"Do you live on the island," Joe asked.

"One thing you should know by now boy is not to be asking too many questions. Specially ones like where somebody lives. Won't nobody tell you the truth anyways, so it's better not to look like you're putting your nose where it don't belong." Cappie looked down at Joe as he spoke. "Relax boy. I'm just giving you a little friendly advice. I will tell you that I caught a fifteen-pound bass on the other side of the island once though. Course that was before these waters got so polluted from the city dumping sewage into it."

Gradually the light of recognition crept into Joe's brain and he realized Cappie was Vic Starboli, the man who'd pointed out landmarks as his family had ridden on the *Columbia* to Boblo Island. Surprised at the chance meeting, he remained silent for a few minutes, processing the information. He looked up at Cappie's eyes again, this time identifying the soft brown color with the young man he'd met years before. The memory calmed him, and his anxiety decreased even more as they continued down the gravel road. Joe had grown many inches taller since that day aboard the *Columbia,* and the illness had taken the baby fat from his cheeks, altering his appearance even more. Not many would have recognized him all these years later.

"What kind of boat do you have, Cappie?" Joe asked.

"I started with just a rowboat earlier this year but I've already cleared enough to buy a power boat and it's a lot easier on the arms," he replied. "Pretty fast one too."

"And I bet it makes it easier to get away from the cops."

"Ha! Not much Coast Guard around here, Joe. And they don't go out when the weather's bad, so if a boat can handle a little tossing around, you're pretty much guaranteed to get to the other side. Now when that Volstead Act is finalized next year, the federal government is supposed to get involved. Things might get a little hairy, but I'm not too worried. In the meantime, we just run across the water like we was running across the street to get some groceries." Cappie smiled down at Joe and clapped him on the back. "You wasn't worried about getting caught, were you, boy?"

"Nah," Joe replied, knowing Cappie could see differently. They'd reached the end of the dirt road and had started down a small path in the woods. The path was new, and they had to push limbs and weeds back to make their way. The wind was mitigated by the trees here, and Joe was thankful for the break from the chilly air.

"Just a little farther," Cappie said when they reached a deep, narrow canal. They turned and walked alongside the canal toward the center of the island. "Let's see . . . it's about two o'clock, so we should get started right when we get to the boat. That'll give us time to load up and everything. Are you hungry?"

"I could eat" Joe replied.

"I've got sandwiches in the boat and some canned peaches. All right, here we are," he said, as they walked up to a small white house on the side of the canal. Tall trees and brush surrounded the little cottage, and no other houses were in sight. The house was new, as was the small wooden dock where a large speedboat was tied. Cappie disregarded the house and walked down to the dock. Joe followed. He jumped in the boat and told Joe to untie the ropes that were holding it to the dock. "You ever ride in a boat, Joe?" he asked.

"One time," Joe said, smiling to himself, his face turned away from Cappie as he worked at the knots.

"Good. Then you already got your sea legs."

Joe threw the ropes into the boat and clambered ungracefully down into the vessel. Cappie started the engine with a roar, startling birds from their roosts. "I been trying to figure out how to quiet that damn exhaust. Might as well shine a light up to the sky saying here I am with all this booze, but I can't get it any quieter. Good thing nobody really cares." He piloted the boat slowly down the canal toward the river.

Cappie pointed Joe to where some sandwiches were in a brown paper bag on the floor of the boat. Joe grabbed one and took a bite. Peanut butter! He'd never eaten a peanut butter sandwich before, and the stickiness in his mouth caught him off guard. Working for the Sugar House for the last year, his mother had packed him a lunch every day. He'd carried it in a small metal pail he'd had when he was attending school at St. Josaphat's. He opened the jar of peaches and grabbed the fruit with his fingers, drinking down the syrup when they were gone. Feeling better with a little food in his stomach, he turned his attention back to his surroundings. They had left the shelter of the trees and were heading out into open water now.

The wind picked up immediately, and Joe pulled his cap down further on his head to cover his ears. "It sure is a lot colder on the water," he yelled above the roar of the engine.

"Sure is," Cappie replied. "Next time you should wear a heavier coat . . . but don't go getting long pants yet. You want to look younger than you are for as long as you can." *Next time?* Joe thought. Was this going to be his new role for the Sugar House? Charlie hadn't said anything to him about a next time. Cappie turned the boat south, and they headed out into Lake Erie. The waves were crashing against the front of the boat, and it felt to Joe as if they would tear it apart. Joe sat down on the bottom to get out of the fierce wind but the waves made him bounce from one side to the other. "It's better if you stand up here with me," Cappie advised. Joe pulled himself up and held onto the wooden side rail. The wind whipped at his face and stung, but he could control his body better as he watched the waves approaching the boat.

"Sure is rough," he yelled.

"It's really not that bad today," Cappie replied. "Gets lots worse than this . . . course sometimes it's smooth as glass too." A boat was approaching from ahead, and Cappie slowed the engine. "Don't worry, Joe. This a friend of mine." A gray speed boat pulled up alongside of theirs and a man threw a rope for Joe to grab. "How's it going, Hatch?" Cappie called to the man.

"Busy day, Cappie. Trying for two runs today. This here's my first . . . lotta thirsty people over on your side of the river." Hatch smiled.

"No doubt about that," Cappie replied. "Safe sailing, Hatch. Gotta get my boy and me going. Promised him some fishing this afternoon."

"Fishing for whiskey is all you two are fishing for. Not a bad idea, Cappie. Maybe I should get a boy of my own to take fishing."

"Now Hatch, you can't be stealing *all* my ideas. If every bootlegger suddenly shows up with a boy in his boat, the coast guard is gonna be all over us."

"I wouldn't double-cross you like that, Cappie. I'm just playing with you. Plenty of business for everyone, I always say. Besides, I couldn't stand dragging a ragamuffin like that across the water every day." Hatch pulled the rope from Joe's hands and waved to Cappie as he accelerated away.

Cappie gunned the engine and headed toward Canada. *Ragamuffin!* Joe thought. *I just bought these clothes last month at Kresge's. They cost me seven dollars not including shoes. Besides, Cappie and Hatch are both dressed in old fishing coats and hats, and who knows when was the last time Cappie went to a barber.*

"Oh don't worry about him, Joe" Cappie said when he saw Joe looking down at his clothes. "He's just razzing you. Hatch is on the up and up."

Cappie pulled the boat into a small inlet and slowed down. A large wharf with a factory rising behind it teemed with activity, as boats pulled in and out of the area in an organized procession. A long chute carried the cargo out of the factory onto the dock, and men grabbed boxes of bottles and carried them to the boats.

"Almost forgot! I need the lettuce." Cappie looked at Joe. Joe stared blankly back at him. "The cabbage Joe. I can't have a boy paying for the hooch, can I?" It took a minute until Joe understood Cappie was talking about the money he'd brought with him. Joe reached deep into his pocket and handed the roll to him. Cappie held up his hand with all fingers extended indicating that Joe had given him five hundred dollars. Joe nodded yes, and Cappie put the roll in his front coat pocket. They waited their turn for a few minutes and pulled the speedboat next to the dock.

"Where you headed?" a short man with a clipboard asked Cappie, as they tied the boat to the side of the pier.

"Mexico," Cappie responded.

"How much?" clipboard man asked.

"Five alive," Cappie answered. The dispatcher indicated to the men standing on the dock to start loading the boat, and Cappie handed box after box labeled Pioneer Distillery to Joe to put into the cutter. It took twenty minutes to load all the whisky inside. Cappie signed for the liquor—using what name Joe didn't know—and they turned back toward Lake Erie.

"How'd you like Amherstburg, Joe?" Cappie yelled over the noise of the wind and the engine when they left Lake Erie and headed back up the river.

"Didn't see enough to know, Cappie," he responded.

"That's all I've seen of it myself, Joe." He laughed. "Pick up that fishing pole, and throw a line over the back of the boat," he said as they neared Grosse Ile. Joe grabbed a pole that had been near the sandwiches and threw the lure on the end of the line over the back end. He held the pole tight and waved at a couple other boats that passed near them. He was shivering, and his hands felt like blocks of ice. The sun was setting behind the island. They pulled into the canal as the last rays fell behind the trees. Joe slapped at a bug that landed on his cheek. "Pull your line in, Joe. There's nobody back in here."

Joe put the fishing pole back on the floor, disappointed that he hadn't accidently caught a fish, and grabbed the ropes to help tie the boat to the dock.

It took a great deal longer to unload the boat then it had loading it. Joe handed the boxes to Cappie, and he placed them on the dock. Then they carried each box to a set of steps that led to a cellar door below the house and stacked them in the corner of the basement.

"Let's cook up something to eat. Being on the water makes a man ravenous," Cappie said, when they had stacked the last box. Darkness blanketed the night when they emerged from the cellar. Cappie bolted the door. They went around to the front of the house and went in. The older man lit a lamp hanging by the door, and Joe could see the interior of the one-room cottage. A wood-burning stove and a stack of logs sat on the wall closest to him. The house had no kitchen per se, but a table and three chairs sat near the stove and a small icebox was pushed up against the opposite wall. There was a small wooden cupboard with a few dishes and cups. A metal bed sat in the corner.

Conspicuously feminine flowered curtains hung from the windows.

Cappie reached in the icebox and pulled out some eggs, bacon, and a loaf of bread. "Can't serve you anything fancy, Joe, but you don't look too picky to me." He grabbed a heavy skillet and fired up the stove.

"I'll cook, Cappie," Joe said, grabbing the eggs off the table. "How many you want?"

"I'll have five eggs and three slices of hog . . . you sure you know how to cook?"

"Sure I do. Got any butter?"

"I think there's a little in the icebox. I'll go check over the boat and fill her up while you're cooking us supper." He headed out the door.

Cappie returned fifteen minutes later, and they sat down to eat. Joe found two forks and a knife in a drawer in the cupboard and placed them on the table. Cappie brought two soda pops from the boat, and they drank them with their meal. After they finished, Cappie showed Joe where to draw some water to wash the dishes. He finished in minutes, grabbed his suitcase, and went around to the cellar to find Cappie.

"Why you got your case?" he asked Joe, looking up as Joe came in.

"I thought we'd be heading back now."

"Not till tomorrow. Didn't Leitner tell you?"

"No, Mr. Leitner didn't say anything about staying overnight. I didn't even pack anything in the case. My mother will be worried sick. I've got to be home tonight."

"Well, nothing we can do about your mama, and nothing we can do about getting you back tonight. We've still got a lot of work to do before morning. No use fretting about it now." Cappie handed Joe a can of white paint and a paint brush.

Easy for you to say, Joe thought, as he started painting over the words Pioneer Distillery. He knew his mother would be uneasy already. He'd been home for dinner every night since he'd started working for the Sugar House, and now he wasn't going to be coming home at all.

Joe painted in silence for the next two hours. Well, *he* was silent. Cappie talked and talked about rum running and boats and Prohibition and cops on the take and dirty politicians and anything else to do with bootlegging. Joe learned that Cappie had been making daily runs down to Ohio since the temperance law first passed in Michigan. Ohio wasn't going dry until the federal government passed the Volstead Act, which was scheduled for the following year. Cappie told him that there'd been so many bootleggers traveling back and forth on Dixie Highway (or the Avenue de Booze as people called it) between Ohio and Detroit, he'd actually gotten caught in traffic jams in the middle of the countryside. The last time he'd driven down, the state cops pulled him over. Although he wasn't arrested, the incident had cost him thirty bucks in bribes. So he quit the land route and opted for the water several months ago and was having an easier time of it.

"Course, working for big cheeses like Leitner and Shorr don't do no harm either," he added. "They's smart men, those two . . . making contacts over in Canada while the other boobs keep trucking down to Ohio."

They finished painting the boxes and Cappie produced a large stencil with the words Braymen's Specialty Candy cut out. He gave Joe a can of black paint and a smaller brush and showed him how to paint the words on top of the boxes. The stenciling took a lot less time, and they finished quickly. Joe noted that Cappie had only opened one of the boxes to inspect its contents but hadn't taken out any whisky and had nailed the box shut.

"Time to tuck in for the night, Joe. I'll throw some more wood in the stove so we don't get too cold." They walked back up to the front of the cottage. "Wind's died down. Should be a quiet night. We'll be up early tomorrow to move the hooch, so I suggest you get some shuteye." Cappie told Joe he could sleep in the metal bed and he'd prop himself up on two chairs. He said he didn't sleep much anyway and Joe could use the rest from the looks of him.

Joe lay down on the lumpy mattress and pulled the thin blanket up over his clothing. The only items he removed were his hat and shoes. The island was as silent as a funeral service, and Joe felt uncomfortable in the quiet. He was used to falling asleep to the sounds of the city: cars, trucks, trains, people in nearby houses shutting doors and banging pots, and the occasional drunk staggering and singing down the alley behind his room. Joe turned toward Cappie and watched him throw a couple of logs into the stove. "Why'd you say we were going to Mexico, Cappie?" he asked. "That guy with the clipboard couldn't have thought we were going all the way to Mexico in your speedboat."

"No, he doesn't think that." Cappie sat down in one of the wooden chairs and propped his feet up on the table. "Our government's angry that Canada won't stop the brewers and distillers, because they think the whole world should participate in Prohibition. The Canadians said they are their own country and the U.S can't tell them what laws they should and shouldn't pass. But instead of having a big old fight about it, the Canadian government is trying to appease the U.S. by declaring that liquor and beer can't be bought for distribution over here. But they really don't care, so if I say I'm taking their whisky to Mexico or Cuba, they just write it down on their list. And when I show back up from my two thousand mile journey two days later, or even the next day, they don't blink an eye."

"The whole thing seems pretty dumb to me," Joe said. "My father drank beer every day and never missed a day of work. So do my uncles and lots of people I know." Joe's heart caught in his chest with the mention of his father. He thought about his mother, who was probably sitting at home worried to death and not sure what to do. She knew better than to go to the police, and he hoped she wouldn't go to the Sugar House and make a scene.

"Yeah, well, I agree with you Joe. But it looks like the whole country is gonna be in it now, and I think any smart man with access to a boat will be making a lotta money if he wants to take a little risk." Cappie turned off the kerosene lamp and closed his eyes. "Goodnight, Joe." He leaned back in his chair.

"Goodnight, Vic," Joe replied.

Cappie jumped up out of his chair exclaiming, "I thought you was him! You're the kid who was going to Boblo with your folks. Devil's pitchfork! You didn't say nothing all day."

"Didn't want to be accused of putting my nose where it didn't belong." Joe smiled and tried to drift off to sleep.

CHAPTER TWENTY FOUR

The smell of coffee woke Joe the next morning. He rolled over in bed and reached for the robe that always hung on the end of his bed. He sat up and remembered where he was. Searing panic shot into his chest. He knew his mother would be in an absolute state of terror. Maybe she thought he was dead. How could Leiter not tell him that he wouldn't be going home last night?

He looked around the room for Cappie and, not seeing him, got his shoes and cap and walked outside. The air was frosty, and a low fog hung over the canal. Joe walked behind the house to the cellar and saw that it was still bolted shut from the night before. *Where's Cappie*, he wondered. Joe's anxiety decreased as anger began to roil up inside.

He couldn't think about eating, so he wandered down to the small dock and sat down, trying to figure out his next move. He could walk back to the train station and try to hitch a ride back to the city, but he didn't have a cent in his pocket. He'd been so worried about carrying the liquor money he had neglected to think of bringing any extra for himself. He could try walking back over the tracks and hop a streetcar. Or maybe someone driving north would give him a ride. But finding the ideal situation could take hours, and Cappie would most likely return before that. And if he left now, Joe knew he'd be canned from his lucrative job and his family would be back in poverty in a week. No, he'd just have to wait for Cappie to return.

The sun warmed the dock, and the fog quickly dissipated. The animals around him sounded their approval of the new day. Cardinals and blue jays flew from tree to tree, singing and calling to each other. A fish jumped in the water below Joe's feet and startled him out of his thoughts. Well, if he had no choice but to wait he might as well try fishing. He retrieved the rod from the boat and went about looking for some bait. He wasn't familiar with lures and wanted to try something that might look more appealing to a fish.

Grabbing a spoon from the cottage he walked around to the side of the cottage where he had noticed moss growing near a large ash tree. If memory served him right from his time in the Upper Peninsula, a treasure trove of night crawlers would be digging tunnels underneath. Within just a few minutes he had two fat worms that he shoved deep in his pocket; the same pocket that had held so much money the day before. Dark guts squirted onto his hand when he pierced the wiggling worm onto the hook and he wiped his hand off on the bottom of his pants. He threw the line as far as he could and sat back to wait. An hour later, the sun warming the dock and the sound of crickets and birds lulling him into a peaceful reverie, he heard a voice from behind him.

"Catch anything?" Joe turned his head and saw Cappie walking up from around the back of the cottage.

"Where've you been?" Joe dropped his pole onto the dock and stood to face him. "Why'd you leave me and not tell me where you were going or when you'd be back!" he demanded. His cheeks were flushed with anger and windburn from the day before.

"Don't get your hose all twisted, Joe. I had to go get the truck. How'd you think we were going take the boxes out of here?"

"Why didn't you tell me last night? You're all treating me like a stooge and I don't like it. I might be a kid but I've got the right to know what's going on, same as everyone else. My mother is probably sick to death worrying about me and—la de dah—you just head off all morning and don't give me a clue!" Joe was furious now, walking toward Cappie with his hands clenched into fists.

"Whoa, hold on Joe. I forgot Leiter didn't tell you all the details. I had to walk back to the train station and over the tracks to Trenton. We hide the car there in a garage so if the cops come by nosing around here it looks to them like this is just a vacant fishing cottage. I give you my word that I'll let you in on everything I know from here on out. OK?" Cappie looked apologetic.

"All right, if you give me your word," Joe replied. Cappie nodded and Joe walked back to pick the pole off the dock. "I caught two fish, but I don't know what they are." He pulled a stringer out of the water to show Cappie the squirming fish.

"Those are nice size perch. Let's cook them up for some lunch, and then we'll head out. I'll cook this time. You know how to scale a fish?" Cappie walked onto the dock, pulled a knife out of his boot, and taught Joe how to scale and gut the perch. They ate a delicious lunch of fried fish and canned pears and loaded up the truck with the boxes. Once the Model T truck was loaded, Cappie locked the cellar door and front door of the cottage. Joe threw a tarp over the boat to protect it from the elements. Cappie drove the truck down a small dirt road Joe hadn't noticed the night before and stopped the truck a few yards further. They climbed back out of the truck and carried a couple dead trees to the opening, where they set them as if they had fallen there. Then they grabbed a pile of brush lying nearby and threw it on top to disguise the entrance to the cottage.

Cappie drove out to the main road toward the north end of the island. They drove onto a small bridge that spanned the river and stopped in the middle at a booth to pay their five cent toll. Cappie turned the truck onto Jefferson Avenue when they reached land and headed north. The truck couldn't go faster than twenty-three miles an hour. Stopping for traffic, streetcars, and pedestrians they made their way back to Detroit in two hours.

Cappie pulled into the large Sugar House garage around three o'clock. Leiter was there to greet them as they climbed down from the truck.

"There you are, boys. Any trouble?" Already three men had walked over to the truck and begun unloading the boxes of Braymen's Specialty Candy.

"No pigs or Coast Guard for the whole two days. Fantastic idea, Charlie, to send the boy. Hatch was a little jealous of your little brainstorm here. Just forgot one thing."

"Forgot what? He brought the whole five to you, didn't he?" Leiter scowled down at Joe, thinking he had pocketed some of the money.

"He brought all the dough, Charlie. You forgot to let him in on the fact that he wouldn't be home till today. The boy still lives with his mama, you know." Cappie smiled and tousled Joe's cap.

"Didn't even think about it. Sorry, Joe. I bet you're in for some real trouble at home. Come up to the office and let me see if I can help you with that." Joe climbed the wooden stairs up to the office, following Leiter. He waved goodbye to Cappie as he went in the door and Cappie winked back at him.

"My mother had pretty much given up on me by your age, Joe," Charlie began. "If I stayed out all night she just cuffed me on the side of the head and I was on my way. How bout I throw you a twenty and you can bring home some nice steaks for your trouble. That should soften her up a little."

"Thanks, Mr. Leiter," he replied, stuffing the money into the same pocket that had held his worms only a few hours before. "Any errands you need me to do before I go?"

"No Joe . . . I'd be heading home straight away. I've seen those Polish women get angry before. I'd rather face two cops carrying long nightsticks in a dark alley than be in your shoes right now. You done good work, Joe. We'll talk tomorrow—that is if you can sit down in that chair and talk to me!" Leiter laughed and waved Joe out the door.

Joe hurried to Eastern Market to buy four steaks before the butcher went home for the day. He quickly found the butcher his mother always bought her meat from and, after grabbing the wrapped meat and pocketing almost eighteen dollars in change, he ran to a streetcar, hopped on, and headed home at last.

His mother greeted him at the door, wrapping him in her arms and squeezed him so tight he lost his breath. When she released him she slapped him across the face as hard as she could. Joe dropped the steaks as his hand went instinctively to his cheek. "I'm sorry, Matka. I had no idea I would be gone all night. Please don't be angry. I didn't know, and I didn't have any way to tell you by the time I did."

"I was so worried about you," Matka replied, reverting to Polish. "I thought you were dead! And that boss of yours sending over all those flowers a half hour ago doesn't change anything. She pointed to a huge arrangement of lilies, roses, and carnations that sat in a vase on a side table in the living room. Leiter had tried to pave the way for Joe's return. Joe smiled inwardly.

"I'm sorry, Matka. Here, Mr. Leiter gave me some money to buy steaks for dinner to apologize, and I have enough left to buy ice cream with. I'll send Frank to the store to get some for after dinner. I know it doesn't make up for you worrying all night. I guess things are going to change from here on out. I promise to let you know that I'm not coming home if I know, OK? But you'll have to promise me that if I don't . . . that you won't worry. Nothing's going to happen to me, Matka. I promise I'll come home."

Matka looked sadly at Joe and replied, "Those were the last words Ojciec said to me." She picked up the package of meat and walked slowly into the kitchen.

CHAPTER TWENTY FIVE

1920

"Push it! They're gaining on us!" Joe yelled into the wind. Cappie was pushing the boat to the limit. The Coast Guard boat was gaining on them. Suddenly, Cappie cut the engine and the boat coasted to a stop.

"Throw out your line, Joe!" he whispered fiercely. Joe scrambled to the back, grabbed his fishing pole, and threw out his line with a lure on the end. His heart was pounding. Almost every day that autumn, he and Cappie made a liquor run to Canada. The bosses sent a man to the island every morning to load the liquor into the truck and drive it back to Detroit. Cappie had outfitted the boat with a light, and they waited in Amherstburg till dusk to return to the cottage. The boat was still loud, but they had only been stopped once by the Coast Guard.

"Gave us quite a chase," the officer yelled as they sidled up to their boat. The officer shined a flashlight at Cappie and then swung it around toward Joe.

"Wasn't racing you, sir," Cappie replied. "Didn't know we were being followed. My boy here wanted to see how fast I could push her. Kids, ya know." Cappie was calm and jovial.

"Yeah, I got a boy his age," the lieutenant replied, eyeing Joe. Just then Joe felt a pull on his line and started to reel it in. The rod bent in a graceful curve and Joe pulled hard. Reeling fast, he brought the fish to the side of the boat.

"Sirs?" Cappie looked inquisitively at the Coast Guard men. The lieutenant nodded yes and Cappie crossed over to help Joe bring the fish into the boat.

"Nice catch, boy!" the officer congratulated him. "That's a nice bullhead you got there." Joe held the fish up so Cappie could pull the hook from its mouth. Soon they were all swapping fish stories.

Joe's hands were shaking so hard that he had to sit on them, but the Coast Guard didn't even bother to climb aboard. The lieutenant sent Cappie and Joe off with a "Thanks for the fish, Joe! Have a good night boys!"

A month later ice started flowing down the river. Joe thought they'd be packing it in for the winter, but Cappie (or was it the bosses at the Sugar House?) had other ideas. The Coast Guard had put their small fleet in dry dock for the winter, giving the bootleggers free rein on the lake. Cappie and Joe would set off in the boat after first light and slowly make their way toward Canada. Joe would stand next to Cappie and watch for blocks of ice floating towards them, and Cappie would skillfully avoid the obstacles. It was cold work, and Leiter had sent his pickup man with thick fur coats for them to wear. The cold air would sometimes catch in Joe's lung. He'd cough ferociously for a few minutes trying to catch his breath. Despite the cold weather, the work wasn't hard except for the fact that Joe was sick and tired of painting boxes every night.

Several times he thought they'd go down with the boat when severe weather struck. Without warning, the sky would turn a greenish black and the wind would roar up, causing the boat to toss and bounce in five-foot waves. Joe would hold onto the sides of the boat and say Hail Mary's and Our Fathers under his breath; the pelting rain hit his cheeks and back like daggers. But Cappie, true to his alias, was a good captain. They always made it safely back to the cottage.

Saturday afternoons, Joe and Cappie would climb into the truck with the pickup man and head back to the city for the night. Joe would head home from the Sugar House with his weekly pay—now fifty dollars a week—eat a home cooked meal for supper, pass out in his bed at eight o'clock, and get up and go to church in the morning with the family. Marya was jealous of her cousin's new wealth but disguised it in an aura of moral superiority, sliding snide comments into conversations over Sunday dinners after church.

"Leaving to go fishing again after dinner, Joe?" she whispered as the two families were finishing their dinner of rolled roast beef and mushrooms. Her bright blue eyes narrowed, and the she arched one perfect eyebrow.

"Enjoy the roast beef, Marya?" he replied, knowing his pay had bought the food she'd just eaten.

When the river froze solid after Christmas, Leiter told Joe and Cappie to make two runs a day over the ice. The fishing ruse all but forgotten for the time, Joe rode next to Cappie over the thick ice in a Packard outfitted with a false floorboard and with the back seat ripped out. They avoided Lake Erie. They drove a mile over the ice, straight across the river, and traveled down a back road to the distillery. This route was shorter but much more dangerous.

Cappie started carrying a crowbar in the front seat of the car when reports of liquor hijackings started leaking into the news. Several gangs in the area deemed it more profitable to hijack a load of liquor from a rum runner than to pay for it themselves. The Sugar House Gang had themselves begun to hijack booze at gunpoint; if anyone resisted, Ray Bernstein or one of his brothers would bash the bootlegger in the face with a wooden board or bat, breaking his cheekbone, nose, or eye socket. Joe was on constant watch for other gangs. His eyes never blinked as they made their way back across the frozen river twice a day, loaded down with whisky.

They were nearing the canal in early February when Joe saw lights flash in the trees. Cappie turned the car north and drove directly to the toll bridge and back into the city.

Leiter sent a couple of his men to the cottage. They reported back that there were fresh footprints in the snow and the lock on the cellar door was broken. But they had found no one. Leiter sent Cappie back to the island with the weekly kickback for the one lone cop stationed on the island; his mission was to decipher whether it had been the cops or another gang sniffing around the cottage. Cappie reported that the cop was happy with his weekly stipend, and the trespassers had likely been another gang looking for an easy score.

Two weeks later, as Joe and Cappie were helping load liquor into the truck with the pickup man, Sam "the Gorilla" Davis, two men came from around the front of the cottage and tried to overtake them. Cappie turned and pounced on the approaching men without hesitation. The hijackers were caught off guard, enabling Sam to grab the crowbar from the truck and whack one of the men hard enough in the arm that Joe heard it break. Cappie held the other man's arms behind his back and started pushing him around to the front of the cottage.

"Joe, take my gun and go to the cellar. Guard the liquor in case there's more of them coming."

Joe took Cappie's gun from his hand, ran down the cellar steps, and shut the door behind him. He sat with his back against the stack of liquor boxes, pointing the gun at the door with shaking hands. Joe heard footsteps on the wooden floor above him as the men entered the cottage.

"Think you're gonna steal our booze?" the Gorilla's voice boomed above him. "Tie up the one with the broken arm, Cappie. We're gonna teach these guys a little lesson about messing with our gang. Joe heard a small scuffle and the man with the broken arm yell out in pain as Cappie tied him to a chair. "Hey, Cappie, hand me that saw from the corner." Joe heard Cappie slowly walk across the floor to the corner of the cottage. Joe had set the saw there that morning after sawing wood for the stove.

"Hold his right arm down, Cappie" the Gorilla said menacingly.

The hijacker started whimpering and pleading with the Gorilla. "No, no, please not my hand. Whadda ya want? I'll pay you. I won't never steal from yous' again. I promise on my mother's life."

"Too late, you son of a bitch. The Sugar House don't tolerate no stealing, and we're sending a message to all you dagos or whoever else thinks about stealing from us." Joe looked up at the ceiling when the hijacker yelled in pain.

"Stop! I work for Capone; he'll pay whatever you ask. I'm his cousin! Please! I know he'll pay!"

"This ain't no kidnapping, dago," replied the Gorilla. You were on *our* property. You go back and let your cousin see what happens to thugs who try to steal from the Sugar House."

Joe heard a loud sob and then a terrifying scream as the saw began to tear through ligaments and bone. He put his fingers into his ears, still holding the gun while trying to block the sound. Without warning he threw up on the cellar floor. Wiping his mouth and replacing his fingers into his ears he started humming a Polish song his mother always sang to him. Joe sat there for several minutes, humming and rocking on the floor. Slowly he pulled his fingers away from his ears. The sound stopped for a moment. Then he heard footsteps on the cellar stairs.

Joe raised the gun as the door opened and pointed it at the man's head. Cappie appeared in the light from outside, trying to adjust his eyes to the darkness of the cellar. A ray of sunlight reflected off Joe's gun, and Cappie yelled at Joe.

"It's me Joe! Put the gun down!" Cappie held his hands high in the air. Joe quickly lowered the weapon and looked up at his friend.

"They're gone, Joe. You can come back upstairs. They won't be back."

The Gorilla walked across the floor above them, and Cappie looked up and back down at Joe realizing Joe had heard everything. Cappie and Joe just looked at one another.

"Joe . . ." Cappie started. "What happened upstairs is not my way of going about things. I prefer to knock them around a couple of times with my fists. You know, black eye, busted lip, couple of missing teeth—no permanent damage."

Joe looked up at Cappie and nodded. He'd heard many of Cappie's bar fight stories while eating supper in the cottage. He'd laughed and laughed as Cappie jabbed the air with his enormous fists and danced around the wood floor reenacting his latest Saturday night fight.

"But the Sugar House don't think a busted lip is gonna stop no one from hijacking their inventory. When the Gorilla asked for the saw, I really thought he was just gonna scare him a little. I'd heard Sam was a little off his rocker, but I really didn't think he was gonna go through with it. I barely made it till those dagos took off. Then I emptied my guts behind the cottage. You all right?" Joe nodded slowly and rose from the cellar floor.

"How bout you give me that gun back now?"

Joe looked down at his hand. He had forgotten he was still holding the weapon. He handed it back to his friend.

"Thought you were gonna shoot my head off when I came down the steps. But I guess I didn't have to worry."

"Cause you knew I'd recognize you, Cappie?"

"No—cause you never cocked the gun, Joe. Guess we'd better have some shooting lessons, huh?"

Joe smiled back at Cappie and followed him out of the cellar.

The Sugar House bosses held a meeting. "That cottage is too exposed," Shorr said.

"I agree," Charles said. "We need a more impenetrable middle-house. Abe, drive down to the island and see if you can find something that'll work. Cappie, you go down to that new city . . . what's it called?"

"Wyandotte," Cappie replied, straightening his tie.

"Yeah, Wyandotte. Find something on the river where you and Joe can run liquor into."

Shorr bought a large estate on the west side of the island and ordered some of his men to dig a tunnel from the basement to the river. He had gun turrets built into the four sides of the house and a tall black fence erected at the property lines. He also bought a house on the opposite side of the river that Cappie scouted out, five miles north, in Wyandotte. Here, he had a boathouse dug from the seawall into the basement of the house.

Joe and Cappie continued smuggling whisky across the ice while the tunnels were being constructed but drove the load back to Detroit every night. Joe was thankful to be once again sleeping in his own bed and especially that he didn't have to paint the whisky cases anymore.

CHAPTER TWENTY SIX

1924

The Sugar House Gang had installed several high capacity brewing plants and stills around the city to increase their bootlegging revenues and had ventured into liquor hijacking for themselves. The Bernstein brothers were put in charge of hundreds of blind pigs and added kidnapping for ransom to their resumes. Ray became known as the strong-arm of the brothers. He was the one who brought in Gorilla Davis to help.

The gang developed a complicated system of bribery and extortion across the city to ensure the safety of their growing enterprise. Beat cops, sergeants, captains, judges, councilmen, and lawyers all had different rates of pay for their silence. Perhaps even the chief of police and the mayor were on the take from the Sugar House. This system allowed the gang to haul beer and whisky from breweries and distilleries and unload it right on the docks in broad daylight. Several groups of men were assigned to drive over the ice to Walkerville, Ontario, across from Belle Isle at the north end of the city. They'd load their cars and trucks with cases of Canadian Club, drive over the ice onto the island park, and take the bridge back to the city. The Belle Isle police, content to have their pockets lined with as much extra cash as their yearly salary never saw anything.

That spring a rash of drownings were reported in the Detroit newspaper when the ice on the river began to thaw, but Cappie had the wherewithal to know when the ice was growing thin. He ceased the daily runs to Canada; only the naive and desperate continued to try their luck across the ice. In the beginning, the Coast Guard rescued the rumrunners whose cars were stuck and trapped in the ice, arrested them, and dumped their liquor. But as the weather turned warmer and the ice thinner, rescue efforts were aborted for the safety of the officers. Drivers and their loads of hooch disappeared under the icy water; days later, bloated bodies would be found drifting down the river. The Coast Guard would haul them into their boats and bring the dead back to the city to be identified. Often, bodies never turned up; they were stuck in the sunken car, caught on the bottom of the river. Others were found on the shores of Lake Erie, too decomposed to identify.

Joe had grown a foot over the last four and a half years. He was almost fifteen now but looked even older from the years in the sun and wind on the river. Gone were the short pants and soft cap that had helped Cappie and Joe portray their father-and-son ruse. Leiter decided Joe would pilot his own boat that spring, doubling his and Cappie's output, thereby doubling Joe's pay to one hundred dollars a week. But the traffic on the river was getting heavy, and with the ratification of the Eighteenth Amendment Joe was concerned that federal agents would become more assertive in their duties to uphold the law.

The week before he and Cappie were to relocate to the Wyandotte house, he went to visit his childhood friend Walt. Walt had followed his dream; he was working on the docks and building speedboats on the side for a team of Gold Cup racers.

"The damn things just make too much noise," Joe was saying to Walt at Jacoby's Bier Garden, a local hangout near City Hall. "I don't know if there's anything you can do about the engine, but the exhaust makes almost as much racket." They'd ordered homemade Wiener schnitzel, spätzle, and potato pancakes and were devouring the German fare as only two teenage boys can do.

"We don't usually try to make them quieter, Joe. Actually we design them to be as loud as possible. The louder the boats, the better the crowd likes it. Makes for a good show while we're racing." Walt took another bite of noodles. "Hey, by the way, how is this a 'beer garden' when they can't serve any beer?"

"Oh, they've got beer upstairs if you want it," Joe replied. "You thirsty? We can take our food up there and drink if you want."

"No," Walt replied with a queer look on his face, "I don't want any I was just wondering. You sure have changed, Joe."

"Not that much. You still see me at church, doncha?" Joe grabbed the last potato pancake and put it on his plate.

"Not very often—not that it's any of my business. And you sure are dressing well too. Seems like last time I saw you at St. Josaphat's you were wearing short pants and stockings and now your all decked out in that fancy suit and overcoat. Bet you didn't buy that at Kresge's or Hudson's."

"No, just this little shop where Leiter gets all his suits. He sent me over there and told me to pick up a few . . . said I looked like an immigrant just off the boat." Joe lowered his voice slightly when he mentioned his boss's name and looked around the crowded tavern. The air was so thick with smoke it almost hid the customers in the corners of the room, and he wanted to make sure he wasn't overheard by any unwelcome eavesdroppers.

"You're going to a tailor?" Walt said incredulously. "Don't you think you'll stand out a little driving a 'fishing boat' back and forth in that getup?"

"I don't wear this on the boat. Come on Walt, who cares about clothes? Whadda ya think you can do about the noise from the boat?"

Walt had changed in the last five years also, not so much in personality or street smarts but physically. He was taller and broader, appearing very much like the seventeen-year-old man he was. His hands were rough and callused from working on boats. Yet his face still held some of the baby fat of pubescence, and a strong Polish accent still permeated his speech. But Joe held his opinions to himself.

"And you sound different too, Joe. I hope you're not in over your head. People around here are talking a lot about your boys."

"They're not my boys, Walt. Geez, you're so serious. So about the boat . . ."

Walt drank a sip of Vernor's ginger ale and thought for a minute. "Yeah, I have some ideas. I'd have to play around a little."

"Great!" Joe replied. "Charlie said he'd pay you fifty bucks a week to make the boats faster and fix them up when they break down."

"Fifty dollars a week! That's more than twice what I'm making now, and I already have a good job!"

"Hey Walt, keep your voice down, all right? I told Charlie that you really know your stuff and he wants to hire you on. He had someone look into the work you're doing for the Gold Cup team, and he was real impressed."

"Now you're calling him Charlie, Joe? Nobody calls Mr. Leiter Charlie. You talked to him about me? Why?" Walt was getting agitated and Joe decided to try another tactic.

"Charlie was asking around the office the other day if anybody knew a good boat mechanic. A couple of the boats are looking rough from fighting the ice this winter, and they need a little upkeep. The exhaust thing is my idea, and I haven't mentioned it because I wasn't sure if you'd be able to do anything about it. If you can swing it, take the idea. I won't say a word."

"I don't want to work for gangsters, Joe. I like my job, and the team is counting on my work for the race this summer. I don't want to go to jail, and I definitely don't want to get killed. Didn't that huckster Johnny Reid just get shot four times in the head last week over in Corktown?" Walt was referring to the area near Navin Field where many Irish immigrants had settled.

"Oh, Johnny—he's got a problem with the women is all. Some dame's husband came home while he was having himself a little visit. Damn Mick was carrying a gun. I think his brother's a cop or something . . . anyways, he got all crazy and started shooting like he was out duck hunting! But Johnny's gonna be all right. He's recuperating in some fancy hospital in New York now." Johnny Reid had come to Detroit from the underworld in Missouri to seek his fortune in bootlegging and had been introduced to the Sugar House by an associate of the gang.

"Well, it doesn't matter, Joe. I'm not interested."

Joe paid for their meal and they walked out onto Brush Street. The sidewalk was crowded with businessmen and shoppers on their way to and from lunch. Joe thought back to a few years before, remembering the horse drawn carriages that had vied for room on the streets with the trolleys and cars. Graceful horses delivering wares and carting the rich around town had become a rare sight on the streets of Detroit. Thankfully, so had what they left behind in their path.

Joe finally managed to talk Walt into going to the Sugar House with him to talk to Leiter. "Just hear him out" was his final argument. Walt grudgingly followed him to the plant and into Charlie's office. Joe introduced the two and set off for the door. "Got a couple of errands to run, Walt . . . just listen to Charlie. It's a good opportunity." Joe closed the door to the office and walked home. He had some things to do before he and Cappie set off for Wyandotte at the end of week.

Joe had saved almost half of his earnings since receiving his raise that winter. He had over three hundred dollars hidden under his mattress, and he took out half and went to find his mother in the kitchen. He found her rolling meat into cabbage rolls and humming an old Polish folk tune. Her face had filled out again, but she remained extremely thin. Joe worried that she'd never truly get over the loss of his father.

"Cze , Matka." He greeted her in Polish.

"Joe, you are home early. I didn't hear you come in. Did Mr. Leiter give you the afternoon off?"

"Things were slow today . . . Matka, you know I have to go to a house down-river in a couple of days, right?" He washed his hands in the sink and grabbed a leaf of cabbage from the boiling pot to help roll the golabki.

"Yes, I know, but I wish you could stay here. I don't understand why Mr. Leiter has to make a young boy go off and live away from his family."

"I told you, Matka, he isn't *making* me do anything. It's just part of the job, and that's where they need me. But I might be gone for a while. I'm not sure when I'll be able to get back. It might be a month or more, so you'll need to send Frank to the Sugar House on Fridays for my pay. It's all arranged, and they'll have it waiting for him." Thirty dollars would be waiting for his brother at the end of every week at the office, and the remainder of his pay would be held until he returned. Joe didn't want his mother to know about his recent pay increase, so as not to arouse any suspicions regarding the increased danger of his job.

"But Joe, that means you'll be gone for Easter! You can't miss Mass. It's a sin to miss on the holiest day of the year! And you'll miss Easter dinner . . . no, you tell that Mr. Leiter that you must be home for Easter."

"Sorry, Matka, it's already been decided. But don't worry; I'll go to Mass. I'll find a church nearby." Joe filled the last leaf of cabbage with the ground pork and beef mixture and placed it in the Dutch oven. He rinsed off his hands and reached into his pocket for the money he'd saved. "Here's some extra money for Easter dinner and to buy new suits for Frank and Stephan to wear to church."

"Joe, this is eighty dollars! Easter dinner and new suits don't cost eighty dollars. I can't take all of this!"

"Then buy a new dress or save it, Matka. Please take the money. I'll feel better leaving if I know you have enough to get by for a while." Joe pressed the bills into his mother's hand. "I have a few errands to run, but I'll be back for supper. I can't wait to eat your golabki- Cappie's cooking is terrible!" Joe kissed Matka on the cheek, grabbed his communion rosary from his bedroom and left out the front door.

He walked the two blocks to St. Josaphat's and entered the quiet cathedral. The school children were in class next door, and the church was empty. He walked down the long aisle to the front of the church and placed five dollars in the offertory box to pay for his prayer candles. He lit five tall red candles; one each for Matka, Frank, and Stephan so God would watch over them while he was away and one each for Cappie and himself to ensure their safety on the river. Joe was sure Cappie wouldn't want a candle lit for him, but he wasn't planning on telling him. He'd had grown close to the man and didn't want anything to happen to him. Lastly he walked over to the candles meant to remember the dead and lit a tall pillar for Ojciec.

"I know God has heard our prayers and you are in heaven Ojciec," Joe whispered. " Matka misses you so much, and so do I. Every day I wish you were here with us, but I'm trying my best to take care of Matka and my brothers. I hope you are proud of me . . . and will you ask God to forgive me for the bootlegging? Take care." Joe crossed himself and out of habit walked to pew number 273 and knelt down on the padded kneeler to pray. Head bowed, he began reciting the rosary. Joe heard the sound of soft footsteps and turned to see Father Gatowski approaching.

"Nice to see you here, Joe," he said, sitting next to him on the hard bench. Joe rose from the kneeler and sat next to the old priest.

"Nice to see you, Father . . . I'm glad you're here. I was about to come look for you. I wanted to make a contribution to the church in honor of my father. Will you say a Mass in his remembrance?" Joe handed Father Gatowski the remaining sixty-five dollars in his pocket.

"That's quite a large donation for a remembrance Mass, Joe."

"Oh, well . . . give the rest to the church, Father. For all they've done for me and my family, I mean."

"All right son, thank you." The priest sat back in the pew and looked at the altar. "You know ,Joe, things are changing quickly in this city. I'm not sure banning alcohol was the best idea our government has ever had. The church is already having difficulties with Prohibition."

"Why is that, Father? I thought the Eighteenth Amendment allowed for sacramental wine?"

"Oh, it does. Unfortunately, that's one of the difficulties. I've already heard rumors about priests in other parishes ordering far above the needed amounts for communion, and I'm pretty sure they're not drinking all the excess alone. I myself have been approached by some of our own parishioners with offers to help 'supplement the church's income' with the sale of any extra wine. Of course if you look at it closely, things haven't changed much since the beginning of time . . . Adam barely hesitated to take a bite of the forbidden apple in the Garden of Eden."

"Yes, but asking a priest to . . ." Joe couldn't finish. "And in church?"

"Is that what bothers you, Joe? That people commit crimes behind the cloak of the church? God doesn't disparage against disobedience and sin with a heavier hand when it occurs in His house. He abhors all sin and evil. The Catholic Church didn't fight for the passing of the Eighteenth Amendment, but now that it's passed we stand by the laws of this country." Father Gatowski's eyes looked directly into Joe's.

"Of course, Father. I've got to get going . . . thank you for the Mass for Ojciec." He grabbed his hat from the pew clip and stood up. Father Gatowski stood also and held out his hand to Joe.

"Take care, Joe, and remember I'm here for confession or just to talk if you need me. God be with you, son." They shook hands. Joe left the pew, walked to the back of the church, and turned around. The priest was kneeling in his family's pew and praying. His mood dampened with the unspoken disappointment from Father Gatowski; he crossed himself and left the church.

Joe hopped a streetcar and headed downtown, back to the Sugar House. The sweet smell of sugarcane permeated the air, in stark contrast to the rough voices and cussing from the workers on the floor. Charlie informed Joe that Walt had been persuaded to work on the boats but had struck a hard bargain. It had been agreed that Walt would never operate the boats himself for rum running or even to the hideout. If a boat broke down, Joe and Cappie would somehow have to get it to the docks in Detroit for Walt to work on. Direct from the conversation with Father Gatowski, Joe's conscience felt a little better knowing that his friend would not be directly involved in the illegal operations that Joe had initiated him into.

Supper was a delicious and lighthearted affair. Stephan spooned his mashed potatoes into a mountain of white spuds on his plate as Frank regaled them with funny stories from school. Joes' feeling of guilt abated as he looked around the tiny kitchen at his family. He was providing for them the best way he knew and fulfilling his promise to Ojciec. God would understand.

CHAPTER TWENTY SEVEN

1927

It was dark when Joe pulled the speedboat into the boathouse in Wyandotte. Cappie quickly shut the door behind the boat and caught the rope Joe threw to him. Electric bulbs cast light on the wooden walls and ceiling as Joe jumped out of the boat and secured the garage door. They had been running whisky from Walkerville for over two years and had it down to a science.

Seven days a week they woke at eight a.m. and pushed carts of whisky and beer through a dimly lit tunnel from the basement of the river house to another house the gang had bought on the other side of the street. When they reached the end of the tunnel, he and Cappie would carry the boxes up the basement stairs to the attached garage at the back of the second house. They loaded it into waiting trucks labeled Fresh Meat, Benny's Breads, or whatever nondescript brand Leiter came up with to disguise the contraband. Drivers took it into the city.

Afterwards, Joe or Cappie ate breakfast in the river house kitchen and then went down to the boathouse to tinker. Walt had designed an underwater exhaust system that decreased the noise of the speedboats by half, but he continually sent notes via the pickup men instructing Joe and Cappie on upkeep or ways to increase the speed. Joe had become an extremely talented boatman, able to evade the Coast Guard with the proficiency of men more experienced than he; but he relied on Cappie for much of the mechanical work. After lunch they'd play cards for a while, and then Joe would read while Cappie took a nap.

On nice days, Joe would meander down to the shipbuilding docks to watch the men construct the giant ships, or he'd walk to one of the two Polish Catholic churches located in the city. Our Lady of Mount Carmel and St. Stanislaus Kostka were sufficient substitutes for his home parish, and if the doors were open he'd go inside and sit for an hour or so, feeling calm and safe in the fragrance of candles and incense. He was unable to attend Sunday morning Mass due to scheduled pickups, but he hoped his silent prayers during the week would suffice for the time being.

Wyandotte was a quiet rural town with quaint streets lined with trees and flowers. Children played in large front yards while prettily dressed ladies sipped tea on expansive porches overlooking the river. But in spite of the tranquil appearance, an intense Italian gang war had begun on those same streets only a few weeks before. The residents were startled from their beds by the sounds of car bomb explosions and loud blasts from sawed-off shotguns blowing bodies to pieces in front of their homes. Burnt corpses were found in nearby farmers' fields, and last week a gift wrapped package intended for an important underboss had detonated inside a drugstore, killing the druggist. But a truce had been tentatively reached, and the last five days the town had reverted to a quiet country atmosphere.

The sky was gray and cloudy that morning as Joe walked to the local grocery store to buy some cottage cheese. Cappie had never tasted pierogi, and he wanted to make some for him. As he neared Vicolli's Fruits and Grocery, several black sedans sped past him up Biddle Avenue in a silent motorcade. When the caravan reached the business block, the pace slowed to a fast crawl. Joe had never seen a hit, but knew the makings of one and leapt into the lobby of the local inn for cover. As he hit the floor the sound of a hundred shots could be heard across the street, shattering windows and splintering bricks and wood. A woman screamed, and the motorcade sped away.

Joe hesitated and then opened the inn's heavy wooden doors. He glanced south at the line of sedans receding and took a deep breath to steady himself as he exited the building. Glass littered the wood sidewalk and street from the windows of Vicolli's and any cars that had been parked in the way. Stepping over bullet casings and shards of glass, Joe looked at the wrecked storefront. A young policeman, not much older than Joe, was propped up in the doorway, holding his leg with his right hand and holding his gun in the left.

"Officer . . ." Joe said when he had reached the storefront. The cop looked up at him with a blank stare. "They're gone, officer. You can put your gun away." Blood was seeping through the man's uniform.

"Get down, boy!" he responded. The young rookie was in some sort of shock. He grabbed at Joe's coat trying to pull him to the ground. Several Italian-looking men ran out the front door of the grocery store and jumped into their cars to track down the motorcade. People peered out of curtained windows and slowly walked over to survey the damage. Joe pulled off his belt and pulled it tight around the policeman's leg above the wound. Joe pinched the belt hard and lightly slapped the young cop on the cheek.

"See? You're all right. You can snap out of it now," he whispered. "These people are counting on you to calm them down." Joe looked into the eyes of the patrolman and then down at the blood that had pooled onto the sidewalk.

The cop's eyes refocused, and he shook his head slightly looking down at his leg. "Damn this hurts! They got me good for sure . . . can you help me up?" He grimaced as he tried to rise. Joe put his neck under the rookie's armpit and pulled him up to a standing position. Several shop owners and citizens had made their way to the grocery store now and had grouped around the patrolman. Avoiding attention, Joe casually ducked out from underneath the wounded man's shoulder and sneaked out of the crowd.

"Back already? Ready to teach me how to make those pie-rogees?" Cappie asked, as Joe entered the side door of the house. He was sitting in a rocking chair in the living room reading the morning paper and didn't look up.

"Had a little problem in town," Joe responded. Cappie jumped up and strode to the kitchen. "What kind of prob— What the hell? Are you hurt? Sit down." He looked at Joe's blood-soaked shirt, and he tried to run his hands over Joe's abdomen, back and arms.

"Relax Cappie, it's not my blood. I'm all right." He pushed Cappie's hands away. He sat down hard in the kitchen chair and took a deep breath.

"Not your blood? You get in a fight? You off someone, Joe? What happened? Oh boy, this is gonna be trouble.

We gotta get you out of here." Cappie stepped toward the small kitchen window, looking outside for the cops.

Joe laughed, "Kill someone with what . . . my brute strength? I never take my gun into town. You know that. There was a hit at the grocery store. I ducked into the inn when I saw what was gonna go down. They hit a cop. He'll be all right, but he's pretty shaken up."

"A hit? Did you see who it was, Joe? What'd they look like?"

"Didn't see no faces. Just three black sedans speeding off." Joe pulled off his bloody shirt and threw it in the trash next to the sink. "I don't think anybody else got hurt. You think they're doing a hit on a rookie cop, Cappie?"

"No, they wouldn't bother with a cop. They'd just threaten his family or give him more money. What grocery store did you say?" Cappie got a glass of water and handed it to Joe.

"Viccoli's." Joe took a long drink of the cool water and set the glass on the table. He looked at Cappie and smiled. "They're probably havin a fire sale this afternoon if you wanta go into town."

"Yeah? Very funny, Joe. How'd you get so bloody if you was in the inn anyway?"

"Umm . . . I helped the cop a little."

"Joe! You gotta think boy! We don't need no one knowing your face around here. We're supposed to stay in the background. Who saw you?" Cappie went to the window again and peered out.

"Relax Cappie! Nobody noticed me, and the cop was too much in shock to remember anything. Let's just make some lunch . . . how about I boil up a couple of wieners? I'll make pierogi next week."

An hour before dusk they headed out in their separate boats toward Walkerville. Leiter had made a deal with the Walker sons, and they no longer bought from the Pioneer plant. Joe preferred the ride to Walkerville because he didn't have to fight the waves of Lake Erie; and seeing the lights of Detroit, even if it was just from the water, made him feel closer to home.

Boating up the river, Joe felt a freedom he had never experienced before. He loved the sound of the engine, the wind and sun on his face, the waves pushing against the bow of the boat. He felt lucky to be out on the water as he passed the factories and warehouses where men toiled away for their meager wages. The muscles in his arms, back and legs had grown strong from carrying cases of whisky up and down the stairs every day, and he had the feeling of invincibility only found in the young.

Not that his job was without stress and peril. Hijackers were a constant threat—more so than the Coast Guard—and he and Cappie now carried.38 snub noses in the waistbands of their pants. Joe was happy for the added protection, especially after the shooting he had witnessed at the grocery store. Cappie had seen his share of violence in the last month also; he'd been shot at twice coming back down the river with a load but had evaded the thugs by hiding out on nearby Fighting Island.

The summer air was humid that evening, and Joe was swarmed with mosquitoes as he pulled into the Walkerville dock. "How ya doing, Clay?" He threw the dock foreman a rope.

"Sweating and swatting at these damn insects, Joey O." Joe had been so young when he started making his runs to Canada that he hadn't thought to develop an alias, so when the gang started calling him Joey O in reference to all the O's in Jopolowski; it stuck.

"It's like trying to swim through a wet blanket out there. I musta ate twenty bugs on the way up here." Joe handed Clay a folded piece of paper with the order for the day.

"That's a lotta hooch, Joey O," the foreman said, glancing at the paper. "Might slow you down a little. You sure about this number?"

"Yep, boss man says there's a lotta thirsty people dying for a drink, and it's our job to help them out. Let's load it up, Clay."

Truth was there *were* a lot of thirsty people wanting a drink in Detroit, but there were a lot of people in the rest of the country that wanted one too. The Sugar House Gang, as the newspapers now referred to them, was supplying booze for much of the country now. Wyandotte was just the starting point of the liquor's long journey. From there, it was driven to Chicago or put on trains headed to the south or west. The Sugar House Gang had formed alliances with gangs in St. Louis, New York, Cleveland, and other major American cities. But their largest shipments were delivered to Al Capone in the windy city. Capone had heard about and seen the brutality of the Sugar House Gang and had decided to work with the Detroit based mob instead of fighting against them. To keep up with the demand, Charlie Leiter sent word that Joe and Cappie were to increase their volume.

"All right, Joey O. All loaded up. Where you headed this evening?" Clay asked, handing the boat's rope back to Joe.

"Looks like Mexico, sir," Joe replied with a smile.

"Have a safe trip."

Joe pulled the long speedboat back onto the river. The sun had faded to the west, and the electric lights from the buildings and signs in Detroit helped guide his way down the river for a while. As he cleared the city limits, the lights from the rivers' edge grew dimmer. He looked to the sky for help, but clouds had rolled in. He had to make his way down the river in darkness. Joe didn't worry. He knew the waterway well. Looking to the east he narrowed his eyes, searching the water. A boat was approaching. It was driving fast and straight towards him.

Thanks to Walt, Joe's boat was one of the fastest on the river. But his cargo was weighing him down in the water and slowing his speed. Joe pushed hard on the throttle to try to outrun the intruders. Speeding over the small waves through the darkness his heart pounded in his chest. Unlikely to be the Coast Guard or a customs officer at the speed the boat was approaching, he thought. He'd be safer if it was. But it looked to him like a rival gang out to hijack his cargo.

Can't be a coincidence I'm getting chased the first night my shipment gets increased, he thought. Joe grabbed for the .38 at his waist with his right hand, steering through the dark water with his left. He'd reached the halfway point, but the other boat was still gaining and he knew he couldn't make it to the boathouse. It was too far to Fighting Island. With nowhere to hide, Joe pushed the boat to the limits of its power.

A shot rang out across the water and hit the boat's transom and splintered the wood. Joe steered the boat in a zigzag pattern while taking care to avoid the shallow areas of the river that hid beneath the dark water. Another shot hit the boat, this time only inches from where his hand held the steering wheel. He threw the .38 under the captain's seat where he could easily reach it; resisting the urge to shoot back. He'd only shot the new gun a few times, and he knew his aim was poor at best. In a split-second decision he cut the power to the engine. He raised his hands in the air as the faster boat approached his portside. A light flashed in his eyes, and he was blinded for a moment.

"Give up, do ya?" an Italian accented voice called from behind the light's source.

"You got me," Joe responded, smiling and trying to chuckle, hoping the hijackers wouldn't notice his trembling hands.

"'You got me'? That's what he says boys." The thug laughed to his comrades. "We outrun him and we outgun him, and all he say is 'you got me'. Well, that's a new one. Usually they are a-crying or a-cussing or threatening me, but I never had a 'you got me' before."

"Your boat's faster than mine. That's all there is to it," Joe replied. "I figure it this way: this time you win. I'll go back to the shop and doctor up my boat, and maybe next time I win; maybe not. A load of hooch isn't worth fightin' over, not when there's so much to go around." Joe reached down slowly, picked up a case of whisky and handed it over to show his sincerity. The man lowered the light from Joe's face and took the wooden case.

"OK boys, grab the hooch. And you keep your hands up, boy. You hear me?" Joe raised his hands again as two Italian teenagers boarded his boat. He recognized the

Licavoli brothers as soon as they stepped aboard his boat. Pete and Yonnie were members of the newly established River Gang that had been trying to gain control of the narrow waterway between Canada and Detroit. Joe quickly glanced down at the men's waists and noted that their belts held no guns, but each had a hammer swinging by his thigh. The Licavoli brothers were recent transports from a St. Louis gang called the Hammerhead Gang, known for hitting their victims over the head with hammers before robbing them.

The brothers unloaded the cargo quickly while Joe stood, hands raised and rocking side to side with the boat. Joe eyed the swinging hammers and tried to continue his friendly tactic. "Warm night," he said, smiling at the older man on the other boat.

"Warm and wet like my first time," he replied, smirking at Joe and laughing. "Course you wouldn't know nothing about that yet, would you, bambino?" His hand rested on the handle of the gun in his waistband.

"I know plenty," Joe replied, trying to figure out who was behind the thick accent. "I know the government hired thirty new customs agents last week, and you're gonna have a hard time docking this load in Detroit."

"Ah, good tip. Guess we'll be taking a ride up the river to St. Clair, boys."

The brothers loaded the last of Joe's liquor into their boat. "Don't know why you'd be helping us avoid the pigs, though. You ain't trying to set us up, are you?" He squinted hard at Joe trying to read his face in the dark.

Joe was sweating from the heat. Perspiration dripped down his back and puddled at his belt. Slowly lowering his hands and putting them on the steering wheel he replied,

"I don't think that fast. Just thought it'd be a waste of good whisky if the cops nabbed it after all the work we've both put into this load. You know how they like to call the reporters and smash all the bottles for the cameras."

"Yeah, this hijacking is getting to be a lotta work. How about next time I let you keep your load and we'll just charge you a river tax?" the Italian had taken hold of the wheel of the boat and his right hand had angled the light he was holding upward. The light flashed for a moment across his face and Joe realized his adversary's identity.

Keeping his expression neutral he replied, "How much is that?"

"Oh, let's say twenty-five percent retail." The brother Joe believed to be Yonnie started their engine and revved the motor. "Good doing business with you," the elder man replied, and they sped off to the north.

'*Twenty-five percent! I wonder what Charlie will have to say about that*,' Joe thought, as he steered south down the river to Wyandotte. When Joe pulled into the boathouse, Cappie was waiting for him inside. Joe related the incident to his friend and they decided that they'd go back to the city with the pickup driver the following morning to explain the situation to their boss.

CHAPTER TWENTY EIGHT

Joe hadn't been to the city in a couple of months. The volume of noise from the traffic, construction, and people was overwhelming. They drove straight to the Sugar House and into the garage. Their load was small, as they were missing more than half, and they unloaded in several minutes. Joe was nervous as they climbed the wooden stairs to the office. It wasn't uncommon for a rumrunner to try to make a few extra bucks by claiming he'd been hijacked with his boss's load and then selling it on the side. It was imperative that Charlie believed his story. His stomach flip-flopped a few times.

"Didn't know you boys were coming back today," Charlie said, looking up from some papers on his desk as they entered the small office.

"Had us a little problem, Charlie," Cappie replied.

"Oh, what sorta problem?" Charlie leaned back in his chair with a smirk. Joe knew that Charlie was trying to appear friendly so he and Cappie would let their guard down. He also knew that his boss's demeanor could turn on a dime and he had to tread carefully.

"I got hijacked last night coming back from Walkerville," Joe responded.

"With the extra-large shipment? Sounds kinda like a funny coincidence to me, Joe." Charlie's smirk remained.

"That's what I thought, Charlie. I think we might have a traitor or a spy in the barrel."

"Yeah? So *you* lose five thousand dollars' worth of booze and it's one of *my* boys. That's what you're sayin'?" Charlie stood up and walked around the desk to where Joe was sitting. Joe swallowed hard and wiped his brow. The office was like a steam bath, and combined with his anxiety he figured he'd lost half the water in his body.

"I don't know, Charlie. You don't pay me to think, and I'm not real good at it. But hear me out for a minute. I get a note from you yesterday morning telling me to increase our load by thirty percent. I don't leave the house till it's time to make the run. We got no telephone in that house, and no one stops by. I run up to Canada like I do every day and hand the order to the foreman. Before I'm halfway back, I'm being chased down and shot at by a bunch of dagos. What's that sound like to you?" Joe's voice grew in confidence and the final question was delivered angrily.

"Hmm, dagos, you say? You recognize anybody?" Charlie returned to the other side of the desk and sat back down. (He looked at Cappie and waved him out of the office.) Charlie would get his side later.

"Yeah, those Licavoli bastards jumped in my boat and unloaded the whole lot. I'll have to wash out the whole damn thing to get the garlic smell out, but I'm not sure who held the gun on me . . . it was an older guy—he had a shiny wedding band on." Joe had to play his hand carefully— he didn't want his boss to comprehend his level of intelligence; better to appear dumb so as not to stand out.

"Yeah? What'd he look like?"

"Like every other dago in this city . . . short, dark . . . stupid look on his face." Joe knew Charlie fiercely hated the Italians. A massive war between two Italian gangs had occurred a couple years before in the city, resulting in the deaths of over a hundred of their members collectively. Charlie liked to joke about how the fighting gangs had saved him so much work by killing each other. Truthfully their ranks had been seriously depleted, allowing the Sugar House to move in with little opposition. Joe had no bad feelings toward Italians himself, thinking they were a hard working group—mostly Catholic like his Polish brethren, but he kept his opinions to himself.

"Licavoli brothers . . . I think I heard their fat sister got married last month. Yeah, they were having a party for her at that blind pig one of them owns . . . the Subway Café. Cops got wind of it and raided it during the reception! I remember because I laughed my ass off when I heard it." Charlie smiled a true smile at the recollection. "She married . . . damn—I can't remember."

"I think one of them might have called the guy with the gun Fran," Joe offered, trying to lead his boss down the right path without revealing his hand.

"Fran . . . Francesco . . . that's it! Frank Cammarato! That dago bastard from St. Louis—that's who married that fat broad! I should've put that together. I thought his racket was robbing banks. Guess he's branching out. What'd they say to you, Joe?" Joe relaxed slightly, although he had to repeatedly wipe his forehead with his handkerchief. Joe related the twenty-five percent "river tax" threat, his invention of the thirty new customs agents, and how Frank had stated they were going take the load up past Detroit to Lake St. Clair.

"Lake St. Clair, huh?" Charlie peered at Joe over the desk. "You're not too dumb are you, boy? Abe Bernstein told me you had a brain about you when we was looking for an errand boy, but truth be told . . . besides the fact that you've managed to get every load delivered, I wasn't convinced. Maybe I better have another look at you. But first I'll send a couple boys up to check out your story. If it checks out and they find your liquor, we'll hijack it right back and smash some heads."

"Anything I can do, Charlie?" Joe asked, rising from his chair. Cappie had returned with the coffee and handed it to Joe. The last thing he wanted was a hot cup of coffee, but he took the mug and drank a small sip.

"Why don't you take a few days off and visit with your family. Cappie's been asking for a few days off to sow his oats in the city, so I guess this is as good a time as any. Here's your last two months' pay," Charlie said, reaching into the desk drawer and handed two thick envelopes to Joe for him and Cappie. "Come back at the end of the week, and we'll have a sit down, Joe. Oh, and on a side note, there's a small issue with a relative of yours that I need to speak to you about."

"A relative of mine?" Joe questioned.

"Yes . . . you got an uncle by the name of Felix, right?"

"Feliks, yes," Joe responded, now having an idea of where this might be going.

"Seems like he's had an awful string of bad luck—got caught not once but twice with his pants down by two different dames' husbands, and there's a little matter of him owing quite a bit of cabbage on some unlucky bets."

"How much?" Joe asked.

"Two dimes," Charlie replied.

Joe whistled under his breath. "Maybe he'll win it back," Joe said.

"It's been a couple months, Joe. I'm a patient man but Shorr isn't. He wants to send a couple of the boys over to help encourage him to get off his wallet."

"If he hasn't paid you, he might not have it, Charlie," Joe replied.

"Then that's even more bad luck, Joe. We've turned our heads to this situation for as long as we can. I've already sent word out to all the gambling joints that we run that no more bets are to be taken from your Uncle Felix. I like you Joe, but business is business, and he's in for a lot."

"I'll talk to him, Charlie. Let me see what I can do, all right? Give me a couple of days?"

"Sure, sure Joe, I'll speak to Shorr. Have a nice couple of days off, and I'll see you at the end of the week."

Cappie and Joe left the office and walked out onto the steaming sidewalk. "How'd it go, Joe?" Cappie asked. The smell of sugar faded as they walked away from the building.

"Pretty good, I think. Gonna send someone up to Lake St. Clair to see if they can get the load back. It's probably already back here in the saloons by now. I'll have to hope they find something that proves my story."

"Don't worry, Joe. I'll vouch for you." Cappie clapped Joe on the shoulder.

"I know Cappie, but you didn't see nothing except me coming back with an empty boat and a couple of bullet holes in the sides."

"Try not to worry, Joe. Charlie likes you and he sure hates dagos . . . I'm sure it'll work out. See you Friday. Say hello to your mama for me." Cappie had met Joe's mother once in the spring when he'd picked him up at his house. He had commented that she looked very young for her age. Joe shook his head at Cappie as they parted ways.

Dressed as he was in fisherman's clothing, he passed without notice among the people on the street. Joe jumped on a streetcar, paid the fare and found an empty seat. Two young women sitting across the aisle observed his poor clothing and twittered and laughed at him to each other. Rolling his eyes at their stupidity, he turned around in his seat and looked out the window.

Beat cops walked down the sidewalk, apparently oblivious to the reverberating jazz music that poured out onto the street from saloons and taverns. Men dressed in the finest suits held doors for women in flimsy short dresses. Bare arms, bobbed hair, and low-cut dresses appeared to be the fashion on a hot summer day for the newborn flappers, as the newspapers called them. Lights and signs flashed from every building, adding heat to the sizzling metropolis. Shiny dark Packards, Chevrolets, Lincolns, and Fords loaded with well-dressed young couples flew past the streetcar honking and weaving their way through traffic.

Getting off the streetcar near his neighborhood he watched two young ladies in short dresses and fashionable boyish caps helping an elderly lady dressed in old world clothing carry her groceries down the sidewalk. The small grocery store on the corner now advertised in both Polish and English, and a little Negro boy manned a shoeshine box near the front door. The sidewalk radiated a heat that felt like a hundred and twenty degrees, and the smell of sweat and body odor overwhelmed his senses. Gratefully, he turned onto his quiet tree lined street and hurried home.

CHAPTER TWENTY NINE

"Joe! Oh my Joe, your home!" Matka dropped the pastry crust she was preparing at the kitchen counter and pulled Joe into her arms. Her pretty face had filled out again, and she was wearing a white apron over a new bright blue dress cut at the knees. "Joe, I never expected you in the middle of the week! I'm so glad to see you. Is everything OK?"

"Yes Matka, just got a few days off. Even a working man needs a couple days of rest and fun now and then." Joe smiled down at Matka, noticing with glee that he had passed her in height. "What's for supper?"

Joe played with his brothers after supper. Matka drew Joe a bath in the new upstairs bathroom. Joe had tried convincing his mother to move to a newer, more modern home; but she had refused, insisting on staying in the house she shared with her sister-in-law. She was comfortable in their neighborhood and felt that was where she belonged. So the year before, Joe paid to have the old house updated with electricity and indoor plumbing. Despite his mother's protests that the updates were not necessary, he found her smiling when she ran the kitchen faucet or turned on the table lamp in the living room. He had already found a fancy new icebox at Hudson's that he was going to buy her for Christmas.

As he lay in the tub of cool water he wondered who Charlie had sent out to St. Clair to retrieve the hijacked load. Hopefully, it was one of the more honest guys . . . one of the boys could find Joe's cargo, take it for himself, tell Charlie he hadn't found anything, and sell it. Of course, if the Sugar House bosses found out, the traitor would be beaten to a pulp and hospitalized or worse. Or maybe Cammarato had outsmarted Joe and taken the load somewhere else. Or maybe they'd landed it at St. Clair and some other gang nabbed it from them.

Joe explored different possibilities in his head until his fingers were as wrinkled as a prune. He toweled off, slipped on a pair of clean underwear that his mother had laid on the sink, and walked across the hall to his room. The sun still hung in the sky; and he could hear his brothers playing on the front porch with Matka, Aunt Hattie, and Emilia, when he fell into an uneasy sleep.

He woke around ten the following morning feeling rested and less anxious then the night before. Whatever was to occur regarding the hijacked load was to be and worrying wasn't going to help anything. Prayer? That was another thing altogether. He knelt next to the bed, hands clasped, and prayed for God's intercession on his behalf. Finishing, he looked around the bare room and noted that his brothers hadn't slept there.

"Where did Frank and Stephan sleep last night?" he asked, entering the kitchen in only a pair of pants and undershirt.

"They slept with me so you could rest," Matka replied. "Would you like some eggs and bacon?"

"Do you have any cereal? It's too hot to cook, Matka."

"Yes, Frank asked me to get some Kellogg's Toasted Corn Flakes; it's in the cupboard. I'll get you some milk." Matka pulled the milk from the old icebox, and Joe noted that all the ice had melted from the heat.

"There's no ice, Matka. What time does the iceman get here?"

"Pretty soon, he's usually here already. What else can I get you? I have sliced ham in the icebox, or would you like some coffee?" Matka bustled around the kitchen, happy to have her eldest son home to take care of for a while.

"Cereal is enough . . . that's all we usually eat for breakfast at the house. Cappie and I usually only cook dinner and then eat that for supper too. Hey, I have an idea . . . it's too hot to cook. Why don't I take you and the boys out to a nice supper tonight?"

Matka blushed and her hands flew to her cheeks, "No, Joe, you do enough for us. I'll cook you something nice for supper. I can get a nice chicken from the butcher."

"No, I have to sleep in this house tonight too, and if you cook in here all day it'll be hotter than Hades. It's decided. Find something pretty to wear, because I'm taking you out for a nice meal."

Matka put the milk back in the icebox and smiled at Joe. "All right, but if I'm getting dressed up I think you should at least get a haircut. You look like a lumberjack." She walked over to the table and tousled his blonde hair. Joe picked up the bowl and slurped down the remaining milk before remembering where he was.

"Sorry, Matka, guess I've been eating with Cappie for too long." He put the bowl back down on the table.

"I hope you don't eat like a wild man when you take us out tonight."

"I'll be on my best behavior, Mrs. Jopolowksi. I'll pick you and the boys up at five o'clock."

Joe stopped at the cabbie dispatch to secure a hired car to pick up his family that afternoon. Then he meandered down the street looking for a barber shop. A spinning red-and-white striped barber pole beckoned him not far from the dispatch office. An elderly black man was shaving a customer in a barber chair near the front window. Two empty barber chairs sat along the wall, and there were no other customers in the shop.

"Hello, young man." A small bell hanging in the doorway jingled as the door shut behind him. "Have a seat, and I'll be with you in jiffy." It was slightly cooler in the shop than on the street , but not much. Joe watched the barber scraping the man's beard off with the long blade. He rubbed his chin and cheeks with one hand feeling for any sign of scruff.

"Needing a shave?" the barber asked, observing Joe's not so subtle search for signs of manhood.

"Yeah. Yeah . . . a shave and a haircut," he responded, unable to hide a smile from the old man. The barber finished with his customer and gestured for Joe to take the seat.

"Slow day?" Joe asked as the barber began to cut his hair.

"Slow every day," he replied. "You're the first white man I've had come in here in a month."

"Why's that? This is a white neighborhood."

"Sure is, sir," the old man replied. "Been here thirty years or so . . . name's Henry Wade Robbins. I always done a good business, but lately they're trying to push me out. Haven't you seen all the help wanted signs that say "White Only" hanging in the barber shop windows around the city?"

"I've been out of town for a few months . . . is this your store?"

"Yes sir. Owned and operated by yours personally for three decades, but I don't know for how much longer. I'm looking to rent a space in Black Bottom. White men won't come in here anymore, and I need to make a living. Don't make no sense. I've given some of the biggest and most powerful men of this city their first shaves. They'd come in here every day, and now they pass by and don't even look in my window. I've listened about their families, their jobs, and the women they want and the women they got for thirty years, and they look right through me now." The old man shook his head and tilted Joe's head slightly so he could trim near his ear without cutting him.

"I thought most barbers were colored," Joe responded.

"Used to be . . . now everybody wants to go to fancy barbershops in the hotels and the train station. Don't help King Gillette invented that safety razor and any old chump can give a shave. Nobody appreciates a close shave anymore. I'm the last Negro-owned shop that's not in Black Bottom. Ha! I thought the Fifteenth Amendment was gonna change my life. Boy was I right . . . just not how I thought." Henry finished Joe's haircut and grabbed a hot towel. Laying the chair back he placed it on Joe's face. The moist heat warmed Joe skin, and he relaxed into the chair. Henry whipped the towel off and started foaming up Joe's face.

"First shave?" Henry asked with a twinkle in his eye.

"Yes," Joe responded, slightly embarrassed.

"Well, by the looks of it you couldn't have waited another day." Henry was stroking Joe's fifteen-year-old psyche, and Joe knew Henry was just being kind. But he appreciated the comment.

"Henry . . . you remember when they ratified the Fifteenth Amendment? How old are you?" Joe asked, enjoying the feel of the cool razor on his young skin.

"Not sure. I was born on a plantation down south. Got sold when I was just a toddler to another master, and I hitched a ride on the underground railroad to Detroit when I was just about your age. I figure I'm somewhere in my late seventies." Henry patted Joe's cheeks with a cooling liquid and sat him back up in the chair. "All done, sir. That'll be a dollar for the haircut and fifty cents for the shave." Joe handed Henry three dollars and thanked him.

"Best shave I ever had, Henry," he said as he exited the barbershop. Joe's eyes now opened from his conversation with Henry, he noted a Whites Only sign that hung in a retail shop window on his walk back home. How had he missed that, he wondered.

The car arrived in front of their house at the appointed time. Joe held the door open for his mother as his brothers pushed past, excited for a ride in a private car. They drove to the thirteen-story Penobscot building, and a black doorman opened the door for his mother when they pulled up to the curb. Matka had worn a pretty lavender dress and her hair was pulled up high on her head. Joe's brothers wore their best suits and had been warned several times that they must be on their best behavior. The Penobscot was one of the first restaurants in the city to have "cold washed air" blown into its dining room. Slabs of ice were placed near the windows, and fans pushed air over the top, cooling the room.

"I wish I'd brought my shawl," Matka teased Joe. Joe laughed, picked up Stephan, and followed the hostess to their table.

They dined on green sea turtle soup, roast veal, halibut, and lobster. Matka tried to argue that the menu was too expensive, but Joe ordered for the table when the waiter came, ending her protests. He also ordered Yoo-Hoos for Frank and Stephan, a beer for himself, and a raspberry fizz for his mother. When she took a sip of her drink her eyes widened, and she looked around the restaurant.

"Joe, this has vodka in it!" she whispered.

"It's all right, Matka. Look. That lady at the next table is drinking one too. The cops won't bust up a fancy joint like this." He ordered bananas with cream and chocolate cake for dessert and drank another beer while Matka sipped coffee from a fine china cup. The cool air felt incredible after the heat of the day and they lingered to avoid going back out into the heat. Matka sent the little boys to the lobby to play with a small toy car Frank had brought in his pocket, while they finished their after dinner drinks.

"Matka," Joe began, "I've been meaning to bring up something for a while now and I hope you'll agree to it."

"Yes Joe?" Matka leaned forward in her chair, giving him her undivided attention. Her cheeks were flushed pink from the raspberry fizz and she looked very pretty in the candlelight.

"I've been thinking about your sister in Poland lately. Whenever I get home to see Frank and Stephan I think how lucky I am to have brothers . . . especially with Ojciec gone."

Tears began to brim in Matka's eyes and Joe worried he had ruined the perfect evening but he pushed forward with his idea. "I've save up quite a bit of money in the last year, and I think it's time we go and look for your sister. The war is over and you still haven't heard from her, and now we have the funds to go and find her and bring her back."

"Oh Joe, I don't know . . . would you leave your job? And I can't leave your brothers for such a long time and I don't know how safe it would be for a woman to travel that far by herself." Matka took another sip of coffee, and Joe noticed her hand trembling slightly. "Not that I wouldn't give my right arm to go and find her. Perhaps I could ask Aunt Hattie if she would take care of the boys . . ."

"I'm sorry, Matka. I guess I'm not explaining myself very well. I meant that we could ask Uncle Feliks to make the trip. He has no wife or children, and I heard he was having some trouble at the plant."

"Do you think he'd do it?" Matka asked. "And what kind of trouble?"

"Oh, just some bad politics with a foreman . . . I'll ask him tomorrow."

A short visit to his uncle would be all that was needed. Joe was sure he'd be happy for a reason to leave the city for a while. Two thousand dollars was a year and a half salary to his uncle, and Joe was sure his uncle wouldn't have a tenth of the debt. The gang wouldn't hold out much longer for payment; Joe's uncle or not, and the betrayed foreman was just waiting for the right moment to have him fired, killed, or both.

Matka agreed that Joe should ask his uncle to make the trip back to Poland, and she grew excited at the prospect of being reunited with her sister. Joe pulled his wallet out to pay the bill and they gathered the boys from the lobby and took the car back home. That evening they played some new records Joe had bought on his way home from the barbershop, and Joe and Matka laughed as they watched the boys dance in the living room.

"I'd like to take Frank to Electric Park today, if that's all right," he asked Matka after breakfast the next day.

"I'll pack you a lunch," she replied, getting up from the table to do the dishes.

"I'll buy us lunch, Matka."

"You are not going to waste money on eating out again," she replied and began to pull out food from the icebox. Half an hour later Joe and Frank were walking toward Woodward to catch the bus. Frank was giddy with enthusiasm, making Joe recall his own excitement when they had walked to Woodward for the first time to catch the streetcar to the Boblo docks. When the double-decker bus pulled up to the curb, Joe thought Frank would burst.

A giant wooden windmill greeted them at the park entrance, and an electric sign blinked The Boardwalk—Just for Fun! Joe bought several tickets for the rides at the ticket booth, and they went inside. The day was cooler, thankfully, and the breeze from the river cooled the park even more.

They walked through the rides trying to decide which one to go on first.

"Let's go on the Big Dipper, Joe!" Frank ran toward the line for the rollercoaster. They sat down in a small car, and Frank grabbed the metal bar in the front of the cart. Frank screamed as the car climbed up to the pinnacle of the first hill and started to descend. Joe laughed and grabbed his shoulder, holding him in the seat.

Next they rode the Ferris wheel, the aerial swings, and another coaster called the Bobs. Frank pointed excitedly at ride after ride, saying, "How about that one Joe? Can we ride it next?" Joe let Frank lead the way, and they rode every ride in the park. Finally, at two o'clock Frank's growling stomach overcame his enthusiasm, and they found a place to eat their lunch near the water. Munching on cold sandwiches and potato chips they watched the large ships traveling up and down the river.

"What'd you like the best, Joe?" Frank asked. "I think I liked the Whip Ride the best or maybe the Big Dipper.

"I liked the swings—it felt like we were flying over the top of everybody. You sit here, and I'll go grab us something to drink, all right?" Joe went to the concession area and purchased two Coca-Colas and two ice cream cones. As he walked back to where they had been sitting, he saw Frank talking to a scantily dressed woman. Hurrying his steps, he strode over to his brother but slowed down as he recognized the young flapper. He couldn't believe his eyes when he realized who it was. Pauline was with her but dressed in more modest attire.

"You should go see the flying trapeze man, Frank-baby," Marya was saying as he walked up. "It's the bees knees."

"The bees knees, huh?" Joe said, turning Marya's attention away from Frank.

"Oh hey, Joe," she said, smiling—or was it sneering—at him. "Nice of you to take Frank out for the day. However did you manage to get away from your important work?" Her voice was clipped yet somehow still retained a very feminine quality.

"Just have a day off, Marya. That's quite a getup you're wearing . . . does Uncle Alexy know how you're dressed?"

Marya pulled at the hem of her dress slightly and fingered her long lavalier. "Don't worry about my father, Joe. I'm an adult now, and I don't need no one watching over me. I've got a date in an hour, and I don't need you for a chaperone." Joe looked over at Pauline, who rolled her eyes and made a disgusted face.

"I don't want to watch over you, Marya. Why'd you bring Pauline if you have a date?"

"My mother made me bring her. Supposed to keep me in line or something . . . here I am all dolled up, and I gotta bring a fire extinguisher with me on my date." Marya pulled a cigarette out of silver case and lit it with a match. She took a deep drag and looked at Pauline.

"Why don't you have your date and Pauline can come with Frank and me to see the flying trapeze man? We'll meet you at eight o'clock at the Old Pier Ballroom, and we'll all go home together." Pauline smiled at Joe, silently thanking him.

"Well, isn't you the cat's meow, Joe? Thanks a lot . . . I'll see you later Pauline-baby," Mayra called, already headed off in search of her date. Joe took Frank and Pauline to the boardwalk to see the trapeze show. They stayed for a second show featuring the Great Chick— a tramp cyclist and comedian. Pauline and Frank laughed at the cyclist's antics until tears rolled down their faces. Afterward, Joe bought some more tickets, and the three rode a few more rides. They decided on hamburgers for supper and sat back down by the river to eat.

CHAPTER THIRTY

"Let's head over to the ballroom and listen to the band," Joe suggested when they'd finished. The ballroom was a beautiful round building built over the water. Detroit's best bands and orchestras vied to play there, and Joe was eager to see what band was playing. The ballroom was fiery with light, and they heard the sound of trumpets and drums as they approached. Joe found a small table near the front of the dance floor and held out a chair for his cousin to sit in. Frank, disappointed that they had to come to a "stupid dance" instead of going on the rides again, was trying not to pout. A young black waiter brought over three waters and asked if they wanted anything else to drink. Joe replied they were fine for now but tipped the young man a dollar anyway.

The Floyd Hickman orchestra was on stage, and their sound was loud, rambunctious, and fun. The eleven black men, all dressed alike, rocked, swayed, jumped, and danced as they played song after song. White couples (black patrons could only visit the park on Sunday evenings) danced to the foxtrot, the Charleston, the shimmy, and the tango until sweat poured down their faces and they had to sit one out. Beads, fringe, feathers, and sequins fell to the floor from the flappers' costumes, and a custodian dressed in white swept the floor when the band took a break so the dancers wouldn't slip on the baubles.

"What's going on with Marya?" Joe asked Pauline when Frank wasn't listening.

"She's driving my mother crazy! Our father is always at the plant—did you hear he got promoted to the line?" Joe shook his head.He hadn't heard, and he was happy for his uncle. But a pang of sadness hit him as he thought about his father and how he might have been moving up in the company if he was still here.

"Marya goes out every night, and she won't even look for a job," Pauline continued, leaning closer. She says her boyfriends will take care of her, and mother is sick with worry. Even when our dad tells her she has to stay in, she sneaks out our bedroom window and doesn't come home till it's almost light out. I don't think my parents know, but it won't be long till they figure it out." Pauline seemed relieved to share her troubles about her sister. Her shoulders relaxed slightly.

"How's she get money to go out?" Joe asked, sure he didn't want to hear the answer.

"I haven't figured it out, but she's always got new clothes and shoes. She says the boys like to give her things, and if they're giving then she's taking."

I wonder what she's giving, Joe thought.

"There's Marya now." Pauline pointed to a corner of the ballroom where Marya was surrounded by three or four men. Joe watched her pull her dress up to her thigh and grab a flask from her garter. Marya took a swig and offered it to her suitors. She looked a little tipsy, and Joe watched the men who vied for her attention. There was no denying that Marya was beautiful, but it was a shame she felt she needed to get attention by acting easy. Joe didn't mind her dress as much as her behavior. Most young women wore shorter dresses and had bobbed their hair, but there was a difference between dressing like a flapper and behaving like a jezebel.

Marya pulled out a cigarette, and the men competed to light it. When one of them struck a match and held it near her face, Joe noticed his cousin had put on heavy eye makeup since she'd left them by the river. The band gathered back on the stage and started their second set with a lively swing dance. Marya led one of the men onto the floor to dance. Joe looked across the table at his two charges. Frank had fallen asleep with his head on the table, and Pauline looked extremely uncomfortable as she watched her older sister twist and sashay around the dance floor. "Pauline, stay here with Frank. Let me see if I can get Marya to leave." Joe walked over to where his cousin was dancing and tapped on the shoulder of her partner. "May I cut in?" he asked. Before the man could answer, Joe grabbed Marya's hand and twirled her away.

"Hey . . . what's the big idea, Joe?" Marya demanded. "The song wasn't over."

"It's time to head home, Marya. Frank is asleep and Pauline wants to leave. Come on, I'll grab us a cab."

"I'm not going anywhere yet! It's not even nine o'clock. Babies stay out till nine. I'm having a good time." Marya pulled away from Joe and walked to the back of the ballroom. She reached for her flask again and took another swig. Joe grabbed the silver plated canteen and took a drink.

"Where the hell did you get this rotgut, Marya? It's been altered and diluted. Aren't you worried about Jake leg or going blind?" Jake leg was a disease that was killing or paralyzing hundreds all over the country. It was the result of drinking contaminated alcohol made from ginger root.

"Geez Joe, you're such a wet blanket. Why don't you try and have some fun? You're younger than me for the love of God. I'll set you up with one of my girlfriends and we can double date." Marya laughed and hiccupped. She was more than a little tipsy now, and Joe wanted to get her out of there.

"Sure, sounds good Marya. Why don't we talk about it on the way home?" Joe tried to grab his cousin's hand but she pulled away.

"I'm not going home now!" Marya pushed past Joe and walked back to her group of admirers. Joe returned to the table where his brother was still asleep despite the loud music. He sat down hard on the wooden chair trying to figure out his next move. He could leave her there and take Frank and Pauline home. After all it wasn't his responsibility to take care of Marya. Or he could send Frank home with Pauline in a cab and try to get her to leave in an hour or so. He sat like that for a few minutes, watching the dancers, as the music grew into a frenzy and they bobbed and jumped over the dance floor.

Just when he was going to give Pauline some money to take Frank home he saw a tall, handsome man approach Marya. It was Ziggie Selbin—newly hired by the Sugar House Gang. Ziggie's job was to manage some blind pigs and collect extortion money from local business owners, but he had ventured off on his own and had been holding up nightclubs and speakeasies up in Hamtramck. Ziggie was a mean drunk, and Joe could see by the looks of him that he'd been drinking for a while.

"Here, Pauline. Take Frank and go get a cab," he said, handing her a few dollars. "I'll go get Marya. Just tell the driver to wait at the curb till I come. This is enough to keep him happy for a few minutes." Pauline woke Frank, and Joe walked over to his sloshed cousin and Ziggie. The other men had slid away when Ziggie approached Marya; he pulled her to a dark corner of the room and was leaning in close as he whispered something in her ear. Marya laughed nervously, trying not to show her anxiety as her eyes searched around the room for help.

"Hey Marya, nadszedł czas, aby wróci do domu ," (It's time to go home) Joe said, as he approached the couple. Ziggie turned his head to see who was speaking to his new fling.

"This here girl is with me, Joe," Ziggie replied, draping his arm around Marya's shoulder and pulling her into him.

"That girl there is my cousin, Ziggie. I promised my aunt I'd have her home by nine and we're late already. Say goodnight, Marya." Joe reached out and grabbed one of Marya's hands.

"You're not ready to leave already, doll, are you?" Ziggie pulled Marya back towards him.

"Umm . . . I better be heading home" Marya slurred. Ziggie pulled a flask from his coat pocket, took a swig, and offered it to Joe.

"I'll get her home, Joe. Don't worry 'about nothing. We's just about to have us a dance, aren't we, doll?" Ziggie faltered a step and grabbed Marya's shoulder to steady himself. "Woops! Looks like I'm dancing already." He laughed uproariously.

"It'll have to be another time, Ziggie. My aunt can be a real mean woman if you make her angry. Then she'll tell my mother I got Marya home late, and I'll have *her* down my throat. I just don't need the heat. I only got a couple of days off, and I don't want the hassle of dealing with a bunch of irate women. There's plenty of pretty women here—whadda ya say?"

"What if I say no, Joe?" Ziggie pulled the front of his jacket back to reveal a .38 in the waist of his pants. Joe looked down at the weapon, smiled at Ziggie, and did the same. "All right, all right . . . no need to get so serious. Take your pretty little cousin home, Joe. I'll see you around." Ziggie stumbled off. Joe grabbed Marya and pulled her out of the ballroom.

"You're gonna get in a heap of trouble if you're not careful, Marya" was all he said as they walked to the waiting cab. Marya sat silently in the cab on the way home, while Frank and Pauline debated which rides were the best. Marya looked slightly remorseful as Joe helped her up the stairs to her house. Frank and Pauline went inside, and Joe told Marya to wait on the porch. He walked around to the back of the house to the old water pump and poured water on his handkerchief. He returned to Marya and wiped the dark charcoal off her eyes as she sat at the top of the steps.

"Thanks, Joe. Thanks for helping me out with that guy. Who is he, anyway?"

"Nobody you want to be talking to, Marya. Why don't you knock off all this going out and get a job to help out your parents? I can probably set you up with a nice salesgirl job at one of the department stores."

"I said thanks, Joe, not hey, Joe, I'd like to be a stiff and stay home every night. You have some nerve acting all morally superior . . . last time I looked I didn't see you wearing a priest collar. You run liquor into this city every day, and you're mad because I go out and have a little fun! How dare you, you pompous ass!"

"It's two different things, Marya. I'm trying to make a living. You're just out for a good time. And I'm a man; women need to behave differently."

"You're younger than me and you sound like you were born fifty years ago, Joe. Times are different now, haven't you heard? Women can vote and work and smoke and drink in bars . . . it's the 1920s not the 1820s. Lord, you sound like my parents. And don't think I'm so tipsy I didn't see you flash your gat at that gangster. Why don't you just lay off and mind your own business?" She pulled herself up from the stoop.

"Didn't think you'd listen, you crabby goat. Do me a favor. Next time you decide to go off and get liquored up, don't bring Pauline along."

Marya slammed the door behind her as she went in.

"Women!" Joe muttered under his breath, as he went into his house.

CHAPTER THIRTY ONE

The following morning, Joe woke to a driving rain and a dark gray sky. He pulled on an overcoat and headed to the Sugar House to meet with Charlie after breakfast. Charlie was sitting in his office as usual when Joe opened the door.

"Come on in, Joe. I've got some good news. Seems that bastard Cammarato isn't only a thief but an idiot too. He believed your story about the new customs agents and tried to unload your cargo in St. Clair. But he had to wait a couple of days till somebody could get there with a truck. Abe and Ray found him just sitting there on the boat with those two stupid goons. So Abe decided to sit on them and watch the loot while Ray headed back to let me know the scoop. So I tell Ray to grab Ziggie and make their way over to Cammarato's house to keep an eye out. That fat sister was hanging clothes on the line in the back when they got there, so Ziggie decided he'd go have a chat with her. Meanwhile, Ray goes in the house and busts the place up good. Ziggie don't touch the fat broad, but he scared her real good, and all the while she can hear all her china being thrown against the wall. They leave for a few hours and go to the speakeasy down the street and have a few drinks. Later, when it gets dark, Ray throws a little bottle bomb through the front window just to make sure we get our point across. Next morning I get here and the dago bastards are driving your load into our garage. Mighty considerate of them, doncha think?" Charlie reached out and clapped Joe hard on the shoulder and laughed.

"They mention anything to you about a twenty-five percent tax, Charlie?" Joe asked, relieved that his story had been corroborated and happy the cargo had been returned.

"Nope. No mention of any taxes, and they've decided to run their operations north of the city from now on, so you and Cappie shouldn't have any more problems with garlic eaters from here on out. They sure must love that fat sister of theirs." Charlie slapped his knee and laughed again. "How about I take you out tonight to my place for a few drinks before you and Cappie head back to Wyandotte?"

"Sounds great, Charlie. I'll meet you there at nine. I've just got one more thing to take care of before we take off again." He shook Charlie's large hand and headed out the door. The air was still cool, but rain fell in buckets. So Joe grabbed a cab to the Ford plant instead of taking the streetcar.

It was lunchtime by the time he reached the plant. Droves of men were heading out of the gates to find a quick drink and a bite to eat. He asked a few of the workers who passed by if they knew of his Uncle Feliks. One man told him that he usually ate at the blind pig on the corner across the street.

Joe knocked on the back door of the building. All the windows were boarded over, and the tavern appeared abandoned except for the sound of laughter and conversation that could be heard through the thin siding. Joe knocked three times on the back door, and an oval flap in the door slid open revealing one brown eye and a very thick eyebrow. Joe said, "sturgeon," the password. He heard the slide of a lock from the other side, and the door swung open. Joe walked into the dark crowded barroom. Smoke clouded his field of view, and he squinted as he searched for his uncle. He found him sitting at a back table eating his free lunch of kielbasa with a side of pickles and chips. An empty mug of beer sat in front of him, so Joe ordered two Stroh's at the bar and carried them over to the table.

"Thirsty, Uncle Feliks?" he asked, setting the glasses down.

"Hey, Joe! Thanks. What are you doing over here? You trying to get hired on at the plant? I could speak to a guy for you . . . you're a little young, but we could tell them you're older." Uncle Feliks took a long drink of beer and wiped his lips. "What are you—fourteen?"

"Almost sixteen. But I didn't come for a job, Uncle Feliks. I wanted to proposition you with an opportunity." Joe took a sip of beer and set it back down. His uncle looked at him, curious.

"Yeah? You got something on the side, Joe?"

"Nah, I don't pull any side jobs. I'm happy just working for the Sugar House . . . don't want no extra trouble. I was thinking about something else entirely. I heard you've had some bad luck lately, and I thought it might be a good time for you to head out of the city for a while." Joe reached across the table and grabbed a potato chip.

"Oh that. Don't worry about your old Uncle Feliks, Joe. Just had a bad run is all. I've got a line on a sure thing and I'll make it all back tonight."

"No one's gonna take your bet, Uncle Feliks. You owe money all over town, and the only reason you don't have two broken legs right now is because you owe most of it to the Sugar House. Besides the angry husbands that are looking to cut off your balls . . ."

His uncle winced. "What do you know about that? That's nothing for a boy to be worrying about, Joe." Uncle Feliks blushed slightly in the dark room and reached for a cigarette in his coat.

"It is when there's a price on your head. This city is smaller than you think, Uncle Feliks, and I don't need you going and getting bumped off for a measly two thousand dollars. I don't think Uncle Alexy could take it after losing . . ." Joe couldn't say *my father*. "Anyway, I've got some dough saved up, and I thought you might like to take a trip till the heat dies down. My mother misses her sister, and I'd like to find her for her. I'll buy your passage to Poland; you go back to your hometown and look for her and bring her back. I'll settle your bets. In a couple of months, everyone will have forgotten about you sleeping in occupied beds, and you can come back. Whaddaya say?"

"I don't know, Joe . . . I never really wanted to go back to Poland." He drained the last of his beer. Joe signaled to the barman to bring over two more beers, though he still had half of his first one. "I'll need to think on it for a couple days."

"No time to think. I gotta head back to work in the morning, and I have to buy your train and boat tickets today. Not sure when I'll get back to the city, and you've reached the end of the line with the Sugar House. I mean it, Uncle Feliks, I met with Mr. Leiter this morning, and he said you've run up too big of a tab to be ignored anymore." Joe finished his first beer and set the empty glass down.

Two of the Sugar House enforcers picked that moment to walk into the saloon and sit down at the bar. One looked over at his uncle with an unfriendly grin, tipped his hat, and waved. Joe looked back at the two toughs and signaled to the barkeep to give them a beer on him. They drank down their beers, tipped their hats again at Feliks, and went out the back door. Uncle Feliks looked a little shaken. Joe ordered him a third beer.

"You can pick up the tickets at my house after your shift, OK?" Joe patted his uncle on the arm. "It'll be a nice trip, and think how happy your brother's widow will be when you bring back her sister. You'll be the hero of the family, and I won't let on about our little agreement?" Uncle Feliks drained the remainder of his last beer and looked at Joe.

"You got my brother's spunk, you know that Joe? Your ma ever tell you he tried to get me to go and fight in the Great War with him?" Joe shook his head no. "'Come on, Feliks—fight for your new country,' he said. But I wouldn't go. Damn coward, I guess . . . shoulda been me that died instead of him."

"Now you can redeem yourself, Uncle. Wait till you see the party they'll throw for you when you bring back Aunt Anna! I'll see you after your shift." Joe grabbed his hat from the table and walked back out onto the street. The rain had abated, but a soft drizzle still fell. The people on the street scurried to avoid getting wet. Joe grabbed a streetcar at the corner and took it to the railroad station.

He exited the streetcar at the entrance of Roosevelt Park, the elegant processional park that led to the entrance of Michigan Central Station. Eighteen massive stories towered over the circular drive, and Joe could hear several trains pulling in and out from behind the grand station. He hurried down the tree-lined boulevard, wishing he'd stopped to buy an umbrella when the streetcar passed through the downtown shopping district. The rain had grown heavier, and he pulled up the collar of his suit coat as he walked up the steps to the station.

Joe walked through a large hall, past several boutiques, a thriving barber shop, and a restaurant, toward the ticket office.

A line of five people deep stood in front of the ticket booth, and he took his place at the back. The line moved quickly. Joe purchased one ticket for New York to depart the following morning. He then found the concierge and purchased passage to Europe for his uncle via telegram.

Tickets safely in his front pocket, he walked to the café for a quick cup of coffee. From here he could observe the crowds passing and enjoy the beautiful architecture. The large copper skylight in the vaulted ceiling provided minimal natural light on such a gray, rainy day, but the station was awash in bright electric light. Pairs of massive columns flanked the hall like soldiers in dress uniform, providing security and an air of regality. Departing passengers carrying suitcases and trunks hurried past him toward the concourse.

Blurred colors of women's dresses reflected in the marble walls, reminding Joe of the young women who had spun around the ballroom at Electric Park. The memory of his drunken cousin cussing him out on their front porch flashed in his head. Marya was really too pretty to be flaunting her body and drinking with strange men. The number of rapes and kidnappings had kept pace with the city's increase in population and illegal drinking establishments; Joe was worried something bad was going to happen to Marya if she didn't change her behavior.

Joe paid for his coffee and grabbed his hat from the chair next to him. As he placed it on his head, he saw a commotion near the long tunnel that led to the train platforms. A group of people at the entrance were vying to get closer and asking for autographs. Curious, Joe walked toward them. He climbed on the pedestal of one of the columns to see over the crowd. A tall man wearing a straw hat stood next to a very small woman in a cloche. He couldn't see their faces, but he realized who the woman was when he heard a gentleman in the crowd call her name.

"Ms. Bow! Please, over here. Can I get an autograph?" A young man was jumping up and down and shouting, trying to get the tiny woman's attention. Just then, Joe caught sight of the woman's pretty face and recalled her image from the cover of the *Photoplay* magazine that fronted the newsstands. There stood Clara Bow right before his eyes! The most famous movie actress of all time . . . the "It" girl, the woman who personified the twenties, female sexuality, frivolous fun, drinking, and the flapper. She appeared slightly disheveled and nervous in the growing crowd; her enormous brown eyes looked around anxiously for a way out. She glanced up at Joe's perch and smiled slightly. It appeared to Joe as a plea for help.

Joe jumped down and entered the mob with the confidence of a police chief at a murder investigation. He pushed the young man who was still shouting at the movie star to the side and reached Ms. Bow and her companion. He turned toward the crowd, took off his bowler hat and waved it over his head to get the attention of the throng of admirers.

"Attention! Ms. Bow has had a long trip and needs to freshen up. If you will kindly gather in the waiting room she will be happy to oblige all autograph requests in a few minutes. Please allow her a few minutes to gather her wits together." Joe crossed his fingers, hoping the crowd would acquiesce. He grabbed the beautiful star's hand and pulled her toward the ladies' powder room; her companion followed. The crowd hurriedly moved toward the waiting room, and as Joe reached the entrance to the ladies' room he turned to the actress and said, "Run!"

The three ran toward the front entrance of the train station and down the steps to a waiting cab. Joe pulled the back door open and gently pushed Clara Bow into the back seat. The tall man with her ran to the other side and jumped in. The rain had finally stopped, and the sun was trying to peek through the gray clouds.

"Jump in, brother!" Clara yelled. Joe opened the front door to the cab and pulled himself in as the cab took off down the drive. He almost fell out as the driver made a quick turn onto the avenue, but he managed to shut the passenger door. The mob had seen the trio making a run for it and had chased after them, but they made it safely away.

CHAPTER THIRTY TWO

"Hot socks—that was terrific!" Clara praised Joe from the back seat in her strong Brooklyn accent. "What's your name, brother?"

"Joey O. Sorry I pulled you so hard, Miss Bow. I hope I didn't hurt you, but that crowd was getting a little wild. I was worried you might get trampled." Joe told the cabbie to drive toward downtown. "Where you headed, Miss Bow?"

"Where we staying at, Gary? Some sorta library, I think."

Suddenly, Joe realized who Bow's companion was. Sitting in the backseat was Gary Cooper, the western movie hero; six foot four, sandy blond hair, handsome, with the body of an Olympic athlete, America's leading man.

"The Book-Cadillac Hotel," Cooper responded, almost so quietly that Joe had a hard time hearing him. For despite all his horsemanship ability, outward virility, and fame, the actor was extremely shy. Joe directed the cabbie to take them to the new hotel. The Book-Cadillac had opened only two years before, and it was the largest hotel structure in the world.

"What brings you to town, Miss Bow?" Joe asked.

"Please call me Clara, Joey O. 'Miss Bow' makes me feel like a old maid. Gee whiz, that was awful smart of ya—fooling all those people. Wasn't it Gary?"

Bow leaned into her companion and Cooper put his arm around her. Joe watched as she reached up to embrace her costar. Her short dress moved, revealing her upper thigh. She didn't seem to notice and didn't reach down to cover herself. Joe could barely move his eyes away from her porcelain skin. Joe was star struck.

"Sure was. Thanks, Joey," Cooper said. "I hate all these crowds. They make me feel like a nun in a nightclub. The studio should send security for Clara. One day she'll get mobbed, and they'll kill her out of love. Man, I hate these press junkets."

"Oh sugar, don't be so dramatic." Bow responded. "We's fine as wine." Clara gave him a kiss on the cheek, leaving a dark red lip print, and turned her attention back to Joe. "We're here to open our new movie tonight at the Fox Theatre. Why dontcha come and see it? I'll leave a ticket for ya at will call." Bow reached into her handbag and pulled out a flask. "Sure could use a drinky-poo after all that hullabaloo." She took a quick drink and offered it to Gary Cooper, who took a swig and then handed it to Joe. Joe took a sip and spit it out on the floor of the cab.

"That's some awful rotgut, Miss—I mean Clara. You shouldn't be drinking that cheap imitation. Why don't we make a quick stop before I drop you at the hotel and get you some real stuff?" Joe felt more at ease now . . . bootleg liquor was his life.

"Why sure, Joey. That's awful nice of him, isn't it Gary?" Bow pulled off her hat, shook her bright red hair, and fluffed it out with her hands. "Didn't know folks were so hospitable in Detroit, did we, sugar?" Cooper only smiled and nodded and looked out the window of the cab at the busy city. Joe gave the cabbie the address of the Sugar House and turned back to look at the beautiful woman-child in the back seat. Bow moved and fidgeted, constantly in a state of motion. Her tiny hands dotted the air as she spoke, and her wide eyes looked about the cab and out the windows, never stopping to rest long on any item or person.

"I saw you both in *Wings* earlier this year. You were both terrific. Actually saw it twice." Joe was referring to the aerial war movie that had played to sold out houses all over the country.

"Isn't that sweet of ya? That's where sugar and I met, right, Gary? Them was some hot nights filming in Texas, wasn't they?" Bow pulled on Cooper's collar, unbuttoning his top button. He blushed and pulled away slightly.

"Clara, let's get somewhere a little more private before you start all that." He smiled and, taking his arm from her shoulders, held her hand.

"Always so proper . . . keeps me in line, he does. Can't stand all the attention, but he became a movie star. Funny baby." She pulled on Cooper's ear and sat back in the seat to look at Joe. "Course you're a mighty fine looking kid yourself. I could get you a bit part in my next movie if you wanna come out to Hollywood, Joey O."

"Aww . . . no thanks, Miss—I mean Clara. I'm not the acting sort. I'm just your average working Joe."

"I'm jest a working girl myself, Joey O." The cab pulled up to the Sugar House. "This where ya work?"

"Kinda . . . you wanna come in? I'm sure my bosses would get a kick outta you coming to the office. They don't like visitors ordinarily, but I'm sure they'll make an exception in your case." Clara looked around at the street and thought for a moment.

"Why not? Seems like the least I could do, seeing as ya saved my hindquarters back there and you're getting us some good hooch. Come on Gary, baby— let's give them a thrill."

Joe gave the cabbie a five dollar bill to wait for them, jumped out of the cab, and opened the door for Bow and Cooper. He led them up the narrow wooden stairs to the small waiting room outside the office. Joe told them to wait there for a minute while he told his boss about their visit. He opened the door and saw Charlie and Shorr bent over the desk discussing profit margins.

"Sorry to interrupt, but I brought you a new customer," Joe said, shutting the door behind him.

"Whadda ya mean, you brought us a new customer? We don't bring customers here, you ignorant immigrant." Shorr stared at Joe angrily.

"I think you'll make an exception for this one." Joe smiled. Charlie looked at Joe's flushed face and bright eyes.

"Who is it, Joey O?" Charlie asked.

"No one but a Miss Clara Bow and Mr. Gary Cooper . . . saw them getting off the train at the station, and they almost got mobbed to death so I helped them grab a cab. They're in need of some good hooch, so I thought you might like a personal appearance. Seeing as all of her movie characters encourage drinking, dancing, and jazz, she's been awful good for our business, I'd say." Shorr and Charlie stared at

Joe, unbelieving. Then Charlie sorta snapped out of it and told him to bring them in.

Clara sashayed into the office followed by Gary Cooper. Her perfect hourglass shape was set off in a tight ivory dress of lace and satin. "How do you do, boys? Thanks for having me. This boy of yours is all right . . . got us out of a tough spot." Clara walked over to Shorr and put her hand on his forearm. She twinkled her enormous eyes at Shorr, and Joe thought he almost blushed.

"Have a seat, Miss Bow," Shorr said, pulling out a chair. "Mr. Cooper?" he asked. Gary declined, and Joe leaned his back against the wall and laughed to himself as he watched his two tough bosses dance around the room, pulling out glasses and bottles of whisky. Ten minutes later, kisses planted on the cheeks of Shorr and Charlie and Joe carrying a case of whisky labeled as fruit, they headed back down to the cab. Clara Bow had charmed, teased, and flirted with the Sugar House bosses, and Gary Cooper had not appeared the least bit jealous. Perhaps it was an act or the handsome actor was just used to Clara's way with men, or maybe it was the several shots of good whisky warming his belly, but Gary appeared to take no notice of Clara's brazenness.

The bosses gave Clara Canadian Club whisky just the way it came from the distillery. But the Sugar House had begun cutting their liquor at various spots across the city to increase their profits. Only the highest end (and highest paying) customers received the unadulterated whisky.

"See ya, baby," Clara called when Joe dropped them at the front door of the Book-Cadillac Hotel. Clara leaned in the passenger window and gave Joe a big kiss on the cheek. "I'll leave that ticket at will call, Joey O."

The taxi pulled away from the curb into the traffic. Joe could still smell the Chanel No. 5 she'd worn. He fantasized about being with a woman of such great beauty and verve. The cab felt empty now, as if a tornado had sucked the air out of it, and there was the eerie silence that followed all fantastic, violent storms.

He ate dinner in silence as his brothers yammered, argued, and fought for his attention. Occasionally he'd nod or grunt, but Frank and Stephan didn't notice that his attention was elsewhere. He ate two fried pork chops, washing down the greasy meat with a large glass of milk, and thanked his mother for the meal. After his brothers were excused from the table to play outside, he stood next to Matka at the sink, drying the dishes she washed.

"Uncle Feliks said he'd be happy to go to Poland to find Anna," he said, wiping a small bowl with the towel.

"Really, Joe? Oh my! I can't believe I'm going to see Anna again." She dropped the dish she'd been washing and hugged him with glee.

"He's leaving on a train in the morning for New York." Joe smiled with pride and then stopped as he looked into Matka's face. Her eyes dimmed as if the sun had passed behind a cloud.

"Why are you upset, Matka?" he asked, as he picked up the shards of the broken dish and threw them in the rubbish bin.

"I'm just surprised that he's leaving in the morning. I would have liked to buy Anna a present and something for your Uncle Feliks's trip. The stores will be closing, and there isn't any time now."

"Sure there is, Matka. I'll run down the street and find a cab to take you to Hudson's. Take this money and find a nice present for Aunt Anna." Deliberately not mentioning Uncle Feliks, who was costing him half of his savings, he held out a fifty-dollar bill.

"Thank you, Joe, but no. I have money saved from my sewing. I'll walk down to Woodward and find a cab myself. Oh dear, I'm such a mess," she said patting at her hair and her simple dress.

"You look beautiful. Hurry now. I'll keep an eye out for the boys and grab a quick shower while you're gone." Matka pulled off her apron, grabbed a small hat to pull over her golden hair, and darted out the door.

After a cool shower, Joe stood in front of the bathroom mirror examining his face. The shave from a few days before appeared to be holding up fine. Apparently his beard hadn't heard that the rest of him was doing the work of a grown man. His shoulders had widened though, and the muscles on his arms and chest were defined and tight from the years of lifting cases out of boats. Joe flexed his biceps several times and laughed at himself. Hair combed back with pompadour oil, cologne applied to all the right areas, and dressed to the nines, he decided that a little facial hair didn't make a difference one way or another. After all, the most beautiful woman in the world had asked to meet him at the theater. Who cares if her boyfriend would be there too?

Joe left for the Fox Theatre when his mother returned from her shopping trip. All smiles and worrying how to wrap her gifts, she sent him out the door without even a question as to his plans. The marquee lights shining from the Fox could be seen from half a mile down the street. An enormous crowd had gathered in front of the majestic theater. Joe worried that Clara might have forgotten to leave a ticket for him. But the ticket agent handed him an envelope containing the ticket and a note from the star.

For Joey O, the real McCoy! Thanks for the giggle water . . . hope you enjoy the show!

Love, Clara

The note was written in big, loopy letters at the bottom of her picture. Joe carefully rolled up the picture and placed it in his front coat pocket. A dark-skinned man in a sharp red uniform opened the door to the theater and ushered him inside. The lobby was more like a ballroom in a castle than a theater lobby. Gold leaf gleamed from every surface, accented by stones that appeared to Joe to be rubies, emeralds, and diamonds. Dashing men and pretty ladies traversed up and down a great staircase that led to the balconies. The top hats and tall, feathered headbands bobbing through the masses on the heads of the movie goers made it look as if exotic animals were performing a mating ritual.

An usher led Joe to a seat on the left side of the balcony. A great gold lion peered down at the rows of seats from above the stage curtain, and a fifty-piece orchestra played a lively rendition of "She's Got It," a song inspired by Clara Bow's movie, "*It*," released earlier that year. The lights dimmed twice, and the young crowd took their seats. The great scarlet curtain slowly opened and Clara Bow appeared, sans Gary Cooper, in the beam of the spotlight. Sparkles of light reflected from the thousands of silver beads that hung from her backless dress, as if she were the origin of all the constellations in the sky. Her fiery red hair had been smoothed and curled, and she looked almost demure as she stood alone on the large stage waiting for the applause to quiet down.

Another spotlight appeared, stage right, and Gary Cooper walked across the stage to join her as the applause roared again. Cooper handed her a massive bouquet of flowers and was rewarded with a big kiss right on the lips. A few rows back, Joe heard a gasp from a woman shocked at such brazen behavior in public. Joe rolled his eyes. What did she expect at a Clara Bow movie? Clara leaned down and said something to the orchestra conductor. He turned to his musicians and waved his baton. They began to play "Gimme a Little Kiss, Will Ya, Huh?" Whispering Jack Smith had recorded the song the year prior, and it had topped the music charts.

A bright light illuminated the aisle, and Joe saw a quartet in candy cane–striped seersucker jackets standing abreast, straw boaters in hand, facing the stage. They harmonized the famous lyrics as they made their way toward the stage.

Gimme a little kiss, will ya, huh?
What are you gonna miss, will ya, huh?
Gosh, oh gee, why do you refuse
I can't see what you've got to lose.

Oh, gimme a little squeeze, will ya, huh?
Why do you wanna make me blue?
I wouldn't say a word if I were asking for the world
But what's a little kiss between a fellow and his girl?

Oh, gimme a little kiss, will ya, huh?
And I'll give it right back to you!"[2]

Clara Bow danced lightly to the serenade. She grabbed Gary Cooper's hand and twirled herself around his towering body. Flashes of skin and beads reflected in the stage lighting, and the crowd applauded loudly, approving of Clara's overpowering sex appeal and lighthearted teasing. Sultry and elegantly feminine, Clara sang a quick verse back to the singing suitors. Joe looked to see where the voice was coming from, for it certainly could not be Clara. In the cab, her Brooklynese had been rough and tough like the gangsters he worked for. This arresting voice was definitely not Clara's, but there she stood, singing and teasing, an exaggerated swing of hips and shoulders tantalizing the already raucous crowd.

Gimme a little coat, will ya, huh?
Sable, or mink or goat Will ya huh?
You know my poor hands are as bare as anything
I could stand a little bracelet maybe a diamond ring

Gimme a little car will ya huh
That would be might nice to do
A Packard or a Lincoln or a Cadillac sedan
Why I'll even take a Rolls and you can add a chauffeur man
But if you give me a little Ford I'll give a kiss right back to you.

The audience stood, clapping, stomping, and whistling as Clara finished the last note, for she had replaced the last line of the lyrics with a crowd-pleasing love-my-Ford reference. The original anti-Detroit lyric—"But don't you give me a little Ford or I'll give it right back to you"—would have offended the many people who relied on Ford for their livelihoods. Clara Bow knew her audience. She wiggled her svelte hips and blew a kiss to the audience, and they continued cheering as she and Gary Cooper took their bows and exited the stage.

The lights dimmed, and the auditorium was dark except for the soft illumination of the ushers' small flashlights as the movie began. Clara Bow appeared as Kitty, a young flapper who tricked her childhood sweetheart into marrying her on a drunken night, at the behest of her avaricious mother, who pressured her to marry for money. The sight of Clara rolling around in a giant bed, her dark, full eyelashes batting at wealthy, despondent Ted Larrabee (Gary Cooper) caused a hot flush of hormones to run through Joe. He looked around to see if anyone could read his thoughts. He blushed at his naivety. Sensing a movement in the alcove walkway near his seat, he peered through the darkness, trying to decipher the situation. His hand reached down to where he had strapped his .38 to his ankle.

Quietly he removed the weapon and placed it under the hem of his sports coat. His neighbors did not notice. Joe looked behind him slowly, wishing he had the eyes of a bat or some other nocturnal creature. Murder attempts were common in theaters, but not in places as crowded as the Fox was tonight. Occasionally a sleeper—a body—would be found when the lights went up and the ushers began sweeping out the rows of seats, the cause of death either strangulation or a stab wound to the back. Theater owners had started installing seats with steel frames to prevent the stabbings, but thugs circumvented them by simply strangling their victims.

The orchestra played on, accompanying Clara's antics on the screen; and the audience shouted out phrases of lust or laughter. But Joe heard nothing other than the beating of his heart. Was it the River Gang? Had they played Charlie, duping him into a false agreement with the intentions of getting revenge on Joe? Or maybe Charlie had duped Joe? It wouldn't be the first time a gangster had lied to one of his own men only to have him knocked off at an unsuspecting moment. Joe saw the movement again and let out a long low sigh. It was only two little boys who must have snuck in and had found an ideal hiding spot to watch the racy movie. On pins and needles now, the magic gone, Joe returned his weapon to its holster and decided to leave the theater.

Glancing at his new Elgin wristwatch he noted he was half an hour late to meet Charlie at the speakeasy. He rushed out the shiny brass doors of the theater and looked down at his watch again. Thump! His shoulder slammed into a gentleman who'd been waiting for a cab outside.

"I'm so sorry, sir; I was looking down" Joe began apologizing, "Hey! You're Ty Cobb! Oh, I'm so sorry, Mr. Cobb." The tall lanky man brushed off the shoulder of his suit coat and looked down at Joe.

"What are you in such a hurry for?" Cobb drawled. "Fire in the theater?" he joked. Joe was so relieved his hero wasn't angry with him.

"No sir—just late to a meeting is all. Mr. Cobb? I'd just like to say that I saw you at the game when you broke the record for the most stolen bases. You were terrific!"

"Thanks, young man. But I never run that fast on the sidewalks, so I'd suggest slowing down off the baseball diamond." Cobb tuned to hail a cab. Joe thought quickly.

"Mr. Cobb? Would you mind signing an autograph for me? Please?"

"Sure. You have any paper?" Joe reached into his pocket and pulled out the picture Clara had left for him at the will-call booth.

"Will this do?" he asked.

"The real McCoy, huh? Seems like you have friends in high places." He signed the back of the photograph. "Goodnight, McCoy." Then he got into his cab and drove off.

CHAPTER THRITY THREE

Hailing a cab was difficult on a Friday night, and it was more than fifteen minutes before one finally pulled to the curb. Joe hoped the surprise visit by Bow and Cooper at the Sugar House would provide a small leeway for his tardiness. His thoughts drifted to the sight of Clara's silky white thigh he'd glimpsed in the back seat of the cab earlier that day.

The cabbie roared to a stop at 121 Davenport. Joe paid the fare and got out. The smell of cigar smoke wafted through the air, creating a foggy atmosphere inside the Powhatan Club. The bar was nearly empty. Most patrons didn't arrive until after midnight. Joe easily found Charlie sitting at the end of the bar. A fine, expensive hat sat next to a full beer on the wooden bar. Joe placed his hat next to Charlie's and took a seat.

"Ah, Joey O . . . here ya are? Beer?" he asked, signaling to the barkeep.

"I think I could use something a little stronger, Charlie," Joe replied, feathers still ruffled at the thought of the River

Gang possibly tracking him. Charlie looked at Joe out the side of his eye, concerned.

"Everything Jake?" he asked.

"Sure, sure Charlie . . . just been a long day is all. Oh, I spoke to my uncle, and I'll have the dough for you tomorrow morning before Cappie and I set off for Wyandotte."

"Good, good. Hey Wes, set my boy up with some of that ten year Canadian Club. He's been out courting celebrities all day. She wear you out, Joe?"

The barkeep set two fingers of whisky in front of Joe.

Joe took a slow sip and set the glass back down. "Like I can compete with Gary Cooper! Nah, I got the heebie-jeebies at the theater, and I started thinking about those damn dagos. You sure everything's on the level with them?" Joe didn't like to ask questions, but he didn't like to imagine the feel of a cold blade on his throat either.

"Doncha worry about them dagos, Joe. Just relax and let's have some fun. I got Art Mooney's Rhythm Kings coming in to play tonight, and I wanna have a good time. Drinks are on me tonight. Least I can do after you helped get that hijacked load back and introduce me to the 'It' girl. Hot damn, does that doll got some gams! Tell me again how you came about having her in your cab." Joe related the story to Charlie and then again as he was introduced to several more men by his boss. A dopey looking fellow named Harry, with wiry black hair, challenged his tale, saying Joe was making it up. Eyes squinted against the smoke, Joe replied he was telling the truth so help him God. Harry laughed and said God who? Charlie stepped in to back Joe, and the situation deescalated. Feeling foolish that he'd let the thug get to him so easily, Joe switched back to beer and ordered some dinner.

The band came in around midnight and set up at the end of the small dance floor. The smoke grew thicker, mixing with the smells of perfume and baby powder in the air. Did every girl who wanted to be a flapper have to wear Chanel No. 5? Joe's one lung felt like it was working overtime in the hazy atmosphere. Money flew over the bar, and beer and whisky poured back out like Niagara Falls. Joe was a little tipsy and was thankful he'd had the sense to eat a good meal. Cappie joined the group just as the band began to play, and Charlie made Joe retell yet again the train station Clara Bow story. The men grew louder and more boisterous and were joined by several ladies who noticed the large amount of cash the group was throwing about.

Blondes and brunettes, tall and short, skinny and chunky drew near like moths to a flame. Charlie had his hand on the rump of a pretty-looking Greek girl, and Cappie was holed up in the corner with a curvy strawberry blonde absorbed in an intense petting session. Couples swayed and danced to the pulsating jazz as the black band sweated and played on and on. A very fair mulatto girl approached Joe and tried to sit on his lap. Flattered and embarrassed, he grabbed her waist and tried to gently push her off. He almost fell to the floor himself. The beer was definitely going to his head now. The girl laughed, and Joe noticed how white her pretty teeth were when she smiled. Joe tried to get the barkeeper's attention to order her another drink. The room grew quieter, and several men stood on the bar rail, craning their necks toward the door. A flash of blonde hair, several low whistles, and Joe was off his seat, pushing past the exotic-looking siren next to him and forcing his way through the boisterous crowd to the back of the bar.

"Damn, I knew it was you, Marya. You can't be in here, you dumb dame . . . the place is full of gangsters and thugs." He grabbed her hand and pulled her outside before any of the Sugar House gang got an eyeful of Marya in her skintight dress. Joe was furious.

"So I guess that's why you's in there, Joe?" she slurred. "Which one is you? Gangster or thug?" That Marya was well past drunk was obvious to Joe despite his own inebriated state. He tried holding her up by her elbow but she pulled away and fell onto the filthy sidewalk. He tried to help her up again, but she just laughed and lay on the sidewalk staring up at the sky. Her dress rose up above her thighs and he quickly reached to pull it down, trying to cover her.

"You can't lie here on the sidewalk, Marya . . . come on, get up!" Several passersby stopped to stare.

"I'll take you home, honey" one bristly fellow offered. "She is *ossified*!" said another. The gawkers erupted in cackles and guffaws. Joe managed to pull her up to a standing position and, holding her around the waist with one arm, dragged her to the side of the building, away from the spectators. He leaned her against the brick wall, and she slowly slid down, landing on her caboose.

"Damn you, Marya! Doncha know those are not the sorts of guys you can fool around with? Don't you gotta brain in your head?" Marya looked up at Joe and shot her best wad of spit onto his cheek. Howling, she held her stomach and hiccupped. Joe wiped the saliva from his face with his handkerchief. "Who were you out with tonight, Marya? Did someone drop you off here?" Marya either couldn't comprehend or wouldn't answer. *How*, he wondered, *could he leave her here on the side of the building and go get a cab?*

Just then Cappie came around the corner of the speakeasy looking for Joe. "There ya are. I wondered where you . . . hey who's this?" Cappie said, noticing Marya giggling on the ground.

"This, Sir Cappie, is my lovely cousin, Marya."

Cappie crouched down next to Marya and held her chin in his hand. He turned Marya's pretty face from side to side and she tried to open her eyes to look back at him.

"She looks like a beautiful baby dove that fell from her nest. Come on, baby dove; let Cappie help you back to your nest." He gently pulled her from the cigarette littered dirt and picked her up in his arms. "Joe, grab a cab and I'll meet you at the street."

Joe hailed yet another cab and whistled to Cappie, who appeared from around the corner of the building carrying Marya as if she were a child. She'd put her arm around the back of his neck and passed out. Cappie softly placed her in the cab, and Joe came around to the other side. "Can you get her in the house, Joe?" he asked. Joe looked down at his sleeping cousin and shrugged.

"If she doesn't wake up, I've got a chance. She's mean as a snake when she's drunk. I'm not Marya's favorite relative, to say the least."

Cappie looked around the street and back at the bar. "I've had enough for tonight anyway. It's getting a little wild in there now. Wouldn't be surprised if the coppers show up for a raid, as loud is it is. I'll help you get her home."

"But what about that good-looking Sheba you were necking with?"

"She's just looking for a Daddy . . . thinks I'm rolling in the dough." Cappie got into the front seat of the cab.

"She was trying to rub up against my front pocket to see how big a roll of green I had. Damn floozies. I've had enough of that juice joint for tonight."

When they arrived at the front of Joe's house, Cappie picked up Marya and carried her up the porch steps. Joe quietly opened the front door of Marya's house, and Cappie set her on the living room couch. "They got an extra blanket down here?" he whispered.

"Geez, Cappie, who cares? We got her home. That's good enough." Joe was getting a headache from all the tap beer, and he was fed up with dragging his cousin home at the end of his rare nights out. Two nights in one week! He'd be glad to get back downriver and back to work. Let his aunt and uncle worry about what Marya was out doing.

"She's your family, Joe," Cappie said quietly.

Rolling his eyes and shaking his head, Joe reached around in the darkness and found a crocheted afghan. He handed it to Cappie. He placed it over Marya's small sleeping frame, tucking the top under her chin.

"Good. The blanket will catch the drool that rolls down her chin. Are you happy? I wantta get outta here before my uncle wakes up." Cappie looked nervously up the stairs. He nodded and followed Joe to the hallway, but just as they reached the doorframe, Cappie slammed his head on the bottom of it, causing an enormous thud. He'd forgotten to duck in his hurry to leave. A light went on at the top of the stairs. They both lit out of the hall, down the stairs, and into the waiting cab.

"You should have seen your face when you hit your big pumpkin head on that doorframe!" Tears of laughter poured down Joe's cheeks.

“Shut up, Joe. I just didn’t want your uncle to come after me with a shotgun is all.” Cappie hunkered down in the back of the cab, crossing his muscular arms across his chest. “Hey, why’d you jump in here, anyway? You should have run into your house.”

Joe broke up laughing again. “I guess that scared look on your face cleared out my brain for a minute.” He turned to the cabbie. “Just drive around to the alley. I’ll sneak in the back door.” He said goodnight to Cappie and jumped over the small backyard fence. He saw the glow of lights in his cousin’s house and heard a loud voice and then Marya yelling as he walked up the back steps. *Oh well, that’s her kettle of fish*, he thought. He walked up the stairs and passed out in his clothes on top of his bed.

CHAPTER THIRTY FOUR

1928

Joe pulled into the boathouse and turned off the engine. Cappie was standing on the dock with another man, talking and smiling that funny grin that made you think of a teenage boy watching his first peep show at the circus. Joe threw the rope to his co-worker. Cappie tied it to the dock and winched the boat up out of the water.

"Hiya Joe!" the stranger called. Joe looked over and saw that it was his Uncle Feliks. It had been almost a year since he had handed him the train ticket to New York that Saturday morning after the crazy night with Clara Bow and Marya.

"Uncle Feliks!" he called, jumping out of the boat and embracing him in a bear hug. "When did you get back? How are you? How did you find me? Did you find Aunt Anna?"

"Hold on, Joe" he smiled. "Let's go inside and get a cup of java and I'll explain everything." Cappie said he'd unload the haul and for Joe to go inside with his uncle. They entered through the secret basement door and walked up the narrow steps. Joe looked around, slightly ashamed at the bachelor pad he and Cappie had been living in. Dirty dishes lay in the sink, on the table, and on the floor, surrounded by old clothes and fishing equipment. Newspapers were stacked on the couch and on the dining room table. Joe cleared a spot for his uncle to sit at the table and tried to find two clean coffee cups. Finding none, he washed two in the sink while the coffee brewed.

"Sorry for the mess, Uncle Feliks. I guess we've been slipping on the housework. They've got us making three runs a night now, and we sleep most of the day. So, are you just back today?"

"No, I've been here a couple weeks. I've been staying with your ma and your brothers." Uncle Feliks looked much thinner but healthier than when Joe had seen him last. His cheeks were tan and his clothes neat and ironed, but his light blue eyes had an aura of sadness about them.

"Joe, I want to thank you for what you did for me. I don't think I showed you the proper amount of appreciation at the time. I was angry that my nephew was helping me out, and I was embarrassed at the situation I had put myself in. I almost didn't go to New York. Oh, I planned on getting on that train with the tickets you had bought but I was going to jump off somewhere east of here and try starting fresh." Uncle Feliks took a sip of the bitter coffee and set it down on the table. He looked out at the river. The sun, just rising above it, created a rosy hue on the water.

"So I was sitting there on the train and trying to figure out the best place to get off when the train stopped. This young woman with two children came up the aisle and sat down next to me. She was traveling back to New York also, and we started talking and I played with her kids to help her keep them occupied. She said her name was Jenney and she was taking a ship back to Europe to meet her husband. They had come to the United States to find the American dream but her husband had missed his native country and had gone back after the war to set up a business and house and he'd sent for her now that he was established."

Joe's stomach grumbled and he smiled at his uncle. "Are you hungry?"

"I could eat."

Joe got up from the table and put a frying pan on the stove to heat. Then he started on the dishes while his uncle continued his story.

"Well, she was worried about traveling all the way to New York alone and then across the ocean with her two little daughters. After a few hours of talking with her, and sharing a lunch she had brought I offered to accompany her. Her ticket for Europe was for the same ship you had booked me on Joe. I thought it was God's way of telling me I needed to follow through with what you and I had agreed to. So, we arrived in New York and then we boarded the ship together. We were both in second class; thank you, by the way, for that, Joe. I wandered down to third and what a sight! Anyway, we passed the days eating meals together and me playing with the girls. She was a kind lady and a very good mother. When the ship reached port we said our goodbyes and I felt rejuvenated—like a new man with a second chance at life. I decided I'd follow through with my promise to you and go find my sister-in-law and bring her back to America."

Joe threw six eggs in the iron skillet with a dab of butter and placed white bakers' bread into the electric toaster

Cappie had bought last month. Cappie came up the stairs, and the men sat down to eat at the now clean kitchen table. Cappie pulled out three cans of peaches and poured them in bowls, reminding Joe of the time he had first eaten canned peaches on the ride to Amherstburg. Cappie said he'd do the dishes when he woke up and headed off to bed. Joe smiled knowingly at his uncle and got up and did the dishes while his uncle continued his story.

"It took me two weeks to make my way to Jastarnia. That whole continent still looks like the war just ended last week, Joe. You wouldn't believe it if I told you. Ancient buildings reduced to piles of rubble, people living in shacks and tents alongside the roads. If you can call them roads. More like paths of mud. I wasn't sure what I'd find in Jastarnia, but the village looked the same as when Alexy, your parents, and I left. Fewer people, quieter, but the buildings were the same, and the church still stood. Feeling like I was starting over to live a good man's life, I went to the old church first seeking confession. There was a young priest there. He didn't remember our family, but he was happy to listen to my sins. After I told him about all the drinking and gambling and, er, women, he gave me absolution and asked why I'd returned. I told him about your aunt, and he asked me to meet him at the front pew of the church. I figured he knew right where she was, and as I opened the door to the confessional I thought about the party your Ma was going to throw me when I presented Anna at your front door."

Joe finished the dishes and made some more coffee. He sat back down at the table to give his uncle his full attention. Joe smiled at Uncle Feliks and poured some more coffee into his cold cup. "The priest had come to the parish only a year before, after the war had long ended. He was trying to unite the town again, as they had lost the sense of community that a fishing village must have to survive. The war had been hard on everyone in Jastarnia, and the people had formed tight-knit groups of immediate family members to survive. In the last days of the war the Prussians had become desperate, realizing the Allies were going to win. The soldiers who had taken over the village decided to flee in the middle of the night, while the people of the village slept. They feared for their lives, expecting a violent retribution from the townspeople. The soldiers had become extremely cruel to the villagers after we made our way to America. They stole their food, raped their women, and beat and killed the men who fought to protect their families. The lieutenant who forced your aunt to marry him was the ringleader, and all despised him. It was he who was leading the exodus, and he decided he could not leave without Anna. Knowing she wouldn't come willingly and his fellow comrades would not consent to dragging a hostile, struggling woman with them, he was at a crossroads."

Joe's eyes grew wide, fearing the end of his uncle's tale.

"The lieutenant cut off all her hair and made her dress in an old uniform of his. He told Anna if she fought him he'd kill her and then come to America and find her family and murder them. He had her pull the cap of her uniform down to her eyes, hoping that in the darkness the other soldiers would not realize she was his wife. They reached the forested hill behind the village, the rendezvous spot where his troops had convened, and he stood in the middle of the group giving directions and orders. Anna silently moved from his side to the outer circle of the group. All the young soldiers were nervous with anxiety and were listening intently to the lieutenant as if his words were their path to safety. She jostled one of the soldiers, lifting his gun from its holster, unawares to him. Anna walked directly into the middle of the circle where the lieutenant was still giving his orders and shot him point blank in the face."

Joe let out a gasp and clapped his hands together. He smiled. But he saw a tear form in the corner of his uncle's eye, and his heart dropped.

Uncle Feliks shook his head and continued. "Anna started to run past the dead lieutenant, trying to make a break for the village; but one of the soldiers fired at her and shot her in the back. They left her there and scattered like mice in an attempt to flee as they had planned. Your aunt lay there for hours, bleeding from her wound, cold on the mossy ground until the sun rose and the villagers came out of their homes to decipher the cause of the gunshots heard in their cottages the night before. They found her lying five feet from the evil man who had forced her to become his wife, pieces of his brain matter and skull within arm's length of her. There were no signs of the other Prussian soldiers except their footprints in the dirt. Two fishermen carried her back to the village and set her on the steps of the church. They could tell by her rasping breaths that she didn't have long on this earth, so they believed last rites would be more propitious than a doctor. The old priest, the same who had baptized her and your mother, was awakened from his sleep. He performed the ritual right there on the church steps. She whispered that she had killed the lieutenant.

She asked for absolution. He granted it to her and thanked her for ridding the world of such evil."

Tears poured from Joe's eyes as his uncle finished the story. What a horrible life his aunt had had to endure in the hands of the lieutenant. And then, days before she would have been free at last from his terrible grasp—for the war would have ended and she surely would have been able to escape him then—she is killed in the same grove of trees his mother had told him she and her sister had played in for hours, watching for their father to return from the sea. Joe was thankful his aunt had received absolution, but a wave of guilt passing over him. He couldn't recall the last time he'd been to church. The tragedy of Anna's sad life was too disconcerting for words.

"I know what you're thinking, Joe, but no. Your thinking if she'd only gone along with the soldiers for a couple of days; if she'd just stayed quiet, perhaps she could have survived till the end of the war. But the troops would have realized that it was her in disguise the minute the sun rose. You see, the lieutenant was mad with desire for Anna. In his desperate desire to keep her with him, he couldn't think clearly. His militia would have insisted on her death immediately upon her discovery . . . especially in their state of heightened anxiety as they tried to make their way back to their homeland.

"I'm so sorry, Joe. I'm sorry I couldn't bring your mother's sister back to her. The young priest took me to where the villagers buried her in the church graveyard. They erected an elegant tombstone in honor of her. I etched a copy for your mother and gave it to her. I had it framed, and she has it hanging in the hallway of your home. It says:

Anna Sczytski
Silna i Piekna
Ukochany corka, siostra I Matka

Joe listened to his uncle and looked out onto the gray rushing river. Now he would never meet his mother's cherished sister. What a waste. At least she had a headstone.

"Wait! Mother? The tombstone said 'Beloved Sister and Mother!" Joe cried, looking at his uncle.

"Yes, Anna had a little girl. She's four years old. That was the other reason Anna had shot the lieutenant and tried to escape back to the village. She couldn't leave her little girl behind with no one to care for her. A neighbor of Anna's brought her little girl to the church steps and Anna got to embrace her and say goodbye before she took a final breath and died on the doorstep of her Maker."

Joe jumped up from his seat and grabbed his uncle and pulled him out of his chair. "Did you bring her here? Did you bring my cousin to America?"

Uncle Feliks laughed and pulled Joe off of him.

"Yes, yes, Joe. Katalina is with your mother as we speak. Let's take a walk down by the water, and I'll finish my story."

The men walked to the river and sat in two rickety wicker chairs while Uncle Feliks told the rest of the tale.

Feliks retrieved Katalina from the family who had taken her in, and they sailed to England for Feliks to find a way to earn passage back for himself and his little charge. He'd hoped he could trade his second class return ticket in for two third class tickets. But the exchange was not equal, and he had to raise more money to afford the return tickets.

Feliks went out every day, taking the little girl with him door-to-door, looking for small handyman jobs that he could perform for the English. After several months, he had almost enough for their fare and was encouraged by a rare sunny morning in the usually gray and rainy city. Feliks and Katalina walked a couple miles to the next hamlet, thinking he could earn the remainder of their passage in a new town. To his shock, the second door they knocked on was opened by Jenney—the woman he'd traveled with from Detroit to England. She let him in, and they made up lost time visiting, as the three young girls played in the garden.

The house didn't belong to Jenney, as he initially thought, but to her aunt, who had gone to a nearby town for some shopping. Jenney and her girls were living with the aunt because her husband had died in an explosion at the factory where he worked, not long after she returned. Her aunt was kind, but Jenney felt as if they were a charity case. She longed to go back to America as she had made many friends there and loved the hustle and bustle of Detroit. She had a little money from the insurance compensation from the factory but not enough to set up a home for her and her girls in the States. Feliks, now in tune enough to know when God was leading him in the right direction, said they should marry, and he would be father to all three girls and be a good husband to her. It took him several weeks of courting and planning and charming until Jenney finally agreed. They combined their savings and bought five third class tickets for America. They had arrived in Detroit two weeks ago.

Uncle Feliks secured a job at a dairy processing plant in the city and had just moved his new family into a little rental house near there. It wasn't in Joe's neighborhood, as his new bride didn't speak Polish; but it was only fifteen minutes away by car. Jenney was a wonderful mother to little Katalina, and they all were adjusting well.

Feliks beamed as he finished his tale. His pride was almost palpable. Joe thanked him for bringing back his mother's niece and congratulated him on his new family. They retreated indoors for a quick lunch of sandwiches.

Feliks noted the exhaustion on Joe's face from being up all night and said it was time for him to leave. Making promises that he would come into the city within the next week to meet Katalina, Jenney, and her girls, Joe reached out his hand to say goodbye.

Feliks grabbed his hand and pulled Joe into his body. Huskily he whispered to Joe," If it weren't for you, my nephew, I'd be at the bottom of that river we were sitting by. You think I don't know it? When I got back to Detroit, first thing I did was got to the Sugar House to talk to your bosses. I told them I've gone straight and I wanted to get set up on some sort of payment plan to pay back my debts. But your boss Charlie told me the money had been repaid a year ago and they had no issues with me. That's when he told me how to find you."

"The money is a non-issue with me too uncle," Joe said. "I'm just so thankful you found Katalina and brought her back so my mother could have a small piece of her sister here."

His uncle squeezed him tighter and whispered in his ear, "I am indebted to you, Joe. I thought I would spend years trying to pay back those gangsters and Jenney and the girls would have to go without. You have given me more than I can ever put into words." His eyes brimmed with tears as he released Joe and went out the front door.

CHAPTER THIRTY FIVE

1929

"What are you doing down here, Walt? Is there a problem with one of the boats?" Joe looked up as his old friend walked in the door of the river house with Cappie. He was puzzled as to why Walt would come down to Wyandotte. In the five years since the Sugar House Gang had hired Walt to work on their fleet of speedboats, he'd never made a visit down the river to work on them. As was initially agreed, Joe and Cappie had brought the boats to Detroit for Walt to fix or alter in a garage the Sugarhouse had built at the edge of the city. Joe was twenty one years old now, and Walt twenty three. Cappie looked as if he never aged, but and he didn't tower over Joe as much.

"No, the Purples are having a shakeup," Walt replied. The *Detroit News* had begun calling the men who ran the Sugar House the Purple Gang. "The coppers are coming down hard on them lately, and the judges take their payoffs and still let them sit in trial after trial. With so many of the boys sitting in jail"—"or dead" was left unsaid—"and the gang having their hands in so many pots, they need more help in the city.

"That's right, Joe," Cappie interjected. "We just come from meeting in the city with them. Things are gonna be changing."

Joe didn't like the direction this conversation was heading. He liked his life downriver with Cappie. It was quiet and steady. Sure they had to maneuver through the federal agents on the river, but they'd been doing it so long it just seemed like an average day at work for Joe. He loved being on the river and running the boat or even hauling ass in the Packard sedan he drove over the ice in the winter. The summer before he had had the ingenious idea to pull the liquor in nets under the boat so if they got pulled over they would just cut the nets and let them sink to the bottom. He attached a block of salt to each net. When the salt dissolved a few hours later, they could return to the same spot and find their load floating on the water and retrieve it. His idea had saved them a least fifty loads and certainly a jail sentence or two.

Walt was correct in saying the cops were coming down harder now. In the past three years the Purples had been hauled into court too many times to count, although the jury almost always came back with a not guilty verdict. Juror intimidation, bribery, and buying alibis had started to take up much of the gang's time. New bosses, henchman, toughs, and bookies had to be brought up through the ranks while others sat in their cells. The Bernstein brothers had so far come out unscathed, but many others had been sent to federal prison or were found floating in the river or had been shot down on the streets of Detroit.

"They had to shut down the boat garage in the city . . . to many snoops around. So Abe said I should relocate down here," Walt continued.

"Abe? He's giving orders now?" Joe said incredulously. "Since when?"

"Since Shorr's been indicted by the Fed's. And Leiter just got off on that extortion case, so he's gotta lay low for a while. Abe, Ray, and Izzy are running things now, along with a couple of other guys." Walt grabbed two beers out of the icebox and sat at the kitchen table. He handed one to Joe and opened his by slamming the cap on the edge of the table.

"What other guys? I work for Charlie, not those damn Bernstein brothers. And certainly not for nobody else."

"You do now, Joe. Harry Keywell and Irving Milberg are running the show with the Bernsteins, and it's all hands on deck, as they say. They want you to report to the Sugar House in the morning. I'm supposed to learn your route tonight. We're supposed to have a little meeting at the distillery with the new owners, and then I'm to drop you off on Belle Isle, where they'll be waiting for you. You can't go against those thugs, Joe. It'll only mean being taken for a ride, and you know it."

Joe did know it. He'd heard rumors that Keywell was at the St. Valentine's Day Massacre and was named by a Chicago landlady as renting a room across the street from the garage where the murders occurred. Harry Keywell had been convicted of extortion, for which he received only probation, and was known as a brute with no conscience. Milberg had been involved with the gang for years but was not widely known.

"So now you're gonna be running booze, Walt? That's against your agreement you had with Charlie. What do you know about this, Cappie?"

Cappie said that he'd heard it same as Walt. Joe was furious. He'd gotten Walt the job, and now he was putting his friend in jeopardy.

"Agreements change, Joe. I'm no baby anymore, and neither are you. I've been thinking about joining the rum running gig for a while now. Don't know if you heard, but I'm married now and got a little one on the way. I could use the kind of dough you've been making." Walt smiled and slugged Joe on the shoulder. "I heard you've been making a killing in the stock market."

"Oh, a little here and there . . . Cappie and I have a lot of time on our hands down here, so we read the papers and play in the market a bit. Seems like it just keeps going up and up. And I heard about you getting hitched. Sorry I couldn't make it to the wedding. Congratulations, I'm sure she's real swell. So you and Cappie are gonna stay down here while I . . . do what?"

"You know I wouldn't be privileged to that type of information, Joe. Just got my orders, and I'm repeating same as I heard them. Well, you ready to take a ride in that fine speedboat of yours?"

The men grabbed their guns and went down to the boathouse for Joe's final run up the river. The late autumn night was cold, and the harvest moon was a glorious orange globe that hung low above the Canadian side. Walt related the details of the meeting to Joe on the trip up to Walkerville. Recently the distillery had begun to allow airplanes to fly liquor out of the country, and the federal agents were getting red-assed from the aerial acrobatics of planes flying over the river day and night. It was against Canadian law to export liquor by airplane, and the Canadian officers were adding heat to the fire. Joe and Cappie were to make an arrangement with the Canadian Club owners to halt the aerial distribution.

Going under the Ambassador Bridge was still a thrill for Joe. He pointed out the large trucks that were most likely smuggling liquor over it to Walt. Joe and Walt pulled into the docks behind Cappie's boat and threw their ropes to the dock men. They climbed onto the shore and were shown a door on the side of the distillery that led to the basement.

Cappie opened a heavy wooden door, and Joe and Walt followed him into a circular room. Warm, red brick made up the walls, and thick wooden beams supported the ceiling. A large bar stood against the right side of the room, and an enormous round table with twelve chairs dominated the space. A painting of a black thoroughbred horse hung on the far wall. Two men in business attire sat at the table and stood when the trio entered. Joe immediately felt like a second-hand player, dressed as he was in his waders and a flannel jacket.

A distinguished man in his forties, Harold C. Hatch had bought the operation from Hiram Walker's sons a couple years before and was training his son Clifford in the distillery business. The self-made millionaire and his son were the no-nonsense type. After offering the three rumrunners a glass of twenty year reserve, they got to the business at hand.

"Where's Bernstein?" the older man asked. "I was told this meeting was going to be with him and his associates."

"Abe couldn't make it. He's got some heat on him in the city, so he sent us. Your men know Joe and Cappie well. This is just a small conversation that never happened anyway, right?" Walt replied. He sounded nervous. Joe gave a look to Cappie to encourage him to take over the meeting.

Cappie straightened out all six foot four inches of his frame in the chair and began, "Mr. Hatch, the Sugar House has come into some heat due to all the aero planes that have been flying in and out of Walkerville. The U.S. government has set up sessions with the Canadian parliament to discuss why they're allowing this to go on when it is against their own laws. Now we've got a good thing going here—all of us—and we don't need no nosy politicians in here trying to make a name for themselves by stirring up a bunch of trouble." Cappie took a sip of the smooth, amber liquid, set it down, and looked Harold straight in the eye.

"I can see your point . . ."Harold began.

"Cappie."

"I can see your point, Cappie, but we'd lose too much profit if we stop our air distribution. And what does your well-publicized acquaintance think about all this?" Hatch said, referring to the Purples' business associate, Al Capone.

"The Purples have been in contact with all the important parties, Mr. Hatch. We're all in agreement that the airplanes must stop." Cappie reverted to the moniker Purples now, because the millionaire had.

"Well, that's all fine and good for you and your underworld bosses, but we've got to make a living too," Clifford said.

"Course you do . . . that's why the Purples and a few other organizations are putting together a political group in the city to discuss the building of a tunnel from here to Detroit. It's to be partially financed by private funds, and the rest will come from the Canadian and U.S. governments.

After all, the Ambassador Bridge is working out well, isn't it?" Cappie took another sip of the reserve, savoring the flavor. Joe watched in amazement at Cappie's bargaining skills. He'd seen him charm and cajole federal agents on several occasions, but this was something else. Either the gang had prepared him extremely well for this meeting or Cappie had been hiding his negotiating abilities as well as Joe had hidden his intelligence from Charlie.

"A tunnel you say? Well, that is interesting. Large enough for trucks to pass through?"

"Bigger—it'll be a two-lane highway right under the river. We just ask that you keep your steady payments to the Canadian police officials on your side, and we'll do the same with the U.S. agents. I don't think there could be a better solution. They're gonna start breathing hard down your neck soon about the plane traffic anyways. Whaddaya say, Mr. Hatch? Can I go back and let the boys know you're in agreement?"

Hatch sat and looked at the men across the table from him. "Let me confer with my son for a moment, won't you?"

Cappie nodded, and the Hatches left the room through the heavy wooden door. Cappie got up and poured himself another glass of the reserve, bringing the bottle to the table and topping off Joe and Walt's drinks. Joe looked around the room, noting how thick the walls were and how no sounds could be heard from above or near the river. Just then his eyes caught on a small round hole in the bricks above Cappie's head.

"Hey Cappie, there's bullet holes in the walls down here. See?" Joe pointed out the one he saw and Walt found another not far from the first.

"Don't worry boys . . . we're not here to cut their pricing. Things only get rough when you try to hit them in their pocketbooks. This conversation is just businessmen discussing roads." Cappie winked at them, and Walt smiled. The Hatches returned to the room and shook hands on the oral agreement. The senior Hatch gave each of them a bottle of the twenty year reserve as a gift, and the trio walked back to their boats.

"Guess this is it for a while, Joe." Cappie clapped Joe on the back. "Soon as I get back into town, I'll take you out for a drink, OK?"

Joe said that would be fine and the men shook Cappie's hand. Cappie started his engine and headed south down the river. So many years together and now they were splitting up. And he'd miss the river—the smell of the wildflowers growing on the banks, the hoots of the owls perched on branches searching for their nightly prey—but mostly he'd miss the quiet solitude of just a man and his boat and the water.

Walt took the wheel and guided the boat the five-minute ride over to Belle Isle. He dropped Joe at the shoreline. Walt told him to meet his pick-up at the Scott Memorial Fountain in a couple of hours. Joe thanked him and wished him good luck. He waved goodbye as Walt headed south. Joe removed his gun from his ankle holster and strapped the bottle of reserve to his leg. *Now what?* he thought, putting his .38 in his coat pocket. Was he just supposed to wander around the park till someone picked him up? He noticed the elaborate arched doorway of the island's aquarium a few hundred yards inland, and he headed in that direction. He knew he could pass an hour or so in the speakeasy in the basement.

"Sturgeon" he said, as the back door opened at his triple knock. *Things don't change that much*, he thought, as the doorman let him in. The smell of salt water and fish drafted down the basement steps. Joe laughed to himself at the irony of it all; if he failed to follow the new Purple leadership he'd be swimming with the fishes.

There were only a few men and a couple of ladies sitting at the bar when he walked up to the bartender and ordered a beer. Joe tipped his hat at the women and took a swig of the cold brew. As he looked up he saw a Detroit policeman coming down the stairs. Joe jumped over the bar and crouched down behind it, pulling out his gun. He heard laughter from the other side, and he looked up at the barkeep who was looking down at him, grinning.

"You want to serve the drinks, do ya young fellow?" he asked. Joe looked perplexedly at the barman. "Isn't that why you jumped over here? You're awful jumpy, boy. We're all friends here on Belle Isle. Why don't you hop back on over and I'll pour you another beer. You spilled your first one all over my clean bar."

Joe replaced his weapon and stood up. He saw that all the customers were laughing at his mistake. The Belle Isle cop smiled, faked a shot at Joe with his hand, and ordered a beer.

Joe walked back around the bar and retook his seat, laughing with the other drinkers. "You sure got me," he said. "Hey, if I tip good can I bring in my own hooch?" he asked the bartender.

"What's a good tip?"

Joe laid a fifty dollar bill on the bar. The barman picked it up and said, "Drink what you wish, young man." Joe pulled up the leg of his pants and grabbed the bottle of reserve he'd almost shattered in his leap over the bar.

"Anyone for some good twenty year whisky?" he asked his fellow patrons. In five minutes he was good friends with everyone in the place, including the man he now knew as Inspector Henry J. Garvin. The regulars returned to their seats, thanking him for the drinks. The inspector sat down next to Joe.

"You're fast on your feet kid . . . what kinda business you in?" the chunky policeman asked amicably.

"Fishing" Joe replied.

"Fishing, huh? Ok, have it your way. Thought I might know a few friends of yours, but I guess I was wrong."

The hairs on Joe's neck stood up, and the muscles in his legs twitched, ready to flee. "Relax boy, I've got friends in high places too, is all I'm saying. I'm just trying to make some small talk with you." Joe recalled hearing the name Garvin before. This was the detective the Purples had helped move up in the police force over the years; thereby ensuring their "innocence" when accusations came through his department. But how had he known who Joe was?

"I heard you were coming over to the city tonight, and I thought I'd just head this way for a drink and introduce myself. See if there was anything I could do for you."

"Did Abe send you?" Joe asked.

"No, he doesn't need to know about this little meeting between two new friends, does he?" Garvin replied. So that was it. The cop was looking for a little extra on the side and had somehow heard Joe would be coming through the park that night.

"I'm not in need of anything at the moment, but I appreciate your generosity. How about you take the rest of this whisky as thanks from me?" Joe slipped a hundred dollar bill under the reserve and pushed it toward the officer.

"Well, that's mighty sweet of you, Joey O," the cop replied as he pocketed the bill and grabbed the remainder of the Canadian Club. "Well, I gotta be heading out. Hope to see you around real soon." Joe took a drink of his beer and gulped it back. Every time he came into the city his nerves unraveled. There was something about the close proximity of hundreds of thousands of people and skyscrapers that added a dash of claustrophobia to his normally even-keeled personality. On the river he could *hear* an enemy approaching, be it a hijacker or an agent. In a city, where the sounds never fall below a low roar and people could approach you from any angle; his senses were dulled and ineffective.

Finishing the last ounce of his cold beer he decided to head toward the fountain and wait where he could at least be outdoors. Enjoying the quiet of the empty park, he reached the fountain in less than twenty minutes and had a seat on a marble step. *Fitting spot for my return to the city.* He pulled his brown flannel jacket collar up to protect himself from the cold wind blowing across the water. The fountain had been commissioned from beyond the grave by an eccentric gambler who was so loathed by the public that it took the city almost fifteen years before they agreed to build it. James Scott was infamous for telling loud, boring tales accentuated with a healthy dose of profanity. That the politicians of the city decided to commission the tower despite Scott's lack of civil respect said much about the current political climate.

Occasionally headlights could be seen driving towards the fountain, but they all turned west. Joe was left to wonder if he should start for the city by foot. According to his watch, it was nearing three o'clock, nearly one hour past the designated pick-up time. A marble lion appeared to glare down at him from his perch on the fountain, and the sculpted frogs jeered at his lonely state. Joe shook off the imaginary antics of the fountain and stood up, resolute that he'd walk back to the city.

"Bang!" Joe saw the flash of the gunshot and a man fall into the lagoon near the fountain, the force of his fall rocking several long canoes that were tied to the shoreline. He ducked back down behind the fountain feeling his leg for his weapon. Damn, it was gone. Remembering he'd put it in his pocket he reached for it as he crawled around the circular monument, trying to locate the shooter. The flash of the gun had blinded him for a moment, and he couldn't see in the dark. Screeching tires rounded the drive by the fountain, and he cocked the.38. The gunman was driving without lights and Joe had to rely entirely on his hearing. Closer, almost there. Joe pointed at what he hoped was the driver's window and shot twice.

"What the hell you think you're doing, Joey O?" rang out a deep, raspy voice. It was Harry Keywell—the obnoxious thug Joe had met that night at the Powhatan Club and his new boss.

"Sorry, boss," he replied, pocketing his weapon. "I had no idea who was flying toward me." Joe descended the steps and opened the door to the Cadillac. He looked over at Harry who still had his gun on Joe. "Honest, Harry—I'm sorry."

"Get in, you stupid Polack, you almost put a hole in my hat."

Joe sat down in the passenger seat, leaning against the door. Actually, Joe had only hit the rear bumper once but he kept his mouth shut and tried to look apologetic. "Like I need more attention from the Belle Isle Bridge Patrol by you shooting off your gun like a maniac." Harry pushed the gas pedal down and headed north on the island.

"I thought we were going back to the city." Joe tapped his fingernail nervously on the door handle.

"We is, but first I gotta make sure nobody heard your rat-a-tat musical display back there. Damn Joey, I go to all the trouble to make that sap strip down naked before I knock him off so the coppers can't identify him, and you go and shoot off fireworks like it's the Fourth of July!"

"Y-you shot him naked?" Joe stuttered slightly.

"Sure, what's the big deal? You knocked someone off before, right?" Harry glared over at Joe as they rounded the avenue and headed back south.

"Sure Harry, a couple of times," Joe responded. *What had Charlie told this goon?* "Just never naked is all." Harry laughed and finally pocketed his gun.

"I just do it so it takes longer for the pigs to figure out who took a swim." Harry slowed the Caddie down as they neared the bridge that led back to the city. A uniformed officer was walking on the sidewalk in the middle of the span and Harry pulled his hat down, as did Joe, to shield their faces as they passed. So many Detroiters had plunged to their deaths from the bridge in suicide attempts that a twenty-four-hour watch had been put in place. "Damn palookas" was all Harry said. He sped back into the city.

CHAPTER THIRTY SIX

"Just ask for their donation, Joe," Abe Bernstein was saying in the Sugar House office. Abe and Harry had decided Joe would be better used in a position where his boyish good looks, charm, and confidence could increase the Purples' profit margin. Extortion. Harry handed him a list of names and addresses and Joe looked down at it.

"But I don't know nothing about collecting." Joe tried not to sulk. "I'm better with boats than people." He was treading on thin ice here. The bosses didn't like arguments.

"You think I don't know how to run a business, Joey O?" Harry stood up from behind the desk and twitched his fingers.

"Course you do, Harry. I just thought. . . ."

"Well, don't think," he growled. "You make the rounds of these stills and bring us our cut, ya here?

"Yeah, Harry. I hear you." Joe shoved the list in his pocket and walked down the stairs into the warehouse. "Damn." He mumbled under his breath. The Purples had realized that they couldn't control all of the liquor that came into Detroit nor the amount that was made there, so they had pushed up their extortion racket to increase revenue.

Joe walked to the Purples' parking garage and found the Buick touring car Abe had given Joe to use to make his rounds, the one with false plates. Every morning he'd leave his house, pull the car out of the backyard into the dirt alley, and drive to the Sugar House. He'd greet Abe and Harry, and he'd be handed a list of addresses and the presumed revenues of the stills. Joe would head off into the city, downriver, or to the north for a day of collections. He hated the work but could rationalize it to himself because the people he was taking money from *were* operating illegally. Other collectors that worked for the Purples had been assigned to rough up the cleaners and dyers operations in the city. If they refused to pay a percentage to the Sugar House, the collectors threw purple dye on the legitimate business owners' product. Joe felt it was a dirty racket and was thankful not to be a part of it.

Most still operators feared the Purples, and an argument wouldn't even arise when Joe paid them a visit. With the ones who resisted, Joe tried different tactics. With the men he'd bring a bottle of whisky and sit with them in their backyards or basements, pouring glass after glass while he sipped his. After several drinks and multiple explanations, observations, examples, and not so subtle inferences, the still owner would concede and part with the obligatory ten percent. Joe remained friendly during even heated altercations, never allowing the men to ruffle his feathers or showing any signs of anger or frustration. If the still owner remained obstinate at the end of the conversation, Joe would leave the bottle as a sign of good will, shake the man's hand, and take his leave.

The following morning, when the obstinate farmer or factory worker awoke, he would find a stick of dynamite with a half burned fuse at his door. When Joe returned a few days later to "discuss the matter again," the operator would have the money ready for him. After all, it was for the owner's protection: fires, thefts, and beatings were commonplace in Detroit, and the Purples only wanted to help protect him.

With the few women Joe was assigned to, he took a different approach. Unbeknownst to his bosses, he'd bring toys for their children or a box of food for their pantries. He'd sit in their kitchens and eat their pastries and play marbles or cards with their youngsters. These women were a poor and lonely lot, making small amounts of gin in their bathtubs and selling it to their neighbors. It was a small price to pay to fork over ten dollars in exchange for a visit by a handsome young man who flattered their tired egos, played with their dirty children, and brought gifts. Joe lost money on his female customers, but his conscience was clean.

CHAPTER THIRTY SEVEN

"Hiya Joe." Marya greeted him as he pulled the Packard into the backyard one evening after a long day of collecting. A snow white crocheted shawl was draped over one shoulder of her crimson dress, as she walked over to his car. "How about a ride, cousin?"

"No dice, Marya. I'm beat, and the family is coming over for supper. Aren't you gonna visit with Uncle Feliks and the girls?" Joe took off his hat and wiped the sweat from his brow.

"And sit here all night absolutely bo-o-o-ored to death? Not on your life! Come on, just drop me at the Kibitzer Club, will ya sweetie pie? Marya flashed her eyes at Joe and smiled demurely.

"Now you're flirting with your cousin, Marya? Can you crawl any lower?" Joe asked disgustedly. "Besides, that's one of the Purples' juice joints, and I told you not to hang out near the gang." Marya let the shawl drop off her other shoulder revealing much cleavage. "Geez, Marya, the sun's still out! Cover up. Are you looking for trouble?"

"Always Joey boy," she replied.

A shiny Cadillac Victoria pulled into the alley as Marya started heading back toward the house. She stopped on the steps to see the visitor's identity. Cappie stepped out of the elegant car and waved at Joe. Joe sprinted over and shook his hand. "Cappie! It's been months since I've seen your ugly mug."

"Got a weekend pass ,and I thought I'd stop in and see how you're faring in our fair city."

"Arent ya gonna introduce me to your friend, Joey?" Marya called, descending from the stairs.

"Well, I would but you've already had the pleasure, Marya. Cappie carried your spifflicated ass home the night I pulled you out of the Powhatan." Marya blushed slightly and held her hand out for Cappie to take.

"My apologies, Mr. Cappie. I must thank you for helping me home then. It seems I'd forgotten to eat that evening, and the champagne went to my little ole head. It was kind of you to assist me home." She batting her eyelashes. "Won't you join us for supper?"

"I thought you were leaving, Marya."

"Why I never said such a thing, Joe. I just wanted to have a quick cocktail before supper is all. How about you, Mr. Cappie? Are you thirsty?"

"It's just Cappie, Miss Marya, and sure I'd be happy to take you for a drink if Joe here don't mind. You are as pretty as a little baby dove, Miss Marya, if you don't mind me saying. Whadda ya say, Joe?"

"Oh, I don't care—but it's your funeral, Cappie. Have fun."

Cappie helped Marya into the Cadillac and darted to the other side. “I won’t have her out late, Joe. I’ll keep a good eye on her.”

“That had better be all you keep on her.”

But Cappie had already shut the door and was pulling away. What could Joe do? Marya was a grown woman, and if she was going to go out with anybody, Joe couldn’t be too upset it was Cappie. He was a good man and had always treated Joe like a son or at least a brother. And Marya was going to do what Marya was going to do anyhow.

Uncle Feliks made raspberry fizzes after supper for Matka and Jenney, and he and Joe drank beer as they sat on the front porch shooting the breeze. Katalina had learned English remarkably fast and she could chant the sing-song rhymes as well as her stepsisters as they jumped rope on the sidewalk. Emma twirled the rope with one of Jenney’s daughters on the other end, as Katalina skipped and hopped merrily through the twirling line.

“She’s adjusted well, Uncle Feliks.”

“We all have, Joe. Seems like this is the life I was meant to live. Jenney is a wonderful woman, and the girls are a joy. Katalina still cries for her mother at night, but not as often as she used to. And Jenney just pulls her into bed with us and cuddles her till she falls asleep. She’s going to start school in the fall.”

“I hope she doesn’t get Sister Mary Monica for a teacher. She used to scare the living hell out of me.”

“We’re not sending her to St. Josaphat, Joe. We want to send all three of the girls to the same school, and Jenney’s girls don’t know Polish.”

"Oh, of course . . . well, I'm sure she'll do great. Maybe she'll go to Marygrove College someday, like Pauline."

Pauline was living at Marygrove College, studying to become a teacher—an education partially financed by Joe. Joe hadn't thought of Katalina attending another school besides St. Josaphat, but his uncle's rationale made sense. He waved to his old neighbor Sam as he exited his house across the street and got in his Model T.

"Sam's doing well, I hear—got himself a job at the Chrysler plant in Hamtramck. I wonder if he's ever gonna leave his mama's house and get married?"

"I've heard he's a bit of a gambler . . ." Feliks looked uncomfortable bringing up a reference to his not so distant past.

"Really? Hope he's a better one than you were!" Joe laughed and hit his uncle in the arm. Feliks chuckled in spite of himself.

"Me too."

Joe looked at his uncle, and a slight pang of jealousy struck him; envious of his quiet, simple life and loving family.

"Katalina! Emma! Josie and Julie! Come inside. I have a treat for you girls," Matka called out the kitchen window. Joe's mother adored spoiling her nieces and would bake for days before the family got together so she could dole out sugary sweets to her heart's content.

"Where'd your brothers take off to after dinner, by the way?" Feliks asked.

"I'm sure Stephan is at the baseball diamond, and Matka told me Frank has a little girlfriend he meets at Sanders on

Saturday evenings. She says they sit at a table for hours and share one milkshake."

"How about you, Joe? You gotta girl you haven't let on about?"

"Oh, I've been seeing this one kinda steady. She's a real firecracker, but we're just having fun." Joe had been dating the mulatto girl he had met at the Powhatan for a few months but didn't want anything serious. Adelaide was a transplant from New Orleans. Each of her parents was half black and half white. She passed for white in the north and held a job as a salesgirl in an upscale women's boutique. Joe took her out dancing a couple nights a week, but they mostly wrestled around in the back of his car.

"Well, be careful Joe. When you play with firecrackers there's a chance you'll get burned," Uncle Feliks said.

Just then Joe and his uncle heard the sound of sirens a few streets over. Uncle Alexy and Aunt Hattie came out onto the porch to investigate.

"That's an awful lot of fire engines," Alexy said. "Hope it's not a big fire."

"No. I think its police sirens," Joe said. He knew it was the police but didn't want to let on how many times he'd heard that sound coming in his direction. The sirens died down, and Matka brought out three more beers for the men. Aunt Hattie went in after her to gossip in the kitchen, and the men sat companionably on the porch. Joe sat on the top step leaning against the brick pillar, sipping his beer and listening to his uncles. He tried not to think how much he wished his father was there. Of course, if Ojciec was here, Joe probably wouldn't have started running for the Sugar House, and his uncle might not have gambled all his money away and slept with married women, and Joe wouldn't have sent him to Poland, and Katalina would still be there living as an orphan. But maybe not . . . only God knew what was meant to be.

A fly buzzed near Joe's ear and he swatted at it, spilling his beer in the process. His uncles laughed, and he got up to grab another from inside the house. A long sedan sped down the street, and Joe turned to yell. "Slow down! There's kids playing here." The car screeched to a stop in front of the walk. A driver opened the door, and Charlie Leiter got out of the back seat. Joe could tell by Charlie's eyes he was there with bad news.

Leiter walked up to the porch and stopped at the foot of the stairs. "Joey, its Cappie. Those dagos hit the Kibitzer. Shot it all to hell. Didn't hit no one inside, but Cappie had just walked out the front door when they started shooting. I'm sorry, Joe. I know he was a good friend to you."

Cappie. It couldn't be Cappie. "It can't be Cappie," Joe said in disbelief. "He's too big. He's an ox. No bullet could take him down. Not Cappie."

"They used Tommy guns, Joey. He didn't stand a chance. Threw himself in front of some dame trying to protect her." Charlie looked up apologetically at Joe's uncles, who were standing uncomfortably on the porch, not wanting to leave Joe yet not wanting to be part of the gangster underworld. Joe looked frantically at his Uncle Alexy and back at Charlie.

"Some dame?" Joe dropped the empty bottle onto the porch. Marya! "Where's the girl?" he demanded. Charlie looked confused. "Where's the dame Cappie stood in front of, Charlie?" Joe yelled bounding down the steps.

"She's in the car. We're taking her to the hospital now . . . I wanted to get her out of there before the cops showed up." Joe pushed past Charlie and flung the back door of the car open. Marya was cowered in the corner of the backseat covered in blood. *Cappie's blood? Her blood?* Joe scooped her up and started toward the house. Uncle Alexy's eyes grew wild with fury, and he bellowed a raw, animal-like growl and jumped off the stoop. He stormed toward Joe but stopped short as he reached Charlie; bringing his arm back, he slugged the gangster, knocking him down. The driver and Charlie's bodyguard were on Alexy in a second, holding his arms behind his back as he hung his head and wailed.

Charlie picked himself off the ground and pulled his gun on Alexy. He looked at Joe holding Marya. "You know this dame?" he asked, trying to put it all together, never taking his gun off of Joe's uncle.

"Marya's my cousin, and this is her father," Joe replied, nodding at his Uncle Alexy.

"Let him go, boys," Charlie said to his thugs. He lowered his weapon. "It's just a flesh wound, Joey. She'll be all right. She's just in shock." Alexy walked over to Joe, who transferred Marya to her father's arms. A weeping Aunt Hattie opened the door for him, and he carried her inside.

"Thanks for not leaving her on the street, Charlie," Joe said.

"Sure. I didn't know she was your cousin, Joey. If I had I would've . . ."

"You couldn't have known, Charlie, Sorry about your mouth. I think my Uncle thought she was dead when I pulled her out of the car."

Charlie wiped some blood from the corner of his mouth with his handkerchief. "Understandable. Well, I'll see you later. Glad your cousin's gonna be all right." Charlie's driver opened the car door and he got in. Joe sat down on the steps as the long sedan drove slowly away. He looked down at his white shirt covered with blood. *Cappie*, he thought. A large tear raced down his cheek.

CHAPTER THIRTY EIGHT

Cappie's funeral was attended by only a dozen men, on a hot August morning on Grosse Ile. Joe insisted that he be buried on the island he loved.

Joe's thoughts drifted to when he first met Cappie—Vic Starboli—on the *Columbia*, when Vic had pointed out the sights along the river to a young Joe. He remembered Vic's wistful look as he gazed at the mansions on the island. "The good life must be really good" he had said.

Charlie Leiter paid for a nice plot beneath a willow tree near the river. Joe had located Cappie's father and driven him to the cemetery behind the hearse.

Four dark cars pulled into the graveyard, each carrying an enormous wreath of flowers on the roof to place on Cappie's grave. A timid minister gave a short eulogy at the graveside, and Cappie's father threw in the first handful of dirt on his casket. The old man seemed unsure of himself, and Joe grabbed his arm to steady him as he leaned over the grave. Joe threw a clump of earth, crossed himself, and said a prayer asking for God to forgive Cappie for any sins he committed and allow him into heaven.

Cappie's mother had died years before, and he had no siblings. So Joe went with Cappie's father to the lawyer's office for the reading of the will. The will consisted of a sheet of paper Cappie had ripped out of the back of a book. He deeded all his investments and monies to his father; to Joe, he left his most prized possession, his boat. Cappie's father didn't understand the stock market. He had Joe help him sell all of Cappie's carefully planned investments and put all the money in a safe under his bed. Joe tried to talk the old man out of it but he insisted.

The stock market had been Joe and Cappie's hobby and they had been putting almost half their paychecks into it and watching their money grow. Every stock they'd invested in and had doubled or better, and they were sitting on a huge pile of money. Joe smiled every time he picked up the paper and read how his shares were increasing. It seemed as if there was no end to the amount of money he could make in the market. Joe shook his head as he pulled up the floorboards under the old man's bed and put the money in a safe underneath. Fifty thousand dollars should at least be in the bank, Joe advised, but the old man refused.

Later that week, Joe took Cappie's boat out of the boathouse and took it south toward Grosse Ile. He knew where he was headed, but he idled slowly, allowing memories of his good friend to sweep over him. He chuckled at the pranks they had played on each other at the Wyandotte house—black paint on the rim of a coffee cup, salt in the sugar bowl, siphoning the gas out of one another's boats. Joe smiled thinking of the stories Cappie would tell, dreams they would share before falling asleep after running whisky down the river all night. Joe held his right wrist, remembering how Cappie had wrapped his sprained joint the time he'd fallen out of a tree trying to catch a glimpse of two girls swimming in the river.

As he neared his destination, tears poured down his cheeks as he envisioned Cappie's wide shoulders jumping in front of Marya in a hail of bullets, pulling her down and covering her with his body. Joe wiped the tears back and pulled into the canal. He cut the engine and there was only silence. No tweeting birds or croaking frogs to break the hot stillness could be heard near the little cottage where he'd spent his first night away from home. He pulled to the dock and tied up the boat. He picked up a rough wooden sign he'd carved after the funeral. Joe grabbed a hammer and nails and jumped out of the boat. When he reached the run-down cottage, he placed the sign above the door and hammered it into the worn siding. Joe had bought the unused property from Charlie and was going to keep it as a fishing camp in remembrance of his best friend. The sign read Cappie's Place.

A month after Cappie's funeral, Joe walked into the Sugar House looking for Charlie. Abe greeted him as he walked into the office, and Harry tipped his hat and fell back asleep in the corner of the room.

"Charlie's had to blow town for a while, Joey O. And Shorr, well nobody's seen him in a few days. I'm running things for now. What can I do for you?" Abe looked up from the newspaper he'd been reading. "Stock Market Dips but No Need for Worry" read the headline.

"I was thinking about taking some time off," Joe told the lanky gangster. Joe had decided he'd had enough of the rum running business. Cappie's death had cut him to the core.

He wanted to get out while he still could. His nest egg could provide him with a cushion until he decided what he wanted to do next.

"Oh yeah? How much time we talking?" Abe put the paper down on the desk in front of him.

"A few months. I've been working for the Sugar House for over ten years now, and I was thinking it might be a good time to take a break. What with Cappie . . ." Joe let his words fall short.

Abe sat up in his chair and scowled at Joe. "You was thinking. You was thinking, was ya? Was ya also thinking how we got about ten guys in the clink and at least that many at the bottom of the river? Was ya thinking how Shorr is missing—maybe kidnapped? Was ya thinking we still got an operation to run here? Was ya thinking that, Joey O?"

Joe took a step back, startled at Abe's sudden hostility. Harry looked up from under his hat and looked at Abe and then back at Joe. "There's lotsa guys who'd take my place, Abe. Hundreds that'd love to make some good dough. You don't need me that bad." Joe sat down uncertainly in a chair in front of the desk.

"You're right, Joey. There's lotsa guys who'd *kill* to make the kind of dough you've been hauling in. I was just saying to Harry that your little brother Frank would probably make a good runner for us. Wasn't I, Harry? He's older than you was when you started here, isn't he, Joey?" Abe bared his teeth in an evil smile. "What's he—seventeen, eighteen years old now?"

"Never mind, Abe. Leave Frank out of this. I don't need a break. It was just an idea. Where you want me to go today?"

1930

Joe continued his collection route but focused his mind on ways to get out from under the Purples that wouldn't affect his family. The stock market had crashed three weeks later. Most of Joe's money had been tied up in stocks, and he lost it all. He threw his plans to leave the Sugar House aside and refocused on trying to earn as much money as he could. The politicians were arguing against Prohibition, and the public supported them. Women's groups had joined the anti-temperance movement, crying that immorality, vice, and loss of faith in the law had been caused by the Volstead Act and that the Eighteenth Amendment should be repealed. This time, Joe could see the writing on the wall.

Violence in the city was escalating. The newspapers ran stories of suicides, floating bodies in the river, and men gunned down in front of their homes daily. The public had not protested the gang wars when they'd only been killing each other, but citizens were getting caught in the crossfire, and the taxpayers wanted some action from their corrupt police department. A small girl aboard the *Columbia* on her way to Boblo was grazed by a bullet when Federal agents chasing a bootlegger opened fire. The Federal agents increased their raids on illegal drinking establishments, but they didn't have the power to shut down the almost twenty-five thousand that operated in the city alone.

Following Black Tuesday, tens of thousands of people lost their jobs, and many more went to work but didn't get paid. Henry Ford cut production and laid people off. Masses of people left for the countryside, hoping to revert to their agricultural roots, while more poured into the city looking for work. The Capuchin priests of Detroit set up a temporary soup kitchen to feed the hungry.

Joe's job had become extremely difficult, as no amount of toys, groceries, charm, or booze could squeeze money out of empty pocketbooks. He'd resorted to lighting firecrackers or small pieces of dynamite behind still owners' houses or under their bedroom windows and blowing them up in the middle of the night to scare the owner to death. The following morning he'd arrive early, while the unlucky bootlegger was still shaken up, and request the Purples' percentage. Fortunately, his only victims were men, as there were so many women cooking gin in their bathtubs now the Purples had decided to look the other way out of fear of bad publicity.

The only thing Joe didn't spend his time worrying about was Marya. Frightened out of her mind and thinking it was God's intervention that she hadn't died in front of that speakeasy, she had joined the Felician Sisters two weeks after the incident. Joe wasn't sure it would last, but with his cousin locked up in a convent somewhere it was one less thing. He'd broke up with Adelaide soon after, too. He thought it was better to let her go than to have her wind up in the crosshairs of his profession.

CHAPTER THIRTY NINE

1931

Joe took a drink of his beer and looked around the Bucket of Blood, a Purple Gang bar deep in the middle of one of the city's poorest neighborhoods. Abe had told Joe to meet his brother Ray at the grimy bar at nine o'clock. Two hours later he was still waiting. In that time he'd seen two fistfights, one knife pulled—countered with a broken bottle—and at least five prostitutes leave with a "date." Red-eyed patrons smoked marijuana and passed around joints (the only legal thing going on in the entire place). Joe kept his mouth shut and sipped his beer, trying to decide how much longer he was going to wait for Ray.

Ray sauntered in twenty minutes later, bought two shots of whisky, and brought them over to Joe's table. "How's it go, Joey O?" he said, laughing at his own joke.

"It'd be better if you'd gotten here two hours ago like you was supposed to."

"Boy, you are wound tight! Abe told me so, but I said nobody who brings in as much dough as you do could be. Am I wrong?" Ray slicked back his hair and looked at Joe; his large dark eyes looked like he hadn't slept in days.

"No, you aint wrong, Ray. So what's the beef?"

"No beef, Joe. Just a little problem we need some help with. Abe thought you'd be just the guy." Ray slugged down his shot and looked at Joe. Joe made a cheers gesture and poured it down his throat.

"Can I get you a beer, Ray?" Joe signaled to the bartender, who brought two frothy mugs to the table. "So what's the scat?"

"There's three guys from Chi-town that have been edging in on our territory. They were working for us at first and giving us a nice kickback too, but they've decided they're too good for that now. They want to go out on their own. They've muscled in on our deal with the River Gang and are selling them the liquor they hijacked from us. Last month they tried shaking down a couple of our gambling rackets, and they owe us more than fifteen G's in back liquor money. Abe's had it. He wants the money now. So he set up a meeting with the three hoods tomorrow at some apartment. They say they got the dough, and all we gotta do is go and get it."

"So what do you need me for?" Joe asked. He looked toward the bar, where yet another fistfight had begun. The bartender grabbed one guy by the neck and pulled out his gun on the other. "Take it outside" was all he said, and the two brawlers left.

"Ain't nobody home in that head of yours, Joe? That's a lot of dough to be pulling out of an apartment in broad daylight. And you never know what the palookas might try. We need manpower in case there's a showdown. I got Harry and Milberg coming, and with you that makes four, see?

We'll outnumber them by one. But not more than that, so they don't get too itchy."

"What time you want me to meet you?" Joe knew better than to fight it. Might as well go along and try to keep his head low.

"Pick us up at the Sugar House at six o'clock tomorrow night. Ya want another beer?" Ray looked at Joe's empty mug.

"Sure," he replied. If he looked like he was in a hurry to leave, Ray would only prolong the meeting. They sat and drank for another hour. Joe listened to Ray's female exploits and made up some of his own for Ray's amusement. Joe left the bar after midnight and drove home. Joe cracked the window of his car and let in some fresh air. Joe's eyes burned from the dope and cigars, and he coughed a few times trying to air out his lung. He looked out at the streets as he drove through the city. Millions of flashing electric lights marred his vision as he passed club after bar after tavern. A cop car sped past him, and he had to swerve to avoid a drunk crossing the street.

A pile of furniture was heaped in the alley two doors down from his house. Another eviction. The landlords were throwing tenants out of their homes at a record rate. It'd been a year and half since Black Tuesday. Things were getting bad. Shoeless children were wandering the streets, and women holding babies begged on the corners.

Uncle Alexy had been laid off from the Ford plant and couldn't find a job. Joe had saved a bit since the crash and was helping them make do, but Pauline had to leave college and find work. Joe had found her a job at a bottle factory; he didn't mention that the Purples bought all their bottles from there. The gang continued to increase their profit margins by cutting whisky with dangerous dilutants in cutting warehouses all over the city.

Joe fell into an uneasy sleep that night, wishing Abe would just leave him his regular work and wishing Charlie would return from wherever the hell he'd gone. He didn't think of Shorr, who he was sure was at the bottom of the river. If he believed the rumors, it had been by Charlie's own hand.

Ray was sitting in the passenger seat next to Joe, and Milberg and Harry were in the back. Joe was driving slowly through the city, fighting the traffic and pedestrians. He drove west on Woodward to the outskirts of the city. Ray told him to turn south on Atkinson Street. Harry was retelling a counterfeiting story that had been in the paper that afternoon. A little girl had walked to the local market and tried to pay for some candy with a quarter. The grocery store clerk looked the quarter over and stated it looked a little funny to him. Ray jumped in saying, "Hey I read that! The little girl says, 'It should be fine. My daddy just cooked it!'" The dark eyed gangster burst into guffaws and Joe turned to look at him. Joe looked past Ray out the car window and saw a house he remembered seeing as a child. It was Ty Cobb's house. Memories of the baseball game he'd gone to with his father came rushing back.

"Hey Joey! Where you going?" Harry yelled from the back. "You gotta turn right here. Damn, Ray! What'd ya have the Polack drive for?" Joe took a sharp right and turned west onto Lawton Street.

"All right, settle down boys. Now listen, Joey O. We're all gonna go up to the apartment together and have a little sit down. I brought some cigars, and we'll light up and make nice. Right before I ask for the dough, I'll ask Joey where Beilman is with the books, see?" Beilman was the Purples' bookkeeper. Ray turned to Joe and continued. "You go down to the car and look around for any wise guys or coppers. If you don't see none, race the engine till it backfires, and lay on the horn. We'll grab the dough and split before they get a chance to change their minds. Like taking candy from a baby." Ray laughed and Harry and Milberg joined in.

"Why do you have to take the dough?" Joe asked. "I thought we were meeting because they want to pay up."

"Geez, Joey. Don't you know nothing? What if it's a setup, or what if they change their minds? Damn. Anything can happen. We's just taking precautions is all."

"Yeah, precautions," Harry said. He laughed again. Joe turned right onto Collingwood Avenue and parked across the street from the apartment complex. Something didn't feel right about this, but he couldn't put his finger on it. A woman in a worn dress walked out the front door of the building, set down an empty milk bottle on the steps, and went back inside. Joe stared at the building, looking for signs of trouble.

"Come on boys, time's a-wasting," Ray said, as he climbed out of the car. The foursome crossed the street in unison, stopping only for a passing car. Harry opened the glass door and held it for the other three. They walked up a filthy stairwell and opened the door to the second floor. The men were silent as they walked down the long hallway. A radio show was blaring behind one of the doors, and the smell of curry and onion reeked out of another. When they reached the end of the hall, Ray knocked on the door of apartment 211. Joe heard a set of footsteps coming to answer Ray's knock. An open can of green paint sat on the floor next to the door.

"Hey, Ray, how ya doing?" said the man who opened the door. "Brought the boys with ya? Well, come on in."

Joe followed the men into the dingy apartment and had a seat on an ugly velour couch. An oriental rug lay on the floor, adding the only splash of color to the drab room. All the men took a seat and Ray began.

"So you boys been keeping outta trouble?" Ray, seated in a small wooden chair, smiled and crossed his legs.

"Course not, Ray. Who's this?" one of the men replied ,looking at Joe.

Joe looked at Ray, unsure if he should introduce himself. "Don't worry about him, Hymie," Ray replied when Joe didn't. "That's Joey O, he's on the level, and you know Harry and Milberg." Joe waved from the couch.

"I'm Hymie, and this here is Nigger Joe, and that's Izzy the Rat."

"How the molls treating you, Izzy?" Ray asked, passing out cigars. The men continued talking about women for several minutes until Ray turned to Joe and asked, "Where's Beilman with the books?" Joe mumbled he'd go outside to look and left the apartment. He ran down the stairs, pushing past the same woman who'd put the milk bottle out on the stoop. She was on her way up the stairs. He crossed the street and got in the car. Joe pulled the car in front of the building and looked up and down the block for any signs of a rival gang or cops. Seeing none he pressed hard on the gas pedal over and over till the car backfired and then he laid on the horn.

Not two minutes later, Ray, Milberg, and Harry raced out the door of the apartment building and jumped on the running boards of the car. "Go! Go! Go!" Ray yelled. Joe put the car in gear and pressed the gas pedal to the floor. He stopped a block later and the three men got inside and he took off again.

"You get the money?" Joe asked as he tore down the side street, passing cars, and dodging pedestrians. Ray laughed and wiped his face with his sleeve. Joe looked at Ray, noticing there was blood splattered on his cheek. Joe turned his head, glancing quickly in the back seat. Milberg looked as pale as a ghost, and Harry was wiping blood off the lapel of his coat with a handkerchief. "What the hell? What the hell happened in there?" Joe demanded.

"I guess you could say they weren't co-operating." Ray laughed again. "Stop the car, Joey." Joe pulled the car over to the curb and, his hands shaking, set the hand brake. *What the hell happened in that apartment?* "Drive out of the city and find a place to burn this hay burner, and then meet us back at the Sugar House in an hour."

With that, all three men got out of the car and started walking in separate directions. Joe sat there for a moment not moving, processing what had just happened. What a fool he was. They hadn't gone to the apartment to get any money . . . It had been a hit the whole time, and they'd made Joe a part of it by driving the getaway car.

"Oh my God," Joe said out loud and made the sign of the cross over himself. Sirens wailed in the distance, and he knew they were headed to the Collingwood apartment. That woman—that woman with the milk bottle—she'd seen his face in the stairwell! She'd be able to identify him.

Another police car sped down the street past Joe's parked car, and he pulled the brim of his hat down. He had to get out of here. He'd go to prison for life for sure! Shaking and nauseated, Joe started the car and drove it to the only place he could think of.

He couldn't go home. He didn't want his family involved in this mess. Anyway the cops would find him there—or worse, the Purples would. Abe might try to bump him off now. He couldn't go to the fishing cottage . . . Charlie had most likely told Abe about it. Anyway he'd had Cappie's boat put in storage. Damn. How brutal to slaughter those men in cold blood like that. What if one of them was still alive? Ray had told them Joe's name. Shit. Things couldn't be worse. Joe parked the car in an alley and covered the back bumper with a couple of cardboard boxes that had been dumped there. He walked down the side of the backstreet, trying to stay in the shadows, until he came to a yard with an old outhouse. He slipped inside the putrid wooden box and crouched on the floor holding his gun at the door. It would be dark in a few hours.

Joe pushed the door open an inch and looked outside. Night had fallen, and the glow of amber light poured out the windows of the house into the backyard. He pushed the door open a few more inches and, trying to remain in the shadows, he crawled in the dirt to the back of the latrine and leaned against the wood. Holding his gun underneath his coat he slowly stood up, looked around, and crawled to the alley. Bright headlights appeared at the end of the street and drove towards him. Joe jumped over a wooden fence and hid in a clump of bushes. His breathing sounded as loud as a train and he tried to take a few deep breaths.

The dark sedan crept down the dirt alley slowly. There were two men sitting in the front of the car. As the car neared Joe, it pulled to a stop. He could hear men arguing but he was unable to make out their words. Then he made out "Damn Polack!" It was Ray Bernstein. When he'd failed to show up at the Sugar House they'd come looking for him. The sound of a car door slammed as someone exited the car. A flashlight swept through the alley and into the trees and brush lining it.

"You really think I'm gonna find some Godforsaken Polack in this city with a flashlight, Ray?" It was Harry speaking.

"Well, he's not at home, and we've gotta find him," the gangster answered back. "The cops are swarming, and we all gotta get out of the city." The car idled for several minutes as Harry walked up and back shining his flashlight into the garbage and furniture that littered the backstreet.

"Who cares about that Polack? He won't talk. He knows if he does we'll grab his little brother," Harry said. "Let's save our own backsides and get out of here." Joe heard the car door slam again, and the sedan drove away.

He waited several minutes until he was sure they were gone and hopped back over the fence. He looked ahead and saw the lights of his destination calling to him. As he took a step forward, a screen door banged shut and he dove behind a pile of garbage. Trembling, he stood back up and sprinted the two blocks down the alley.

He pulled on the great wooden door but it was locked. Joe prowled around the back and tried the smaller door. It too was locked. Joe lightly knocked on the back door.

Nothing. He tried again and then he heard the sound of a lock turning.

"Joe! What's the matter?"

"Please, Father, I need your help," he pleaded to Father Gatowski. The old priest looked behind Joe into the darkness and opened the door. He slipped inside, and the priest locked it behind him. Joe followed Father Gatowksi into the church and up the steps of the altar. The priest walked across the altar and opened the door to the sacristy. Joe followed him in. Crosses, linens, and priestly vestments hung from the walls; gold plates and chalices sat on a table in the corner. The gray-haired priest turned and faced Joe.

"What happened, Joe?" Tears poured down Joe's face and he couldn't speak. How could he tell the kindly priest what he'd been a part of? The shame from his criminal life burned hot in his heart, and the sinfulness of it exploded in his gut. "Son, tell me," he said gently. Joe sat down dejectedly in a wooden chair and summarized the last ten years of his life—the boats, the whisky, the Sugar House, the extortions, Cappie's death—ending with the events of that day. Tears flowed down his cheeks during the entire oration. Father Gatowski sat across from him and listened silently until he finished.

"Where's the car?" the priest asked. Joe looked up at the priests face for the first time. The car?

"It's down the alley a couple blocks. I threw some boxes over the back of it. But Father, didn't you hear me? Those men in that apartment are . . ."

"I heard you, son. Give me the keys, and go in there and wait for me." The priest pointed to a small door leading off the sacristy. Joe handed him the car keys and looked at him questioningly. "I'll be back soon. Wait there." Father Gatowski went out the door of the sacristy.

Joe entered the tiny dark room and shut the door. He found a light switch and flipped it on. Elaborate golden doors lined the back wall, and a large cross hung above. He fell to his knees on the tiled floor and held his head in his hands. The priest had hidden him in a room with God himself. This is where the church kept the blessed Eucharist . . . the body and blood of God. Joe knelt on his knees, crying and praying for forgiveness. Finally, he fell into an exhausted sleep on the floor.

Father Gatowski gently shook Joe to waken him. "Come, my son" he said. Joe got up and followed the priest out of the sacristy into the church. He led Joe to his family's pew and they sat down on the wooden bench. Joe felt a slight calming warmth sitting in the familiarity of the church.

"Joe, what you've been doing is wrong, and you'll need to beg for God's forgiveness. You've performed illegal acts, extorted money by threats and fear, caroused with women, witnessed a murder and didn't report the culprit, *and* contributed to the murder of three men. But almost worse, you lost your faith." The priest looked at Joe and took his hands in his.

"I know, Father, please take my confession now. I'll turn myself in in the morning, but please give me absolution before I go." Joe buried his face in the priest's wrinkled hands.

"There will be a time for confession, son, but it is not now." Joe looked into the priest's eyes. "What you have done is wrong, but this murder the Purples committed is not of your doing. You say you had no knowledge of their plans, and I believe you. I've taken your car to the convent—a donation to the nuns. The police will never question that it belongs to them. Morning Mass is to begin in twenty minutes. You will stay in the sacristy until it has ended. Then I will take you in my car to a train station a couple hours from here." Joe wiped his eyes disbelieving what the priest was telling him.

"You want me to run?" he asked incredulously.

"You're not running. You're going on a retreat to find God, a pilgrimage. I'll visit your mother and let her know you are safe but you will be unable to return for some time. I'll send a letter with you to take to the Sacred Heart Church in Calumet. That's the parish you attended when you were a boy, correct? The monsignor there is Father Luke, a friend of mine from the seminary. He will see that you are taken care of. He'd written me just last week asking if I knew of any young men who were in need of work. His parish has gone through several divisions in the last few years, and he is in need of someone to help keep up the church and the rectory. In exchange, the church will provide you with room and board and—most importantly Joe—a place for you to find your way back to God." The priest sat back in the pew and looked up at the altar. "I believe you will find your way. I have faith in you."

Joe listened to the Mass from the sacristy and thought about the old priest's words. This time he did not pray. He needed to prove to God that he could change his life and be a good man before truly asking for forgiveness. Two hours later, at the train depot north of the city, Joe embraced Father Gatowski on the wooden platform as the train pulled into the station.

"Thank you, Father," Joe whispered fiercely, holding tightly to the old man. The old priest released Joe and looked into his deep blue eyes.

"Joe, you've tried to take care of your family the best you knew how since your father died. You've taken care of your mother and your brothers and even your Uncle Feliks and your little cousin Katalina. And I know joining the convent was not the direction Marya had been heading. Your father would be very proud. You haven't always made the right choices, but you have a good heart, Joe." Father Gatowski embraced Joe a final time, and Joe stepped onto the train's first step.

"Thank you for helping me, Father," he said. "I promise to make you proud, too."

"I know you'll keep your promise Joe—just as I have. Your Ojciec came to me the day he left for the army and asked if I'd watch over you if something happened to him. I believe I've fulfilled that promise tonight, as I know you will fulfill yours to form a new life for yourself and be good in your faith to God. Take care, Joe," he said, as the train began to pull away from the station. "I'll be praying for you."

Joe waved, boarded the train, and found a seat. He looked out the window and felt the first sense of peace he'd had in years. His shoulders relaxed, and he took what felt like his first deep breath in months. He smiled softly to himself and whispered, "Thank you, Ojciec. I love you too."

EPILOGUE

Joe sat looking out over the blue water of Cranberry Lake and cast his line thirty feet from the boat. Cappie's boat was old, but he was too sentimental to buy another. Though his hair was white, his blue eyes still held their fantastic hue as he looked at the cottages that dotted the lakeshore, perched on small rises. Their appearance was similar to the homes that fronted Keweenaw Bay in the Upper Peninsula, where he'd spent five years at the Sacred Heart parish before returning to Detroit. Father Gatowski had been right to have faith in him. Joe found God again.

Joe worked hard fixing up the old church and rectory. He replaced the worn floor of the church board by board, fixed leaky pipes, rewired the electricity, and did any other job that needed to be done. He taught himself these new skills by trial and error as he approached each new task. Father Luke had been welcoming and asked no questions of Joe. It wasn't till a couple of years later that Joe approached Father Luke in the confessional and bared his soul. He waited till he felt he'd proven his worth for what God had provided to him and saved him from.

He didn't socialize with the people of the parish, for fear one would recognize him from his days there as a boy, but he needn't have worried. Most if not all of the people who would have remembered Joe had left by then, and if any remained they had their own troubles to contend with and didn't ponder the quiet, handsome man who had shown up suddenly one autumn morning.

During the drive to the train station, Joe had told Father Gatowski where he'd hidden his nest egg and had asked him to give it to his mother as he boarded the train. He'd wanted to give some to the church but worried his family would not have enough to survive on. Instead he deeded the fishing property to St. Josaphat, and Father Gatowski housed several homeless families there during the Depression. After Prohibition ended Father Gatowski had written to him letting him know that it was safe to return to the city. The Purples had self-destructed after Ray, Harry, and Milberg were convicted of committing the Collingwood Manor Massacre and were sentenced to life in federal prison. The woman who had put the milk bottle on the porch of the apartment turned out in the end to be his redeemer. She'd told police that before she heard the volley of bullets on the second floor she'd seen a blond man going down the stairwell, thereby clearing him of the murders. The city was awash in so much crime and poverty that the police had much more pressing circumstances on their hands; they closed the case of the getaway driver.

Uncle Alexy, rehired at the end of the Depression, secured Joe a position at the Ford plant when he returned to Detroit from Sacred Heart, and he moved back in with his mother. Frank and Stephan also worked at Ford, but Frank had married and moved out of the house. Joe and Stephan financed a new home in the suburbs of Detroit and moved their mother out of the city. They traveled together to work and back until Stephan also met a lovely Polish girl and settled down. Joe dated sporadically but focused his spare time on his work with the newly formed U.A.W. and volunteering at St. Josaphat. Father Gatowski passed on shortly after Joe returned to Detroit, and Joe was able to attend the massive funeral held in his honor.

In 1937, Joe protested Ford's fight against the union with hundreds of others on an overpass near the River Rouge Plant. He was severely beaten by one of Ford's henchman, and a photographer who caught it on film published it in the *Detroit News*. Thinking he'd lost his job for protesting against his employer so publicly, he went to work the next day only to get his pink slip. The public was so outraged at the photographs in the papers that Ford had to issue an apology (of sorts), and Joe was able to keep his position.

When the Second World War began on that infamous December 7, 1941, Joe went with thousands of others to the recruiting office to enlist. He was turned away due to the loss of his lung and was bitterly disappointed he could not follow in his father's footsteps by fighting for his country. He later learned his childhood friend Sam had perished fighting for his country. When Ford announced they were to cease building cars to help in the war effort and would build an airplane factory in Ypsilanti, just west of Detroit, Joe was one of the first line workers to request a transfer.

He was given the position of foreman at the Willow Run plant and was assigned to supervise the hundreds of women that were hired to build the airplanes. True Rosie the Riveters, they were a loud, spunky, hard-working group of women, and he had his hands full most days. Joe started dating a little brunette that worked on his line and tried to keep it under management's radar, as fraternizing with the line workers was forbidden. The white-collar bosses never noticed; but a tall, blonde beauty who worked down the line from Joe did.

Suddenly the little brunette began to refuse any offers of a date with Joe, and he found himself in the arms of the lovely blonde Polish girl. It wasn't till years later that he found out the woman who was to become his wife had let the brunette know under no uncertain terms that Joe was to be hers.

Blanche loved to fish. Joe would take her out on Saturdays in Cappie's boat, and they would troll the Detroit River and Lake Erie for hours, fishing and talking. They married in St. Josaphat's before the war ended and moved into a house down the street from Joe's mother. They had two boys and a little girl and sent them to Catholic school as Joe had been sent. His friends from work would laugh when they visited for backyard barbeques when they saw the picture of Clara Bow that hung in his small hallway, saying they didn't believe Joe had ever met the "It" girl. Ty Cobb's signature remained hidden on the back of the photograph. One day he planned to give it to his youngest son, who loved baseball as much as he did. He'd lived a good life and he hoped he had atoned for his sins in the eyes of God.

The sound of children laughing and splashing in the shallow water nearby shook Joe out of his memories, and he pulled in the empty hook. He looked over at the small cottage he had bought after he'd retired and saw his nine granddaughters playing and swimming together near the dock. One screamed shrilly and jumped off the wooden dock out as far as she could leap. "Did you see that, Grandpa?" she called, as he neared the dock, her blonde hair shining in the sun. "I almost touched heaven!"

"Yes, I think you did," he replied.

ACKNOWLEDGEMENTS

When a first time author sits down to write her very first story it takes a very supportive group of friends and family to bolster her with the courage to put her thoughts down on paper and then show them to the world.

To my husband, Todd who always believed I could write a "pretty good" novel. You are my rock and my home.

To my children, Katarina, Max and Julianna- who listened hours and hours of 'the fascinating history of Detroit' and helped me to write from the perspective of an intelligent curious young child.

To my parents who have always supported and encouraged me in all my adventures- Thank You will never be enough!

To my sister, Jodie, whose energetic encouragement helped me keep writing on those tough days when it's hard to be a mother of three and concentrate on a vision.

Thanks to my very first editors – Randine Scheffler, Hugh Madden, Terri Parks and Debbie Papalia. Your feedback and praise was much needed.

To my youngest supporters for their unending enthusiasm – Emily Madden and Nico Carnago. The Mrs. Scheffler T-Shirts are on order...

To my Aunt Mary Ann for providing the beautiful picture of my Grandfather for the cover of the book.

To Karrie Ross, the Book cover, and interior designer. Thank you for all the advice, patience and for the final push I needed!

And to all my Ya-Ya sisters and especially my best friends, Debbie Papalia, Cheri Molino, and Eileen Wilson. Our blood might not be the same but our hearts are connected forever. Thank you for ALWAYS believing in me and pushing me to accomplish my dreams!

ABOUT THE AUTHOR

ean Scheffler is a first time author. She lives "South of Detroit" with her family. She welcomes visitors to her web site, www.JeanScheffler.com

Notes:

[1] Published in 1902, music by George Evans; lyrics by Ren Shields.

[2] Lyrics by Maceo Pinkard, 1919. Public domain.

Made in the USA
Middletown, DE
31 July 2020

14220346R00239